Escaping the Shadows

Aleah Donald

Copyright © 2025 by Aleah Donald

All rights reserved.

No part of this publication may be reproduced, distributed, or transmitted in any form or by any means, including photocopying, recording, or other electronic or mechanical methods, without the prior written permission of the publisher, except as permitted by U.S. copyright law. For permission requests, contact Aleahdonaldauthor@gmail.com.

The story, all names, characters, and incidents portrayed in this production are fictitious. No identification with actual persons (living or deceased), places, buildings, and products is intended or should be inferred.

Book Cover by Get Covers

Edited by Jessica Fortenberry, enchantedinkwell.com

First edition 2025

For my husband, who showed me what real love looks like, and for every woman discovering that God's plan for her life is greater than her pain.
Psalm 34:18

Contents

Author's Note

Escaping the Shadows deals with sensitive topics including physical and emotional abuse and alcoholism. Though this is a fictional story, for many, it reflects a very real truth.

This story includes painful moments—but it also walks through a realistic journey of healing, returning to God, and discovering what real love looks like.

My characters aren't perfect. They struggle, they fall short, they wrestle with choices. But through it all, my prayer is to show the thread of redemption, grace, and restoration that only God can bring.

With love and prayers,

Aleah Donald

Chapter 1

"ASHA, WHERE DO YOU think you're going dressed like that?" My boyfriend, Russell Steffens, narrows his eyes at me.

I tilt my head at my reflection in the vertical mirror hanging in our bedroom. My chocolate-brown silk dress stops right above my knees, with matching heels accented by gold accessories: hoop earrings, bracelets that line my right arm, and rings on three fingers. I see nothing wrong with what I'm wearing—in fact, I think it complements my brown complexion beautifully.

"It's Zara's grand opening tonight, remember?" I ask. "I've been talking about it for almost a year now. She's my best friend, Russell. I can't miss it." Not only is she my best friend, but we've known each other since we were infants. Our mothers were close friends, which automatically made Zara and me just as close.

Tonight, Zara is accomplishing her wildest dreams. She's opening her first art gallery right here in River Falls, North Carolina. I'm so proud of her. "After years of planning and dreaming, tonight is finally the night. I told you this already." I look over my shoulder at Russell, who is sitting on the edge of our king-size bed holding our one-year-old daughter, Olivia.

"I think I would remember us having that conversation." His stare causes my spine to stiffen. *God, please don't let him start an argument, not tonight.*

His jawline is sharp beneath his goatee, and even sitting down, his tall, broad-shouldered frame commands the room. His dark brown skin is smooth under the soft lighting, and his hair is neatly trimmed close to his scalp. But his eyes make me nervous—dark and cold, lingering on my face.

I purse my thick lips together, unsure of what to say next. I don't want to argue. Because if we do, he might put his foot down and demand I stay home, or else I'll be in a bad mood the rest of the night. But there's no way I'm missing out on her grand opening of Creative Souls Art Gallery. I can't do that to her.

"We just talked about it last week. I asked if you wanted to go so I could ask Ms. Mildred to babysit Liv, and you said you didn't want to."

"Asha, what did I just say?" Russell tilts his head to the side as his nostrils flare.

I lick my lips, afraid to say anything further, because I can't do this right now. "You're right." The lie tastes bitter as it leaves my lips. "I must have forgotten to tell you it was tonight." But I know we spoke about it because I remember begging him to come.

Somehow that discussion had started an argument. He yelled at me, telling me how much I don't respect him. He backed me into a corner until I started crying. When he saw the tears leaving streaks of mascara down my cheeks, he walked away.

But tonight, my mascara is still neatly applied. A golden shimmer from my body cream glistens on my warm brown skin. My amber eyes evaluate my outfit once more. My dark brown hair is rich and voluminous, my thick lips coated with gloss, eyeliner accentuating my eyes.

"Who all is going to be there?" he asks, as if I know every single person on her guest list.

"I don't know. I'm pretty sure Zara's family will be there. She sent out special invitations, and she posted a lot of advertisements."

Russell bounces Olivia on his knee, his eyes locked onto me. He scans me up and down, his lip twitching upward slightly. "Why are you all dressed up like that?"

I look down at my outfit, eyebrows raised. I'm not sure what he's trying to imply. Tonight is a special occasion, and I want to look good. It's my first night out in a long time. Because I'm a stay-at-home mom, most days when I leave the house, Russell constantly wants to know my every move.

I usually wear sweatpants or leggings and oversized sweatshirts. So yeah, I want to dress up because I'm going out. I haven't been on a date since Olivia was born, and Zara and I mainly hang out at each other's houses.

"Do you not like it?" He watches me like a predator eyeing its prey. "I can change into something else." I step toward the closet before his free hand grabs my wrist. My breath catches in my throat as his grip tightens.

"Nah, it's cool." Russell bites his lower lip. "You look good, is all." The compliment feels tainted as if he thinks how I look tonight will pique someone else's interest. Even if it did, I'm not interested in anyone else. The only man I want is him.

"Thanks, baby."

His hand slides to my back, then he pulls me close to him. He holds me like a trophy, positioned between his legs. When his eyes flutter to my lips, I give him a kiss. It's quick and rushed.

His hand holds me in place as I try to take a step back. "Don't stay out too late." The words come out like a warning.

"I won't," I promise. I turn my attention to Olivia, whose doe eyes are full of joy. "Mama loves you, baby girl." I bend down, planting a kiss on her chubby cheek.

Olivia babbles, "Ma-ma." When her arms stretch out, reaching for me, I feel weak. I want to cancel going out, pick up my daughter, and hold her all night long, but I can't miss Zara's opening.

No one warned me about mom guilt, but it's a real thing. Even though I'm with my daughter all the time, my chest aches for leaving her home. But tonight isn't just about the grand opening; it's a chance for me to get out of the house.

With Russell working full time as a detective for the River Falls Police Department, he's barely home, and when he is, he's tired and frustrated. Hence why he's snappy tonight.

"I'll be back soon." I kiss her again, then rub my hand over her wild, curly hair.

I look in the mirror one more time, tucking a stray coil back into place and checking my makeup. My oval face looks even under the soft light, brows arched and thin. I give a quick smile, catching a glimpse of my straight white teeth, then I rub my favorite perfume onto my wrist, pat my dress carefully over my curvy hips, and grab my purse.

"Asha," Russell calls as I make my way toward the bedroom door.
"Yes?"
"Text me when you get there," he commands.
"I will. I promise."

***

CREATIVE SOULS ART GALLERY is packed within minutes of opening. A sea of people squeeze shoulder to shoulder as they navigate their way inside. I knew tonight would be a success, but seeing so many people here to support my best friend has me on the verge of tears. The place is full of life, and the energy in the building is almost electric. A thrill travels up my spine as I stand on the stairs, watching Zara and her husband, Akin, greet everyone with warm smiles.

Zara started as an instructor at The Art Institute four years ago while pursuing her dream of becoming an artist. Her big break came when the famous painter John Dior noticed one of her pieces in a contest in California. He bought the artwork, featured it in his show, and suddenly, everyone wanted her creativity. This isn't just her career—it's her life.

Witnessing this night means the world to me, and it takes everything I have not to cry from pure joy. I'm standing at the top of the stairs, witnessing her prayers come to life. The crowd is here to see her and her work, along with a few pieces by other local and well-known artists.

I watched the gallery transform during renovations, but the final product takes my breath away. The sage-green walls create a soothing atmosphere, complemented by plants arranged in the corners and along the walls. Black benches and soft cushioned chairs invite visitors to sit and admire the art. All the details were carefully planned and beyond what I could have imagined.

Servers dressed in all black weave through the crowd, carrying trays of sparkling water and mocktails. Zara's mom and stepdad, Irene and Manuel Ramirez, help greet the guests. I scan the room, searching for Zara's stepbrother, Malachi, but I don't see him. He's probably running late.

Tonight, Zara shines in a long-sleeve brown shirt tucked into flared black jeans and red heels paired with red dangling earrings. Earlier this morning, she got her nails done, and the red stiletto-shaped acrylic completes her look. Every outfit she wears looks as if it belongs in a fashion magazine. Her creative touch doesn't just apply to her artwork but her wardrobe as well.

I can't stop smiling as I watch my best friend. She's beautiful. Her smooth dark skin, long box braids, and symmetrical features give her a natural beauty that's impossible to ignore. Before leaving the house, she always does her makeup to such perfection she could be like those women who do tutorials on YouTube.

Having already seen most of the exhibits, I sip on my mocktail while lingering near a sculpture that I hadn't fully appreciated before. It's an incredible sculpture of a woman with dreads breastfeeding an infant. Her wrist, bound in chains, pulls the strings of my heart. Her eyes are full of sorrow, and I can't believe how real she looks. The longer I stare at it, the more depth the weight of her story has on me. I can't look away. The small plaque at the base reads: *Chains of Sacrifice*.

As I study the sculpture, a familiar presence appears beside me. The scent of spicy, earthy cologne fills the air. I inhale deeply before I hear a voice—deep, rough, and slightly teasing. I wipe at the corners of my eyes.

"Need a tissue, Ms. Tate?"

I don't have to turn to recognize the six-foot-four man hovering over me like the Eiffel Tower. It's Malachi Ramirez, Zara's stepbrother.

"No, I don't," I reply confidently, squaring my shoulders.

"Good. Crying women make me uncomfortable," he admits.

Over the years, I've lost count of how many times he shut his bedroom door to avoid my emotional venting sessions with Zara.

"I figured you'd be late tonight," I say, keeping my eyes on the sculpture.

"To my sister's grand opening? That hurts my feelings." He clutches his chest dramatically.

"You'll probably be late to your own funeral," I tease.

"Now that, you're right about." He chuckles.

When I finally turn to look at him, he meets my gaze. His rich brown skin and deep brown eyes remind me of dark sand on the beach.

Malachi is in a black tux and matching dress shoes tonight. He looks good.

We're standing right in front of each other, his brown eyes looking down at me.

"Wow," he says, studying me.

"What?" I ask, swallowing hard.

"Nothing. It's just . . . I don't think I've ever seen you not dressed like a college frat boy."

I burst into laughter. "You've hurt my feelings," I say, pinching my fingers together. "Just a little bit, though."

"Just a little bit?" he mimics, laughing. "But seriously, you look beautiful tonight."

"Thanks, Mal." My cheeks warm, so I turn away.

As I descend the stairs, he follows close behind, his cologne lingering.

"I'm so proud of our girl," I say as Zara poses for a photo with a guest.

"Me too," he says, adjusting his collar with a grin. "She's following in her big brother's footsteps."

"You wish. Zara's paving the way for her own success. Just because you opened your own business first doesn't mean she's following you." I chuckle.

Malachi holds out his hand, helping me navigate the long, curved staircase in my pointy heels.

"You're right. Tonight is all about our girl."

We reach the bottom of the stairs just as Zara takes her last photo with an excited fan.

"You're practically famous now, sis," Malachi says, pulling Zara into a tight hug and planting a kiss on her forehead.

"Not yet, but soon." She smiles. "But thank God you got here on time. I was looking everywhere for you."

"Why does everyone assume I'd be late to my baby sister's big night?"

"Because you're late to everything," she reminds him. "You were even late to my wedding." Zara pulls back, crossing her arms over her chest.

"I was late but not late-late." He shrugs. "I think it's time for you to get over it."

"Never," Zara replies. "Now move—I need to hug my best friend."

"I thought I was your best friend." Malachi shoves his hands into his pockets.

"She likes me more than you." I smack at his arm, nudging him aside so I can get to Zara. "Z, I'm so proud of you!" I squeal. She opens her arms, and we embrace tightly.

"I'm so glad you're here. Now I can finally breathe." Zara inhales deeply, then exhales as she places a hand on her stomach. "I honestly thought I was going to pass out."

"This is amazing. I can't believe how many people are here!"

Zara's eyes shine as she scans the room. Guests wander through the gallery, admiring the beautiful artwork while mingling and sipping their drinks.

"It feels like I'm dreaming," she says.

"Soak it all in, sis," Malachi tells her, wrapping an arm around us both, pulling us to him. "You deserve this."

Her eyes well with tears, and right on queue my own tears follow.

"Oh no." Malachi steps back. "Why do women always cry?" He quickly excuses himself from the emotional moment.

I pull Zara into another hug, hoping she can feel how proud I am.

"All the late nights and hard work were worth it," I whisper.

"Girl." She clears her throat, dabbing at her eyes. "You're going to make me ruin my makeup." She fans her eyes with her hands.

We laugh, looping our arms together, and stroll through the gallery. As we reminisce about the delays and doubtful days it took to pull this off, Zara stops occasionally to admire her artwork. Every few minutes a guest will run up to her to congratulate her, and I sip on my drink, watching her shine.

Zara is outgoing and friendly while I tend to stay in the background. Social interactions are not for me. I spend so much time at home with my toddler, I forgot how to make new friends. Zara's family feels like an extension of my own. They're the only friends I need.

Irene is running around like a chicken with its head cut off, ensuring the guests are comfortable and directing them to refreshments or the restrooms. Manuel is standing in the middle of a large crowd, entertaining everyone with his humor. He's a funny man with a heart of gold.

Manuel came into Zara's life when she was one year old, bringing an energetic, curly-haired two-year-old named Malachi. The people who truly matter to her are here—except Olivia, who is home with Russell.

Malachi stands near a large potted plant, chatting with a woman who's leaning in close and laughing a little too loudly. Her pale hand rests on his shoulder, and for a moment, I wonder who she is. But knowing how women throw themselves at Malachi, she's probably working up the nerve to ask for his number.

As the night winds down, Zara ascends the long staircase while I hang back near the white reception desk. She asks for everyone's attention before taking her place at the top, where Akin proudly stands behind her. All eyes are on her.

They're a beautiful couple. Together for nearly four years, they're two of my closest friends and Olivia's godparents. Akin, with his tall frame, muscular build, and rich complexion, exudes confidence. His long dreads are freshly retwisted, and tonight he's wearing a striking red suit with a black shirt and red tie. His hand rests on Zara's lower back as he gazes at her with unmistakable love.

"Where do I even start?" Zara's voice cracks as she addresses the crowd. "Thank you all for coming tonight. It means the world to me and my husband." She glances back at Akin briefly before continuing. "I couldn't have done this without your support and prayers.

"I want to thank my husband, Akin. All my sponsors, my fellow artists, my parents, Irene and Manuel. My amazing brother, Malachi, my mentors, and my best friend, Asha, for helping me. Most importantly—" she pauses, her voice thick with emotion "—I want to thank God. Without Him guiding me, I don't know if any of this would be possible."

She wipes her eyes, and tears spill down my own cheeks. My throat tightens as waves of happiness wash over me. God has answered her prayers, and I know this is just the beginning for her.

"Again, thank you all for coming. I hope for your continued support and love. I can't wait to see what else God has in store for our community."

As she finishes, a hand settles on my shoulder. Somehow, I know Malachi is standing behind me.

"Here you go, crybaby," he teases, handing me a tissue. I'm grateful despite his playful banter.

"Thanks," I whisper.

As I listen to Zara's heartfelt speech, a phone dings beside me, and I remember my own phone, buried in my purse, its ringer off. I haven't checked it all night. *Crap.* I forgot to text Russell to let him know I arrived, which was a little over an hour ago.

I quickly pull my phone out. The screen lights up before I can unlock it. Three missed calls and five text messages from Russell. My heart sinks, and fear freezes me in place.

"You all right?" Malachi whispers in my ear, his breath warm against my neck.

"Yeah," I manage, clearing my throat. "I'm fine."

But I'm not.

Chapter 2

I sit in the car in front of our house for a few minutes, dreading the moment I have to get out. I silently pray that Russell is asleep, but the uneasy feeling in the pit of my stomach tells me otherwise. After Zara finished her lovely speech, I asked Malachi to let Zara know I had to leave. His eyebrows drew together, but I rushed out the door before he could question me.

Now that I'm home, my heart might just explode. No matter how many times I experience Russell's anger or witness his frustration and rage, the nervousness never fades. On his bad days, I remind myself of the good times we've shared and hope there will be more in the future. But right now, all I can focus on is how terrifying he looks when he looms over me. His dark eyes are always sharp, cutting into my soul.

I know Russell wants to make sure I'm safe and okay, or at least that's what he tells me. But sometimes, I feel like it's more than that. Our recent arguments replay in my mind—his voice raised, his hands flying up too close to my face. Every argument ends with me cowering and flinching. The memories send a shiver down my spine. It's not just his words or the volume of his voice; it's the fear of things escalating further.

I've learned how to de-escalate our arguments, even though that rarely works anymore. My main goal is to avoid them altogether, which requires me to walk on eggshells.

Like tonight—I should have remembered to text him. But I was so caught up in admiring my best friend's hard work that it completely slipped my mind. Now, all I can do is brace myself for what's to come.

My days are spent questioning every word I say, every action I take. If I say the wrong thing or burn dinner, will that spark another argument? And yet, there's always this glimmer of hope. Maybe he'll come home in a great mood, plant kisses along my cheeks and neck, and offer to do something thoughtful for me. I live with two versions of him, and I never know which one I'm going to face.

But lately, I've been getting the version of him I dread the most—the one that yells and curses when I forget to tell him I'm out running errands or visiting Zara. It's such a stark contrast to the man I met three years ago. Back then, he was so thoughtful, so careful, treating me as if I were as delicate as glass. He was understanding and kind, and those moments felt endless. Now, they are distant memories. Yet, I know that version of him still exists. I catch glimpses of it in the rare moments he holds me late at night, his arms wrapped around me as though he's afraid to let me go. Or when he cooks breakfast for Liv and me, smiling as he hands me my plate.

The uncertainty wears on me. My chest tightens, the familiar ache of anxiety gripping me. My head throbs from the constant overthinking, the endless questions and what-ifs swirling in my mind. I crave the ability to feel safe and at ease in my own home.

I swallow the large lump forming in my throat as I climb the steps to the front door. I say a quick prayer, hoping that tonight won't end in an uproar. My hand hovers over the doorknob. It's locked, which I take as a small sign of hope. Russell usually locks the door before going to bed, so maybe he's already upstairs under the comforter in our king-size bed.

When I walk inside, the house is dark except for a faint sliver of moonlight pouring through the windows into the kitchen and living room. The silence is heavy and suffocating, but a breath of relief escapes me. I lean against the door, letting it close softly behind me. If he is asleep, I don't want to risk waking him.

My feet ache, so I kick off my heels and wiggle my toes.

I rub them briefly before heading to our bedroom upstairs. I stop by Olivia's room. Her pink door is slightly open, and I peek inside to find her sound asleep in her crib. She looks so peaceful, her tiny chest rising and falling with each gentle breath. She's wearing her favorite purple onesie paired with fuzzy socks that barely stay on her wiggly little feet. My girl is beautiful.

The urge to pick her up, to cradle her against me and inhale her soft baby scent, tugs at my heart. But I know better. If I do, she'll be up for hours, wide-eyed and full of energy, and I'm already running on fumes.

Our bedroom door is closed. I hesitate, my heart thudding in my chest. I take a steadying breath before finally pushing it open. I expect—no, hope—to see Russell lying in bed under the sheets, already asleep. But the bed is empty.

My breathing quickens, and a familiar tightness grips my throat as I push the door open further. There he is, sitting on our gray love sofa. His figure is dark and shadowy, illuminated only by the faint moonlight spilling through the blinds. A beer bottle dangles loosely in his hand. Two empty beer bottles sit by his feet on the carpet, evidence that tonight may be worse than I imagined.

"I'm sorry for not texting you. I forgot," I say quickly, trying to get the words out before he can speak.

Russell takes a slow swig from the bottle, his gaze never leaving me. His voice slurs slightly as he mutters, "Where've you been?"

Confusion settles on my face. "You know where I've been. I told you; I was at Zara's grand opening."

"So, you couldn't text me, huh? I don't get it, Asha. Why'd you like making me so upset?"

My stomach sinks, the familiar knot of anxiety twisting in my heart. I take a slow step forward, the space between us thick with pressure. "It was an accident. I meant to text you, I just . . . forgot."

His eyes narrow, and he leans back, his expression hardening. "Admit it. You were ignoring me. I know you saw them."

The words catch in my throat, but I force myself to speak calmly. "I swear, I didn't see it."

Russell leans forward, his gaze dark and intense. "You're lying. It's not hard to send a text to let me know you're okay. You think I'm stupid?" He curses under his breath.

Guilt and fear churn inside me, and I feel sick to my stomach. I know I messed up, but it wasn't intentional. "I was trying to celebrate my best friend's grand opening and got caught up in the moment. I would never ignore you."

But now, that moment of happiness is lost beneath the weight of Russell's frustration.

The words fumble from my lips. "I'm sorry," I say again because I don't know what else to say. I know my words hold no value, but they're all I have to offer.

Russell stands up suddenly. His eyebrows furrow, and his nose and lips twist as his anger boils over. He practically slams the beer onto the dresser. "What am I supposed to think when I don't hear from you for hours?"

My feet instinctively take a step back, as if distance could somehow protect me from his rage. But Russell is fast. He strides toward me, and I brace for impact. I'm fully convinced that tonight will be the night he finally hits me, but instead, he slams the door shut with such force that I pray Liv doesn't wake.

My heart pounds against my chest, and my palms drip with sweat. His face is mere inches from mine. The heat of his breath brushes my skin, and for a moment, I think the room is closing in on us. My mind races, trying to make sense of how something so small has led to this. No matter how many times I mentally prepare for these arguments, I always feel just as helpless and speechless as the last.

"I—"

"You always do stupid stuff like this," he sneers, interrupting me. I press my trembling hands to his solid chest, trying to put more space between us. Tears creep at the corners of my eyes, but I don't want them to fall.

"I know," I whisper. Although I don't agree with his way of handling things, deep down I wonder if he's right. Maybe if I were a better girlfriend or mother, we wouldn't be having this conversation. Maybe the fights wouldn't happen so often. "I'm sorry."

His arms tighten around my waist, pulling me against him. The smell of beer and sweat hits me like a baseball to the head. His breath is sharp and sour, stinging my nostrils.

When Russell and I first started dating, he never used to drink much. He'd have a beer or wine on special occasions. But now, it's every week. Almost every day. When he comes home from work, I smell the alcohol before I even see him.

The smell is repulsive and pungent. I want to pull away, to escape from his heavy embrace, but his posture tells me he's starting to calm down. If I pull back now, I'll only reignite the storm—more yelling, more cursing. So, I stay still. My body stiffens, and I let his hands roam over me even though it feels wrong.

"I love you, baby," he slurs into my ear. "I don't want to be angry at you. You know that, right? I was just so worried."

I swallow hard and nod. Words fail me. My mouth is dry, as if I've eaten a spoonful of cotton. I press my lips together to hold back the tears that threaten to spill. He buries his nose into the curve of my neck, his breath tickling my skin.

"Tell me you understand and that you love me." His voice cracks. Most of our arguments don't end this way, but tonight, I blame it on the several bottles of beer he's had. The alcohol is probably taking its toll on him, pulling him into a vulnerable state. His grip tightens around me, almost desperate.

"I understand." I sniffle through the words. "I love you."

The words don't feel like my own, but I say them because it's easier. I do love him, with all my heart, but understanding him—especially in moments like this—is hard. There are times when I think I'm starting to understand him, but then nights like these make me lose hope.

While Russell holds me, I can't help but think about reaching out to Zara. I want to ask her for advice, but I can't bring myself to tell her the truth. Russell can be intense, but I can forgive him. I'm not sure she could. She won't understand, and I don't have the words to help her understand. Do I stay because of Liv? Or is it because I love him so much and I hope this is just a phase? That once we're engaged or married, things will change . . . that *he'll* change. I cling to the hope that God will make it better.

Russell's eyes soften at my response, but I still feel uneasy. He presses his forehead against mine, his breathing slow and uneven. His hands tighten around me as if he fears losing me. And just for a moment, I wonder if he will.

Chapter 3

"ASHA! IT'S SO GOOD to see you again. And look at little Liv!" Miss Justine says. She's my favorite front desk receptionist at the River Falls Police Department.

"Hi, Miss Justine. It's good to see you too," I say with a smile.

Miss Justine steadies herself by gripping the edge of the counter as she leans down, her face lighting up at the sight of Liv. Wrinkles line her cheeks and around her eyes and neck. She has curly bright-white hair and glasses that sit on the bridge of her nose. She gently pinches Liv's cheek. "Hey there, sweet pea," she coos.

Liv smiles shyly, ducking behind my leg. "How are you doing today?" I ask.

"I'm doing all right, honey. How about you?" Miss Justine replies.

"I'm good. I stopped by to see Russell. Is he in?"

"He's around here somewhere. You can go back if you'd like," Miss Justine says with a knowing smile.

I nod, gripping Liv's hand as we wait patiently for her to shuffle her frail body around the counter to let us into the restricted area. At the metallic click of the lock, I guide Liv inside. Though I've only been through this section a few times over the years, I know exactly where Russell's desk is located.

Around us, the area buzzes with activity. Detectives and officers in uniform rush back and forth like busy bees in a hive. Clicking boots and serious conversations fill the air. The place is crowded. I find myself slightly overwhelmed and out of place.

Loose papers and case files are scattered across Russell's desk. Empty water bottles line its edge, while crumpled trash lies beside the bin instead of inside it.

Among the clutter, a picture frame catches my eye—a photo of Liv and me. I'm sitting on the couch, holding her in my arms. She had to be at least two or three months old in this photo. Somehow it feels out of place in the middle of all this mess, but I smile at the picture.

A half-eaten doughnut sits on a napkin next to a coffee cup, its surface dull and cold. Russell must have had a busy morning, so busy he couldn't even finish his breakfast.

I'm not sure how Russell works in this environment. I wouldn't be able to get any work done with how messy the space is. My fingers itch to tidy up, but I know he'd be upset if I touched anything on his desk, so I force myself to look anywhere else but there.

"Asha," a deep voice calls from behind me.

I turn to see Darnell Collins, Russell's partner, holding a packet of papers in his hand. He strides toward his desk, situated opposite Russell's. But unlike Russell's cluttered workspace, Darnell's desk is tidy and clean. Case files are stacked neatly, and the trash is where it belongs. A framed photo of him and his wife on their wedding day sits beside another picture of their three boys.

"Hey, Darnell," I say with a grin while scanning the area for Russell.

He places the papers on his desk and shrugs on his coat. His gaze shifts to Liv, his smile wide. "Olivia's getting so big. She looks just like you."

"You think?" I glance down at my baby girl, who's holding my finger tightly. With her dark brown curly hair and wide doe eyes, I can see the resemblance. But most days when I look at her, I see her father.

"Absolutely," he says, nodding.

"Well, thank you." I chuckle softly. "How are Trina and the boys?"

"Woo." Darnell groans, rubbing a hand over his exhausted face. "They're all doing good, but man, those boys eat like an entire football team."

I laugh, recalling the times I've met his family. During the cookouts last summer, his boys kept coming back for more hamburgers and chips. "I bet they keep you busy."

"Oh, you have no idea. And guess what?" He pauses, a proud smile spreading across his face. "I don't know if Russell told you or not, but we're having another one." He rubs a hand over his thick mustache.

"No way!" My jaw drops. "Liv is a lot; I don't know how Trina manages three boys while being pregnant."

"Yeah, but this time we finally got our little girl." His voice grows louder with excitement. I have to tilt my head to look up at him. Adjusting his collar, he grabs his briefcase. "We're done after this. She's our last one," he adds confidently.

"Well, tell her I said congratulations. I'm happy for you both. Maybe we can get together again soon. It's been a while." When Russell was first partnered with Darnell, we went out with him and Trina a few times. Trina and I hit it off instantly, but for some reason, Russell hasn't brought up going out with them again.

Darnell nods but then pauses, a look of confusion crossing his face. "I invited you guys over for Drew's party last Saturday, but Russell said you were sick."

My eyes narrow, and my head tilts slightly to the side. "Sick?" Russell never mentioned any invitation to me, and I haven't been sick.

"Yeah," Darnell continues. "Russell stopped by, brought a gift and everything. I think he said you and Liv had a stomach virus."

My mind races with questions I know I won't get answers to. *Why didn't Russell tell me about the party? How many other things has he kept from me? And why would he make up some story about us being sick?*

I force a tight smile, playing along. "Oh, right," I say, covering for him. "We're much better now. Maybe we can plan something soon. How about next Friday?"

"Sure," he replies with a warm smile. "I'll check with the missus, but it shouldn't be a problem."

"Great!" I respond before fully thinking it through. I don't know why I invited them over without talking to Russell first, but the fact that he lied about Liv and me being sick frustrates me. *Have things really gotten so bad that he doesn't want to be around us?* But that doesn't make sense either.

I've been blaming his drinking on the stress of the job, but now I'm not so sure. My thoughts spiral as I wonder just how many events we've missed because of his lies. He knows I've been wanting to get out of the house, to do more, but he kept this from me. The thought gnaws at me, leaving a bitter taste on my tongue as Darnell turns off his desk lamp and locks his computer.

"Have you seen Russell?" I ask, remembering why I bothered driving all the way over here. I hold up the tray of food. "He told me he's working late."

Darnell scratches the back of his neck, and his gaze darts away from mine. "I think he stepped out for a bit."

My brow furrows. "But don't you usually know where he is? You're his partner. I thought you shared the same caseload."

Darnell shifts uncomfortably. "Yeah, but he's been handling some extra work on his own lately. I'm not always in the loop." He forces a laugh. "I'm not his babysitter, but he's probably out there saving lives."

I'm not sure if he's being sarcastic, so I try to keep my face from scrunching up further. My grip on the tray tightens. "Oh, okay." I smile, but it doesn't reach my eyes. "I'll just leave it here on his desk, then."

Darnell nods, his expression unreadable. As he turns to walk away, a question lingers on the tip of my tongue, one I hesitate to ask. But I can't help myself. "Darnell?"

He stops and spins on his heel. "Yeah?"

I pause, weighing my words carefully. "Is there something going on that I should know about?"

***

AFTER LEAVING THE POLICE station, I call Russell and then text him. No response. As the minutes pass, an ache settles in my chest. I replay my conversation with Darnell, trying to make sense of what he said. He assured me there was nothing to worry about, but his words didn't ease my fears. Something about the situation doesn't sit right with me. Where was Russell, and why wasn't he responding to my calls?

And why didn't Russell tell me about the party? Why didn't he at least take Liv with him? She doesn't have any friends her age, and it would have been a perfect chance for her to interact with other kids. Plus, spending time with other couples might have been good for us too.

Since Russell and Darnell are close, I figure he and his wife are a great couple for us to spend time with, like we used to. It makes sense to me, especially since Russell doesn't seem to enjoy hanging out with Zara and Akin as much. He refers to them as "my" friends.

Zara and Akin have invited us over countless times, and each time I have to fight tooth and nail to get him to agree. Once Russell agrees to come, things seem to go fine—great even. But then every time I bring it back up, we're at square one.

As I sit here, I can't help but think about where Russell might be. He could be working. *But if that were true, wouldn't Darnell know where he was? Wouldn't Darnell be with him? He wouldn't lie to me too, would he?*

The only other explanation that comes to mind is that he's at some bar, throwing back beers. Beyond that, his routine is a mystery to me. It's unsettling, realizing how little I know about where he spends his time. I hope he's not drinking, because I don't want him coming home and picking a fight. I pray to God that he's just out working on a case like Darnell said.

Anger bubbles just beneath the surface. There's nothing I can do about it right now. I want to confront him, but I already know how that conversation will go. It's a dead end unless I'm ready to deal with the intoxicated version of him, and I'm not. I never am.

When I pull into the driveway, I check my phone again, hoping to find a notification from him. But instead, a text from Zara asks if I'm home because she misses me and her goddaughter. I exhale sharply. Maybe this is how he feels when I forget to check in.

Ten minutes later, Zara's sitting at the kitchen table, feeding Liv leftover mashed potatoes with a purple baby spoon.

I sip a cup of tea from a nearby barstool. I hoped the tea would calm my nerves, but my leg continues to bounce. My eyes drift to Zara as she pretends the spoon is a train, eliciting hysterical giggles from Liv. Her laughter tugs a smile from my lips despite the anxious sensation in my chest.

Watching my best friend bond with my daughter melts me in a way that leaves me speechless. Knowing Liv feels safe and comfortable with her means everything to me. I focus on my daughter's giggles, trying to drown out the persistent thoughts of Russell.

Zara glances up from her antics, her gaze meeting mine. Her playful smile fades slightly. "Everything okay?" she asks softly.

I raise the mug to my lips and allow the heat to wash over me. "I'm fine," I say, yet my voice cracks.

It's difficult hiding the uneasiness brewing inside of me, but the truth is written all over my face. Setting the mug down, I wrap my hands around it for comfort. "It's nothing, really," I mumble, though I know Zara isn't buying it.

She feeds Olivia the last bite of mashed potatoes before standing up to put the dirty dishes in the sink. "Fine," she says over her shoulder. She turns on the faucet and begins rinsing the dishes. "You don't have to talk to your best friend if you don't want to. But now I'm wondering if there's another best friend out there that you're venting to."

A small laugh escapes me. "You're my only best friend. I don't talk to anyone else."

She turns the faucet off. "Well, you're definitely not telling me everything. I know when something's bothering you. Is it about Russell? Have you two been arguing?"

"Is it that obvious?"

Zara places the dishes into the dishwasher, dries her hands, and picks up Liv before coming to sit next to me. "Asha, all couples argue. Even Akin gets on my nerves sometimes." She snickers.

They're so in love, I can't imagine them yelling at one another.

"We have our fair share of heated disagreements. It's normal. The longer you're married, the better you get at hiding it." She winks at me.

I consider the possibility of Zara hiding the difficulties of her relationship from me like I am with her. I've been doing my best to keep the cracks from showing, but I don't know how much longer I can do that.

Her reassurance doesn't bring the hope I longed for. Instead, it causes more uncertainty. Our arguments aren't just disagreements—they're intense and unpredictable, leaving me feeling small and scared.

I glance at my best friend, wanting to tell her everything, to release this heavy burden, but shame holds me back. *How do I explain something like this without sounding weak or foolish?* I clench my mug tighter, willing the heat to melt away my growing discomfort.

Zara gently tickles Liv, who giggles in her lap.

"Yeah, I guess you're right."

"We're sisters. Just know you can always talk to me—about anything. I mean anything," she says, placing her hand on my shoulder.

"I know," I whisper. But for now, it's easier to keep pretending that everything is fine.

Chapter 4

BEING IN CHURCH HAS always lifted my spirits. I'm not sure if it's the music, the warm smiles from friendly people, or the power of the preached Word, but something about being within these four walls causes me to feel lighter.

Growing up, my late mother, Wilma Tate, made sure I was in church every single Sunday and Wednesday night for Bible Study. As I get ready for church this morning, I remember how she'd brush my coils into neat pigtails tied with white ribbons, but instead of wearing those itchy dresses she constantly bought, I choose a dress that's more comfortable.

When she passed away just after my nineteenth birthday, I lost my way. My faith wavered, and I drifted from God. I left behind His comfort and strength, because losing my mother left a void in me that felt impossible to fill.

Meeting Russell didn't exactly help; he isn't a man who prioritizes faith or church. He's a hard worker and a great father, but he rarely steps foot in church. I made it my mission to ensure Liv and I went to church when we could. I wanted to raise her the way my mother had raised me. She taught me that when the world felt too heavy, I could always turn to God. So that's what I'm trying to do. Not just for me, but for Liv too.

Russell sprawls across the bed, one leg dangling off the edge, his lower body covered by the ruffled sheets. His soft snores fill the room, a trail of drool glistening at the corner of his mouth. I'm glad he's still asleep because I can't hide the anger in my eyes as I glance his way. I wonder what time he got home last night. I stayed up till midnight waiting for him but couldn't fight sleep any longer.

We haven't been talking much since he stormed into the house a few nights ago, furious after Darnell called to tell him I'd stopped by looking for him. The argument spiraled into Russell accusing me of embarrassing him. He went on about how I had no business showing up at his job unannounced or speaking to his coworkers without him there. He said everything except the truth I was looking for. Where had he been? The smell of liquor on his breath told me what I already suspected: he'd been drinking at some bar. Since that night, "working late" has taken on a whole new meaning.

I force my gaze from him, hesitant to let the bitterness linger any longer. Instead, I focus on sliding my baby-blue dress over my curves. I drape a white cardigan over my shoulders for the crisp September morning air. I pair it with plain white heels and my silver cross necklace, adding small diamond studs to complete the look.

Despite my efforts to fix my relationship with God and raise Liv in church, my increasingly strained relationship with Russell is one of the main reasons I got out of bed this morning.

When we pull into the church, the parking lot is crammed, cars filling every spot, so I have to park at the very back along the grass. I rush to unbuckle Liv from her car seat, frantically grabbing the diapers, bottles, and snacks that tumbled out of the diaper bag, but we're still late.

Getting myself ready is one thing, but getting a toddler ready means starting at least an hour earlier than usual. I finally shove everything back into the diaper bag and scoop Liv up onto my hip only for my luck to run out. The bag tips, and everything spills out again because, of course, I forgot to zip it. A loud, frustrated grunt escapes me, and my eyes roll to the back of my head.

"You look like you could use some help."

I glance up as Malachi approaches, his shoes crunching against the gravel as he closes the distance. Without waiting for a response, he bends down, picking up the scattered items. Hands full, he places everything neatly back into the diaper bag.

The morning sun hits him just right, causing his light brown skin to shimmer. Malachi is half Latino and half Black. His hairline and beard are freshly trimmed, giving him a sharp, clean look. His dark curls are crisp and neat. He's wearing a simple sweater that clings to his broad shoulders paired with well-fitted blue jeans.

"Here, let me," he says, sliding the bag off my shoulder and zipping it closed. Malachi's always been kind, but for some reason, I'm caught off guard. Maybe it's because embarrassment stings my cheeks.

"Thanks," I mumble, shifting Liv on my hip. Her face lights up at the sight of him. Her tiny hands reach out for Malachi, and she lets out a squeal of excitement. I chuckle at Malachi's wide eyes as he stares at her, momentarily frozen.

"Guess she missed me?" he says with a teasing grin, carefully reaching for her.

I can't help but laugh. He takes Liv into his arms as if he's afraid his large hands will hurt her. He's always been gentle with her. When she was first born, he was nervous to hold her, but he took his time to learn how to support her head and neck properly, keeping her close to his chest. He's careful now, adjusting her in his arms as she giggles, and he relaxes quickly. It warms my heart seeing how natural he's become with her over the months.

"Maybe you should come around more often," I say with a smile as we walk toward the church entrance.

"So I can be outnumbered? Between you, my sister, my mom, and Liv, that's a bit too much female energy." He laughs.

"What is that supposed to mean?" I say playfully as he opens the church doors.

He chuckles, stepping aside to let me through. "I'm just saying, women can be a lot to handle."

"You're ridiculous." I roll my eyes, still smiling. "If you're afraid of women, just say that."

"I'm not afraid of women; I just grew up with too many," he replies with a wink. Malachi's family is full of female cousins and aunties. He's the only male cousin on their side. So his statement is full of truth. While he wanted to play football, his sister and I, along with his cousins, wanted to dress up our Barbie dolls.

We step into the sanctuary, and I glance around. Church has already started, but the praise team is still singing. The voices sound heavenly, their harmonies filling the air, while the piano plays a soulful melody. The drums send a vibration through the room, making me want to clap my hands.

Zara and Akin sit on the back row, and surprisingly there's space for us to join them. Zara grins, immediately sliding over and reaching for Liv, who eagerly jumps out of Malachi's arms to get to her.

Malachi shakes his head in disbelief at my daughter's sudden betrayal. He gets over it, fist-bumps Akin, and takes a seat next to his sister. "Guess she likes Zara more than me," he whispers in my ear.

"It's a girl thing," I joke.

The church is medium sized with at least two hundred people filling every available seat. Long wooden pews stretch out across the sanctuary, creaking occasionally as people rise to their feet. At the front of the church, a large stage is set up with microphones, instruments, and a large backdrop where a cross is displayed. Looking at the cross sends a chill through me.

Above the stage, the name of the church, Truth Center Ministries, is painted in bold, black letters across the top of the sanctuary. The letters stand out clearly, reminding me of the mission and heart of this church.

The congregation is diverse, with young and old members from various backgrounds and races, all coming together for the same purpose.

As the music continues to fill the room, peace washes over me. I close my eyes, meditating on the words being sung. It's like medicine to my aching soul. This is exactly what I need. I try to force the stressful events of the past few days out of my mind, but the worries seem to be stuck. Every time I try to surrender them to God, they creep back in like an unwanted guest.

I give up on my attempts to forget about the past few months and simply focus on the presence of God. As Pastor Quinton steps behind the pulpit, his voice fills the sanctuary, calm yet powerful. He dives right into the Word, speaking with such conviction that he grabs all my attention. He teaches the scripture with boldness, and my eyes well up with tears.

"All things are working for your good!" Pastor Quinton exclaims, his voice rising as he declares the promise. "Everything works together for those who love God and are called according to His purpose!" The congregation erupts in applause and shouts in agreement.

He talks about Joseph from the Old Testament—a man whose life was filled with betrayals, lies, and hard times. Yet through it all, God used everything he went through for His good. The details of Joseph's story flood my mind as he speaks. When I was a little girl, I learned about him in children's church. The familiar story takes on new meaning as Pastor Quinton brings it to life. He reminds me of things I once forgot.

"Storms come and go! You may not understand why you're going through your storm," he says, "but you have to trust that God has a plan bigger than what you can see. Stop worrying about what you feel, and focus on what you know. You know that God is good and faithful, that He will never leave you nor forsake you."

I lean forward, the weight of his words sinking deep into my spirit. I absorb as much of the Word as I can, because when I leave here, I want to take it with me. I want to carry it in my heart on the days I feel uncertain about my future, on the days when the world feels heavy and my faith seems small.

I close my eyes, saying a quiet prayer in my heart. I ask God to help me and to give me the strength to endure what's ahead. I hope He's listening to me, because right now I can't help but feel like I'm speaking into an empty void. The uncertainty is overwhelming, but I hold on to the hope that somehow He hears me, even after I left Him.

Once church is over, I still sit there. I'm stuck in the moment, and I don't want to leave. Because I'm afraid His peace won't go with me.

"Hey, Ash. You good?" Zara asks. She's still holding Liv, her head resting on Zara's shoulder with droopy eyelids.

"Um, yeah," I say after a moment, shaking myself out of the trance. "I'm fine."

"We're all going to Rita's Diner if you want to join us," Zara offers, giving me a warm smile.

As much as I want to go, I know I can't. My thoughts drift to the reality waiting for me at home. I glance at the clock hanging on the wall. It's already after noon, which means Russell will be awake, expecting a home-cooked meal. The weight of it hits me all over again, but I try my best not to let it pull me under.

"Maybe next time," I say, pursing my lips together.

"Fine, but we're going out again soon."

***

WHEN WE GET HOME, I expect Russell to be lounging on the couch, a football game blasting from the sixty-five-inch TV hanging in our living room. I imagine him with a beer in hand and annoyance plastered on his face as he waits for me to start cooking. But when I open the door, the savory scent of garlic and onions wafts from the kitchen.

I lay our sleeping daughter on the couch, then make my way into the kitchen. Russell hovers over the stove, stirring something in a pot. I pause, taken aback, because it's not like him to be in the kitchen.

I'm thankful that Russell can cook, but that's usually a duty he leaves for me. I cook every day because Russell doesn't like to waste money on takeout, and he works a lot.

"Hey, baby," he says casually as he looks over his shoulder.

I stand there for a second, wondering if I'm dreaming. "Hey," I whisper.

"I was hoping to be done cooking before you got home." He lowers the temp on the stove and turns to face me. "I wanted to switch things up today—surprise you," he says.

My heart flutters at the sight of him genuinely doing something nice for me. My mouth drops open, and my words fail me. "Babe—" He slides his hand around my waist, pulling me closer to him. The gesture feels so foreign that it takes me a minute to relax in his arms. It's a rare moment between us that I never want to end—because I'd forgotten how good it feels to be held by him.

"Don't make it into a big deal," he says sharply.

"I won't." I exhale. "So, what'd you cook?"

"Loaded potato soup. One of your favorites."

I look up at Russell, a grin spreading across my lips at his thoughtful actions. The version of him that stands in front of me is what assures me that things will get better. *Hopefully.*

"Loaded potato soup, huh?" I tease lightly. "You're really trying to win me over, aren't you?"

Russell laughs, a twinkle in his eye I don't see often. "Maybe a little." He pauses, lifting my chin with his index finger. "I just wanted to do something nice for you."

I gulp, and my knees become slightly weak. I look into his eyes, and I let myself believe him, despite how things have been recently. "Well," I say, taking a step back to glance at the pot on the stove, "it smells amazing."

"Good." His voice is deep and low. "I hope you like it."

"I'm sure I will. Thank you, Russ," I respond, planting a firm kiss onto his cheek.

"How was church?" he asks, which he rarely ever does.

"It was great," I say with a raised eyebrow.

Russell nods, turning back to the stove as the aroma of the soup fills the room. "Good to hear. I might join you next Sunday."

My mouth falls open again, and I wonder if Russell is feeling okay. I lean against the counter, watching him work. He's never volunteered to go to church with me. If I hadn't heard him say the words myself, I would've never believed it. I pray that this version of him shows up more often.

I can't shake the nagging feeling that this might be like a shadow—brief and fleeting, disappearing as quickly as it appeared, leaving me wondering if it was ever really there. "Are you serious?"

"Yeah, I want to go. Think it'll be good for me."

Chapter 5

RUSSELL ALREADY SEASONED THE burgers and tossed them on the grill by the time Darnell and Trina arrive to join us for dinner. I still can't believe he was fine with having them over.

When Trina walks through the front door, I can't help but notice her round belly pressing against me as we hug. "Oh my goodness, it's so good to see you, Trina. You look amazing!"

"I don't feel amazing, but I'll take the compliment!" She laughs, rubbing her belly with a tired but genuine smile.

Her movements are slow and a bit clumsy as she struggles to remove her jacket. I'm about to offer help, but Darnell is already at her side. He carefully guides the jacket off her shoulders.

"I'm so huge I can't even take off my jacket," Trina jokes, shaking her head.

"You're not huge, and you're doing great," Darnell reassures her, draping the jacket over his arm. "But I've got you."

"Thanks, babe," Trina murmurs, placing her hand along Darnell's cheek with a soft grin.

"So, when are you due?" I ask as I lead them further into the living room.

"Three months," Trina replies with an exaggerated sigh, "but I feel like I'm about to explode." She waddles toward the couch like a penguin.

I remember those days—the aching back, swollen feet, and sore breasts.

Darnell, being attentive to her every need, places one hand on her back and the other on her forearm. He gently supports her as she lowers herself onto the firm cushions.

A grunt escapes her as she plops down, a mix of relief and exhaustion. "Russell around?" Darnell asks, his eyes sweeping the room.

"Yeah, he's out back checking on the burgers," I say, jerking my thumb over my shoulder toward the back door.

Darnell heads out back, leaving Trina and me alone in the living room. "Can I get you some water or anything?"

"No, I'm fine. Thanks." She rubs her belly absentmindedly.

My eyes linger on her circular stomach, and I can't help but think about my own pregnancy with Liv. I miss those little moments—feeling her tiny feet kicking inside me, the reassurance that she was safe from the outside world. Of course, labor was another story entirely. The pain was excruciating, and the exhaustion pushed my body to limits I didn't think possible. Russell was there but was just as nervous as I was. I had always imagined my mom being there to help me, to comfort me—but Zara had come, held my hand, and tended to my every need. I don't think I could have done it without her. But in the end, it was all worth it.

"How have you been?"

Trina looks at me with a tired but kind expression. Her short black bob frames her face, highlighting her puffy cheeks. Despite her discomfort, there's a glow about her that reminds me of how beautiful pregnancy is, even in its hardest moments.

"As good as I can be." Trina chuckles. "Raising three boys while being pregnant has shown me a whole new meaning of exhaustion."

"I can only imagine. I just have Liv, and she keeps me on my toes as it is." A tender laugh escapes my lips.

"Girl, I'm sure you could manage just fine. But my parents are a huge help," she says with a grateful tone.

I shift in my seat, my thoughts wandering to my own mom again. I wonder how different life would be if she were still earthside—how close she and Liv would've been. It pains me to know they never got the chance to meet, but I like to believe Liv met her before God placed her in my womb. I know that sounds crazy, but it brings me comfort.

"How are you and Russell?" Trina's question pulls me back to the moment.

"We're doing good," I say, which isn't a lie this time. Surprisingly, things have been better. I don't want to get my hopes up as it's only been about a week, but Russell has been so intentional lately. I can't help but think that maybe God is answering my prayers.

"Where's Liv?" she asks, glancing around the room.

"She's with Ms. Mildred, the babysitter."

Before I can say more, Russell and Darnell enter the living room. The aroma of garlic butter and burgers swirls through the air as they walk past us. They chat about work while making their way into the kitchen. As I look at them with smiles plastered on their faces, I can't stop the reminder of betrayal when I learned that Russell didn't tell me about their son's party. But if I want things to continue the way they have been, I may never get my answer.

The doorbell rings, interrupting our conversation.

"That must be Zara and Akin," I say, rising to answer the door.

Russell's recent good mood has been a pleasant shock. I expected him to be upset about me planning this dinner without running it by him first, but to my surprise, he didn't put up a fight. So I took a chance and invited Zara and Akin, and he hesitated for a moment before shrugging his shoulders and saying, "Sure, why not?"

I smile to myself as I head to the door, hoping the evening continues on this positive note. But when I open it, my smile falters briefly. It's not just Zara and Akin standing there as expected. Behind them is Malachi, hands shoved into his trench jacket. Standing beside him, however, is the beautiful woman I noticed at Zara's grand opening—the one who had her hand resting on his shoulder, laughing as he spoke.

Her presence catches me off guard. She's dressed in a tight black dress with heels, and her golden blonde hair falls in perfect waves over her shoulders.

"Hey!" Zara chirps, stepping forward to hug me, completely oblivious to my surprise of two extra guests. Although Malachi's been here plenty of times, I've never met this woman.

"Uh . . . hey," I manage to say. My eyes shift to Malachi, my brow arching in silent inquiry. He offers a casual nod, a faint grin tugging at his lips. He's just as oblivious as Zara.

"I hope you don't mind," Zara says, looping her arm through mine as she steps inside, the others following close behind her. "Malachi is staying at our place for a few months because a water pipe burst in his apartment, basically ruining everything. But I figured he could join us for dinner, and his girlfriend was stopping by, so . . . is that cool? Akin brought extra salad."

I blink, caught off guard yet again. *What? He has a girlfriend?* Malachi is practically like family—of course I don't mind him joining us, but I didn't even know he was dating someone. *When did that happen?* Russell had been fine with the four guests I'd told him about, but adding Malachi to the mix with a random woman is sure to be a problem. My stomach flips.

Russell's standing over the stove, his gaze landing on Malachi and the unfamiliar blonde at his side. "What's going on?" he asks, his tone steady but curious.

I force a smile, gesturing toward our guests. "Oh . . . um, Malachi and his girlfriend . . . uh . . ." I trail off.

"Phoebe!" the woman says enthusiastically.

"Right, Phoebe," I repeat, turning to Russell. "They want to join us for dinner. Do you mind?"

For a moment, Russell's facial expression changes—a dense look that flashes in his eyes, accompanied by a large vein in his forehead. But it's gone just as quickly as it appeared, replaced by a polite smile.

"Of course I don't mind," he says. "The more the merrier." His tone is laced with tension that only I notice. He turns back around, putting his attention on the stove. Darnell, standing beside him, waves to everyone. Darnell and Trina have met Zara, Akin, and Malachi a few times at the occasional cookout and dinners.

Despite him agreeing that they can join us, something about his expression leaves me flustered. I try to ignore it and focus on entertaining the guests.

***

"SO, ZARA AND AKIN, any kids in your future?" Trina asks, poking pieces of romaine lettuce and spinach onto her fork. She sits between Zara and Phoebe, with Akin, Darnell, and Malachi sitting across from them while Russell and I sit on opposite ends of the long table.

Zara covers her mouth as she swallows a bite of her cheeseburger. "One day, but not right now."

"With the art gallery just opening and me taking on more clients at the marketing firm, we think it's best to wait. At least another year or so," Akin adds.

Zara looks up at him with a smile full of radiant love. I know they both want children someday, but because of Akin's upbringing, he wants to be financially stable first. The way they adore Liv, I know they'll be wonderful parents when the time comes.

"Man, wait as long as you can. Travel, date, and enjoy life together," Russell says. My head snaps toward him at the hint of regret in his tone. I clear my throat and perch my elbows onto the table, but I don't respond. I can't—not with everyone here and not with how good things have been going.

"I'll admit, things change when you have kids, but it's not the end of the world," Darnell says.

"Right. I mean, we still date and travel. It's different now, but life is great," Trina says, placing her hand affectionately on Darnell's. "Instead of laying up at the beach being freaky, we're building sandcastles and playing in the water."

"Well, obviously you two are good in that department." Malachi laughs, nodding toward her bump.

Trina winks at Darnell, and we erupt in laughter.

"When the time is right, we'll know," Zara reiterates.

"I've always wanted kids," Phoebe chimes in, her voice bright and bubbly. The cheerful tone immediately draws our attention as she continues. "I have three sisters and four brothers, so I grew up in a big family. I want one just like it."

It doesn't take long for me to come to the realization that Phoebe is a talker. She's definitely an extrovert. Even though I still feel weird about not knowing Malachi had a girlfriend, I like her. She's a ray of sunshine, and I think Malachi might have found someone good for him. His track record hasn't always been the best in the dating department, but Phoebe gives me hope.

Even though Phoebe just met the rest of us, she talks as if she's known us forever.

Malachi takes a sip of his water, staying quiet as Phoebe speaks. I can't help but notice his eyes widening slightly, and I wonder if they've had this conversation before. But given the relationship being so new, they probably haven't.

"How long have you two been dating?" I ask, genuinely curious.

Phoebe grins, her red lipstick accentuating the curve of her lips. "Just a few weeks now. Well, we just made it official, but we met three months ago." Phoebe flashes Malachi an encouraging smile. "Babe, tell them how we met."

All eyes shift to him, and he rubs the back of his neck, a faint hint of discomfort crossing his face. His brown eyes briefly meet mine before settling on his plate.

"Um, it's not much to tell," he says with a low voice.

"Brother, please do tell." Zara chuckles, eager to hear the story as much as the rest of us.

He clears his throat, sitting straighter. "Well, we met at the coffee shop."

"That's it?" I ask. If so, that's not an interesting story at all. I have a feeling he's holding back, skipping important details.

"Fine, I'll tell them." Phoebe grins as she leans forward on her elbows. "Okay, so it's seven in the morning, and I'm running on energy drinks and granola bars after working a double shift at the hospital. I decide to stop by his coffee shop, which I'd never been to before, but I saw it in passing. I'm already running late to my dental appointment when I notice this handsome man behind the counter." She takes a moment to look at Malachi, her eyes twinkling with affection.

"As Malachi grabs my cup of coffee to hand to me, he bumps into one of his employees and hurls the entire cup right onto my scrubs."

The table erupts into laughter as Malachi groans, sinking back into his chair. "It's not my fault. I didn't see the newbie coming behind me. But it was iced coffee. It could've been a lot worse."

"I'm standing there, soaking wet and covered in sticky syrup, while he stands there frozen like a deer in headlights," Phoebe continues, her hands flying in the air. "Then he grabs a stack of napkins and starts patting me down like we're on a first-name basis."

"I wasn't trying to pat you down," Malachi protests as everyone continues laughing. "I was trying to help clean you off."

"Oh, sure, Mal, whatever you say." She winks. "He offered me free coffee for two months as an apology, which I think he did on purpose to make sure I came back."

"That's a smart move, man." Darnell laughs, nudging Malachi with his elbow.

"After I came in a few times, he finally asked me out on a date." Phoebe clasps her fingers together dramatically as she finishes her story. A smile tugs at my lips as I envision Malachi doing something so clumsy. I can picture him noticing her beauty, getting distracted, then spilling coffee all over her.

Malachi owns the Good Brew, a cozy coffee shop downtown nestled near all the aesthetically pleasing franchises. It's not too far from Zara's gallery.

His coffee is rich and strong; it's my favorite. But I don't get to drink it often, because Russell has a strict budget for me to follow. When I am rewarded with the luxury of buying a coffee, I go to his shop. Not just because we're friends, but because he has the best coffee in town.

"How did you two meet?" Phoebe asks me, her bright eyes meeting mine as she digs into her salad. She's vegetarian, which is why I'm glad I prepared a fresh salad and fries to go with the juicy burgers. And it's a good thing Akin brought additional salad mix.

The question throws me for a loop, and I can feel Russell's eyes on me. Everyone knows how we met except Phoebe. It's not something I like to talk about much.

Russell traces the rim of his beer. His eyes loom at me, awaiting my response.

"Um, we met at a restaurant."

"You holding out on me, Asha?" Phoebe playfully raises her eyebrows in suspense. "Give me all the deets!"

I shrug. "I was on a date, and it wasn't going well. Russell was there with some friends from work, and he stepped in to help."

"The guy was a douche bag." Malachi speaks up. "I begged Asha not to go out with him, but she insisted."

He did in fact tell me not to date him. When I think about it, he's warned me not to date half the guys I went out with throughout high school and college. He'd been right about most of them, surprisingly. I'm sure he can recognize the crazies, given his history of unhinged girlfriends.

"He wasn't even cute," Zara adds, shaking her head with a laugh.

Trina laughs while rubbing her belly. "What happened after that? I can't remember, pregnancy brain and all."

"Well," I begin, pushing a tomato around my plate, "Russell jerked the guy up and threw him out on the sidewalk."

Darnell laughs, clearly remembering the story because he was there. Even though it happened a few years ago, I still think about that night. At first, I'd admired how Russell stood up for me, but now his actions have taken on a new meaning. When he's frustrated or annoyed at me, the same spark of anger flashes in his eyes that he had that night. His quick, impulsive reaction to defend me was a glimpse of something deeper. Something I didn't know would be evident in our future.

I wonder if the warning signs of his anger problems were always there. I guess I chose to overlook them because he was there when I needed him.

"My date was trying to feel me up."

Malachi shifts in his seat before I can continue. Specifically, the guy slid his hand up my thigh even after I asked him to stop. I tried to pull away from him, but he was stronger than me. When I raised my voice to make my wishes clear, all eyes turned to us. That's when Russell jumped from his table—tall, dark, and intimidating. I'd even been scared.

"After that, he made sure I got home safe," I say more quietly. Russell's five years older than me, and at the time, I was living on my own. I was a young, stupid girl just trying to figure out adulthood.

I glance at Russell, his gaze unreadable as I speak.

"He would have lost his job if that guy had pressed charges." Darnell takes a swig of his beer and grimaces as it travels down his throat.

"Well, good thing he didn't." Russell rubs a hand over his beard. He looks down at the table. "But for Asha I'd do anything." His words make me shift in my seat.

After we all finish eating the delicious food, we gather in the living room. Zara lounges on the couch, Akin sitting on the floor between her legs as she plays with his long dreadlocks. Trina sits beside Zara as Darnell rests on the arm of the couch. His hands move gently, massaging the knots in her shoulders. Trina leans back, her eyes heavy from the late hour and satisfying food. Phoebe and Malachi are on the opposite couch, her hand resting on his knee. I stand next to the recliner where Russell is sitting, and without a word, he pulls me down onto his lap.

"How come you two aren't married yet?" Phoebe asks with that same glowing smile never leaving her face. Before the end of the night, I'm pretty sure Phoebe will know more about us than we do ourselves.

I glance at Russell, silently giving him the chance to respond. He runs his hand down the side of my leg, meeting my gaze. "Just have a lot going on," he says. I break his gaze and look down at my left hand.

My acrylic nails are painted with white French tips, and I can't help but wonder how I'd look with a ring on.

Zara huffs. I don't look at her, because if I do, I'm pretty sure she'll have a scowl spread across her face. She knows how badly I want to get married. I want to do things the right way. The way I was taught, even though I went astray after my mother passed.

But my desire for marriage has never wavered. I want to be a wife, not just a girlfriend or baby mama. "Miss Wilma would be rolling over in her grave if she knew her daughter was playing house," Zara says jokingly, but her words sting.

My mother had always taught Zara and me the importance of saving ourselves for marriage and not giving our bodies to just anyone. She'd met my father at church, they got married after a year of dating, and she had me the following year. He passed away before I was born. Never got the chance to know him. I wonder often if he'd approve of Russell or if they had similarities.

When Russell and I started dating, things moved quickly. I hadn't expected to get pregnant so soon into our relationship, but it happened. I felt so guilty, scared, and condemned. I had no idea how I was going to get through it, but with the help of Zara and her family, I did it.

Russell's body tenses at the comment, his countenance changing. "I think she'd be happy to know I'm taking care of her daughter." The room is silent for a moment, his words sinking deep into my mind.

Would she really be happy? I wonder.

Trina, eyes half closed from exhaustion, asks, "You don't want to get married, Asha?"

I take a moment, trying to choose my words carefully, because I can see the growing tension in Russell's body even if no one else can. His grip tightens along my leg, enough for me to feel it but not hard enough for it to hurt. His eyes grow dark, and his jaw tightens. "Of course I do, but I know Russell will ask when he's ready. Our love is still strong with or without a ring." I say it with so much confidence, I hope it's believable. Lately our love hasn't felt as strong as it once had, but with my wide grin, no one would ever know.

Russell leans forward, pulling me closer while reaching for his beer on the table. He takes a swig, and the bitter smell of the drink matches the sour turn in the conversation.

"I'm going to the bathroom. I'll be right back," I say, trying to escape the pressure. If I stay gone long enough, hopefully the conversation will shift. Enough about Russell and me. Maybe one of the guys will bring up football or Phoebe will ask Trina a bunch of questions about her pregnancy.

As I walk down the hall, heavy footsteps following me catch my attention. When I look behind me, Russell is inches from me. His stare is intense. "What was that?" he whispers as his fingers dig into my arm. He jerks me toward the wall, and I hit it with a soft thud.

I gasp. My heart pounds in my chest so loud I can hear it in my ears. "What are you talking about?" I sigh, knowing our friends are just out of earshot.

"I'm talking about how you tried to embarrass me in front of everybody." The accusation stings, and I try to process how he could jump to that conclusion. I would never do that.

"No, of course not. I was answering their questions," I explain, but his grip on me only gets stronger. My skin throbs where his fingers dig in. His short-clipped nails pierce into me. It hurts so bad that I bite my bottom lip to keep from screaming.

"You keep it up, and I swear—"

"You're hurting me," I groan, hoping he'll listen. I try to pry my arm from his grasp, but he pushes me into the wall, closing the gap between us. I can't escape. My friends are down the hall in the living room, and I can call for them, but what then? *What will they think or say?* I want them to like Russell, so I keep quiet. "I'm sorry," I say in an attempt to calm him.

Before Russell can respond, Malachi's voice cuts through the tension. "Everything all right, Asha?" He's standing a few feet away, arms folded across his muscular chest.

I take a sharp breath, surprised to see him there, wondering how much he saw. My heart is still racing. As Russell's hand drops from my arm, I nod quickly, forcing a smile, masking my pain.

His hand now slides up my neck and he plants a kiss on my lips, pretending we were just sharing an intimate moment. I flutter my eyes at him, going along with the facade. When I glance at Malachi, the scowl on his face is unwavering.

"Everything's fine, man," Russell says with a coerced laugh that doesn't ease the tension.

"Is it?" he asks, waiting for me to answer.

"Yeah." But my voice cracks, betraying me.

Chapter 6

I'VE BEEN ON THE phone with Zara for the past ten minutes. She's giving me an earful about what Malachi saw between Russell and me the other night. "It was nothing, I swear." I say, sitting cross-legged on the floor in my daughter's room.

Liv's beside me, her chubby hands trying to stack the pink and purple blocks on top of each other. She keeps pausing to shove one into her mouth, babbling happily.

Zara's voice carries a hint of skepticism as she speaks. "Why would my brother lie about something like that?"

I glance at the phone, which is resting on the floor on speaker. My fingers fumble with one of Liv's blocks as anxiety wraps itself around me.

"He said Russell was grabbing your arm, and you looked as if you were about to cry."

I swallow hard, my mouth suddenly dry. The image of last night's events plays in my mind like a reel—Russell's tight grip on my arm, his voice raised in anger after our guests left. The kind, sweet version of him vanished the moment the door closed behind them. He accused me of embarrassing him, though I couldn't understand what I had done wrong. For the next hour, he berated me and made me feel so worthless.

It was all my fault. Whatever I had said or done caused him to lash out. I replayed every conversation in my mind, but nothing hinted toward his embarrassment. "Zara, it's not like that. It was a misunderstanding."

Her sigh crackles over the line, heavy with doubt. "Mal wouldn't lie about something like that. If something's going on, you can tell me."

I hesitate, realizing I could tell her the truth about everything—how Russell's grip had left five tiny fingerprint-shaped bruises on my arm and how his words cut deeply.

But the words refuse to come. Instead, I say what's easier. "Like you said, all couples argue. That's all it was—a little disagreement." I don't know what goes on in anyone else's home, but I have come to the conclusion that maybe every relationship is like ours.

The silence stretches between us. I visualize Zara sitting at her desk, her acrylic nail caught between her teeth as she debates whether to push further or not. "Whatever you say. Malachi already doesn't care too much for Russell, and this was the cherry on the top for him."

"Well, Malachi has never liked anyone I've dated. Ever."

"Because he can see through their crap," Zara snaps. "You know how I feel about Russell, but if you're telling me everything is fine, I'll drop it."

A sigh of relief escapes me. The last thing I want is to keep talking about my relationship or to hear more about how much my closest friends dislike him. While Akin has never openly expressed any animosity toward Russell, he's also never been eager to have him around. Zara, on the other hand, has been vocal about the changes she's noticed in me since Russell came into my life—how I don't go out with her as much anymore, how often I have to check in with Russell when I do go out, and how some days I can't hide the sadness on my face after one of our arguments. She thinks I'm unhappy. And sometimes, I wonder if she's right.

Malachi is another story entirely. He's always been protective, not just of Zara, but of me and any other woman in his circle. He has this expectation that we should be treated like queens, with love and respect. And to his credit, I haven't always chosen the best boyfriends either.

Most of those relationships were meaningless anyway. But when I met Russell, things were different. I thought he was *different*, and a part of me still clings to that hope.

But Malachi doesn't see it that way. He's mentioned to Zara more than once that there's something off about him. The only reason any of them tolerate him is because of me and our sweet girl.

Throughout all their disdain for him, it's pushed me to try harder to get them to see what I see—to like him.

He's always going to be in my life; we have a daughter together. We live together. Our relationship is what it is, and I've become skilled at keeping our problems hidden. Yet as I glance at the faint bruises on my arm, I'm not sure how much longer I can keep up the charade.

I hate lying to my friends, pretending things are fine when they're not. But I can't bring myself to tell them the truth—especially when, deep down, I feel like it's my fault. If I could stop saying or doing stupid things, he wouldn't get so angry.

Desperate to shift the focus, I ask, "So, are you ready for your birthday party?"

Zara's mood changes immediately. She squeals on the other end of the line, and I let out a giggle. Liv jumps slightly, startled by the noise. She then returns to gnawing on her block.

"I'm so excited. I can't believe I'll be twenty-seven in a few short weeks. It feels like just yesterday we were playing with Barbie dolls and sneaking out of the house to go to parties," Zara says with a laugh, her voice full of nostalgia.

I chuckle as countless memories flood my mind like a projector casting images on a wall. "Those were the good old days."

"Yes, if only we could be sixteen again," she exclaims. "But I have most of the plans figured out already. I think I want to keep it simple this year and save the big blowout for my thirtieth birthday."

"Whatever you decide, I'm sure it'll be amazing," I say as Liv stands up on her wobbly little legs and toddles over to me. She plops herself into my lap, laying her head against my chest. Her sleepy eyes tell me she's ready for her nap.

"Of course it will."

"How's it going with Malachi living with you?"

"It's actually not as bad as I thought it would be," Zara admits. "I figured it'd be like when we were kids—you know, him leaving his dirty clothes everywhere, his room smelling like onions and sweaty socks. But I guess adulthood has made him cleaner."

I smile at the mental image of a younger, messier Malachi. How I'd have to squeeze my nose every time I walked past his bedroom door when we were teens. "How long is it going to take to fix his apartment?"

"We have no idea." She sighs. "The damage was to his entire floor. They've got to do drywall removal, replace the flooring, and gain access to the pipes to figure out what happened and do repairs. Honestly, I told him he might as well start looking for a new place to live. He can't stay here forever. Me and my man need our alone time. I hate knowing Malachi is in the next room over."

"Phoebe seems nice. I like her."

"She's super sweet," Zara says warmly. I hear shuffling in the background, probably her rearranging something on her desk.

"How come I'm just now finding out about her?" I finally ask the question that's been plaguing my mind.

"Malachi told me not to say anything. He said he wasn't sure how things were going to go with her, but I guess they are going pretty good."

"She's very pretty," I add, trying to ignore the part about him telling Zara not to tell me.

"I like her too, but that woman can talk. Malachi says it's like that twenty-four-seven. But hey, I've got to get back to work. I'll call you tonight, okay?"

"Yeah, talk to you later," I reply, ending the call. I glance down at my curly-headed daughter, her eyes now closed. Her chest rises and falls in a steady rhythm. She's fast asleep.

I stand and gently place Liv in her crib, covering her with a thin blanket.

With Russell still at work and Liv asleep, it would be the perfect time for me to take an hour or two to relax, but I can't relax until dinner is ready. I have no idea if Russell will get off early and come home in a mood. So instead of curling up with a good book, I take out the chicken that has been marinating in the refrigerator since this morning. I put on a sermon on the TV while I prepare dinner.

***

THE CLOCK ON THE wall ticks loudly, each second never-ending as I sit at the kitchen table. The plate I prepared for Russell is cold now, untouched. I've already fed Liv, bathed her, and put her back to bed, and Russell's still not home. Normally he'll text or call to let me know he will be home late, but that hasn't happened tonight, which causes me to worry. I shower and then make my way back downstairs. Still, there's no sign of him.

It isn't until an hour later that I hear keys jingling at the door. Russell's shirt is untucked, his tie loosened, and his eyes are red. I know this look. It's his *I just got done drinking* look.

"You're late," I say, keeping my voice as calm as possible.

Russell shrugs, his eyes barely meeting mine. He tosses his keys onto the kitchen island, and they land with a clatter. "I had a long day."

"I made dinner," I say, gesturing to the plate across from me. "I can heat it back up."

"Nah, it's fine," he mutters, slumping into the chair. He rubs his face. "I ate already."

I press my thick lips together as I fight the urge to say more. If I would have known he was coming home late and had already eaten, I could have taken time to relax. It's rare that I get opportunities to do something that I enjoy, something that helps me unwind. "You could've called. Or texted. I was waiting—"

"Waiting for what, Asha? For me to come home so you can nag and get on my nerves?" he snaps. His voice is slurred but pointed.

I blink, taken aback, because the man who made my favorite soup in the kitchen has disappeared again. "I wanted to make sure you were okay."

"Now you see how I feel." He grunts. "But I'm fine. I don't need you hovering over me like I'm some child. I'm the man of this house."

His words slap me across the face.

Don't say anything stupid, I tell myself. I refuse to fight tonight. "I'm going to bed," I mutter, getting up and leaving the kitchen before he can stop me.

I crawl into bed, pulling the covers up to my chin as I try to block out the sound of Russell moving around downstairs. Moments later, the door creaks open, and his uneven footsteps approach the bed.

He yanks off his shirt and jeans before collapsing onto the bed beside me. The strong smell of alcohol hits me instantly.

"Asha," he mumbles, his hand resting on my hip.

I remain quiet, praying he'll assume I'm asleep and leave me alone for the night. My body stiffens like a brick as he inches closer to me, the smell becoming unbearable. I hope that Russell will fall asleep, allowing the intoxication to pull him into a deep slumber. It isn't until I feel his breath on my ear that I realize he has other plans in mind.

"Russ—" My voice cracks. "Please don't." One thing I've been struggling with lately is the reality of our predicament. I know what the Bible says about fornication, and yet I chose to live in it for so long, even had a child from it. But now that I'm trying to better myself, strengthen my relationship with God, and show my daughter the right way, I've been trying to avoid doing something I'd done plenty of times. Conviction eats at my insides as I say a quick prayer.

"What?" he whispers.

"Just don't," I say firmly, grabbing his arm and lifting it from my hip.

"What's the matter with you?" he snaps. "You don't want me anymore? You don't love me?" His question is full of venom. "You think you can just push me away whenever you feel like it? We haven't done anything in weeks."

"I'm not doing this. I can't," I say, sitting up. I decide that it'll be best for me to sleep on the couch or in Liv's room. I don't want to be around him right now.

"Oh, you're not doing this?" he yells, his voice rising. "You don't get to decide when we 'do this,' Asha. You don't run this house. I do!"

My own anger bubbles to the surface, but I do everything in my power to suppress it. God knows my heart and how badly I want this relationship to work. He also knows how much I want to do what pleases Him, but nothing I do feels good enough. "I know, baby. I don't want to fight, and I'm tired."

"You're tired?" He chuckles. "Tired from what? I'm the one getting up every morning to work long hours to keep your nails done and put food on our table. I'm the one providing for this family."

Russell climbs out of bed, staggering to his feet. My eyes dampen, and I'm glad the lights are off. I don't want him to see me cry.

I may not work, but it's not because I don't want to. He was the one who wanted me to stay home and raise our daughter. He was the one who didn't want Liv going to daycare.

I cook every single day, do all the laundry, mop, sweep, vacuum, and take care of Liv. I go grocery shopping, run errands, make all our appointments and attend every last one. I may not provide financially, but I provide in other ways. My duties as the woman of the house are just as important as his, right? If so, why can't he see that? Should I be doing more?

"I contribute to this family," I whisper.

"Whatever. You can't do what I do every day!" he yells.

"You're right." Before I can stop myself, the words spew from my lips. "I could never come home drunk picking fights every single day!"

My hand shoots up to my mouth as realization kicks in, and I regret my words instantly.

Russell's face twists in anger. "What did you just say to me?"

"Nothing," I stammer. "Nothing. I didn't mean it." I lie because I'm scared of what will happen if he thinks otherwise. Scared that the bruises on my arm will be nothing compared to what he'll do if he blacks out from rage.

"You think I want to drink? That I want to feel like this?" He slams his fist against the wall, and I flinch.

Everything in me screams to run or hide, but I'm frozen in place. Fearful that any sudden movement will cause those fists to hit me instead. I pray that he never hurts me in that way, but lately, the idea has been looming in the back of my mind like a dark cloud.

He punches the wall again, and this time his fist goes right through it. The drywall breaks and falls to the ground. The sound is so loud it wakes Liv. Her cries echo from her bedroom.

"Russell, stop!" I scream. "You're scaring me!"

He holds his white-speckled hand close to his chest and sinks to the floor, leaning against the bed. His shoulders begin to shake. "I'm sorry." His voice cracks. "I didn't mean to scare you."

I sit in silence for a moment as Liv's cries dissipate, but the sound of my pounding heart is evident. He falls apart, tears streaking down his face. His eyes fill with pain.

"I'm sorry, baby," he says again. "Come here."

I don't want to. I'm terrified. But my body betrays me. I crawl across the bed in my pajamas, coming to sit beside him. He places his good hand on my knee, and he rubs it up and down my leg. "There's this case," he starts, "a little girl . . . assaulted by her mother's boyfriend. She's almost the same age as our baby girl. And all I could think about was . . . how someone could do something like that. What if someone hurt Liv like that?"

Tears roll down his cheeks, and he struggles to catch his breath. "The photos, Ash. I see stuff like this every single day, and it's getting to me. I don't know what to do—how to handle it anymore. I just needed to stop thinking, so I went to grab a drink."

My chest contracts as conflicting emotions swirl inside of me. Anger, pity, exhaustion, sadness, love—all battling for dominance. I caress his damp cheeks, bringing his face to look at me. "Russell," I say softly, "I understand that you're scared, and I'm scared too. But this . . . the drinking—it's not the way to deal with it. You can't keep shutting me out and taking it out on me. You have to get some help."

He nods weakly, his face crumpling as he leans into me. He lays his head on my chest. "I'm sorry, Asha. I love you so much, I don't want to lose you. I need you. With work and being stressed all the time, it makes me act this way, and I just need you to be there for me. Can you do that?"

I nod, struggling to swallow the lump in my throat. I exhale deeply, my own tears threatening to spill again. I don't know how the conversation turned from him lashing out at me to him finally opening up, but I'm grateful. This is the first time he's ever talked about work with me, and somehow, I want to call that progress.

I don't know what it's like to do his job, but I can imagine the toll it takes on a person. Relief washes over me, knowing he's given me a sneak peek as to what goes on in his head. It's important for me to know that he's capable of acknowledging his need for help and realizes he can't keep turning to a liquor bottle. But then I feel anger, pity, and sadness that, even though Russell is a witness to violence all day, he has no problem bringing it home to us.

As he lays his head on my chest, his tears soak into my night shirt. I look at the wall where his fist left a hole just minutes ago. "Asha," he cries, "I know I can yell a lot, but you don't have to be scared of me, okay. I'd never hurt you. You know that, right?"

I wrap my arms around his broad shoulders, examining the damage. I don't know how to answer his question, because the bruise on my arm is a revelation that he has in fact hurt me.

Chapter 7

RUSSELL LEFT THURSDAY MORNING for a biannual training in Georgia for a refresher course on the use of deadly force and de-escalation techniques. He's set to return Sunday night, and the thought of him coming home is slightly nauseating. I hate to admit it, but things have been peaceful—quieter—without him here. The house doesn't feel heavy. *I don't feel heavy.*

He checks in frequently, texting every few hours. *How are you and Liv? What are you doing? What's Liv up to? What are your plans for the day?*

Not one message reads *I miss you* or *I love you.* Instead, it's a string of questions that feels insincere.

Part of me wonders if he's checking in because he misses us, but the more cynical part of me believes he's trying to keep tabs. Even from two states away, he still wants to know my every move.

As I sit on my bed, Liv in my arms, my eyes focus on the hole in the wall. Liv drinks from her sippy cup, and she's watching me. Every time I look at the damaged exterior of the wall, it's like a reminder of everything I've been trying to ignore. When I pass it, his fist connecting with the drywall echoes in my ears. I can't stand looking at it any longer, and I have to get it fixed before he gets back. I need it gone.

My first thought is to call Malachi, because he's always been reliable and handy when Russell isn't available. He helped me repair a leaky sink and busted pipe and came to my rescue when my battery died, leaving Liv and me stranded at the store. He's always been there.

He helped with the construction for his business and Zara's, so I'm pretty sure this would be nothing compared to that. But I hesitate. I can already picture his reaction. His eyes will scan the damage, his lips will press into a thin line, and his jaw will clench as he tries to figure out what happened. It won't take him long to put everything together, and he will explode. He'll get so angry that he'll probably drive all the way to Georgia to confront Russell.

Instead, I scroll through my contacts and call Akin. He's the calm and level-headed one out of the bunch. He's always been like an older brother to me. I trust that Akin won't tell Zara if I ask him not to. He won't make a big scene or demand an explanation. Oh, he'll be angry for sure, but he won't yell. He'll show concern and offer some brotherly advice and reassurance. But he'll also trust me to handle the situation.

When I call him, I leave out the details. He agrees to come by as soon as he gets off work.

Akin's SUV pulling into the driveway sends a ripple of nerves through my body. I peek through the blinds, watching as he steps out, toolbox in hand. He's dressed in a plaid shirt and worn jeans.

I open the door before he can knock. I greet him with a genuine smile. "Thanks for coming, Akin."

"No problem, sis," he says warmly, stepping inside. "Where's Russell and Liv?"

"Russell's at training for a few days, and Liv is playing with her toys in her room."

Akin nods, then follows me to where the damage is.

His boots are heavy against the hardwood floor as we enter the master bedroom. The moment we step into the room, his gaze lands on the gaping hole in the wall. He exhales slowly, setting his toolbox down beside him.

Akin chews on his bottom lip. He's silent, but his eyes say a lot when he jerks his head toward me.

I shift uncomfortably and go stand by the closet door with my arms folded across my chest. I wear a long-sleeve sweater and pull the sleeves with my hands. I purposefully picked a shirt that would cover the fading bruises, still not wanting to acknowledge that they came from Russell.

I don't understand how he could hurt me. His grip was so tight, it felt so intentional. But it had to be an accident, right? And if Akin saw them, well that would be another story.

Akin runs his fingers over the jagged edges. "It's not too bad," he murmurs. "I'll have it patched up in no time."

As he works, I sit in the armchair, and the entire room spins on a tilted axis. Liv toddles into the room. Apparently, she's lost interest in her toys, preferring my comforting arms instead. I stroke her curls absentmindedly, letting Akin work in silence.

Minutes pass. Then, without looking up, he speaks. "You gonna tell me what happened?"

My breath catches. I keep my focus on Liv. I hope that rubbing my palm over her back will somehow steady my own nerves, but of course, it doesn't. "It's nothing," I whisper. "Just . . . an accident."

Akin stops what he's doing and turns his head slightly. "An accident?" he repeats with a firm tone.

I nod quickly. "Yeah. Just a stupid accident." I play it off with a chuckle.

Akin doesn't seem to fall for it. He gives me that *do you think I'm stupid* look. "Accidents don't usually leave holes in walls, Asha."

Suddenly, my mouth no longer works. *How do I respond to that?* My throat becomes dry and suffocating. It tightens until it aches.

He sighs again, setting down his tools and turning to face me fully. His expression isn't harsh or demanding—it's caring, like always. "Listen, I'm not one to judge or pry. You know how I am. But if there's something going on, you know you can trust me, right?"

I know that. It's exactly why I called him here. I knew Akin would ask questions. That he'd express concern, because he wouldn't be himself if he didn't. Still, at the weight of his words, my heart aches. All I can do is nod, hoping it will be enough to ease his worries.

He watches me for a moment longer, running a hand over his beard. "I'm not going to say anything to Zara or Mal, because you're a grown woman. But . . ." He pauses, his voice lowering. "I look at you like my little sister, and Liv—she's my goddaughter. I love that little girl to pieces. And I need to know you're both okay."

His words hang in the air like a lifeline, and I almost grab onto them. *Almost.* But instead, I look down at my hands, my fingers fiddling with the hem of my sweater. "We're fine," I say quietly. "Really." The smile I plaster on my face isn't enough to reassure him, but he doesn't pry further.

"All right, then," he says, turning back around to finish fixing the wall. "But if you're not, that's okay too. You don't have to pretend to be, not with us. We've got your back."

His words bring a comfort I didn't think was possible. My friends have always been here for me, but to hear Akin acknowledge my doubts causes my eyes to become glossy. I sniffle. Liv glances up at me again with those perfect eyes and gives me a bright smile.

"How much do I owe you?" I ask Akin as he loads the toolbox into his SUV.

He chuckles. "Asha, you don't have to pay me."

"But I want to," I insist, thumbing through the cash Russell left for me.

He shuts the trunk with a thud and shakes his head. "I'm not taking it. Keep your money. You might need it to bail me out of jail one day." His dark joke isn't lost on me, and I force a small smile. I don't want anyone fighting my battles or getting themselves hurt because of me. "But seriously," he adds. "Don't worry about it."

I hesitate, then tuck the money away. "Thanks, Akin."

"Don't mention it," he says, climbing into the driver's seat and starting the engine.

I pause before calling out, "Akin." He stops, one hand on the wheel, and turns his gaze back to me. "Don't tell Zara," I say, even though he already told me he won't.

He grinds his teeth together and looks away for a moment. "I won't—for now. But if something like this happens again, promise me you'll tell me the truth."

I swallow hard and nod, pursing my lips together. Because deep down, I don't know if I would.

He studies me for a beat longer, and when he realizes I won't give him a verbal response, he nods before pulling out of the driveway. I watch until his taillights disappear down the street before I go back into the house.

Upstairs, I step into my bedroom, my eyes landing on the spot where the hole once was. Akin did a good job—the white patch stands out against the wall, but it's smooth, the damage erased. Tomorrow night I'll repaint it with the can of paint still sitting in the garage. I tell myself that once the wall is whole again, I'll forget it ever happened. When Russell returns . . . things will be different. This won't happen again. *Ever.*

***

BY THE NEXT EVENING, two even coats of paint cover the patch. The wall looks normal again, as if nothing had ever broken it. But standing there staring at the freshly dried paint, I realize something unsettling. Fixing it didn't ease the queasiness in my stomach. It didn't change what happened.

Because even though the hole is gone, I remember that it was there. I remember that Russell's hand put it there.

I recall those same hands that once held me gently, guiding me across a dimly lit dance floor on our third date. How warm his palm was against mine as he pulled me to my feet. His dark burgundy button-up made his smile brighter, and his cologne wrapped around me like a blanket. We had just finished eating—thick burgers and loaded fries at a bar on the outskirts of town. I laughed when he dragged me to the dance floor, my protests falling away the moment he spun me under the low golden lights.

I felt safe then.

I close my eyes, pressing my palm against my chest. I struggle to level my breathing. That version of Russell—the one who danced with me, who whispered in my ear, who kissed my forehead like I was something precious—he existed once.

But so did the version who put his fist through this wall. The version of him who put a bruise on my arm. And I don't know which one will come home to me on Sunday night.

After losing my mother, learning to navigate life without her seemed impossible. Even with Zara, Malachi, and their parents filling in the gaps, it still hurt. My heart held a hollow space that nothing could fill. I withdrew, isolating myself to process the cruel reality that she was gone. I couldn't understand how I was supposed to live in a world that no longer had her in it. And in that isolation, I drifted from God. Not because I stopped believing, but because I didn't know how to find comfort in Him when I was so lost.

Then I met Russell.

He was a breath of fresh air. He was the first person to make me feel something different since my mother's passing. It was new and enticing. Maybe that's why things moved so quickly between us. I clung to him because he offered something no one else could—an escape from my pain. He never knew my mother, so he couldn't remind me of her. Russell filled the emptiness, dulled the loneliness, and for a while, that was enough.

That night, we danced slowly for hours, the world narrowing to just the two of us. When he tilted my chin up, his gaze locked onto mine, and my mind turned fuzzy. Then he kissed me, and for the first time in so long, the weight of grief lifted. The darkness that had followed me since losing her faded into the background.

But somewhere along the way, the dizzying, intoxicating love became something else entirely. And now, I find myself grasping at memories, desperate to get back to the way things used to be.

Ring. Ring. My phone cuts through the silence, pulling me from my thoughts. My eyes flicker to my bed, where Russell's name glows on the screen.

I take a slow breath. I force my fingers steady before pressing the green button. "Hey, baby," I say, injecting as much passion into my voice as I can muster.

"Hey," he exhales. He sounds exhausted. "What are you up to?"

I tuck the phone between my ear and shoulder and head downstairs. "I just put Liv to bed. I'll probably clean the kitchen and head to bed myself. How's training going?"

He groans, the sound heavy and irritated. "A waste of time. They could've sent someone to our precinct to cover all this in one day. But it's all right."

I grab the dirty dishes from the table and begin to rinse them in the sink. "Are you ready to come home?" I don't know why I ask, but I'm genuinely curious. I want to know if he misses us.

"Of course I am." His response is sharp.

I place the rinsed dishes in the dishwasher. I close it and lean against the counter. "Liv misses you," I say. "She's been asking for you."

I sense the smile in his voice when he responds. "I miss her too. I miss both of you."

The simple words hit me harder than they should. They're exactly what I've been longing to hear since he left. Yet at the same time—I worry about him coming back.

"I miss you too," I say softly. And though the words feel distant, I mean them. Through all the uncertainty—I want him back home.

A silence settles between us. It's not awkward, just heavy. It stretches on for a few seconds before I hear movement on his end.

"Asha."

"Yeah?"

He swallows audibly, as if gathering his thoughts. "Are we good?"

I close my eyes, inhaling deeply through my nose. I let the question ruminate. Recollections of the fights and yelling crash over me like a violent wave. But I don't let them pull me under, and I force myself to focus on the good days—the moments when his laughter filled the house, when he played with Liv, and when I caught glimpses of the man I first loved.

"Yeah, we are," I eventually answer, hoping the words will reassure him. Hoping they'll reassure me too.

"Good." Relief is evident in his tone. "I was thinking . . . when I get back, maybe we could have some one-on-one time. Go out to eat, see a movie, just us."

My heart lightens at the suggestion. "Seriously?" I ask, caught off guard.

We haven't been on a real date in over a year. *I wasn't even sure he'd realized how long it'd been.* Between his long hours, raising a toddler, and the chaos of life—the idea of going out together just the two of us seems unrealistic.

"Yeah, babe. I want to get out of the house. Do something fun together. Would you like that?"

"Yeah, of course." The words rush out, full and eager.

"All right, it's a date. When I get back, I'll check my schedule and plan something nice. Just the two of us, like old times."

"Like old times," I echo, a giddy smile pulling at my lips. And for a moment, I feel like a schoolgirl again—blushing, hopeful, remembering what it's like when things are good. When they feel right. When they feel like us again.

Chapter 8

WHEN I WALK INTO the venue Zara rented out for her birthday party, it's immediately evident that she decorated it herself. It's a small building located in the country that most everyone in town uses to host events. No one else could've made this bland and dull building as extravagant as she did.

Balloons float everywhere, filled with swirls of purple and gold confetti. Streamers hang from the ceiling, and a large sign stretches across the room, boldly declaring: *Happy Birthday, Zara!*

Every detail is flawless. Her creativity and elegance are evident as I glance around the room. Thick purple cloths drape the tables, each adorned with golden floral centerpieces and flickering artificial candles. At one end of the building, a balloon arch frames a glittery backdrop for photos. Beside it, a table overflows with neatly wrapped gifts, all waiting for the birthday girl.

Speakers blast the cha-cha slide, and as expected, half the guests occupy the dance floor. Everyone moves in perfect sync. Despite being in their early sixties, Irene and Manuel dance as if they are teenagers again. Irene places her hands on her knees, laughing as Manuel stands behind her, encouraging her as she playfully backs into him. The sight of their seasoned love tugs a smile onto my lips. That's what I want for Russell and me someday.

Russell stands in line at the food bar, piling his plate with a second serving of ribs and mac and cheese. Meanwhile, Zara moves gracefully through the crowd, chatting and laughing with her guests with ease. She practically glows in her sparkly purple fairy dress and gold pumps, her waist-length braids swaying behind her as she walks. *Zara Boyd, my best friend, is that girl!*

Akin stands nearby, engaged in conversation with a few of his cousins, all of whom bear a striking resemblance to him: tall with rich dark skin and long, neatly maintained dreads. Even the women in his family wear their locs beautifully. They look like queens.

The energy in the room is vibrant and full of love because everyone is celebrating Zara. It doesn't take long for the space to get warm. Sweat trickles down my back, and I'm not even dancing yet.

I sit alone at the table, savoring another bite of the banana pudding. The smooth, creamy sweetness pairs perfectly with the crunch of the wafers. It's so good that I want to go back for another serving, but I decide against it. Instead, I scrape the last bit from my plate with the plastic spoon and twirl it into my mouth.

"Is it that good?" Malachi's voice pulls me from my thoughts.

I glance up as he approaches with Liv perched on his shoulders, her tiny fingers gripping his hands for balance. Her face is lit with pure joy, and a grin stretches across his face as he carefully lifts her down and settles into the chair beside me.

"It's really good, actually," I say, laughing as I cover my mouth to finish swallowing.

Liv stares at me, her big eyes gleaming. "Ma-ma," she coos sweetly.

I reach for her and snicker at the smudges of purple frosting on her lips. "Looks like someone got into the birthday cupcakes."

Malachi cracks up, rubbing Liv's back. "Don't tell Z. She wanted a cupcake." He shrugs.

I shake my head, wiping the remaining icing from the corners of her mouth. "You do realize she's going to be bouncing off the walls now, right?"

He smiles, sinking deeper into his chair. "Nothing wrong with that."

"Oh, yeah?" I raise a brow. "Well, when she's too hyper to go to bed tonight, are you coming over to stay up with her?"

He places his hand on the back of his neck and lets out a deep laugh. "Yeah . . . I'm not so sure about that."

"Didn't think so." I giggle, shifting Liv on my lap. My eyes scan the room. "Where's Phoebe? I haven't seen her much tonight."

"She's around here somewhere. Probably taking a work call." He glances toward the back of the venue, unconcerned.

I nod, licking my lips.

"So." Malachi leans in slightly, smirking. "Are you planning to sit here all night, or are you finally going to join us on the dance floor?" A layer of sweat seeps through his shirt, clinging to his back.

I shake my head with a grin. "I think I'll sit this one out."

He laughs. "It's only a matter of time before Zara drags you out there."

I roll my eyes playfully. "You're probably right."

His expression shifts into one of amusement. "Hey, remember when you and Zara did that dance to 'Waterfalls' at the talent show your sophomore year?"

A laugh bursts out of me before I can stop it. My cheeks warm at the memory. "Oh my goodness, how could I forget? I fell in front of the entire school!"

Malachi grins wide, his laughter mixing with mine. "At least you played it off. Nobody even noticed it wasn't part of the routine. Except me."

"Yeah, but I had a red knot on my forehead the size of a ping pong," I remind him. We both erupt into laughter as we reminisce about the event from over ten years ago. "It's not funny," I protest, swatting at his arm.

"Then why are you laughing too?" he teases.

He has a point, and I wipe the tears gathering at my bottom lashes. "Fine, it was funny. But also super embarrassing."

Before Malachi can respond, a familiar voice cuts through the music and chatter. It slices through the fun moment like a knife cutting through cake.

"What are you two laughing about?" Russell asks.

I clear my throat, instinctively sitting up straighter. Malachi, on the other hand, doesn't move. His elbows rest casually on his knees, but his eyes darken as he glares up at Russell. The smile that had been on his face just moments ago is gone.

I press my lips together before answering. "We were just talking about high school."

Russell sets his plate of food down and takes the seat opposite me. The way he and Malachi stare at each other causes me to stiffen. The tension between them is thick and suffocating.

I know exactly why.

Malachi doesn't trust him. Doesn't *like* him, I suppose. And even though I tried to assure him what he saw in the hallway was nothing . . . he clearly doesn't believe me. Because he could see through the lie.

"Oh, really?" Russell's voice drips with skepticism.

"Yeah, really," Malachi replies with the same tone.

I clear my throat again, forcing a light chuckle. I retell the story, hoping to draw out a laugh from my boyfriend, but he doesn't even crack a smile. Instead, his eyes stay locked on Malachi, his head tilting slightly.

"Is there a problem?" Russell asks, his voice calm but carrying an undercurrent of something dangerous.

"Is there?"

"You look like you got something to say," Russell answers.

Malachi's lips curl into a slow, devious smirk. "Nah, man." He leans back, the smirk still covering his face as if he's teasing Russell somehow. I can tell Russell doesn't like it by the tick in his jaw. Malachi's gaze flicks to me. It's subtle, but I know what it means.

Are you okay?

It's unspoken, but I hear it. I give him the smallest nod—an assurance, a silent *I'm fine.*

After a moment, Malachi stands. "Enjoy the rest of the party," he says. As he disappears into the crowd, he glances back over his shoulder once more.

Russell laughs under his breath, shaking his head. "What's his problem?"

I shrug, chewing my lower lip.

"I don't think he likes me," Russell says, taking a bite of his food.

"Why do you think that?"

"It's obvious." He gnaws slowly, eyes narrowing slightly. "He's probably still worked up about that night we got into it."

I shift in my chair at his comment. "He was just worried about me," I say carefully.

Russell scoffs. "I don't care. He needs to mind his business and worry about his own family."

But he is my family. The thought clings to my mind, though I don't dare say it out loud. Besides Russell and Liv, Malachi and his family are all I have.

Russell throws his fork down. "I take care of you two. I don't need him snooping around, trying to make assumptions about what we have going on."

"It's not like that, Russ—" I try to explain, but he cuts me off.

"Are you defending him? Picking his side over mine?"

His words are quick, sharp, laced with bitterness. I tread carefully. Since he's been back, things have been . . . good.

He hasn't kept his promise yet to take me out on a date, but I keep telling myself he will soon. I want to believe that. But if tonight ends in an argument, I don't know where that will leave us.

"Of course not." I sigh, rubbing Liv's back. "You're right. It's none of his business, and I know you'd never hurt me."

The words slip out smoother this time, more easily than they should.

Russell's muscles relax, the tension in his shoulders fading. "Thanks for having my back, baby." His hand finds my cheek, giving it a soft pat.

I can't believe he just did that.

"And I haven't forgotten about our date. I'm just catching up on some paperwork, and then I'll plan something nice for us. I promise."

"I know. I can't wait."

Deep down, I do want date nights and private moments. But the weight of the tension between Russell and Malachi has left me disturbed, like something was about to happen.

"Asha!" Zara's voice blares over the loud music. "Come dance with me!"

She's in the middle of the dance floor, swaying her hips and waving her hands in the air.

I peek at Russell impulsively, searching his face for some kind of unspoken consent. I don't know why I always do that. It frustrates me.

"Go. I'll hold Liv," he says, wiping his hands clean. He reaches for our daughter, and she starts to whine. When she quickly sees the plate of food in front of her, she settles. One thing about Liv—she loves to eat.

Reluctantly, I stride to the dance floor. Zara grabs me and pulls me closer to her. My hand shoots up to my face in mock embarrassment.

I'm not a dancer at all. Whatever rhythm my parents had didn't pass down to me. The only reason I even joined the high school talent show was because Zara begged me to. But as the upbeat music pulses through the room, I do my best to find the tempo. Even though I think I'm the only one dancing like a worm on a hook, something inside me loosens.

Akin dances beside us, moving like a robot. I throw my head back in laughter.

"Esa es mi niñas!" Manuel shouts. That's my girls! He pretends to take a photo with his index fingers and thumbs pinched together.

I follow Zara's lead, letting go for just a moment. I don't want to care about anything else. I just want to dance and have fun—something far too rare these days.

"You get those moves from me," Malachi teases as he slides through the crowd, a bead of sweat trickling down his forehead.

"You *wish*!" Zara shouts back, laughing.

I smile, genuinely happy to see her enjoying her celebration. Her eyes shine as she twirls in excitement. Just as I'm about to tease her, Akin steps in, effortlessly stealing her away from me. He pulls her against his chest as the music shifts into something slower, something softer. The energy in the room shifts with it. Couples draw closer, bodies swaying in sync with the beat.

I take a step back, brushing my dark brown curly hair behind my ears. I plan to slip away from the dance floor, because Russell isn't going to offer a dance, and I'm literally standing in the middle of the floor with couples caressing one another. Just as I'm about to push my way through the crowd, I suddenly find Malachi standing in front of me.

For a moment, neither of us move. We're the only two left standing still. Music fills the room, and my heart does this weird fluttering thing. A wave of awkwardness washes over me.

Malachi extends his hand with a teasing grin. "Come on, don't leave me hanging."

Before I open my mouth to speak, he twirls me around carefully. A surprise laugh escapes my lips as I spin. Everything blurs until I land back in front of him. His hand settles on my waist lightly. He's standing so close that the heat radiating from his touch warms my skin.

For a second, I forget everything else. I forget about Russell sitting at the table. About the heaviness of the past couple of months. I forget about the arguments, drinking, and bruises. Right now, I'm just me.

But then reality creeps in. Russell's voice from earlier echoes in my head. *Are you picking his side over mine?* My stomach knots. I know how this will look to him. Even though this is nothing, just a friendly dance with a close friend—my best friend's brother—he may not see it that way.

I stop moving and take a step back, but his hand still rests on my waist. "You tired already?" he jokes.

"I should check on Liv."

His lip twitches as if he's disappointed, but he doesn't say anything else.

Before I can walk away, Phoebe emerges through the crowd in a yellow dress that complements her fair skin. She looks radiant. Her grin is wide as she hooks her arm around Malachi's, and his hand drops from my waist and to his side.

"Hey, Asha!" she says in her joyful tone. "Let's dance, honey!" She tugs him toward her, and for a moment, Malachi hesitates. His gaze lingers on me, but then he lets Phoebe pull his attention away. I turn quickly, weaving through the crowd.

I stand on the sidelines like some stood-up teenager on prom night, watching everyone dance together. That should be Russell and me out there letting the music wrap around us like a warm embrace.

Glancing toward our table, I expect to find Russell sitting there holding Liv, but his seat is empty. My eyes sweep across the room searching for him, but he's nowhere in sight.

I spot Liv sitting with Zara's cousin Bryana. She's playing peek-a-boo with her while her younger sister, Mariah, chats with their mom. A strange unease settles in my chest as I make my way over. Crossing my arms, I ask, "Where's Russell?"

Bryana barely looks up as she bounces Liv on her knee. "He asked if I could watch her for a minute. I think he might've stepped outside."

"He went that way," Mariah chimes in, pointing toward the side door leading to the hallway.

My pulse ticks up a notch. *Why? Did he see Malachi and me dancing? Oh no.*

"Thanks. Can you keep an eye on her for a few more minutes?"

"Of course," she responds, continuing to play with her.

I head toward the door Mariah pointed to. The music gradually fades as I walk down the hallway and step outside. The door clicks shut behind me. The chilly October night air hits me, sending a shiver up my spine. I scan the area and spot Russell near the edge of the building.

The streetlight casts a warm glow over him, stretching his shadow wide and intimidating against the gravel pavement.

He's pacing back and forth, one hand shoved in his pocket, while the other lifts a silver flask to his lips. The crunch of my heels against the gravel fills the space, and Russell snaps his head toward me. "What are you doing out here?"

"I was looking for you," I say with a shaky voice. I try to remember why I wanted to find him in the first place, but it's vanished from my mind. Seeing him sneaking outside to drink alcohol undoes something in me. "Why are you out here drinking?"

His eyes dart around, and I realize he's intentionally avoiding my gaze. "Why are you questioning me? I'm a grown man."

I bite my bottom lip until it throbs. I'm not going to argue with him. Not here. This is something we'll have to deal with later.

"I'm tired of you always questioning me," Russell spits, striding closer. I instinctively take a step back. "I'm ready to go."

"What, why?" I ask.

He stomps back inside without answering, and I follow, the music growing louder as we reenter the room. "Asha, get your things. We're leaving," Russell commands. My heels click against the floor as I attempt to catch up with him.

He picks up Liv and grips the diaper bag. He walks toward the front entrance, and I grab my purse and phone. On my way out, I stop by the dance floor where Zara and Akin are still dancing. Irene and Manuel are watching, along with a few others who heard Russell.

Zara finally notices me, her smile slipping as she eyes the purse and phone in my hands. "Are you leaving?" she asks.

I nod, my voice apologetic. "Yeah." I pause, searching for something to say, then add, "Russell got called into work, so we're going to head home. Sorry, Z." *Here I go, lying to her again.*

Disappointment lingers in her eyes, and Akin places a hand on her shoulder. Both of their faces are filled with concern. "Everything okay?" I know he's asking because I promised I'd let him know if things weren't.

"Yeah." But my reassurance doesn't do anything to ease their worried expressions.

"Do you really have to go so early? The party is just starting." She sounds as if she's about to cry, and my own eyes become glossy.

I'm such a bad friend. "I know, but he has to go to work. I'm sorry."

Zara pulls me into a tight hug. "You owe me," she whispers into my ear, her voice teasing but with a hint of pain.

I force a chuckle because I don't want them to worry. I catch Akin's glare over her shoulder, and I know he's watching Russell, who's growing impatient with me.

"I got you, girl," I say, trying to lighten the mood.

Zara returns to dancing, but disappointment still flickers in her eyes. She'll do her best to enjoy the rest of the night, but I know it stings. I'm her best friend. I should be here to the very end. I should be here when they sing happy birthday and eat the cupcakes.

Akin lingers for a moment, his hands shoved in his pockets.

"Call me if you need me," he says quietly.

"I will."

Chapter 9

WHEN I WAKE UP, the first thing I notice is the raw burning in my throat. My body is on fire, yet chills trail over my skin. My head is heavy like a brick. My nose is stuffy and each breath ragged. I can't remember the last time I felt this sick.

Just getting out of bed is a struggle, but Liv needs to eat, so I force myself into the kitchen. Every movement is unbearable; it takes all my energy to simply stir a bowl of oatmeal.

Russell was already gone when I woke up. I've been calling him, but it goes straight to voicemail. Either way, I doubt he'd leave work because I'm sick. Nothing can pull him from his job. Not even me. But I wish he'd put me first, just this once. I feel wiped out, barely able to keep my eyes open. I send a quick text to Zara, telling her how sick I am.

By the time I finish making Liv's breakfast and find a spot on the couch to feed her, my hands are shaking. Before I know it, Zara's unlocking my door with the spare key hidden under the potted plant outside.

"Aww, babe, you look awful." She drops her purse and keys onto the coffee table before rushing to my side. Zara presses the back of her hand to my forehead, her brows knit together.

"I feel terrible." My voice comes out hoarse, barely more than a whisper. "I'm sorry for pulling you away from work, but Russell's not answering, and I just . . . I can't do it today."

"Don't even worry about it. I got you," Zara says without hesitation. She scoops Liv up from my lap and gently takes the oatmeal bowl from my unsteady hands. "I'll get Ma to bring over her herbal juice."

Relief washes over me as I sink into the couch. I don't have the strength to even thank her. My eyelids are clumsy, which allows my body to give into exhaustion easier. I don't try to fight it when sleep pulls me under.

While I float in and out of a strange slumber, faint chatter echoes in the background. The voices seem distant, almost dream-like. I don't know if I'm imagining them or if they're coming from inside the house.

My mind tries to pull me awake, but my body resists, dragging me back into the heavy fog of sleep. This is the only time I feel relief. Each time my eyelids flutter open, the feverish ache returns.

I don't know how long I've been asleep when a gentle shake pulls me from the depths of my exhaustion. Blinking, I find Irene leaning over me with a cup in her hand.

"Here, sweetheart, take a sip of this." I don't know when she arrived, but here she is, pressing the rim of the cup to my lips. I take a small sip of the deep purple liquid. A mix of ginger, berries, and something bitter coats my tongue, making me grimace.

"It'll make you feel better in no time," she assures me.

I force myself to take another sip, knowing from experience that Irene's herbal juice works wonders. I drank this same concoction when I was younger, back when she'd make a jug of it for my mom every flu season.

Irene gives me a kind smile, her hand running over my wild curls that have become a knotted mess. I don't look forward to detangling it later.

When I glance up at her, my vision is almost blurry. Her smile slips, and for a moment I begin to worry. I must look exactly how I feel. *Miserable.*

"Zara, where are the rags?" she asks, setting the cup on the table.

A few moments later, Irene returns with two damp rags. She places one on my forehead and the other on my neck, and the icy relief immediately chills my burning skin.

My throat is raw as I swallow and croak out, "Has Russell called?"

"No, we haven't heard from him. I tried calling, but he didn't answer," Zara replies from somewhere behind me. "I'll see if Akin can get in touch with Darnell."

"Thank you," I whisper. I lick my chapped lips and close my eyes again.

Liv's cheerful giggles echo in the background, and I can imagine Zara making weird faces or tickling her, causing her to laugh. Despite how awful I feel, a small swell of gratitude fills my heart. Without Zara and Irene, I don't know how I'd be managing right now. They stepped in without hesitation, and I don't take that for granted.

"You just get some rest, sweetheart," Irene says softly before disappearing from my sight.

I'm too exhausted to turn and see what they're doing, but their voices continue murmuring behind me. Zara is on the phone with one of her employees talking about a shipment that's supposed to arrive sometime today.

A flicker of guilt stirs in me. Zara should be at her gallery, working on her art and greeting the customers. She shouldn't be here, Russell should.

Whatever I have, I don't wish it on my worst enemy. Since I don't get out of the house much, I'm not sure where this sickness came from. I pray that Irene's juice starts working quickly, because I'm not sure how much longer I can take it.

A loud ringing causes my head to throb. It takes a moment to register the sound. It's Zara's awful ringtone. It sounds like retro elevator music. Her voice cuts through my feverish haze. "Russell? Where have you been? We've been calling you all morning!"

My eyelids flutter open, but my body feels too weak to move. Zara's frustration is evident as she presses the phone to her ear, pacing the room. Then, she puts him on speaker.

"I'm at work, Zara," Russell's voice booms over the speaker, irritation filling his tone. "I'm handling a homicide. I can't just leave."

She forces a breath through her nose before crossing her arms over her chest. "Asha is really sick, Russell. She has a fever, chills, and can barely keep her eyes open. Irene is here helping me take care of her and Liv. She needs you right now."

Russell sighs. "It's probably just the flu or something. How bad is it? I mean, you and Irene are there, right? She's not alone."

Zara's fist tightens, evidence that she wants to punch something. Irene shakes her head from where she's holding Liv on the couch opposite me. "Yeah, we're here," Zara bites out, "but that's not the point."

"I get it, but I can't just leave in the middle of a case. This is serious."

"So is this."

"If it's so serious, then take her to the hospital." It's clear he's already made up his mind. He's not coming, and that knowledge shatters something in me. "Look, I'll come when I get off. Just make sure she stays hydrated and let her rest."

Irene mutters something in Spanish under her breath. Even if she spoke up, I wouldn't understand. After more than twenty years of marriage to Manuel, she's fluent in his language. I may not know the words, but the sharp shake of her head tells me—whatever she said wasn't kind.

Zara presses her lips into a thin line. "That's what we're already doing. I just thought you'd want to know so you can be here with her."

He exhales on the other end, followed by a stretch of silence. Then, his tone shifts slightly. He speaks more softly when he says, "Zara, let me talk to her."

She looks down at me, hesitating before holding the phone close enough for us to hear each other. My body feels weak, my throat dry and scratchy. I don't want to talk because I'm so exhausted. I take a shallow breath and manage a gruff whisper. "I'm here."

"How are you feeling?"

"Terrible."

"Did you take anything?"

"Irene gave me something." Every time I talk, it hurts. I rub my throat, praying that he stops asking questions.

Russell pauses for a moment. "All right. Tell Zara to give you some medicine out of the cabinet. I'll be there soon."

A part of me wants to ask him when that will be, but I already know the answer. He'll be late. So instead, I just nod weakly, even though he can't see me. His dismissive behavior causes my eyes to water, but I'm too sick to meditate on it. "Okay," I murmur.

There's another pause, and for a split second, I think he might say something more. But then, all I hear is noise before the call disconnects.

Zara pulls the phone away, shaking her head with an annoyed sigh. "He's unbelievable sometimes," she says, shoving the phone into her pocket.

Irene clicks her tongue, shaking her head too. "That boy—" She stops herself, inhaling sharply through her nose as if biting back whatever she really wants to say. Instead, she sighs and stands, effortlessly shifting Liv against her chest. "I'm going to put this little one down for a nap."

Zara settles onto the edge of the couch, holding the cup to my lips. "Try to drink all of it," she urges gently.

It takes a few slow gulps, my throat burning with each swallow, but I manage to finish. As soon as I do, Zara is ready with a dose of liquid medicine. I grimace at the taste. "If you're not feeling better soon, I don't care what you say—I'm taking you to the hospital."

I nod, then I let my heavy eyelids drift shut, sinking into the feverish haze of sleep once more.

When I finally wake again, golden sunlight streams through the blinds, casting a warm glow over the room. The scent of chicken noodle soup lingers in the air, somehow breaking through my clogged sinuses. My body still aches, but the insufferable burden from earlier has decreased. My throat, however, still feels raw—like I've swallowed a dozen needles.

"How are you feeling?" A deep voice pulls me fully from my fog.

I blink, turning toward the sound. A slight gasp escapes me when I realize Malachi is sitting in the recliner beside me. His brown eyes trace over my messy coils and full lips, and his forehead creases with concern.

I swallow, wincing at the pain. "What . . . what are you doing here?" My voice is raspy, and I'm pretty sure I sound like a grown man who just woke up.

Malachi doesn't answer because Zara appears from the kitchen, holding a bowl of steaming soup. "I called him," she says, setting the bowl on the coffee table. "After Russell said he wasn't coming home, I got a little upset and needed to vent. You know how I am." She gives an apologetic shrug.

Malachi leans forward, his elbows on his knees. The way he looks at me causes me to rub a shaky hand over my face. "You look awful, Ash," he says jokingly in an attempt to draw a smile. It works.

I manage a weak chuckle, but it comes out more like a cough. "Geez . . . thanks for that."

I try to sit up, but my muscles protest, every movement sending a dull ache through my body. Malachi reaches over immediately, his large hands sliding under my arms. He lifts me effortlessly, and his touch sends a flutter through my entire body.

"I hate to see you this way," he whispers into my ear, worry etched into his voice. "If I had known earlier, I would've come sooner."

"I'm okay now. A little better," I rasp, though it's clear I'm anything but.

Malachi watches me carefully as Zara helps me adjust the bowl in my lap. His eyes darken slightly. "Next time you're sick like this, call me."

His words hang in the air. I manage to eat most of the soup, and Malachi takes the bowl from my hands when I'm done, disappearing into the kitchen. My throat still aches, but the warmth of the soup soothes it slightly. I shift under the blanket, pulling it up to my chin.

"What time is it?"

Zara pulls out her phone, glancing at the screen. "Six thirty."

My eyes widen. There's no way I slept the whole day away. Then it dawns on me—Russell still isn't home. My stomach twists, but I dismiss the thought, because even though he isn't here, Zara has been since this morning. *Crap.*

"Zara, you've been here all day," I say. "And Irene. You two should go."

"Mom left about an hour ago, but she told us to call if we needed her." Zara hesitates, chewing on her lip. "I think I'll stay a little longer, until Russell gets here. He may still be a few more hours."

I give her a weak smile. "Z, you've already done enough. I'll be okay."

She still doesn't seem convinced, but after a moment, she sighs. "All right . . . but I'll take Liv for the weekend."

"You don't have to—"

"That's my godchild. Besides, I was going to ask to get her tomorrow anyway." She waves a dismissive hand and gives me a look that says not to argue. "And you need to rest."

I nod, knowing she's right. Liv adores Zara, and because I'm still not 100 percent myself, she may be better off going with her godparents. I can't do anything for her feeling the way I do. Plus, I don't want to get her sick.

From the kitchen, Malachi speaks up. "I'll stay until Russell gets home."

My heart skips, my head jerking back to look at him. "Malachi, you don't have to do that. Russ—"

"If Russell has a problem with it, then he should have come when you called. Besides, I don't mind waiting. You're still sick, so I'm staying till he gets here."

I chew on the inside of my cheek, a rush of nervousness coming over me. I don't know if this is a good idea. Although I don't want to be alone, I don't want something to pop off when Russell gets home to find Malachi here . . . with me . . . alone. The tension between Russell and Malachi has only been growing.

Zara kneels in front of me, placing a hand on my knee. Her braids are pulled into a high ponytail and exhaustion covers her face, but despite her own tiredness, she's putting my needs first. One of my favorite things about her—she's always so caring. "Just rest, okay? Call me if you need anything."

"I will." She presses a kiss to my forehead before heading upstairs to get Liv. No need for her to gather her things, because Zara's house is stocked with diapers, clothes, and toys. As badly as I want to hold Liv before she leaves, I don't risk it. So I blow her a kiss instead. "Thanks, Zara."

"Anytime," she responds as the front door clicks shut behind them.

A quiet stillness settles over the house. Now, it's just Malachi and me.

He locks the door and turns to me. "You need anything? Another blanket? Water? Tea?"

"Tea is fine," I whisper, pulling the blanket tighter around my chest. I listen to the soft shuffle of his feet as he moves around the kitchen. He knows his way around just as well as Zara does, so I don't have to guide him. The clinking of a spoon against a mug and the faint sound of water pouring fill the silence.

A few minutes later, he returns with a steaming mug and hands it to me. Then he carefully lays another blanket over me.

"Thanks." I bring the mug to my lips. The minty, slightly bitter tea soothes my aching throat. Warmth spreads through my chest as I take another sip.

Malachi sits at the edge of the couch where my feet rest.

"I wouldn't get too close. I don't want you getting sick too."

"I'll be fine."

I study him, taking in his black sweater that enhances the curves of his muscles, khaki jeans on his long-built legs, and black Jordans. His gold watch shimmers under the soft lighting, and his chain hangs low against his chest. He's watching me too. I wonder what he's thinking.

"What?" I rub my hand over my hair—because there is no way my fingers are combing through these tangled curls. I sneak a glance at the mirror hanging beside the TV. My full lips are chapped, my face dry and bare. I haven't showered, combed my hair, or brushed my teeth. At this point I don't know if the nerves in the pit of my stomach are from Malachi being this close in proximity and seeing me this way or knowing Russell could come home any minute.

"Nothing," he says, but his gaze lingers. There's a look in his eyes, but I can't quite place it. "How are you feeling now?"

"Better," I say as I cough lightly. The house has been so quiet all day, but now that I'm awake, I crave conversation—something to occupy my mind. "How are things between you and Phoebe?"

He exhales deeply, rubbing his hands together. "Things are . . . good."

I arch a brow, waiting for him to explain.

"She's a good woman. Attractive and kind," he adds.

I feel like there is a "but" coming. And there it is.

"But I don't know. I guess since it's still so new, I'm trying to see where this will go. She's different from the other women I've dated before."

A chuckle escapes me before I can stop it.

Malachi's lips twitch. "What's so funny?"

I shake my head, still smiling. "Just admit it—you're in love, aren't you?"

He rubs a hand across his face with an iffy smirk. Licking his lips, he responds, "I'll admit I do like her. But—" He pauses.

I'd be lying if I said Malachi wasn't an attractive guy. The fact that I even acknowledge that in my mind causes me to look away from him entirely.

"How come you didn't tell me about her?" The question comes out rushed.

"Honestly, I don't know."

"I mean, it's not like you have to tell me who you date. It's none of my business, but I guess I was just surprised, that's all."

"Surprised, why?"

Before I can search my mind for an answer, the front door swings open.

A gush of cold air sweeps into the house as Russell steps inside. His presence causes me to jump. His low fade haircut is slightly disheveled, exhaustion engraved into his face.

He removes his trench coat, hanging it on the coat rack, but his eyes remain on me. His shirt is untucked, the sleeves rolled up just past his forearms. Then he looks over to Malachi. I gulp at his expression.

Malachi shifts but doesn't move. He's not intimidated.

"Where's Zara and Irene?"

"They left a little while ago," I whisper. "They were here all day."

Russell gives a slow nod, saying nothing as he runs a hand over his eyes as if he's trying to make sense of everything. "So, you two have just been chilling—alone?"

"Zara called you. Told you that Asha wasn't feeling good. So, I stopped by to check on her. They had to leave, so I stayed." Malachi's hands are folded in his lap. He's leaning back in the chair, unbothered.

"I was busy working a homicide. Can't just leave a crime scene like that."

Malachi licks his lips and chuckles, but the irritation is evident. "Whatever you say, man."

"Well." Russell motions toward the door. "I'm here now."

Malachi doesn't move for a minute. *What is he doing?* Russell made it clear that he needs to leave. Finally, he stands and rolls his shoulders.

Glancing down at me, he says, "Hope you feel better. I'll check in on you later."

I nod, offering an appreciative smile.

"That won't be necessary," Russell whispers to Malachi as he walks to the door. I almost don't hear him over my thudding heart.

He huffs and looks back at me but doesn't respond. Russell opens the door and slams it shut when Malachi exits.

Fear crashes over me. He paces momentarily before he pops his knuckles and exhales. Without a word, he lowers himself onto the couch and gently guides my head into his lap.

My body tenses at the rare softness in his touch. But then, his fingers brush lightly against my forehead. I find myself struggling to relax in his arms. This is a stark contrast to the way I thought things would play out after he returned home.

"It's been a long day . . . but I'm here now. I'm going to take care of you."

The words should bring me comfort. And in a way, they *almost* do. But a small voice in the back of my mind whispers, *Yeah, but where were you hours ago when I needed you most?*

Chapter 10

THE CRISP MORNING AIR fills my lungs as we step out of the car. Golden rays of sunlight trace my skin, reminding me just how much I've missed its warmth. The breeze dances around me like a soft lullaby, and I inhale deeply though my nose, letting the clean air wash over me. Relief floods me—I can finally breathe normally again.

After days of being sick and anchored to the couch, it feels good to be outside. My body is no longer weighed down by invisible stones. The pressure in my chest has lifted, the raw sting in my throat is gone, and the fever and chills have finally passed. I'm still a little drained, sure, but it's nothing compared to how I felt before.

Reflecting on this past week, I'm grateful for my village. Zara, Irene, and Malachi were so helpful and present. Of course, I knew Zara and Irene would show up. I wouldn't have expected less. Liv was well taken care of, and I never had to worry. Akin even dropped off more soup, and Irene and Manuel called every day. But Malachi . . . he's been there too, but this time felt different. He was present in a way he hadn't been before. He must've taken Russell's stern words into consideration because he didn't check in, but I know he would have.

Russell kept his promise, staying by my side the next two days while I recovered. He surprised me, taking care of me in ways I hadn't expected at all, and his presence made me feel even more grateful despite the growing chasm between us.

And things have stayed surprisingly good this week. He has been coming home right after work, playing with Liv, taking the trash out and cleaning up after we eat. He's been attentive and present, something he hadn't been for the past several months. Over the past few weeks his love had felt overbearing and hollow, but lately it feels as light as a feather.

Russell shifts Liv in his arms as I adjust the small bow clipped to her curls before we walk into the entrance of Truth Center Ministries. His other hand is firm around my waist, pulling me close. Even though his grip is a little tight, I don't mind it. I'm excited because today, Russell is finally joining us for church. I lean into his grasp, planting a kiss on his cheek.

Seeing him dressed in a crisp, clean suit causes me to realize just how handsome he is. Maybe it's the suit—because he really does look good in it—or maybe it's the fact that he's here, in church, that has me swooning.

We arrive earlier than normal, and a few church members greet us as we step inside. "Good morning, Detective Russell."

"How are you, brother?"

"Good to see you, man. We appreciate everything you do for the community."

Russell shakes hands and nods with that charming smile of his, the kind that makes people want to get to know him more. The same smile that made me fall in love with him. "Just doing my job."

A prideful smile spreads across my face as he interacts with everyone.

"You really do a lot for the city," an older woman praises, her eyes warm with admiration. "We need more good men like you."

Russell chuckles, adjusting Liv once more. "No need to thank me. Just trying to keep the streets safe, ma'am."

Russell has a tough job, but having people come up to him and thank him for his hard work must make it all worth it in the end.

"It's good to see you at church. Hopefully we'll see you around more often," the older woman says.

Russell hasn't attended church much over the years, but his job as a detective keeps him connected to the community. He knows people I haven't even met. The way they confide in him with their concerns and troubles is evidence enough that they trust him. As members of the church flock to him, it brings me comfort. Everyone seems to see the good in him . . . the good that I've always seen in him and wish to see more of. I wish my friends could see it too.

Of course, he isn't perfect. No one is. But he's a good man even though we have our differences. I love him—and I want to spend the rest of my life with him. At least, that's what I think I want. *Right?*

Russell smiles and nods politely. "Yes, ma'am," he responds casually.

My jaw drops, a flicker of hope flashing across my face. If Russell agrees to attend church more, then God is answering my prayers more quickly than I could've imagined. The more Russell comes to church and hears the Word of God, the better our relationship will be.

The man I love talks with ease and pride, and my heart swells with something complicated. Moments like this remind me of why I fell in love with him. When he's like this—present and composed and respectable—it gives me hope that he is capable of change.

Before I can dwell too much, the doors open again. Akin, Zara, Malachi, and their parents walk in. Malachi is dressed sharply in a navy-blue suit, his gold chain peeking out just above his collar. The suit looks as if it was tailored just for him, sculpting his wide shoulders. I find myself studying the curve of his smile as he notices me, his eyes holding mine. I blink and look away as Russell's hand slides around my back and to my side again.

Zara walks beside Malachi, looking effortlessly beautiful. Akin follows close behind.

Russell's grip contracts slightly, and his body stiffens. I glimpse up at him, but his expression remains indecipherable. Although his smile has disappeared, I can't figure out what he's thinking—what's caused his entire mood to change.

Akin nods at Russell, and Malachi is still staring at me. He doesn't even acknowledge Russell, which given their last interaction, I didn't expect him to.

"Hey, Liv," Zara coos, stepping up to take Liv from his arms. Liv goes willingly, wrapping her arms around Zara's neck as she presses a kiss to her cheek. "Hey, Russ." Zara says, her attention already focused on our sweet girl.

"What's up," he responds, adjusting his sleeves. "We should take our seats."

He guides me down the aisle as everyone else follows behind. We're early enough to sit close to the front without being too close. As we move into the pew, Russell's hand firmly pushes into my back, directing me into my seat. I press my lips together, smoothing out the bottom of my dress. *I hope no one saw that.*

Russell drapes his arm around my shoulders. His fingers draw tiny circles on my skin. I peek toward the row behind me where Zara and Akin sit. There's room on our row, yet my friends decided to sit behind us. Knowing it's because of Russell, I try not to let it affect my mood. When he isn't here, we always sit together.

Liv grabs one of Akin's long dreads and begins to pull it with a wide grin. Malachi's standing at the end of the row. His eyes dance across my face before he looks away. Irene and Manuel move closer to the front, deciding to sit with a group of their friends.

I exhale slowly as the choir begins to sing. Shifting my focus to the service is a battle, because no matter how hard I try to concentrate on the singing and the Word, I can't help but sneak glances at Russell.

He's held the same expression since Zara and everyone else arrived. It's unreadable, yet it causes me discomfort. His eyes are fixed ahead, and his lips are in a neutral line.

Does he understand what the pastor is talking about? Do the choir's voices send a chill over his body the way they do mine? Does he feel what I feel every time I come here? The peace, the gentle tug on his heart?

Or does he feel nothing at all? Is he just sitting through the service for me? But is that such a bad thing? That he's trying, even if it's just for my sake? The fact that he's here at all is a miracle, and for now, I'll take it. Even if his heart isn't open yet, I pray that one day, God will reach him.

Russell doesn't say much as we exit the sanctuary. He checks his phone a few times, but then as we make our way out the door, more people surround him, eager to speak with him. Most of them convey their thanks for his hard work, and others simply want to share their concerns about the community. They speak to him like he's on duty, and yet, he doesn't seem to mind. He smiles warmly as he nods without a trace of frustration.

I step aside as he effortlessly falls into professional conversation with a man on the city council.

"He's quite the superstar, isn't he?" Zara teases, nudging me lightly.

I glimpse at Russell, then back at her. I can't hide the smile tugging at my lips. "Yeah," I murmur. "I guess so."

"Did you guys want to join us for dinner?" Akin asks, now holding Liv in his arms.

"I'll have to ask Russell."

"I'm making my famous jerk chicken and mango salsa," he says with a tempting grin, knowing it's one of my favorites. Every time he makes it, I lick my plate clean. Akin is practically a chef in the kitchen, and just the thought of the sweet and savory flavors has my mouth watering.

I stride back over to Russell. When I approach him, I place my hand on his chest to gather his attention.

The man Russell is speaking to acknowledges me with a smile, then says, "Thank you so much, Russell. I'll send over some documents and maybe we can set something up. I'd love to have you be a guest speaker."

"Sounds like a plan," Russell says, finishing his conversation. He's beaming so brightly it causes me to smile. I prepare to ask him what engagement the councilman wants him to speak at, but before I can, Russell says through a tight-lipped smile, "What's your problem?"

My forehead creases, and my eyes narrow. "Excuse me?" I whisper.

Russell's hand finds my arm, and he gives me a tug that sends a jolt of pain up to my shoulder. I think of the night he grabbed me, how he left those bruises.

"I was in the middle of an important conversation, and I think you'd have the common decency to wait till I'm finished talking." From a distance, someone might think that everything is fine and that we're just a happy couple talking. But in reality, behind his smile hides a scowl that cuts deep. His grip tightens, and tears threaten to spill out of the corners of my eyes.

"I'm sorry," I stutter. "It won't happen again. I didn't mean to interrupt you."

It takes a moment before Russell finally lets my arm go. My eyes dart around the crowd of people heading to their cars, and for now, it seems like no one saw the little dispute we just shared.

"What was so important that you had to interrupt me?"

I lick my lips, afraid to speak. I want to explain that no words had even left my mouth. I was going to let him finish his conversation before asking if he wanted to join Akin and Zara for dinner. "It was nothing." My voice comes out too low.

"Asha, what is it?" Russell checks his watch.

"Akin invited us over for dinner. He wanted to see if we'd like to join them," I say, rubbing my sore arm.

He exhales, slipping his hands into his pockets. "You interrupted me for that?" A condescending chuckle leaves his throat. It sends a cold shiver down my neck. "You and Liv go ahead without me."

He's never been one to spend much time with my friends, but things have been good between us lately—until now, whatever this was. I was hoping he'd say yes because I want him to join us, to have another chance at building a relationship with them.

He holds my eyes for a moment before glancing away. "I'm going into the office for a bit anyway. After talking with everyone, I realize there are a few things I should catch up on."

I chew the inside of my mouth, knowing that's not the whole truth. All his efforts this past week seem to slip from my grasp when I look in his eyes. "Are you mad at me?" I ask, choking back tears of disappointment.

Russell doesn't respond right away. He finally takes a step toward me, brushing his fingers across my cheek. "No," he says dismissively.

A part of me longs for something more—to know that my little slipup didn't send us back to square one. It's always my fault.

"I promise not to work too late, okay?"

I nod, but deep down I wonder if he wants to go to work so he can get away from me. If I made him so upset he'd rather go busy himself than spend the evening with me. Or if he wants to go drink. Maybe he's going to some bar to throw back beers until the sun goes down. But then there's the possibility that he just doesn't want to be around my friends.

Since Akin patched up the wall Russell punched, he hasn't looked at Russell the same. The worry is evident in his expression. And I think Russell knows it. Maybe that's why he's choosing to stay behind. Maybe it's easier to avoid them than to pretend. That's what I tell myself, hoping it's the truth. Because I don't want to think about him being mad at me . . . *again.*

I force a fake smile while still processing his choice to stay behind.

"Can you ride with Zara and Akin?" he adds.

"Yeah, I'm sure they won't mind. Plus, they have a car seat for Liv in their car."

"Good." He lowers his lips to mine briefly and whispers, "I'll see you later tonight." The kiss is so quick, his lips barely brush against mine.

He gives me a final glance before going to his car. My eyes follow, and I rub my arm as he disappears down the street.

If I would've waited for his conversation to be over, maybe he would have said yes. My mind starts to spiral, running through endless scenarios of where he could be going or what he could be doing. I don't want to let myself consider the possibility that "working on his day off" might really mean he's heading to a bar to drink. Despite his drinking problem, Russell is a good detective. So many people here today had such good things to say about him. So, I try to hold onto that.

He's been doing so well lately. I refuse to let my imagination ruin the ease between us. I have to trust him—believe that he's telling me the truth.

"Everything all right?"

Malachi's voice pulls me back to reality. He's standing with Zara and Akin, Liv nestled in his arms. They're all watching me, waiting.

"Yeah," I say quickly, but I'm not sure the mask I'm wearing will hide the hurt brewing inside. "He had to go to work."

Their nods feel hesitant, their expressions hard to read. The way they're watching me causes my stomach to twist. *Do they suspect something? Do they feel bad for me?*

Before I can overthink further, Liv's tiny voice cuts through the tension. "Eat! Eat!" she says clear as day, her eager grin lighting up her face.

Our attention shifts immediately to her.

"My girl is as hungry as I am." Zara laughs, kissing Liv's cheek.

"Well, what are we waiting for?" Akin smirks. "Let's go."

***

LAUGHTER AND THE CLINKING of silverware fill the dining room as we relax around the table, full and satisfied. Akin's jerk chicken and mango salsa hit the spot. Liv ate a piece of chicken and a few bites of the mango salsa. The food was so good, it put her to sleep, and she's now lying in her crib in her godparents' bedroom. If I were home, I'd be asleep too. Nothing like a good meal after church to send a girl into a deep slumber.

Akin paired the dish with Caribbean rice so delicious that I licked my plate clean.

"Man, I'm done," Malachi groans, leaning back in his chair and rubbing his stomach. "That's it for me."

"It was amazing," I add, picking up a piece of mango and popping it into my mouth. "I could eat this every day."

"Not too much on my man's cooking," Zara teases, taking the last bite of her chicken. "His services are exclusively for me."

Malachi smirks. "Well, you could at least share the recipe."

Akin chuckles, shaking his head. "What, you gonna put it on the menu at the coffee shop?"

Zara snickers. "You know he's got a woman now, so he has to learn how to cook real food instead of just baking cookies and brownies."

"It's a good thing she doesn't eat meat, so he doesn't have to learn much." I chuckle.

Akin grunts and says, "Man, I don't know how people live without meat. No chicken? No steak? No burgers?" He shudders dramatically. "That's just . . . sad."

Zara scoffs as she rises to clear the empty plates from the table. "Some of us have evolved beyond our caveman days, Akin. Not every meal needs meat. All that seasoning and grease can cause serious health issues."

"Well, that doesn't apply to this household." Akin flexes his muscles. "I need my protein. Give me chicken, cows, deer meat, rabbit, all the animal kingdom."

I laugh with a grimace. "That's disgusting."

"Don't knock it till you try it," Akin says.

I gaze at Malachi, who has a toothpick nestled between his lips. "Speaking of Phoebe, where is she?"

"Probably at home sleeping. She worked late last night." He checks his phone even though it hasn't rung.

I tilt my head slightly, resting my elbow on the table.

"I hope this one lasts. She's at least likable, unlike the last one," Zara calls from the kitchen.

Malachi doesn't talk about his relationships much unless prompted. He's always kept his love life private. He'd introduce them, and then in a couple weeks he'd simply explain how the relationship didn't work because they were a little crazy. Women have followed him around before. One tried hacking into his phone, and one tried to run him over after he broke up with her. But Phoebe doesn't seem crazy. Not yet anyway.

He shrugs. "We'll see where it goes." He grabs his glass of lemonade, bringing it to his lips.

"Be honest, Malachi—does Phoebe have my brother-in-law hooked already?"

Malachi sits up straighter, biting his bottom lip as he sets his glass down. "Nah, nothing like that. Things are just good. I'm taking my time."

Akin pulls his beard with his index and thumb. "Man, when you know, you know. When you find the one you want to marry, it's like—fireworks going off. There was no hesitation for me." He glances at Zara walking back into the dining room. "I knew within a few weeks of dating that I wanted to marry your sister."

Zara presses a hand to her chest, and her eyes soften. "Aww, babe." Then she gives Malachi a pointed look. "See? Some men don't waste time."

I force a small laugh, but Akin's words stir something inside me. *When you know, you know.*

Russell and I have been together for a few years. We have a child together, and yet he still hasn't proposed.

The thought stings, and I wonder if Russell knows what he wants—if he wants me. *What if he doesn't want to marry me? What if he does but is just waiting for . . . I don't know . . . waiting for things to be less stressful? For a promotion? For Liv to get older?*

Malachi exhales, scratching at his eyebrow. "That's not the case for everyone," he says. "Some people just want to be sure they're making the right choice. That when they get married, it's to the person they can't live without."

Lost in thought, I don't realize Malachi is watching me intently until our eyes meet for a brief second.

"I want to marry someone that I love more than I love myself," he continues.

I close my eyes, but I still feel his gaze on me. Shifting in my seat, I nod in agreement with his heartfelt words. But the reality of my own relationship clouds my mind like fog.

How do you know if you're making the right choice? Could I live without Russell? Do I love Russell more than I love myself?

"That's the smartest thing I've ever heard you say," Zara teases, playfully smacking the back of Malachi's head as she leaves the room again. "I'm gonna go check on Liv."

As soon as she walks out, my phone buzzes on the table. My stomach tightens at the sight of Russell's name on the screen. Without excusing myself, I stand and head into the living room to answer.

"Hey, babe," I say softly.

"Hey," Russell replies. "How was the food?"

"Really good. I wish you would've joined us." I hope he hears the disappointment in my voice. "We are having a good time."

"Yeah? Maybe next time." There's a pause before he adds, "I just wanted to let you know I'll be working late. Don't wait up."

I frown. "It's your day off. You shouldn't be working at all."

He sighs. "I know, but I have things to catch up on. I'm under a lot of stress. You understand, right?"

I do. But I also want him home. I nod as if he can see me. "Yeah," I finally say.

"See if Zara can take you home."

"I'm sure she can."

"Good. Kiss Liv for me. I'll see you later."

The call disconnects before I can say anything else.

A heaviness settles in my chest. My mind instantly goes back to the time he told me he was working late—but he wasn't at work at all. He was drinking.

What am I supposed to think now?

Lately, he's been trying. He came to church with me. He helped me while I was sick. But now that I'm well again, I can't shake the feeling that the other version of him—the one who can't keep his promises—is creeping back.

The thought terrifies me, though I hate admitting it.

I take a deep breath, smoothing my hands over my dress as I prepare to ask my friends for a ride home later. I already know they'll have questions, and I'm not sure how I'll address them without magnifying their concerns.

As I step back toward the dining room, voices stop me in my tracks.

"I don't know, man. I just feel like something's off," Malachi whispers firmly.

Akin sighs. It sounds like he's tapping his fingers against the table. "Yeah. I've been thinking the same thing."

Malachi hesitates. "I don't want Asha to get hurt." It's obvious he's still thinking about the time Russell grabbed me in the hallway at our house. Or is something else troubling his mind? Knowing Malachi, it could be anything. He's so observant that maybe he saw one of our disputes without me knowing.

"Have you seen the way he talks to her sometimes? It's like he's always got a problem." Malachi's voice raises slightly.

"Trust me, I've noticed," Akin responds.

"I try not to overstep because I respect her. I care about her, but I'm not sure how much longer I can keep quiet."

Silence stretches between them, thick with unspoken worries. Just as I think the conversation is over, Akin lets out a slow breath.

"I never said anything before, but . . . Asha called me—"

My heart leaps into my throat. I know exactly what he's about to say, and I can't let him do that. *He promised me he wouldn't say anything.* Everything is fine. I'm fine.

Before he can finish, I rush into the dining room, almost tripping over my own two feet. I smile, sliding into my seat. "Anyone want dessert?" I ask, but my voice is a little too bright and forced.

Malachi clears his throat, and Akin grabs his cup, pretending that he wasn't just about to tell Malachi *our* secret.

I keep my head down, avoiding their eyes. *Are things really that bad? Bad enough that they feel the need to have secret conversations about me?*

About my relationship? Malachi is worried that I'll get hurt, and for a moment, a quiet thought creeps into my mind—*should he be?*

If they've seen how Russell talks to me—and they think something's wrong with it—then maybe I'm not as good at hiding it as I think.

Maybe . . . something *is* wrong with it.

Chapter 11

I APPLY ANOTHER LAYER of sheer rosy lip gloss, the soft tint bringing out the pink undertone of my thick lips. My lashes are curled and coated with voluminous mascara, and a hint of cherry blush warms my lifted cheeks. I'm wearing an off-the-shoulder sparkly red dress that hugs my wide curves in all the right places.

I straightened my naturally curly hair, careful not to set the temperature too high. So when I wash it again, the strands will soak up water like a sponge and spring back into curls. My coils usually rest above my shoulders, but when straightened, my hair falls past them—sleek and smooth.

Tonight, I'm not dressed up to go to an event with Zara or to attend church. No, tonight I'm dressed up because Russell is taking me on a date. *Finally.*

I move around the bedroom, searching for my silver jewelry and red-bottom heels to complete my outfit. Excitement flutters in my chest as if we're going on a very first date. I'm nervous and hopeful all at the same time.

Liv is with Ms. Mildred, our go-to babysitter when her godparents aren't available or for spur of the moment occasions. She rarely gets out of the house, and she enjoys Liv's company. Luckily, Ms. Mildred eagerly agreed to watch her for a few hours so Russell and I could have a night to ourselves.

I have no idea where we're going, but I know it must be somewhere nice. Russell sent me a text this morning, reminding me to dress up. I can't even remember the last time we wore fancy clothes and went somewhere high-end. Most of the time if we go out to eat, it's to the small diner down the street that sells greasy burgers and loaded fries.

I can already picture it—the flicker of candlelight, the warmth of his hand resting on my thigh, the way we'll dance the night away after indulging in a wonderful but overpriced meal. Warmth bubbles in my chest that I can't contain. Because a part of me hopes that *tonight is the night*.

The night I've dreamed of since I was a little girl. Regardless of everything, I want this life with him. A two-parent household full of love and joy. With our complicated relationship, I want this not just for me, but for Liv.

The front door opens. I quickly gain my composure and smile to myself. He's home. Any second now, he'll come upstairs, pull me close, and kiss me like he's missed me all day. Then he'll hop in the shower to get ready for our date.

Footsteps echo up the stairs, growing louder.

But the second Russell's solid frame steps into the bedroom, I know something is wrong. His posture is tense, brows furrowed deeply, eyes dark and unfocused.

My smile falters, but I try to shake off the unease creeping up my spine. *Maybe he just had a long day.*

"Hey, baby." I tread lightly toward him, placing a gentle hand on his firm chest.

He doesn't return the smile. Instead, he grabs my wrist, throwing my hand aside with ease. He pushes past me with a loud sigh.

"Baby, listen . . . change of plans. I have to go back in."

His words are a slap to the face.

No . . . no, he wouldn't.

"What?" I blink, sure I misheard him.

He blows out a deep breath, digging through his drawers as if this is just a regular night, as if he *didn't* just shatter me. "I know, I know. This wasn't the plan, but something came up. It's important."

Important? Is this date not important to him?

I stare at him in disbelief, my mouth agape. My heart plummets into my stomach. No way he'd do this to me—to us.

"Russell, are you serious right now? We were supposed to go out. You promised."

He doesn't even look up at me as he responds, "Asha, I know." His voice is distracted, as if his mind is elsewhere. "I swear I'll make it up to you, babe. Just not tonight."

Giving him a disbelieving glance, I stand frozen, unable to process the sheer audacity of his words. It took hours to get ready for tonight. From finding something to wear, to shaving, to straightening my hair. I'm dressed up. For him. For us. And he doesn't even care.

How many times does this have to happen before I stop believing him? Nothing's ever going to change, is it? I want to ask but don't.

Tears sting my eyes, but I refuse to let them fall. "Not tonight?" My voice shakes with contained rage as I gesture down at myself. I'd been looking forward to this all day, and he cancels it with no remorse. He was the one who sent a text early this morning about it.

Blinking rapidly, my lips curve into a frown. I try to force the anger down. *If not tonight, then when?*

"Huh?" My voice is louder than I intended, but I don't care. "When, Russell? Because every time it's 'not tonight.' Every time it's 'I'll make it up to you.' And I just—" My voice cracks, and I swallow hard.

Russell finally stops. His hands clench into fists at his sides as he turns to face me. His head tilts, and his top lip curves upward.

Something in his eyes—something dark—sends a chill down my spine.

"Asha, you need to calm down," he warns in a deep tone.

My chest heaves, but I shake my head. "Don't tell me to calm down, Russell! I have every right to be upset!"

He grinds his back teeth, and his eyes narrow dangerously.

"You always do this," I continue, my voice rising against my will. I try to put the lid over my anger to contain it, but it bursts free. *No, it explodes.* "You make promises you don't keep, and I'm supposed to just smile and be okay with it? I got dressed up for you! Am I not important to you?"

Russell's expression shifts in an instant—his patience snapping like a twig. "Oh my gosh, Asha, stop acting like a spoiled child!" His voice booms through the room, and I flinch despite myself.

"Are you serious right now?" I stare at him, heart pounding.

"Yes, I'm serious!" He throws his hands up, and I jump. "You think I want to be working late? You think I enjoy this? I bust my behind every day, and all you do is whine because I don't take you out enough! You don't understand the pressure I'm under! The life that I'm trying to give you and Liv means putting in the hours! I'm tired of this. Working a job that I hate, but I do it for you, for Liv! Get over yourself!"

I press a hand against my stomach in an attempt to calm the nerves. *He hates his job. How did I not know that?* He's mentioned how hard it is being a detective a sparse number of times, but he's never told me he hated it.

When the people at the church came up to him, thanking him for his services, I saw pure bliss.

"That's not fair," I whisper, voice trembling. "You're making this about you when I'm just asking for something. Asking for your attention. For one night where I don't feel like I mean nothing to you. I want to know you love me . . . care about me." It takes everything in me to pour out the feelings I'd been keeping bottled up only for Russell to take in a sharp, irritated breath.

He rubs a hand down his tired face. His eyes blaze with frustration as he peers at me. "You don't get it, Asha. You never do. And honestly? I don't have time for this right now."

"Make time!" I cry. The tears that I fought back escape and run down my cheek. I had gotten my hopes up for what? To be let down again and again.

"I promise I'm going to make it up to you, and I mean that. I get it, you're upset, but my job is important!"

I cross my arms over my chest, lip trembling as if I'm cold, willing myself not to say anything else, because if I do I know what will come next. The version of him I've been afraid of, the one I've tried to convince myself no longer exists, will rise.

"I'm tired of this." The words slip out before I can stop them, barely above a whisper. I pray he doesn't hear me. But he does.

Russell's head snaps toward me, his jaw tightening. "What did you just say?"

"Nothing," I stammer quickly, shaking my head. "I didn't say anything."

A muscle ticks in his jaw. He takes a step toward me, then another. My pulse jumps, and I wince when his hands shove against my shoulders *hard*. "Say it again!" he spits out.

I stumble backward. My heel catches on the rug, and suddenly, I'm falling. The sharp edge of the wooden bed frame slams into my hip. Pain radiates through my side as I try to catch myself before hitting the floor with a hard thud.

What just happened? My body feels disconnected from my mind. Shock—or maybe fear—paralyzes me. My breath comes too fast, too shallow.

I look up at him, wide-eyed, my heart pounding against my ribs.

He's never done that before. It doesn't feel real, like my mind doesn't want me to believe what just happened . . . what I just saw and felt. Or maybe it's my heart that's trying to deceive me.

Russell scowls, bottom lip tucked under his sharp teeth. He looks away from me, head down, his clenched fist resting on his hip. "I didn't mean to do that," he mutters.

My hip throbs. My hands tremble against the floor, but I don't move. The sting in my skin is already turning into a deep, tender ache. It's as if my throat is suffocated with pebbles; my voice is consumed whole by the lump forming there.

Russell groans, his foot tapping against the floor. "I'm just stressed, all right? You should've listened to me. I told you to drop it. You always do this. Make things into a big deal." He extends a hand, as if expecting me to take it, as if he didn't just put me here.

I cower at his offer and turn away from him. The floor is easier to look at than his demeaning gaze.

"Asha—"

His phone buzzes in his pocket. He curses under his breath and yanks it out, and it's as if I no longer exist. "This is important," he says. "We'll finish this conversation later."

Tears roll down my cheeks. My body simmers in frustration and confusion. The air around me sizzles like boiling water on a cold surface. The weight of realization settles deep in my chest, sharper than anything I've ever felt before.

Russell doesn't kneel beside me. He doesn't help me.

Instead, he steps over me, pressing the phone to his ear. He leaves me on the floor.

***

With unsteady hands and tears blurring my vision, I drive to Zara's place the moment Russell is gone. My fingers clutch the steering wheel so tight I think I'm going to break it in two. My mind replays the moment over again like it's set to rewind every fifteen seconds. Each time, I notice something new—the anger in his voice, the fear and exhaustion in my own, how the spark I'd once felt is slowly dying.

As I pull into Zara's driveway, I realize my mind subconsciously guided me here without awareness of stop signs or red lights. I just drove with a destination in mind, needing my best friend more than ever.

My tears have dried, leaving behind dark streaks of mascara staining my cheeks. My heart is still thudding dramatically in my chest, and my stomach shudders with nerves. *What am I even going to say? I can't tell her the truth. Can I?*

How do I explain that Russell shoved me, causing me to fall? How do I tell her I let him do it, and that he stepped over me like I was a piece of trash on the floor?

I can't tell her, despite the pull in my heart begging for a chance to release all the pain and frustration. I suck in a shaky breath, trying to steady myself. *It was just an argument,* I tell myself. That's all Zara needs to know. *Because that's all it was, right?* Heated discussion. Heat of the moment. An accident?

I tap on the door softly, then wrap my arms around myself, trying to stop the shaking. Tonight, the November air is cool, but the chill in my chest isn't from the weather.

A few seconds later, Zara swings the door open, her eyes lighting up until they land on me. The excitement fades from her face like color from a dying flower. Concern washes over her expression, and her eyes widen. "Asha?" She says my name as if she's looking at a ghost. Zara gently tugs me inside.

As soon as I cross the threshold, something in me breaks. The warmth of her home should be comforting, but instead, it nearly drowns me. It's too safe. Too calm. The chaos inside me grows louder. I shouldn't be here. I should be on my date with Russell, sitting across from him at some dimly lit restaurant, eating expensive steak and feeling special, important—*loved*.

Instead, I'm here.

"What happened? What's wrong?" Zara's words come out rushed and worrisome.

"I need to sit down." My voice cracks, exposing the pain inside. My legs feel like bricks are tied to my ankles as we walk to the sofa.

Her perfectly arched brows knit together. "Did Russell do something?"

When I sit, I try to hide my hands under my thighs, but I can't stop the slight tremble in my hands.

Zara reaches for them, holding them steady. "What's wrong, Ash?" she asks again.

I inhale, blinking back more tears. "Russell and I just . . . got into it." The words taste bitter. Like a lie. *Just an argument.* That's what I tell her. That's what I force myself to believe.

Zara's almond-shaped eyes glare at me so attentively, as if she can read my thoughts. "How bad was it?"

I force a laugh, shaking my head, desperate to minimize the situation. I don't know why I'm doing this, but I am. I tell her, "Bad." I press my palm to my forehead.

Zara immediately pulls me into a comforting hug. Her small arms wrap around me, and at first, I stiffen, but the longer she embraces me, the sincerity of it unravels something in me. I sink into her, the lump in my throat growing painful, my vision blurring again.

"Asha, you can talk to me," she whispers softly. "We're sisters."

I nod against her shoulder, squeezing my eyes shut as fresh tears spill down my cheeks. "I know."

She doesn't let go, doesn't rush me. We sit there in silence, my body trembling against hers, until she finally speaks. "Whatever it is, Ash, I'm right here. You're not alone." Zara always knows what to say.

She reaches for the tissue box on the coffee table, pulling out a few and dabbing gently at my cheeks. *How'd I get so lucky to have a friend like her?* The tissue comes away smeared with foundation, mascara, and hopelessness. I know I look a mess right now, but I don't care. She's seen me at my worst, and yet she still stays by my side.

When I can finally breathe again, I clear my throat, my voice soft. "I don't know what I'm doing—what *we're* doing." My fingers tighten around the tissue in my lap. "I love him so much, Z, but I don't know if he even understands that."

She studies me carefully, like she's trying to read between the lines. Between the words I won't say. "What happened?" A quick trace of disappointment flashes in her eyes, because she'd tell me anything, yet I'm holding back.

I sit up a little, pressing my palms against my thighs. I take a deep breath in an attempt to still my voice. With Zara, I know I can trust her—tell her the truth—but I don't want Zara to see Russell the way I'm starting to. I don't want her to despise him. *I should've just let it go. Should've told him it was fine. I should've understood instead of pushing his buttons.*

I exhale slowly. "We were supposed to go out tonight, but . . . he got called back into work. We haven't been out on a date in so long, Z. Tonight was a chance for us to find our spark. To figure things out."

Zara frowns. "Can't he ask Darnell to cover for him?"

I shrug. "I appreciate everything he does for me and Liv, but sometimes I just feel like he puts his job first." I hesitate, staring down at my lap. What I really want to say is, *sometimes I'm afraid of him.* The truth presses against my tongue, desperate for escape.

But I don't say it. *How can I fear the man that I love so much?*

"Russell does put his job first. I hate that he does that, but maybe it's time you two try couple's therapy. It won't hurt. If anything, maybe a therapist can help shed some light on why Russell feels he has to work so much."

"Yeah, you're right," I respond, but I don't know if that'll change anything. *Change him.* I smile weakly, like I didn't just fall apart in her arms. "I just needed to get out of the house for a little while. I didn't want to be alone."

Zara doesn't push. She just nods, squeezing my hand. "You can stay as long as you want. I'll find you something to change into—something more comfortable. I'm sure Mal won't mind." She gives my hand one last reassuring squeeze before disappearing down the hall toward the guest room. Zara's clothes would never fit me. She's petite with a much smaller chest than mine, so borrowing something from her brother is the next best option.

Left alone on the couch, I sit in silence, my fingers absentmindedly shredding the damp tissue in my lap. My thoughts churn, an endless loop of emotions I can't seem to quiet.

I'm furious at Russell—for canceling our date, for putting his job before me again, for *shoving* me. But beneath the anger, there's frustration—at myself. *Why can't I just be a good girlfriend?* He's so stressed, so overwhelmed, and I don't know how to make it better. *I don't know how to help him. Help us.*

Then, the sharp, humiliating realization that cuts deeper than anything else hits me: I'm the one sitting here with an aching side, a bruise probably already forming beneath my dress. *He* should be the one apologizing, begging for my forgiveness. But instead, *I* want to apologize. I want to tell him I'm sorry for how I reacted, for making a big deal out of tonight. I want to press rewind and start the entire evening over—to do it *right*.

I squeeze my eyes shut, trying to push the thoughts away, but they cling to me like this dress. I want to rip it off and set it on fire.

The sound of the front door unlocking makes me jolt. For some reason my brain tells me it's Russell, even though I know it's not. He doesn't know I'm here.

"Z!" Malachi's voice fills the apartment as he steps inside, struggling to shut the door with his foot. His arms are full. He's balancing a tray of food in one hand and a cup holder of drinks and a milkshake in the other. I completely forgot that he would be here, since he's been crashing here while they work on his apartment.

He's too preoccupied to notice me at first, but when he turns around, our eyes meet.

He freezes.

His brown eyes scan my face, my posture, the way I'm sunken into the couch. He glares at the shredded pile of tissue on my lap.

"What happened?" he asks.

Chapter 12

"ASHA?" MALACHI'S VOICE IS laced with urgency and worry. He sets the food and drinks down on the entryway table and quickly crosses the room, not hesitating to lower himself beside me on the couch. He sits close—close enough that his warmth blends with the heat of my own frustration.

The corners of his eyes soften as he stares at me. I'm sure he notices the slight downturn of my lips, my glossy and anguished eyes. I know Malachi sees straight through the mask I've been trying to wear.

I shift, straightening my posture and rolling my shoulders back. Sitting up taller, I run my hands over my hair to make sure my silk press still looks decent. Why? I don't know. I sniffle, wiping at my face for any lingering bits of tissue.

"Hey, Mal." My voice comes out hoarse, like I've been screaming for hours.

His eyes stay locked on me, as if he's afraid if he looks away, I'll vanish. I drop my gaze to my hands. His presence is comforting, but my cheeks burn beneath his stare. I don't want him to see me like this.

"You okay?"

I nod quickly, swallowing hard. "Yeah, I'm fine."

"Don't lie to me, Ash. Please. What happened?" The question I know he's dying to ask comes out raspy. "Did Russell hurt you?" His brow furrows, and his jaw tightens.

I press my lips together to keep them from trembling, holding myself together by the thinnest thread. Malachi brushes my hair behind my ear, tilting his head to meet my expression.

"Asha." The crack in his voice nearly undoes me. "If he hurt you, I'll handle it."

And that's exactly why I can't say anything. If I tell him about the argument—about how Russell pushed me—I know Malachi won't hesitate. He'll rush out that door to find him.

I can't let that happen. I wouldn't be able to stop him.

"Mal, I'm fine," I manage to say.

He lowers his head, chin touching his chest. His shoulders rise and fall with slow, deep breaths. It's as if he's holding himself together too, like looking at me longer might shatter something in him too. His knuckles clench between us.

"Did he hurt you?"

My heart seizes. Without thinking, I reach for his hand, curling my fingers lightly around his. I need him to believe me when I withhold the truth, when I say the words that sound right, the ones that'll keep him here with me. "No." I squeeze my eyes shut, already regretting it.

"Then what's wrong? Why are you upset?"

Being near him eases the ache in my bones. I glance down at our hands, now gently intertwined like we've done this countless times, even though we have never done this before. "I'm fine. We just got into an argument, but nothing else happened."

Malachi shakes his head. "Don't do that."

"Do what?" I whisper.

"Pretend like you're fine. You don't have to pretend with me." His voice is thick, pleading.

I force myself to meet his eyes, even though it's the last thing I want to do. But when I do, something in me cracks. The tears that have been threatening spill over, breaking through the dam I've built inside.

"I'm sorry, Asha—that he makes you cry."

For a moment, silence hangs heavy between us. I need relief—some way to break the tension. Forcing a weak, wobbly smile, I say, "Aren't you going to run to your room to get away from the tears?"

Malachi exhales sharply, the vein in his forehead becoming more defined. He looks away for half a second, then back at me. His brown eyes are glossy now too. "Not this time."

My breath catches. My palms start to sweat. My stomach does that weird flip thing I try to ignore. His words, the sincerity in his gaze, the way he's looking at me—it's all too much.

"I'm not going anywhere."

I press a palm to my mouth to muffle a sob trying to escape. I close my teary eyes as he wraps his arms around me, strong and sure, pulling me close.

My head rests on his chest, and my tears soak into the fabric of his shirt.

"It's okay," he whispers.

I want to say something—anything—but before I can, the door swings open.

Phoebe steps in, snapping me back to reality. Instinctively, I pull away from Malachi's embrace, like a child caught doing something wrong. Her eyes bounce between us. Her wide grin falters. "Asha, what's wrong?" She shrugs off her fluffy pink coat and tosses it on the rack, crossing her arms over her small frame.

"Russell and I just had a fight. I needed to get out of the house for a bit."

She studies our faces, probably searching for the truth, but my tears tell enough of the story. "Oh no, girlie. I'm so sorry. Arguments are the worst. Maybe a movie and popcorn will help take your mind off things. We were just about to have a movie night."

That explains the food and drinks Malachi brought in earlier.

I shake my head, forcing a controlled laugh as I wipe at my face. "I . . . uh. I don't want to intrude. I can come back later."

As I stand, a sharp pain stings my side, and I wince before I can stop it.

"What was that?" Malachi's eyes drop, his expression hardening. "Are you hurt?"

I shake my head fast. "Nothing. I'm okay."

He doesn't look convinced. His eyes scan me, taking in every detail. His hands twitch, like he wants to reach for me, but he holds himself back. If Phoebe weren't here, maybe he would.

"Asha—"

"I'm fine," I say through gritted teeth.

Before he can argue, Phoebe jumps in. "Asha, you should totally stay. It might help take your mind off things."

I hesitate, torn between the warmth of their invitation and the overwhelming urge to curl up alone with my thoughts. I'm in no mood for a movie. What I really want to do is cry and eat ice cream. Then I want to pick up Liv and hold her while she sleeps, letting her little breaths soothe the ache in my chest. Besides, I feel bad for showing up unannounced, crashing their planned movie night. The last thing I want is to drag everyone down with my bad mood.

I can't help but wonder if I wasn't invited because of Russell. Like he said, they are my friends—not his.

"No, but thank you."

"Asha, I think it's best if you stay," Malachi says, standing up.

"Are you sure?" I ask, glancing between them.

"Yeah, of course!" Phoebe beams, effortlessly cheerful as always. "By the way, I love your dress. It's super gorg." She grabs the tray of food, setting it on the coffee table in the middle of the living room.

Sometimes I imagine I'd see butterflies and rainbows crowning her head if I looked closely enough—she's always in a good mood, and honestly, I envy that about her. I want my life to be that bright and stress-free.

"Thanks," I whisper, forcing a grin.

Just then, Zara returns, a bundle of clothes in her hands. "Here, these should fit better than anything I own," she says. "Sorry, Mal, I had to give her your clothes."

He doesn't respond, but Phoebe lifts her head at me briefly before continuing to her task of separating the food and drinks.

Zara tilts her head toward the hallway, and I nod, silently following her.

Even as we walk away, I feel Malachi's eyes on me. It takes everything in me to not turn around to confirm it.

"I also have some slippers you can wear." She says, handing me a pair of large black bedroom shoes.

Once the bathroom door shuts behind me, I press my back against it. My body sinks to the floor as the weight of the night consumes me.

Salty tears spill down my cheeks, my chest rising and falling as I struggle to breathe. It as if I'm suffocating. I claw at my neck because I don't know what to do. I don't know how to feel.

It takes a full minute before I find the strength to move, to peel off the dress clinging to my skin. My legs tremble as I walk to the sink. I hesitate before looking in the mirror, because I'm scared that my skin will be bruised. If there is one . . . this will be real. More real than I want to admit.

I swallow hard and finally force my gaze downward.

On my hip, an ugly red mark is blossoming, darkening into a deep purple. It's about the size of a golf ball and growing.

I squeeze my eyes shut, tears escaping. My shoulders quiver as I sob. I try to tell myself that he didn't mean to hurt me, that it was an accident. I tell myself that the bruise only happened because I fell.

But the reality of it all forces me to confront a truth I don't want to face. That I don't understand. *How could he hurt me if he loves me?* That's all I want to know. *How could he do something like this? How could he push me like I meant nothing to him?*

I wipe the makeup from my face, erasing the tears and smudged mascara. Brushing my hair behind my ears, I take a steadying breath and grip the edge of the sink like my life depends on it.

My phone dings on the counter. My heart leaps for a split second, but when I look at it, it's a notification from my email. For some reason, I was expecting to see a message from Russell. And that realization alone confuses me. Disappointment and anxiety creep into my chest.

Why do I want to hear from him after what happened? Why am I searching for reassurance from the person who just hurt me?

I don't know how long I stand there, lost in my thoughts, before a sudden knock startles me. "Asha?" Akin's voice filters through the door.

I cough, clearing the sadness from my throat. "Yeah, I'll be right out."

Quickly, I drape my dress over the railing, slip off my heels, and change into the fresh clothes Zara gave me. They smell like him . . . a woodsy, spicy fragrance.

When I swing the door open, Akin is standing there, his arms crossed over his chest.

"You straight?"

I nod. "I'll be fine," I say, but my voice lacks conviction.

His sharp eyes study me for a long moment before he asks, "Did he hit you?"

I freeze. My gaze drops to the large slippers on my feet, suddenly unable to meet his eyes. Akin knows something that neither Zara nor Malachi do. He knows about the punched wall. He knows what Russell is capable of—without me ever having to say it.

Russell pushed me, but not on purpose . . . right? He was frustrated, upset, and I just lost my balance. It was just an argument—things got a little heated. That happens in relationships . . . doesn't it? I'll keep telling myself that until I believe it.

"It wasn't like that. We argued, and things got . . . tense. But then he left. So, I came here." I give him the same version I gave Zara and Malachi; the same one I'm trying to believe.

"A misunderstanding?"

"Yes." I twist my fingers together.

Akin exhales, and his nostrils flare as he flicks his nose with a curved index finger. "I've kept quiet for your sake, Asha. Because you asked me to. Because you won't tell me the truth." His voice is low, but frustration etches his tone. "But I don't know how much longer I'm willing to. If he's hurting you, then you need to tell me the truth. I'll help you. All of us will. So, I'll ask you one last time. Did he hurt you?" His question comes out sharp and pointed.

I blink back the tears threatening to spill, no longer wanting to cry. I just want to forget about tonight. But the dull ache in my side is a reminder I can't ignore. "No," I finally say, because if I say yes, what then? "I'm fine," I assure him. "I don't need any help."

I want to pull my hair out, because I could've told him the truth, but I didn't. Instead, I lied to them all—to protect Russell, not myself.

He takes a step forward, his tall frame hovering over me like an overprotective brother. "I pray there never comes a time when you do. And even if you don't think you need it, I'm here. We all are. That's not changing."

I manage a tight-lipped smile that hurts my cheeks. "I know."

He nods, although I know there's more he wants to say, but he never presses. With that, we walk back down the hall.

Malachi and Phoebe are on the couch. She's curled up next to him. Her feet are tucked beneath her, while a hand rests on Malachi's leg.

Zara is sitting with an empty spot beside her, and Akin takes it. He pulls her close to him and plants a reassuring kiss on her cheek.

My gaze drifts to the only available seat—a chair opposite them all. Instead of squeezing in beside someone, I lower myself into it, sitting alone.

Malachi's eyes follow me. His brows pull together, his nose scrunching slightly. I force myself to focus on the screen instead.

The movie starts. It's an action film filled with fight scenes and gunfire. It should be distracting enough to pull me out of my thoughts, but the ache in my side intensifies.

I shift in my seat, pulling my knees up to my chest, wrapping my arms around them as if that will make me feel less alone. But instead, the loneliness presses in harder.

Resting my chin on my knees, I steal a glance at my friends. Zara and Akin are shoving their faces with salty, buttered popcorn. Malachi must feel my gaze because he looks up at me. Our eyes meet, but he doesn't look away until Phoebe lays her head on his shoulder.

I drop my gaze.

Toward the end of the movie, my phone vibrates against the armrest. I hesitate before checking it.

Russell: *I'll be on the way home shortly.*

That's it. That's all he has to say.

I stare at the message, waiting—hoping—for something more. Maybe an apology. Maybe reassurance. Maybe . . . anything that proves tonight meant something to him. That what happened wasn't just another forgettable argument.

But there's nothing.

His message lacks everything I want—everything I need to hear.

I swallow hard and lock my phone, exhaling slowly. My stomach twists, and suddenly I'm queasy. Leaving is my only option because if he gets back before I do, that may spark another argument.

The thought quickens my pulse.

I clear my throat. "I should probably head out," I say, pushing to my feet, wincing slightly but hiding it better.

Zara frowns. "Already? The movie isn't even over."

"I know. I have to pick up Liv from Ms. Mildred's." Which isn't a lie. I need to pick her up before heading home, hopefully before Russell gets there.

Akin tenses beside Zara. Malachi looks as if he wants to jump to his feet. Even Phoebe perks up a little, but she's not looking at me. She's staring at Malachi.

"You sure you don't want to stay a little longer?" Malachi speaks up.

I shake my head, rolling my stiff shoulders back. "No, I should get going, but thanks for letting me crash your movie night." I smile.

Zara sighs, getting up to embrace me. "Text me when you get home."

"I will," I whisper, giving her a tight squeeze. It takes a moment before she lets go. When she finally steps back, I give her one last soothing smile before heading toward the door.

As I step outside, the chilly air nips at my skin, and I pull the oversized sleeves of the shirt over my hands. I've barely reached my car when I hear footsteps behind me.

"Asha, wait."

I turn just as Malachi jogs up, my dress and heels clutched in his hands like a gold medal. His pace slows until he stops in front of me. "You forgot this." He holds the items out for me to grab.

I blink, momentarily caught off guard. "Oh, thanks." His fingers feel like feathers as I take the dress from his hands. That's when I realize—I still have his clothes on.

I open my mouth to say something, but before I can, he shakes his head. "It's fine. Keep them."

I hesitate, searching his face. "Are you sure?"

"Yeah, I don't need them."

"What about your slippers?" I say, lifting my toes up.

"It's fine. I promise." He chuckles. "Just . . . get home safe, okay?"

I nod. "I will."

"And Asha?"

I hesitate, then say, "Yeah?"

Malachi rubs the back of his neck and then shakes his head. "Never mind."

He doesn't move right away, and neither do I.

Then, after a moment, he steps back, his hands slipping into his pockets. He walks backward as I turn to open the car door and slide inside.

When I finally start the car and pull off, Malachi is standing on the side of the curb, still watching. His scent lingering on his clothes brings me comfort the entire way home.

Chapter 13

I BARELY HAVE TIME to get Liv in bed and change clothes before Russell barges in the house. I placed Malachi's clothes in the hamper, planning to wash them and return them to him. I'm downstairs cleaning—mind racing, hands needing something to do. Sleep won't be visiting me tonight. I already know that much.

I keep my head down as I scrub the counter, but I can hear him. His movements are quick and agitated. His shoes hit the floor with a loud thud, followed by the heavy stomp of his feet crossing the living room. I close my eyes and pray he keeps walking. Just go upstairs. Let me have this night alone. Let me sit in my thoughts, in this ache he caused.

But tonight is not my lucky night.

Russell storms into the kitchen and tosses something on the counter. I wince, startled, unsure what it is until I glance over.

A box of chocolates and a bent bouquet of flowers sit at the edge of the counter, carelessly thrown, petals already bruising. My grip tightens around the dishrag. Whatever fight I had in me hours ago has dissolved. I say nothing. Just keep wiping the same spot in slow, endless circles.

The air is heavy with tension. Whatever peace I found earlier—at Zara's house, in Malachi's arms—feels distant now, like a dream I had to wake up from.

What am I supposed to do? Say thank you? Pretend he didn't shove me?

Russell brushes past me and heads straight for the fridge, grabbing the last beer without a word of apology.

"I got your favorite chocolate," he says, motioning toward the box. I reach for it, fingers grazing the plastic cover, lips pressed tight to hold back a frown.

They're caramel-filled. I hate caramel. *After all this time, how does he still not know?*

"You can put the flowers in a vase. Set them right there on the windowsill," he suggests, pointing with the neck of his beer bottle before taking a long swig.

His promise to quit drinking is long forgotten. Every case of beer has been "the last," but it never is.

"So when you're washing dishes or cooking, you can see them."

See them? All they'll do is remind me of why he bought them in the first place.

I pick up the wilted bouquet and bring it to my nose. The scent doesn't register. There's no sweetness in this gesture—just an attempt to cover the bruise on my side. A bruise he doesn't even know about. And he never will.

Because I won't give him the satisfaction of knowing how badly he hurt me. How fragile I've become.

He steps closer. For a split second, I wonder if he'll apologize, tell me he didn't mean to hurt me, or say something that might sound like love. Instead, he presses a kiss to my temple and runs a hand down my back. My breath stills.

I glance up at him with wet eyes, searching his face for something—anything. A crack in the mask. A sign that he's still the man I once knew.

He meets my gaze for a beat, then looks away. "I'll make it up to you," he says.

But the ache in my chest tells me the truth: he won't.

He walks off, grabbing another beer before disappearing up the stairs.

The moment he's gone, I drop the flowers on the counter and shove the chocolates into the trash with shaking hands. A choking sound escapes me, and I slap a hand over my mouth to muffle it. My body trembles with quiet rage. I want to throw something, to smash every glass in the kitchen, to tear down every lie I've framed and hung on these walls.

My eyes land on a photo—Russell and me at a cookout, back when I was pregnant with Liv. I pull it from the wall, studying the frozen moment. I'm smiling, clueless. Things were already unraveling back then, but I ignored it. Pretended the distance wasn't growing. I trace my smile behind the glass, wondering how I didn't see it.

This isn't the life I pictured. When we first started dating, he used to bring me flowers before every date. We used to laugh, touch, talk like we had forever. But the flowers stopped. The dates stopped. His love grew cold—and somehow, I didn't notice until I was already drowning in it.

I press my back against the wall near the steps, trying to wipe away the tears before heading to bed. But they won't stop.

My legs give out, and I slide to the floor, sobbing uncontrollably.

***

THE FLOWERS HE BOUGHT sit in a vase on the kitchen windowsill, withering away. I stare at them with a scowl as I unload the groceries onto the granite countertop. With Thanksgiving a week away, I make it a point to shop early, dodging the chaos of packed aisles, traffic, and frustrated moms searching for items in bare sections.

This morning was peaceful. I had the store mostly to myself. Russell stayed home with Liv, who was still asleep when I left. Grocery shopping may be a chore, but for me, it's become a small escape. A moment of quiet. That is, until Russell texted me before I checked out, asking—no, telling—me to bring home a case of beer.

I wanted to say no. I wanted to ignore it. But I didn't.

Because keeping the peace has become my priority. So, I bought the beer, resenting every step from the cooler to the checkout.

The bags are full of sweet potatoes, cinnamon, butter, fresh greens, ingredients for cornbread, mac and cheese, turkey wings, and more. Zara's bringing potato salad, creamed corn, and drinks.

Next week, I'll be surrounded by the people who love me and Liv unconditionally. People I never have to guess with. Even if things aren't perfect, the thought of being with them fills me with thankfulness.

Zara and Akin always join us for Thanksgiving. Malachi too. But this year, I'm not sure if he's coming. Things between him and Russell have been strained—tension brewing like a thunderstorm that never breaks. I wouldn't blame him for skipping it, but it wouldn't feel the same without him here. Still, I hope things go smoothly. I'm not worried about Zara or Akin. Russell, I fear, will ruin it.

I pull out my phone and call Zara. She picks up on the second ring. "Hey, sis, I'm putting you on speaker," she says.

"Hey. What you up to?" I ask, organizing the groceries by dish, cradling the phone between my shoulder and ear.

"Finishing up in the studio. You?"

"Unloading groceries. Trying to get ahead for Thanksgiving next week."

"Please tell me you're making sweet potato pie," she says, hopeful.

"I'm making three. One you can take home."

"This is why I love you," she sings.

I laugh. "You talk to Malachi?"

"Yeah. Why?"

"Just wondering if he's still coming this year."

She hesitates, then sighs. "I don't know. He usually comes, then we head to Mom and Dad's after. But he hasn't been too keen on being around Russell lately."

So, it's not just me.

"Can you find out for me?" I ask, trying not to sound too desperate. It shouldn't even matter to me, but it does.

"Sure," she says, though her tone is cautious.

"Phoebe's welcome to join too," I add quickly.

"As long as I get a pie to myself, I don't care who you invite." She laughs. "But I'll let her know."

Just as I'm reaching into another bag, the front door swings open.

"Man, what?!" Russell's voice booms.

I freeze, carton of milk still in hand. A deep breath settles in my lungs.

He walks into the kitchen, eyes glued to the football game on his phone. I exhale slowly, tension uncoiling just a little.

"Hey, Z, I'll call you back," I say quickly.

"Talk later," she replies before the line goes dead.

"Hey, babe," I offer gently, not wanting to disrupt his focus.

"Hey," he says without looking up. "Need help?"

"Um . . . yeah."

Russell finally moves toward me, unloading groceries with one hand, the other still holding his phone. "Is Liv still asleep?" I ask.

"Yeah, upstairs. I was in the backyard watching the game. Didn't know you were back yet. What took you so long?"

"I just made sure I got everything we needed."

He hums and nods. "That's good," he murmurs, pulling out the beer. "I see you grabbed my beer."

"I did." *Even though I shouldn't have.*

He nods, seemingly satisfied, and keeps unpacking, laying everything on the counter. His eyes flick toward me, and then suddenly, he moves in closer.

"You look beautiful today," he murmurs, fingers trailing along my cheek and down my neck. His touch is as light as a feather, and it sends an involuntary shudder through me.

I manage a smile. "Thanks, honey." I'm in high-waisted jeans, a cropped long-sleeve shirt, and white New Balances. I don't know what's so special about my outfit today. It's something I've worn a million times before.

His gaze lingers on my face, unreadable. Then his eyes narrow slightly, brows pulling downward.

"You make any extra stops while you were out?"

Even though he isn't outright accusing me of something, it feels as if he is. My stomach clenches. His nose flares just slightly, and I realize he's studying me for any tell.

I force a chuckle, thrown off by the question. "No. I was at the store and came straight home."

Russell doesn't respond right away. My pulse ticks up even though I'm telling the truth. He tilts his head and says, "All right, then."

His tone is light, almost sweet. But something about it feels off.

I turn away, and my eyes land on the small vase on the windowsill.

The flowers he bought me are wilting. Their deep purple and white petals have curled inward, the edges browning.

The sight tugs at my chest, but before I can dwell on it, Russell follows my gaze and clicks his tongue.

"Guess I'll have to bring you fresh ones," he mutters, shaking his head. Then, turning toward me, his expression softens. "Can't have my woman looking at dead flowers, can I?"

I swallow, forcing another smile. "You don't have to do that." *Because I really don't want you too.*

"I will," he says smoothly, stepping even closer. His fingers find my wrist, rubbing small circles against my skin. "You deserve fresh flowers, Asha."

I should appreciate the sentiment. I should feel happy. But instead, my stomach knots. *Do I not deserve more than that?* I ask myself.

I nod, murmuring a quiet "thank you" before slipping from his grasp, pretending to busy myself with the rest of the bags. My hands move on autopilot, but my mind lingers—caught between the warmth of his affection and the cold shadow of doubt creeping in.

I shouldn't feel uneasy.

I should feel gratitude.

But it's misplaced—lost somewhere beneath the weight of our last argument, buried under the silent bruises his love sometimes leaves behind.

Chapter 14

LIV'S PIERCING SCREAMS FILL the room, sharp and loud, cutting through the silence like a siren. Her tiny fists flail as hot tears stream down her cheeks, her breath coming out in hiccupping gasps. I hold her close, pressing a kiss to her damp forehead. I whisper soothing words and rock her, but nothing helps.

She doesn't have a fever. She doesn't want her sippy cup. She won't take a nap. And she refused to eat all her dinner—pushing her plate of food away.

I pace the floor, bouncing her gently, humming a lullaby that usually works. It doesn't. And I am becoming a little discouraged. The frustration isn't with her—it's with me. I'm her mother. I should know how to calm her. But tonight, I can't. And the longer she cries, the heavier my exhaustion feels.

The smell of turkey seasonings still lingers in the air, the half-prepared meal for tomorrow's Thanksgiving dinner sitting untouched on the counter. I wanted to get a head start, but I can't focus on anything except the weight of Liv in my arms and the sharp ache creeping into my temples.

"Mama's got you, baby girl," I whisper into her ear. "Mama's here."

As tears threaten, the door opens abruptly. The sound startles me, but Liv doesn't even notice—her screams just grow louder.

Russell steps inside, slamming the door shut behind him. His badge is crooked at his waist, his shirt untucked. His eyes—red-rimmed and sunken—flicker toward me.

"What's wrong with her?" he asks, voice tense. He stumbles slightly, tossing his keys onto the counter.

I don't answer immediately, just tighten my arms around Liv.

He lets out a sharp breath. "I could hear her from the driveway."

"I don't know," I say, shifting her weight. "She's just . . . fussy."

Russell rubs a hand over his face, sighing. "Maybe she's gassy or sleepy." His voice is flat, tired. "Hand her to me."

My grip tightens instinctively, holding her slightly closer to me.

I glance at the glowing numbers on the oven. It's a little after nine, and he's just now getting home. *Working or drinking—I don't know anymore.* But the sway in his step, the way his words are slightly rushed and slurred, gives the impression of the latter.

"What's wrong with you?" His eyes narrow. "You heard me. Hand her here."

I swallow hard. "Are you drunk?" The words slip out.

He tilts his head, amusement in his eyes before they darken. "Are you serious right now?"

I don't answer. His scowl steals my breath, tightens my throat. His nostrils flare, and his mouth opens.

Russell steps closer. "I'm her father, Asha. If you don't give me my child—" His voice is threatening and demanding.

Taking a step back, I gulp. His eyebrows furrow deeply, and his hardened chest rises and falls. His jaw clenches as he yanks Liv from my arms. I reach for her but stop myself from fighting back. I don't want to hurt or scare her . . . or make things worse.

Liv whimpers, then buries her face in his chest. Her cries soften into a silent sob. The moment she settles, relief flashes across his face.

He looks up at me with a sly smirk because he knows he was able to do something I couldn't.

A lump rises in my throat. I hate this. Hate how that feels—watching her calm in his arms while I stand here, useless.

But I'm grateful too. At least she stopped crying. At least one of us knows how to soothe her. And at least she's comfortable in his arms.

I wrap my arms around myself as he moves toward the couch. He flops down, Liv resting against him, her tiny fingers curled into his shirt.

"I'm not drunk," he mutters, keeping his eyes locked on the blank television screen. "Had one beer. That's it."

The faint scent of alcohol lingers in the air, clinging to him. Although faint, it's unmistakable. Even if it were one beer, I'd rather it be none.

I bite the inside of my cheek until I taste blood. Maybe I'm imagining the way he swayed. Maybe I'm overreacting.

Or maybe I'm not.

A heavy silence fills the room as I stand there. Russell looks up at me. His gaze locks onto mine.

"Do you really think I'd ever hurt her?" His voice is soft. Almost wounded.

The guilt hits me instantly. *Hard.* "No," I whisper. "Of course not."

His stare lingers before he nods. "Good."

I dig my nails into my arms until it hurts. *But you've hurt me before.* The thought slams into me like a whispered admission I'm too afraid to utter out loud.

I should feel relief, grateful that Liv is finally settling. But worry brews in the pit of my stomach. Because right now, at this moment, I feel like I've done something wrong—as if trying to protect her, trying to calm her, trying to make sure Russell wasn't drunk, was a mistake.

Russell shifts his attention back to Liv, his fingers tracing slow, gentle circles on her back. She relaxes further against him. She looks just like him.

I can't stop staring.

I can't stop feeling the war raging inside me.

I love that he's comforting her.

Yet, a part of me wonders—*how can his hands be so gentle with her . . . but so violent toward me?*

The thought is dangerous.

I force it away, blinking back tears. Instead, I try to focus on how comfortable Liv is in his arms, on how—even though he just got off work—he's there for her.

Maybe that's what matters most.

"You gonna finish cooking or keep looking at me?" His voice cuts through the silence.

I nod quickly, turning toward the kitchen counter. "Yeah," I whisper. "I'm sorry."

The scent of cinnamon and nutmeg lingers in the kitchen as I smooth my hands over my apron. My sweet potato pies are cooling on the counter, golden and perfect. But my mind is far from here.

I'm standing in the middle of the kitchen, willing myself to focus—on the warmth of the oven, the quiet hum of the fridge, the distant sound of the wind outside. Anything but the thoughts clawing at me. Thoughts of Russell.

I'm exhausted.

My body aches from all the stirring, chopping, and mixing. The weight of a toddler who fought sleep with the energy of a wild animal still lingers in my arms. Every inch of me begs for rest, for the comfort of my bed and the quiet of sleep.

I roll my shoulders, twisting my neck from side to side, trying to work out the stiffness—until a set of warm hands settles on them. The hands knead me like dough. Strong, rough hands.

Russell.

His hands slide down to my waist, his chest pressing against my back. His lips graze my shoulder, his voice low and hushed.

"Liv's asleep," he murmurs. "After a long day at work . . . I need you. I miss you."

I stiffen, my fingers tightening against the counter's edge. His lips trail along my neck, slow and soft. This used to melt my mind and body. I used to long for this, crave it.

But now?

Now, it feels different.

His touch doesn't send electricity down my spine—it sends tension through my limbs. His arms don't feel like safety; they feel like control. I still don't understand these feelings, but they're present. Terrifying. Consuming.

A deep breath escapes me as I take a small step forward. I slip from his grasp as gently as I can. "Russell, wait . . ."

His hands fall away, but I can still feel his looming presence behind me. His eyes study me. "What's up?" he asks, a trace of aggravation in his tone.

I wring my hands together, staring at the counter. I should just say it. Tell him how ever since I've been going to church more, spending intimate time with God, I've felt conviction about what we're doing. How we need to do things the right way.

But more than my faith is holding me back.

Fear is too.

A piece of me is scared of him. Scared to be intimate with him when he's hurt me. I'm scared to let those same large hands that left bruises on my skin caress me.

I open my mouth, but the words feel stuck. I clear my throat, my body tensing. I say the easiest thing. The safest thing. "I'm tired."

A moment of silence passes between us. Then he scoffs with a deep sigh. I turn slightly just in time to see his eyes darken. "You're tired?"

I nod slowly.

His tongue prods his cheek. "So what?"

I shift uncomfortably as he closes the space between us again. He puts his hands on my hips, pulling me into him. Before I can say anything, he presses his lips against mine, but they feel cold and distant.

His grip tightens, and his fingers dig into my skin. My stomach churns, and chills spread over my body. I lean into the kiss because I have to--because I need to. But it feels fake. Hollow. And I wonder if he can sense it too.

When his hold starts to hurt, fear creeps up behind me like a dark shadow, and I pull away.

"Russ—"

He swears under his breath, stepping back, heaving. "What is it?"

I keep my head down, not sure what to say. "I'm tired," I whisper into the crook of his neck. "It's been a long—"

His laugh cuts me off. It's not a happy or playful laugh. It's a bitter and condescending one. He shakes his head, running a hand down his face. "You can't be serious." It's evident his patience is thinning.

"I work every darn day," he snaps. "I don't get to be tired. I don't get to say 'not tonight.' You think I don't want to just come home, drop everything, and do nothing? But I don't." His voice rises. "Because I have a family to provide for."

My pulse hammers in my ears. My hands are shaking, so I shove them into my back pockets.

His nostrils flare. "And all I ask—all I need is this. You." He steps closer again, his presence overwhelming. "And now you're holding out on me?"

I gulp, forcing myself to keep his gaze even though my eyes are watering. "I'm not trying to—"

"The least you could do," he grits out, "is do your part."

My stomach drops.

But I'm not your wife. The part he wants me to play—isn't mine to give. The thought cuts through me like a blade.

I hesitate. "I just . . . I mean, we're not—" I stop myself, shaking my head. "Never mind."

Russell exhales sharply. "Don't forget who takes care of you and Liv. You wouldn't have anyone or anything without me."

I know that. I know Russell does so much for us, even though he doesn't have to. When my mom passed away, he helped me figure things out. When I got pregnant, he didn't hesitate to take care of me. He's been taking care of us ever since.

"I know," I whisper, wiping my eyes.

For a moment his gaze softens. A small grin pulls at his lips, and his eyes lighten. "Then why are you doing this to me?" he whines.

I flinch as he lifts his hand and taps his index finger against my temple. "Don't let those friends of yours put these thoughts in your head."

But the truth is they don't really know much about our relationship—except for what I tell them. They haven't put any thoughts into my head. They're coming from me. From somewhere deep inside me that I can't control.

"I'm sorry." I whisper, placing my hand along his chest.

"I love you," Russell whispers. His lips brush my temple, then my cheek, then right below my ear. His right hand cups my neck, his thumb tracing my collarbone. His grip tightens slightly.

The heat of his kisses doesn't warm me. It chills me. "Come on, baby . . . don't do this to me." His voice is smooth now, persuading. Gentle in a way that makes it hard to say no. "You know how much I need you."

His lips move lower, planting tiny kisses along my jaw and neck. I stand there, frozen, hands trapped at my sides.

I should say no. I should push him away.

But when I do nothing, he takes it as permission. And when he takes my hand, leading me toward the stairs, my feet move even though my heart screams stop.

Each step feels heavy.

By the time we reach our bedroom, my stomach is twisted so tight it aches. I hesitate at the door, but Russell doesn't notice. He tugs me forward, tilting my chin up with a crooked finger.

"I take care of you, don't I?" he murmurs.

I nod. Agreeing makes things easier. If I argue or ask any more questions, I know it'll result in a fight. Liv's door is cracked open, and I don't want to wake her. I don't have the strength to fight tonight.

Still, the guilt is there. The shame. The fear.

And as he pulls me close, my eyes shut, and I whisper in my head, *God, what am I supposed to do?*

But I don't stop.

I don't say no.

And I don't know if that makes it my fault or not.

Chapter 15

Table set. Check.

Dinner cooked. Check.

Pies ready. Check.

House clean. Check.

Liv dressed in her adorable orange dress with tiny turkeys on it and matching bows. Check.

This morning felt like a race against time. After waking up early to clean, fold laundry, wash dishes, finish the last of the cooking, and take care of Liv, I'm exhausted.

Meanwhile Russell is exactly where he's been for the past hour and a half—stretched out on the couch, watching a football game. His phone is in his hand, and his fingers idly tap the screen. With all the work that needed to be done, it would have been good to have his help.

He's wearing a dark green sweater that draws out the warmth in his skin, paired with khakis and crisp white Nikes. A silver chain rests on his collarbone, catching the light as he shifts upright. He looks handsome—undeniably so. His looks were never what drew me in, but they once made my heart race. Now, they just make it ache.

Liv sits beside him, shaking his car keys like they're the most fascinating toy in the world. It's funny how kids work—it's never the things made for them that capture their attention, always the off-limits objects. Boxes, spoons, mail, or shoes. Boring objects.

She looks absolutely precious in her little dress, bows, and pristine white stockings. Zara picked the outfit out months ago. I couldn't be more satisfied with how cute she looks. I pull out my phone, snapping a few quick pictures before Liv can make a mess on herself.

With the last of the food finished, I rush upstairs. When I glance at myself in the mirror, I almost jump at my reflection. I look like I've been fighting for my life in the kitchen all morning.

My dark brown hair is frizzy and tangled. My face is bare and could use some moisture. Food stains are splattered on my oversized T-shirt and sweatpants. Which, I've been meaning to throw them out anyway due to the tiny holes in them.

I take a quick shower, barely letting myself enjoy the warmth of the water. For the sake of time, I only dampen my hair just enough to work in some gel. I smooth it into a side swoop and a low bun. I apply a little mascara, some lotion and foundation to even out my skin, and then a layer of lip gloss. *That'll do.*

I slip into a silk beige dress that flows down to my ankles, cinched at the waist to give me some shape, and step into a pair of matching closed-toe heels. My gold jewelry—hoops, rings, necklace—adds the final touch.

Just as I reach the bottom of the stairs, a loud knock echoes through the house. Russell doesn't move. Doesn't even glance toward the door. He just sits there, completely absorbed in the game.

After last night, I haven't said much to him.

I shove the thought of last night's events away before it can form a dark cloud over my head. Last night happened. And all the confusing, conflicting emotions it stirred inside me haven't settled. They've only grown stronger. But now isn't the time to deal with them. Right now,

I need to be a good host. I need tonight to go smoothly—better than our last gathering.

Russell was hesitant to have everyone over again, but he agreed . . . for me. They join us every year, and it'd be too weird if we didn't uphold the tradition. So, I have to make this right. Despite everything, I still want my friends to like Russell, and maybe one day he will like them too.

I take a steadying breath and open the door.

The sight of Zara immediately lifts my spirits. She matches Liv! Akin stands beside her, wearing a peach-toned button-up under a dark trench coat, light jeans, and boots, with a fresh re-twist.

A slither of disappointment creeps into my chest when I realize Malachi isn't with them. I guess he decided not to join us after all.

Akin lifts a bag of ice and jugs of sweet tea and lemonade. "For a second, I thought nobody was home," he jokes.

"Sorry about that," I say quickly, stepping aside. "Please, come in."

Zara steps in, grinning with several containers in hand.

"If I'd known you were matching Liv, I would've asked for a matching dress too."

Zara gasps dramatically. "Oh no, you can't copy me and my girl."

I don't really mind that Zara and Liv match; fashion is her thing. I'm just happy someone cares for Liv the way Zara does. If anything ever happened to me . . . I know my baby would be okay. Zara would make sure of that.

She pulls me into a hug, her embrace tight as if she knows somehow I need it.

And for the first time all day, I find myself relaxing—just a little.

"Hey, Russell," Zara chimes as she walks in front of the television.

Russell sits up slightly, a flicker of irritation crossing his face until Zara moves from his view.

Russell gives a nod. "What's up."

"Hey, baby girl," Zara coos as she moves past him to scoop Liv into her arms. My daughter practically leaps toward her, arms stretching eagerly.

Akin sets the items on the kitchen counter before settling onto the couch across from Russell, just as engrossed in the game. The two men acknowledge each other with a simple nod, a quiet understanding between them most men seem to have.

"Girl, it smells amazing in here!" Zara squeals as she takes a seat at the island, balancing Liv on her knee. "I'm starving."

"Thank you," I say, licking my lips. "I just hope it tastes as good as it smells. I've been cooking all day."

There's nothing left for me to do, but my hands won't stay still. I start adjusting things on the counter, shifting plates an inch to the left, and refolding an already neatly folded towel.

Zara watches me for a moment, then lowers her voice. "So . . . how are things with you and Russell?"

I hesitate. *How in the world do I answer that question?* My first instinct is to say *good*. I'm so used to pasting on a smile and pretending everything is fine. But I can't keep lying to my best friend—shutting her out feels wrong. She might not know all the details of our relationship, but she knows things haven't been great. And honestly . . . keeping her in the dark is starting to feel harder than just telling the truth.

"Things could be better," I admit, carefully folding the towel. "But . . . we're figuring things out."

Zara's brows pull together. "You wanna talk about it?" she asks carefully, as if she's bracing herself for me to shut her down like I always do.

Glancing toward the living room, I ensure Russell is still glued to the game. Then, swallowing my pride, I whisper, "Sure."

Zara's eyes widen in surprise, and she sits up straighter, fully tuned in.

I take a deep breath. Saying the words out loud makes them heavier, more *real*. "It's just . . . he's been different lately," I start, speaking as low as I can. "One minute, he's extra sweet—like, bringing me flowers just because—" I motion toward the wilting bouquet still sitting on the windowsill. "Then the next, he's mad at me over little things."

Zara tilts her head. "I mean . . . couples argue over little things sometimes. Like, Akin leaves his dirty clothes right beside the basket instead of in it. And I always leave the cabinet drawers open. Drives him crazy." She chuckles, shaking her head.

I want to laugh with her, to brush this off as something *normal*, something *every* couple goes through. But I can't.

Because our fights aren't about dirty laundry or cabinet drawers.

I inhale deeply, pressing my lips together before shaking my head. "No, it's not things like that," I say. "It's . . . it's different. Like he becomes a completely different person."

Zara's face shifts, the amusement fading from her expression.

"He wants to know my every move." I shrug. "I can't do anything without running it by him first," I say, omitting how he grabbed my arm so tight it left bruises. I don't tell her about how he's always yelling so loud it terrifies me, or how he punched a hole in the wall, or how he pushed me that night I came crying at her doorstep. The list of things I haven't told her is growing. I shake my head again, struggling to put it into words.

Instead, I force a weak smile and say, "I just don't understand it—him."

Zara studies me, her gaze soft but serious. "Asha . . ." she starts, her voice cautious.

I swallow hard, brushing my hands across the smooth, clean counter. I don't give her time to speak when I whisper, "Does Akin ever act like that?"

"No," she says quickly.

One word. One syllable. But it feels like a cold splash of water to my face.

My head falls down to my chest, but I quickly regain my composure. Pressing my lips together, I exhale from my flared nostrils. A deep sinking feeling travels through my entire body. I grip the counter, composing myself.

I've always told myself that *all* couples argue. That every relationship has its ups and downs. That what Russell and I go through is just . . . part of loving someone.

But now, I'm starting to wonder if I've been lying to myself.

Things are becoming a little clearer—the dust is settling, and for a brief moment, I catch a glimpse of how things should be. But just as quickly, the image blurs again, clouded with doubt.

This is just a phase of our relationship that we have to get through, I tell myself. Because at some point, things weren't this way. We were in love. We were happy. And he wasn't like this.

Things can go back to that, can't they?

This is just a phase; I repeat it in my head. But the words don't quite reach my heart.

Zara is saying something, but the words don't register. My mind is tangled in its own web of thoughts, so much so that I don't even realize Russell is looking at me over his shoulder.

Thankfully, the doorbell rings just in time.

"I'll get it," I chime, rushing toward the door. The first thing I notice is a flash of red—Phoebe's bright red dress and lipstick.

"Asha!" she squeals, wrapping me into a hug before I even have time to open the door fully.

"Hey, Phoebe." I smile. Over her shoulder, I spot Malachi, a Tupperware bowl in hand, his scarf tucked neatly into his coat. He wears an apologetic grin. *He came.* Zara had asked him if he was coming, but he hadn't given her a definite answer. And that had bothered me for some reason, but I'd remained hopeful. Seeing him here right now sends a wave of bliss through my heart.

"Thanks for having us over! I'm so excited!" Phoebe scurries past me, inviting herself in with her usual enthusiasm. She makes her way to the living room, greeting the guys with the same passion.

"Sorry about that," Malachi murmurs.

"It's fine." I chuckle.

He lifts the container toward me. "Happy Thanksgiving."

I take it, peeling back the lid. The familiar scent of bananas and wafer cookies fills my nostrils.

"You bought me banana pudding?" I ask, grinning.

"No, I didn't buy anything. I made it."

I freeze for a moment, my chest tightening at the gesture. It's so small—so simple—yet it warms me.

"You didn't have to do that," I whisper, closing the lid and holding the container close to my chest.

"Yeah, but I wanted to," he says, stepping inside and shutting the door behind him. "I remember how much you liked the one at Zara's party."

I recall eating the creamy and crunchy sweetness as he approached my table. I wanted to go for seconds, but with Russell's voice echoing in my ear about how I've gained weight, I didn't want to appear greedy.

"Thank you, Mal. And I'm glad you came."

"You really thought I wasn't going to come?" His eyes search mine. I shrug. "I'm not going to let anything or anyone stop me from coming around. Plus, there's free food," he says, rubbing his stomach with a deep laugh.

Playful, I roll my eyes at him.

As we enter the living room, Malachi and Russell lock eyes. The air stiffens slightly. It's subtle, but I feel it. Russell's lip twitches. His gaze lingers on Malachi a little too long for comfort. Malachi, to his credit, doesn't waver. He simply nods before he shifts his attention to Zara.

She's walking to him with a smile. He pulls her into a hug, planting a kiss on the top of her forehead and then Liv's. Malachi grabs Liv from her arm and cradles her close to his chest.

Before the silence can stretch, Phoebe claps her hands together, her voice bright and cheery. "So! Who's ready to eat? Because I am starving."

That breaks the tension, and soon enough, we're all gathered around the table, plates filled with food. The aroma of seasoned turkey wings, mac and cheese, greens, and cornbread fills the room.

I glance at Russell, hoping he'll offer the blessing, but he's already chewing. Clearing my throat, I extend my hands.

Russell looks up, cheeks full, and swallows.

"I'll bless the food," I say.

When his hand slips into mine, his grip tightens. A wave of discomfort crawls up my spine, but I bow my head and push through. "Thank you, Lord, for this meal, for family, for keeping us another day. Amen."

"Amen," everyone else echoes. Russell is already back to eating.

Akin takes a bite of the turkey and groans dramatically. "Asha, this is amazing. I swear food is the key to my heart."

I laugh, shaking my head.

Zara wipes the corner of her mouth with a napkin before smiling at me. "This pie reminds me of your mom's," she says softly. "She would be so proud of you."

A lump forms in my throat. Thanksgiving was always Mom's favorite holiday. Cooking was her love language, and you could taste the love in every dish. I push past that void growing in my heart and nod. "Thank you."

Russell lifts his glass of wine. "Well, I'm grateful to be with a woman who cooks as well as she does."

My head snaps to him. He rarely compliments me in front of my friends, and after the past couple of days, I hadn't expected him to say anything like that.

Despite my confused expression, I finally smile. It only feels right to say something kind in return, so I say, "And I'm grateful to be with a man who provides for me and protects the community."

Liv, sitting in her highchair beside me, babbles happily, slapping her tiny hands on the tray.

Phoebe tilts her head, her eyes flicking toward Russell. "Speaking of that, what's it like working as a detective?"

Russell exhales sharply, setting his fork down. "It's a job."

His tone is sharp. But then, as if realizing how that might sound, he leans back in his chair and sighs. "It's not easy. People think they know what we go through, but they don't. It's split-second decisions that could cost you your life. It's stressful. You try to do the right thing, and people still find a reason to hate you for it."

I shift in my seat.

He looks around the table with a blank expression. "But it's whatever. It's what I get paid to do."

My heart falters at his words. Being his partner, I've seen firsthand how stressful his job can be, but after all this time, I still don't know how to be there for him. I've tried, but it doesn't seem to be enough.

There's a dismissiveness to his tone, as if he doesn't care whether anyone sympathizes with him or not. He's not looking for their approval—he's just making sure I know how hard his life is.

I press my lips together and glance at Zara. Her eyes are narrowed, head tilted as she studies Russell.

Phoebe, ever the peacemaker, pipes up with a bright smile. "Well, I think it's good you care so much. We definitely need good officers out there!"

Russell smirks slightly, picking up his fork. "Yeah. Sure."

Akin clears his throat, taking a sip of his sweet tea. "I heard about that big drug bust last week. That was you, wasn't it?"

Russell nods, and I realize I have no idea what they're talking about.

"Yeah, I was working a homicide, and it ended up leading to an operation that was bigger than anything I've ever seen," he says with pride. I recognize that look—he enjoys talking about himself, about his job. It's the same look he had at church when everyone was treating him like a superstar.

"That's amazing, honey," I say, placing my hand on top of his. I brush my thumb along his hand, offering him a small smile. *He's not the only one who can pretend.* "I had no idea."

Russell turns his hand over, lacing his fingers through mine. "It wasn't easy," he says, his voice tender. "But I get through the rough days because I have such an amazing woman by my side."

His words settle over the table, pulling everyone's attention toward us. I blink, taken aback. His words feel almost . . . deliberate. As if he wanted them all to know just how much he values me. A sense of happiness creeps in, but it's layered with uncertainty. The way we are admiring one another, it would be easy to assume this is a normal occurrence from the outside looking in. But in reality, this is all pretend.

Malachi nods, setting down his fork. "I agree. Asha's an incredible woman," he says simply.

A strange heat creeps up my neck, and I inhale. The way Russell's fingers tighten slightly around mine causes my pulse to quicken.

He turns his head, catching Malachi's gaze for half a second before looking back at me, his expression unreadable.

Why would Malachi say something like that? Does he mean it?

"She really is," Russell says smoothly, his grip firm but affectionate. "I don't say it enough, but I'm a lucky man."

The words should make me happy. They should make me feel cherished. Instead, my body tenses. He's trying to convince everyone else, but the words are distant.

I force a smile. "Well, I'm lucky too," I say, though my voice lacks honest admission. "I'm grateful for you all."

At some point, the conversation shifts to football, which I expected given the guys' love for anything sports. It's the only thing they have in common. I take a breath, relieved by the change in topic. Russell surprisingly stays engaged, even though he doesn't typically talk much with the guys. The dinner is going well, better than I expected, and I silently hope it stays that way.

Zara, Phoebe, and I fall into an easy conversation about shopping, recipes, and holiday plans. Liv made a mess of her food, half of it ending up on her dress, but she ate well. I smile to myself, grateful for the pictures I took earlier.

"Asha, can you pass me the greens?" Akin asks.

I nod, leaning over to hand the dish to him, and my arm brushes against Russell's glass. Before I can react, it tips forward and spills right onto his lap. A gasp escapes from my lips as it soaks through his jeans.

"Oh my gosh, I'm so sorry," I say quickly, reaching for a napkin. My hand trembles as I dab uselessly at the mess. My heart pounds, heat crawling up my cheeks. Everyone's staring.

Russell pushes my hand away, his jaw clenched tight. "Stop," he hisses under his breath, eyes dark. He forces a laugh through gritted teeth. "It's fine. Accidents happen."

But I know it's not fine. Behind that smile is a scowl that could cut flesh. I lean into him, whispering, "I'm really sorry."

"We'll deal with this later," he mutters so low that no one else hears him.

"Later" comes sooner than I expect. As soon as the door clicks shut behind our guests, pain explodes across my face. The force sends me stumbling back against the wall, my breath catching in my throat.

"What did I say about embarrassing me?" Russell yells.

For a moment, I can't move. I can't think. My ears ring, my vision blurs, and all I can process is the sharp sting blooming across my cheek.

Russell just hit me.

Chapter 16

HOURS LATER, I STILL feel the sting of his hand across my face. A burning, lingering heat spreads across my cheek. It feels swollen, but when I glance in the mirror, there's no deep bruise. It's barely noticeable, but I know it happened. I felt it. I still feel it.

It doesn't seem real—like maybe I imagined it, like maybe my mind is exaggerating it and twisting things. But that's not true. The bruise on my arm from before, the shove, the hole in the wall . . . I let myself believe those things were accidental. That he lost control for a second. That he didn't mean it.

But this? This slap wasn't an accident. It was intentional and precise.

The memory replays in my head, and no matter how much I try to push it down, it keeps surfacing. One moment, we were standing in the doorway, saying goodbye to our friends, and the next, a pain so sharp and searing, exploding across my face.

I hadn't even seen it coming.

Russell—*my Russell*—hit me.

My mind spirals, grasping for something to make sense of it, for something to justify it. But no matter how I try to piece it together,

I can't understand how the man I love—the man who's supposed to love me—could do this.

I didn't mean to spill wine on him. It was an accident. I'd never do anything to intentionally embarrass him.

Tears sting my eyes again as I remember his face. The anger in his eyes. The way his jaw clenched. The way he warned me not to embarrass him.

After he hit me, he kept talking and yelling. I couldn't hear him over the ringing in my ears. I just stood there, too stunned to speak.

And then he left. He left me standing there, my body shaking, my mind racing, my heart breaking.

I sank to the floor, small and alone. Feeling like my whole world had shifted under my feet.

Now, in the quiet of the morning, I should have clarity. I should know what to do. But every conclusion I come to feels impossible.

There's no bruise. No physical evidence. If I called the police, what then? He is the police. Would they believe me? And if they did, what happens next? Would they arrest him? Would he post bond and come back even angrier? Would I be safe?

Would Liv be safe?

A shudder runs through me as I glance at her, peacefully asleep in her crib. She's so small. So innocent. She has no idea that something in her world just changed.

I don't know what to do.

If I call Zara, she'll be furious. She'll show up with Malachi and Akin. And then they'll all tell me to leave him, demanding that I pack our bags and come with them.

But how can I be safe if he knows where we are?

And what if that only makes things worse?

What if I'm overreacting?

I swallow hard, my stomach twisting with guilt even as the thought enters my mind.

It was just a slap, right?

Just one slap.

Not that big of a deal.

He was angry. Frustrated. Maybe he didn't mean it. Maybe he won't do it again.

I don't know.

And that uncertainty, that not knowing, is worse than anything else.

Because if I admit this is what it is . . . if I admit that Russell is the kind of man who hits the woman he claims to love . . . then what does that mean for my future?

For our daughter's future?

I close my eyes, willing the thoughts away, but they won't leave me alone. I don't know what else to do, so after lunch, I get Liv in the car and I drive without thinking.

And somehow, I end up here.

Truth Center Ministries.

The parking lot is mostly empty except for a black SUV parked near the entrance. For a second, I think maybe I should turn around, but before I can change my mind, I exit the car and get Liv out. The church door swings open, and Mrs. Charlene Tate, the pastor's wife, appears, holding the door ajar.

She waves, motioning for us to come inside.

Mrs. Charlene is a thin woman with short soft curls and affectionate eyes. Wrinkles line the corners of her eyes and forehead, with tiny freckles dancing across her cheeks.

A lump forms in my throat as I adjust the weight of the diaper bag over my shoulder and shift Liv on my hip.

I don't know why I came here. I just know that I don't want to be alone. I don't want to sit in that house and pretend everything is fine. I don't want to keep drowning in my thoughts, convincing myself this isn't what it is.

Maybe I just want someone to tell me what to do.

God, can't you just tell me what to do?

Mrs. Charlene greets me warmly, her smile kind, but as she takes a closer look at me, I wonder if she can see it. The faint redness on my cheek. The way my shoulders are hunched. The way I'm holding Liv just a little too tightly, like she's the only thing keeping me together.

"Hey," she says gently. "Can I help you?"

The kindness in her voice nearly undoes me. My chest tightens, my throat burns, and suddenly, my eyes water.

I try to swallow it down, try to keep it together, but she places a firm, reassuring hand on my back and guides me inside.

"Here, sweetheart. Have a seat."

I sink onto a pew, clutching Liv to me as I fight to catch my breath.

Footsteps echo behind me, and Pastor Quinton steps into the sanctuary. "Everything all right?" he asks, his eyes flicking between us.

His wife nods. "Yes."

"If you need me, I'll be in the study," he says before disappearing down the hall.

Mrs. Charlene chuckles. "Forgive him. These days we have to be extra careful."

I nod, understanding exactly what she means.

"I—I'm sorry," I manage to say. "I didn't know anyone was here. I just . . . I was hoping to pray. I didn't know where else to go."

"You don't have to apologize," she says. "That's what the church is for."

I sniffle, wiping my sleeve across my nose. She gets up and hands me a box of tissues. "If you need some time to talk to God alone, I'll leave you to it."

"No—" I blurt out, my voice raw, desperate. "Can you please sit with me?"

She nods, settling beside me. "Take your time," she says. "We can talk whenever you're ready."

We sit in silence for a while, and I don't know why, but her company makes it easier to breathe.

Liv drifts off in my arms. My tears slow. Finally, after what feels like forever, Mrs. Charlene shifts, facing me fully. She reaches out and gently squeezes my hand.

"I don't know where to start," I whisper.

"Baby girl, you don't have to say a word if you're not ready. But let me tell you something—sometimes, a woman's pain will speak for her."

Swallowing hard, I look down at Liv and stroke her soft curls. My hands tremble.

Mrs. Charlene studies my expression in a way that makes me feel seen, like she's gazing straight into my soul.

"Plenty of young women have come through those very doors," she continues. "Some of them came in with bright smiles but eyes full of sorrow. Some walked in just like you—carrying this weight too heavy for one person to bear. And you know what the saddest part is?" She pauses, waiting for me to look at her. "They always think they gotta carry it alone."

I press my lips together, holding onto her every word.

She sighs, shaking her head. "I'm not trying to be in your business. So, I hope you don't take what I'm about to say personal. But love is never supposed to make you afraid. Love is never supposed to make you question your worth. And love? *Real love?* It doesn't make you cry tears of pain."

My jaw clenches, my throat burning. *How does she know all of this?* There's so much I want to say, but it's as if Mrs. Charlene is inside my head, because she's saying everything I need to hear.

She adjusts in her seat. "Now, I ain't saying you gotta tell me what's going on. That's not my place to do so, but whatever answer you're searching for . . ." She tilts her head. "Maybe you already know what you need to do, but you don't wanna say it out loud yet."

Tears slip down my cheeks before I can stop them.

She sighs again, her voice softer this time. "The hardest thing a woman can do is admit when she's standing at a crossroads. Because once you see the problem, you can't unsee it. You either keep walking the same path, hoping the darkness doesn't pull you under . . . or you turn toward the unknown, praying there's light on the other side."

"How do I know . . . what to do?"

Mrs. Charlene leans forward, looking me right in the eyes. "You don't have to know yet. But when the time comes, you'll know what to do. When you're ready, you'll know." Mrs. Charlene offers to pray for me, and I let her.

I close my eyes, resting my chin on top of Liv's head, listening to Mrs. Charlene talk to God on my behalf.

***

RUSSELL COMES HOME RIGHT after work today, which I didn't expect. We haven't spoken a word to each other since he hit me and stormed out of the house.

Mrs. Charlene's words still tug at my heart from earlier. Each sentence repeats in my mind like a broken record. I had hoped that after speaking with her and praying, God would give me some clarity, but I'm still on edge—unsure of what to do, what to believe.

But despite the burn on my cheek and the suffocating weight of Russell's presence, I ground myself in Mrs. Charlene's words and the small comfort of knowing God is still here. Even if I can't quite feel Him, I have to hold on.

Sitting in Liv's room, I play with her on the floor. Her laughter soothes me, and right now, this room feels safer than anywhere else

162

in the house. I made sure to eat dinner early just to avoid Russell. The idea of sitting at the table together pretending to be this happy couple is exhausting. I pray Russell will eat the dinner I left on the table, shower, and either go to bed or stay downstairs long enough for me to crawl under the covers before he does. I don't want to face him. I don't want to see those dark eyes that seem so empty.

His heavy footsteps move around downstairs, pausing, then starting again. When they grow louder, climbing the stairs, my heart slams against my ribs. I pull Liv onto my lap, holding her close, forcing myself to focus on her smile, her joyful eyes. *Take a deep breath.*

I don't turn around, but I know he's there. The weight of his stare presses into the back of my head. Then Liv peeks over my shoulder, giggling.

"Dada."

My stomach contracts. I inhale a sharp breath before looking over my shoulder. "Hey, how was work?"

Russell leans against the doorframe, his gaze locked onto me. In his hand is a bouquet of fresh flowers—white, yellow, and pink petals. *Flowers again? Is this what I should expect after every argument and altercation?*

"Work was work," he says plainly. "I stopped and got you some fresh flowers on the way home."

"Thanks," I say, squeezing my lips together. "They're beautiful."

"I'll put them in a vase for you." He takes a step back, but his eyes never leave me. "You need anything?" His voice is casual, as if last night never happened. As if he didn't hit me.

I swallow hard, willing myself to stay calm, to fight the urge to cry. "No, thanks. I'm fine."

"All right. I'll put these in water."

The second he walks out, relief crashes over me. The tears I've been holding back spill, rolling down my cheeks. I stay in place, clutching Liv in my arms until she squirms free, distracted by something on the floor.

Even though my body feels weak, I force myself up. No matter what I'm feeling, no matter what I'm going through, I'm a mother first.

I've already fed Liv dinner, so after reading her a book, I bathe her and lay her down for bed. Standing over her crib, I stare at her, her tiny lashes resting against her cheeks. My voice is a soft whisper as I sing a lullaby, stroking her back until she falls asleep. I fight the urge to pick her back up and hold her against me. In just a few minutes quiet snores reach my ears.

Gently I close her door, leaving a small crack before slipping into my bedroom. The TV hums downstairs—Russell is still up.

I rush into the bathroom, shower quickly, then slip into a nightgown. Crawling under the covers, I pull the blanket up to my head, willing myself to fall asleep before Russell comes to bed.

But sleep doesn't find me.

I hear him moving around, the TV shutting off, and the sound of his footsteps coming up the stairs. Then the door opens.

His clothes hit the floor with a thud. I wince. He climbs into bed behind me, his body pressing against mine, his arm wrapping around my waist. His lips brush against my bare shoulder, then my neck.

"I love you," he murmurs against my skin. "You mean everything to me."

I stay still.

"I was thinking," he continues, pressing another kiss near my ear, "we never got to have our date. So, I want to make up for it tomorrow. Me and you. This time I won't cancel. I'll even get off early."

A response is stuck in the pit of my throat. I continue lying motionless like a statue, my breath shallow and controlled.

"We'll have a good time." His arm tightens around my waist. "It'll be the best date I've ever taken you on."

Chapter 17

I DON'T PUT AS much effort into my appearance like last time. It took me hours to get ready only for Russell to cancel at the last minute. Doubt creeps through my core, because I don't know if he'll actually keep his word, or maybe it's because the memory of his hand connecting with my cheek drained the excitement from me.

But this time, Russell surprises me.

He gets off work early as promised. He comes home, showers, and dresses in a black tux. I can't deny the fact that he looks handsome, well put together. I'd be proud to be out in public with him, arm looped through his, making a statement that this is my man . . . but things don't feel that way anymore.

When I glance down at myself, at the dull purple loose-fitting dress that's been hanging in my closet for longer than I can remember, something in me shifts. I shouldn't care. I don't want to care. After everything he's done, after the way he made me feel small and insignificant, why should it matter what I wear?

And yet, it does.

A deep part of me that still remembers the good in him, the part that still foolishly loves him despite everything, wants his approval. I want to see that flicker of admiration in his eyes.

Russell steps out of the bathroom, adjusting the cuff of his sleeve, and his stare lands on me. His expression is unreadable at first, his lips pressed into a neutral line, but then I see it—the slight crease of his brows, the way his eyes scan over me like he's looking through a microscope. It's subtle, but I recognize it.

He's disappointed and unsatisfied with my choice of fashion for our *big date*. For the date that's supposed to be the best one yet.

It's not in the way I would notice if it were someone else, but I know Russell. His approval and disapproval aren't always spoken outright. Sometimes they come in uncomfortable glances that linger just long enough to be felt.

I force myself to look away, pretending I didn't see it, pretending it doesn't sting.

But it does. And that makes me angry.

But before I can force myself to care less about his opinions, I mumble something about changing and slip into the closet.

I sift through my clothes, pulling out a dress I'd been saving for a special occasion. It's formfitting, elegant and long. As I slip it over my body, a lump rises in my throat. *Why am I doing this? Why do I care if he thinks I look good?*

I tell myself it's just for the sake of the evening. That it's easier this way, easier to avoid whatever tension might come if I stay in the old dress. The one that makes him grimace.

When I step back out, Russell looks up from his phone, and this time, his gaze lingers longer. His lips curl into a smirk, and his eyes look hungry.

"That's better. You look beautiful, baby."

No words come out. Instead, I offer him a grin, grab my purse, and call Ms. Mildred so I can check on Liv one last time.

The drive is quiet. The city lights blur past the window as we head downtown, the weight in my chest growing heavier with every mile. My hand rests on my stomach. I inhale the air coming in from the cracked window to ease the queasiness.

When we pull up to Ironwood Grill, my eyes widen.

I've always wanted to come here. It's expensive, one of those places any woman would dream of being proposed to. On several occasions, I remember asking Russell if we could go, and he'd say the place wasn't worth the hype.

Russell parks and turns to me with a knowing look. "I figured you'd like it," he says.

He did?

And for a second, my chest warms with stupid, dangerous hope that maybe, just maybe, this is his way of making up for everything.

But my mind remembers.

I remember how he shoved me and smacked me. And I try to remind myself, despite the fluttering feeling in my chest, that fancy dinners don't erase the past even if I want them to.

The large brick building towers over us, its modern exterior relaxed by the warmth of golden outdoor lights casting a soft glow onto the street below. As we step through the heavy iron doors, the rich scent of sizzling steaks and smoky wood fills my nostrils.

Inside, the restaurant is a perfect blend of rustic elegance and modern culture. Deep oak wood accents the interior with steel beams crisscrossing the high ceilings. Expensive leather chairs invite guests to sink into their embrace. The rooftop dining area—intimate and radiant under dim candlelight—feels like something out of a dream. The air is damp with a chilly breeze, but the signature outdoor heaters keep the space comfortably warm.

I've passed this place so many times, longing to step inside, to taste the food people rave about. But because of current circumstances, I can't enjoy it the way I want to. My stomach is in knots, my hands cold despite the heat. This isn't just about a nice dinner. This isn't just a date for me. Tonight, I want to talk to Russell—to try to fix what has shattered between us. To figure out how I can make this better. Because I can't keep doing this.

Russell was quiet on the drive here, but now, across from me, his lips curve into a flirtatious smile as he chews on his lower lip, his eyes never leaving mine. "You look amazing," he murmurs, and I wonder if he really means it.

After everything, after all the times his love felt more like a chokehold than an embrace, why do I still yearn for his approval? "Thanks," I whisper.

The server arrives, breaking the moment, and I barely register the menu in front of me. Russell, however, scans the options, his eyes moving over the high-priced meals. I wonder if he's worried about the bill. He makes decent money, but this place isn't exactly in our tax bracket.

"I'll have a glass of red wine," he says smoothly.

My hands tremble at the thought of him drinking tonight, of possibly getting drunk. A sober Russell is better than a drunk one. He's kept his promise of finally taking me out, and maybe soon he'll keep his promise of cutting back on drinking.

Clearing my throat, I scratch behind my ear. His gaze flicks to me, and for a moment, irritation flashes in his eyes before he masks it. I'm hoping he'll change his mind, but he doesn't.

The waiter turns to me. "And for you, ma'am?"

"Water with lemon, please."

As the server walks away, I force a breath into my lungs.

"How are you feeling?" he asks, his voice soft.

"Fine." The lie slips out easily. Or maybe it's not a lie at all. Maybe I'm fine and not fine at the same time. I want to be honest tonight, but there's always that fear. *If I say the wrong thing, will he get angry? Will he shut down? Will the kindness stop and be replaced with his cold, suffocating silence?*

The waiter returns, and I realize I still don't know what I want to eat. Russell orders, and before I can speak, he takes the liberty of ordering for me. "She'll take the rib eye with a Caesar salad and a loaded baked potato."

I bite the inside of my cheek, tasting metal. "I could have ordered for myself."

"I know, but you were taking too long." His response is casual, dismissive, as he sips his wine.

Why would he think that is okay? Does it not register in his mind that I'm my own person that can do things for myself?

The tension between us thickens, but then he smiles. "Do you remember our three-month anniversary date?"

I nod, the memory surfacing. "I remember."

His grin widens. "That burger joint on North Pine Street. We both got food poisoning."

I let out a laugh, covering my mouth. That night was a disaster filled with vomiting and fevers. Although we were miserable, we spent those awful three days together, curled up, laughing through the nausea. For a moment, it feels good to remember something that isn't tainted by pain.

"Those were good times," he says, his expression turning nostalgic. "I want more of that. I want us back."

"I want that too." And I mean it. But wanting something and believing it's possible are two different things.

"I'll do anything to make it happen." His eyes are slightly glossy, and I want to believe he's sorry, that his words hold truth, but how can I when he hasn't even apologized?

Now is the perfect time to bring the hard conversation up, but I don't. His expression is remorseful, like he's hurt by his own actions or the way things have been between us. I don't want to ruin the night and instead decide to bring up the conversation later. Possibly when we get home.

Dinner passes in a blur, and when the check comes, Russell barely flinches, slipping his black card into the folder.

"Let's dance," he says, standing and holding out his hand.

I hesitate before sliding mine into his, letting him lead me to an open space near the edge of the rooftop. As we sway to the soft jazz playing in the background, I rest my head against his chest, listening to the steady beat of his heart. His heartbeat sounds foreign, even though I've lain on his chest countless times. It used to soothe me, especially on nights when I cried myself to sleep thinking about my mom.

For a moment, I let myself believe in this version of him—the one who holds me gently, who whispers against my hair, who wants to fix things.

Then he stops moving, stepping back just enough to reach into his pocket. My breath hitches. When his knee hits the ground, the world tilts. I'm going to pass out.

The small navy-blue box in his hand sends ice through my veins.

He opens it. A ring. A 4-carat diamond, glistening under the soft glow of the restaurant lights.

A hush falls over the rooftop.

"Will you marry me?"

I can't breathe. My hands tremble, my mind races. The world around me blurs. *What's wrong with me?* I've wanted this . . . prayed for this. *Is this God's answer?* I should be happy.

But instead, I'm suffocating.

God, help me. What should I say? I search for an answer, for a sign, for anything—but there's only silence.

Russell's gaze locks onto mine. He looks like he loves me. But hasn't he looked at me with the same tenderness before shoving me against the wall? Hasn't he whispered "I love you" before making me feel like I was nothing?

The past and present blur together, and I should say no.

With a shaky breath, I whisper, "Yes."

Chapter 18

THE RING ON MY finger catches the light, sparkling like something out of a dream. I want to feel elated, but the reality won't settle the way I need it to. I try to convince myself that this is what I've always wanted. That this is what I've been waiting for. And yet, the more I stare at it, the heavier it feels.

I'm engaged. It feels surreal, as if I'm living someone else's reality.

Zara should be here celebrating with me, gushing over every detail of the proposal, but I haven't told her. I should be posting pictures, letting everyone see how Russell finally *chose* me. But I haven't told anyone. Not Zara. Not Malachi. Not Akin. Not even Irene, who I know would have a hundred things to say, whether I wanted to hear them or not.

After Mom passed, I'd promised at her funeral that when the day came, I'd visit her and tell her all about it, but it feels wrong. All of it.

A part of me whispers that I should be grateful. Russell has been sweet lately, attentive in a way he hasn't been in a while. He tells me he loves me, touches me more, buys me things just because. *And isn't that what I want? A family, stability, and love?*

But I also want honesty. I want trust. I want to know for certain that it won't happen again, that the drinking won't spiral, that his anger won't turn on me when things don't go his way. If I'm going to marry him, I need things to change. But how do I even begin to tell him that?

I press my fingers to my temples, squeezing my eyes shut. Maybe I'm overthinking it. Maybe this is just nerves, the way every bride-to-be feels at the beginning. Maybe if I just hold on, things really will get better.

Or maybe, deep down, I already know the truth and I'm just too scared to say it out loud.

For a brief moment, I wish I could stay home, just avoid the whole day. But I can't. Every year Zara and I go Christmas shopping together. Plus, I need this time away from everything to keep my mind from spiraling.

"I'll be back in about an hour," I say, adjusting my coat.

Russell sits at the kitchen table, typing away on his phone. "Where are you going again?"

"Christmas shopping with Zara."

He looks up at me, eyes studying my entire body. I know he's observing my outfit, making sure I'm not showing too much skin or that my clothes aren't too tight. "Don't be out too long."

"I won't."

As I button up my coat, his chair scrapes against the floor. "Did you tell Zara yet?"

I freeze for half a second, my fingers fumbling with the button. "Tell her what?"

Russell crosses his arms, leaning against the counter. "About the engagement."

My shoulder tenses as I reach for my purse. "Not yet."

"When are you going to?"

"I will," I assure him, finally looking at him. "Soon."

Russell watches me for a moment before he nods. "All right. Do you have a date?"

"A date?" I blink.

"For the wedding."

I blink again, the weight of the question pressing against me. "I . . . I haven't thought about it yet."

"Well, I have," he says, stepping toward me. "I want to do it as soon as possible."

His certainty unsettles me. *What's the rush?* We just got engaged, and I haven't had time to process it yet.

I open my mouth, but before I can respond, he kisses my forehead. "We'll talk about it when you get back."

I nod quickly, mutter a goodbye, and leave before he can say anything else.

***

THE STORE IS PACKED, Christmas music playing overhead as Zara and I weave through aisles, searching for gifts. I've kept my left hand shoved into my pocket as much as I can, because I don't know how to tell her.

Hey girl, did I mention the shocking news? I'm engaged!

Do I just hold out the ring for her to see? Ugh, it's so frustrating.

I spot a row of pink baby clothes, tiny sweaters and dresses, and immediately think of Olivia. A little farther down, I find some toys I know she'd love.

Zara holds up a sleek leather wallet. "This would be perfect for Akin. For some reason all his wallets keep getting holes in them." She shakes her head in amusement.

I smile, glad at how easily she picks out gifts for her husband. Meanwhile, I hesitate, unsure what to get for Russell. Nothing feels right—I don't know what he'd like or want.

"How are things with Malachi and Phoebe?" I ask casually.

Zara smirks, her eyes darting my way. "Things might be getting pretty serious between them."

I raise an eyebrow and gulp. "Serious as in . . . engagement?"

She laughs. "I'm not sure about all that, but they seem happy. It's just Mal. He's never dated anyone this long. I'm shocked."

I inhale, then nod, picking up a hat that Russell may like, even though I'm not sure I've ever seen him wear a hat. "That's good."

She glances at me. "And things with you and Russell?"

The smile I'm forcing hurts my cheeks. "Things are good." My voice cracks. Zara stops, her head tilts, and eyes narrow. She doesn't speak, but it feels like she's reading my mind.

Now is the perfect opportunity to tell my best friend about the ring I'm hiding in my pocket, yet I find myself hesitating.

I take a deep breath and finally say, "He took me out on a date and . . . he proposed."

Zara's eyes grow so wide I fear they'll pop out of their sockets. "Shut up!" Zara squeals, reaching for my hand. "Oh my gosh, let me see!"

I reluctantly pull my hand from my pocket and show her the ring, and she gasps. I can't tell if she's excited for me or worried. "Asha! How come you didn't tell me?"

Her tearful eyes gaze up at me. *I'm the worst friend ever.* Shrugging, I manage to say, "It's complicated. I wanted to, but it took me a while to process it."

"Well, it's beautiful." She holds it closer, admiring it.

Her smile falters as she studies my face. "You don't look happy. Are you?"

My face freezes, and I don't know what to say. *How do I explain the confusion inside me? How do I tell her that, yes, I'm happy, but . . . not fully? Not yet? Not until I'm sure about everything.*

"I . . . I don't know," I say finally. "It's just . . . complicated." I realize I said that already, but it's the only word that makes sense right now.

Zara's face softens, and she places a hand on my shoulder. "Asha, I just want you to be happy. Whatever that looks like."

I bite my lip, trying to hold back the flood of emotions. With the large crowd of people racing past us to grab items off the shelf, I withhold the contents of my heart. I can't tell her here.

Desperation claws at my insides, but I can't formulate words to express what's inside.

"I don't know if I'm ready for this. For the wedding . . . for any of it," I confess, my voice breaking.

"Haven't you been waiting for this since we were little girls?"

I know I have—in middle school, we dreamed about our weddings and promised to always be there for each other. But now, as I think about that future, I'm not so sure Russell is the man I imagined being with. Everything feels so complicated. The love I once believed in is now shadowed by fear and pain. I wanted this badly, yet now it's like an impossible decision. And I've already given him my answer. "Yes . . ." I whisper, trailing off.

Zara's eyes meet mine, and in unison with my unspoken thoughts, she adds, "But it's complicated. Things have always been complicated with him." Tears build in the corners of my eyes, threatening to spill. "If you don't want this—if you're not happy—then you should say something."

I laugh nervously and wave my hands dismissively. "Zara . . . it isn't that easy," I continue, my voice shaking as I search through the chaos in my head. "I love him, but sometimes . . . I'm not sure what

I feel. Aren't I supposed to feel this . . . unimaginable joy? I mean, shouldn't I feel like a princess in a fairy tale?"

"It feels different for everyone, Asha. When Akin proposed, I was ecstatic—he's the one person I want to spend the rest of my life with. But if you feel even a sliver of doubt, maybe you should rethink it."

I know she's right, but I've already accepted the ring. Part of me clings to the memory of the good times, the compliments he used to give me. I want to explain that if things were different, I'd be excited—happy, even. But with Russell hurting me, I can't fully embrace that happiness.

"If you're happy, then I'm elated," Zara says, her smile softening and then melting into a frown as she studies my face. "But if you're not . . . then neither am I. Whatever you decide, I've got your back, sis."

"Thank you," I croak, my voice barely audible.

Then, in a moment of trembling hesitation, I add, "Please, Zara, don't tell Malachi." The thought surprises me; I'm not even sure why I worry about him knowing. But the fear of judgment, of being exposed, is too strong. I'm worried about what he'll think or say, I guess.

Zara nods, her eyes darkening with concern. "I promise, Asha. I won't say a word. But the person you need to be worried about finding out is Mama."

She's right. I know Irene will give me an earful, and I don't know if I can handle that right now.

When I get back home, Russell is waiting for me. The second I step inside, I see him glance at his watch, his expression neutral as he notes the time. My stomach knots. He knows exactly how long I've been gone.

"Where are the things?" he asks, his tone casual but laced with suspicion.

I shift my purse higher on my shoulder. "In the trunk," I say. "I'll get them later."

Russell nods slowly, then leans against the table, watching me. I take a breath, preparing myself. "Can we talk for a minute?"

His brow lifts slightly. "Sure," he says, stepping away from the table. "Liv's upstairs. She's down for a nap."

I pause. I don't want to argue. I don't want this to turn ugly. But I need to say this. I need him to hear me. To understand.

Moving to sit across from him, I reach out to take his hands. He lets me, his palms warm against mine. I squeeze lightly, more to brace myself than anything else.

"I want this," I begin, my voice softer than I intend. "I want us to work. I want the marriage, I do, but—"

His eyes narrow. "But what?"

I swallow hard. "If we're going to do this . . . I need you to promise me something."

He doesn't blink. "Okay."

"You can never hit me again, Russell." And as I speak, it registers deeper, like a truth I've tried to ignore.

Something flickers in his expression—dark and quick—but then it's gone, replaced by that gleaming, charming smile.

"Baby." He leans forward. "You know I never want to hurt you. It was an accident."

I'm not convinced it was, I think to myself.

I press on before I lose my nerve. "And I think you should do counseling."

His smile doesn't falter, but the air changes.

"For what?"

"Your job is stressful," I say carefully. "And I think it could help with . . . the drinking too."

There it is. The flare of anger. His jaw clenches for a fraction of a second, his fingers twitching against mine. Then, just as quickly, he smooths it over.

Russell exhales, shaking his head with a small chuckle, like I said something ridiculous. Then he lifts my hands, kissing my knuckles.

"I'll do anything for you," he says, his voice warm, sincere. "If that's what it takes to make you mine."

What does he mean by 'mine'? Like I'm something he could own?

Relief rushes through me, but it doesn't settle the war inside. Russell pulls me toward him, wrapping his arms around my waist, his lips brushing against my ear.

"Now that we've got that out of the way," he murmurs, "I want to pick a date."

I tense slightly, still processing everything. "A date?"

"For the wedding."

I pull back just enough to look at him. "Already?"

He grins. "I was thinking about Valentine's Day."

My stomach drops. "That's in two months."

"Exactly," he says. "Not too far away."

"That's not enough time to plan." My voice sounds thin, stretched between panic and uncertainty.

Russell shrugs. "I'll take care of everything. We'll do something small, just us and Liv."

That familiar sensation of being backed into a corner overwhelms me. The pressure tightens around me, squeezing until there's no space left to breathe.

Russell watches me, waiting for me to decide.

And I realize, with a sinking certainty, despite his promise to do what I've asked, I don't know if I can agree. Not yet.

Chapter 19

THE GOOD BREW IS packed this morning, transformed by a festive Christmas vibe. Twinkling lights and garlands drape over the windows and counters, while cheerful ornaments and holiday wreaths lend the space an inviting glow.

The rich aroma of freshly brewed coffee, cinnamon rolls, and buttery pastries engulfs me as I step inside. The place is decorated with chiseled wooden tables and walls adorned with local artwork. The paintings, photographs, and hand-written scriptures are framed on the wall. Every detail, from the warm tones to the subtle jazz Christmas tunes, summonses me to slow down and savor the moment.

A swell of pride fills me as I take it all in. It's clear Malachi has poured his heart into this place. What once was a modest coffee shop has transformed into a community hub.

Malachi is behind the counter greeting regulars and directing his staff with professional ease. Observing him in charge and being friendly makes me realize just how good of a person he is.

I wrap my brown furry coat tighter around me and head to the counter, my engagement ring loose in my pocket. I wonder what he'd think if he knew I was getting married soon. His eyes glimmer as he hands a coffee to a customer, then he strides toward me.

"Hey, Asha. I'm shocked to see you here."

"Yeah, it's been a while. The place looks amazing," I reply.

I haven't been here much lately. Since I don't have a job, Russell's money dictates our outings.

"Thank you. You know, Zara put her little spin on everything in here," he adds, his gaze drifting around the shop in admiration. "So, can I get you something? We have some winter special drinks, sandwiches, and fresh cookies."

I bite my lower lip. "I'm actually here to get something for Zara. She's busy at the gallery and asked if I could come by and pick it up."

He nods, crossing his arms. "Ah, yes—it's in my office. You can follow me. Be careful—the floors can be a little slippery."

He leads me behind the counter as I carefully dodge baristas as they pull espresso shots and load the baking racks with fresh pastries. The vibrant energy here is infectious. I know it has everything to do with the atmosphere Malachi created for this place . . . it's admirable.

When we enter his office, I pause to take in the space. The room is neat, with walls painted a sleek black. A swivel chair and a tidy desk scattered with a few papers and a computer sit in one corner. Pictures hang on the wall: snapshots of Malachi with his parents; a photo of Zara and Akin. Then, unexpectedly, I spot a picture that takes my breath away—it's of me, Malachi, and Liv. It was taken the day after I gave birth, and I had almost forgotten that Malachi was there.

Russell left early that day. He went home to shower, grab something to eat, and get some rest before heading back to the hospital. I remember Malachi coming with Zara and Akin—how he immediately washed his hands, his eyes glistening with a quiet, almost terrifying awe as he took a seat next to me. He hesitated before reaching for Liv. It was obvious he was nervous. But he was careful, supporting her tiny head, and I guess Zara had snapped a picture.

My curls were in disarray, dark circles under my eyes from exhaustion, and Liv, the most beautiful and precious baby in the world. And Malachi—that man never changes.

Malachi clears his throat. "It's one of my favorite pictures of us. I hope you don't mind."

A thought tugs at me—Phoebe is not on the wall—but I keep it to myself. I know Phoebe and Malachi are still newly dating. Besides, it's none of my business.

"I love this picture. It's beautiful," I whisper as I trace the frame with my fingertips, careful not to disturb it.

After a moment, Malachi digs through his desk and finally hands me an envelope.

"So, what's in here?"

He grins. "Two tickets for Akin and Zara to attend an art show in three weeks."

I blink, surprised. "I didn't know about that."

His tone is light, edged with excitement as he explains. "I gifted them the tickets as an early Christmas present. They're going to see one of her favorite artists do a live painting event the day after Christmas."

"That's sweet of you, Mal," I say softly.

He adds, "Yeah, because I'm the best big brother ever."

A giggle escapes me before I can suppress it.

"Are you still planning on coming over to Zara's on Christmas Eve?" he asks.

"Of course. If I don't, Zara's going to kill me."

"Just a heads-up: they bought Liv so much stuff." He shakes his head slightly.

"I know. They keep spoiling her, but I'm not going to complain." I shift my feet, standing a little closer to him. "Will you be there too, or do you have other plans?"

"I'll be there," he says. I smile faintly and nod. Before I leave his office, Malachi offers, "You haven't been here in months. The least you could do is let me make you one of my best-selling coffees."

I pause, then agree. "Fine, as long as you promise not to spill it on me," I tease.

"That only happened once," he reminds me.

Before Malachi closes the door behind us, I glance at the photo on the wall again. Malachi's eyes in the picture are soft and caring as he holds Liv—looking at me. My heart flutters, and I gulp.

I wait behind the counter as Malachi effortlessly mixes espresso shots, blending white chocolate and java chips into a cup. He squirts something into the coffee, then hands it to me with a smile. I hold it to my lips. The coffee is smooth and velvety, like Christmas in a cup.

"Mal, this tastes amazing," I say, taking another sip. Its warmth spreads through me.

"I'm glad you like it. Here," he says, reaching for a freshly baked cookie and placing it in a brown paper bag, then hands it to me.

"Cookies are my weakness," I say, taking a quick sniff of the ooey-gooey chocolate goodness.

"I know. I remember when your mom would make them, you'd eat half the batch."

I playfully roll my eyes.

"Then you'd lie and say I ate them all."

"I did not!" I squeal.

"No, I'm pretty sure you did. I actually remember you doing that on multiple occasions."

He probably was telling the truth just a little bit.

"Mom did make the best cookies," I say, staring at the brown bag in my hand. I miss my mom's baking. I'd do anything to bring her back, to have her for just one more day.

Malachi's eyes scan over me briefly before he clears his throat. "Anytime you want a cookie or coffee, just stop by. It's on me," he offers.

I nod, my eyes failing to meet his gaze. "Thanks."

After leaving the Good Brew, I head to the gallery to drop off the tickets for Zara. The gallery is alive with color and movement. Zara is busy hanging new pieces, while her mom, Irene, lends a steady hand. I offer a few suggestions about moving one of the paintings, a piece that should be positioned a little higher and slightly to the right for better balance.

"Thanks, Ash," Zara says, accepting the envelope.

"No problem."

"I would've gotten it myself, but as you see I've been super busy." Zara's assistant approaches, handing her a clipboard and papers to review and sign. She scans them quickly, then scribbles her signature.

Just then, Irene steps forward and pulls me into a quick hug. "How are you and Liv doing, Asha?"

"We're good," I reply, managing a small smile. Irene's kindness reminds me of my mom, comforting and nostalgic.

As Irene steps back, her hand finds mine. Her finger brushes against the ring on my left hand, and my heart skips a beat. I'd put it back on once I got in the car, afraid I'd forget before heading home. I follow her gaze to my hand, and for a moment, I'm exposed. Zara shoots me a quick, knowing look before she rushes down the hall.

"Zara!" I call after her, but she only shakes a finger in the air and hurries off.

"Good luck!" she yells back over her shoulder.

I knew Irene would eventually learn the truth about my engagement, but I'm not ready for that conversation today.

After a pause, she speaks softly but firmly. "I'm trying to figure out when this happened?"

I take a deep breath, the memory of that rooftop proposal flashing uncomfortably in my mind. "I was going to tell you, I swear. I just . . . was waiting for the right moment," I murmur, dipping my head down.

"Girl, I know this man didn't propose and you didn't tell me."

My eyes glisten with confusion and fear, and I'm on the verge of crying. "I'm sorry."

Without a word, Irene pulls me into a warm, steady embrace and plants a soft kiss on my forehead. "Asha," she whispers, "what are you saying sorry for? I'm just teasing. But I hope you know you can tell me anything."

I choke on the words before they can form. "I know, but I . . . I know you don't really like him." My voice is barely audible, loaded with uncertainty.

Irene chuckles, though her tone quickly shifts to tough love as she places her hands firmly on my shoulders. "It's not about whether I like him, even though you're right. I don't, but that's beside the point. It's about you making the right choice for you and Liv. Only you know what that choice is. I wouldn't be who I am if I didn't tell you this: you need to really, truly pray about it before you do anything impulsively."

I want to tell her about everything—the nights I've been scared, how Russell's anger has left marks that I try to hide, the way I'm constantly wondering if I'm enough. But I hold back. *Again.*

Irene is the closest thing I have to a mother figure, and I long to share every painful detail with her. I wonder if she'd give me the same advice my mom once would have. But for now, all I can do is nod silently, letting her words sink in, even as I struggle with the conflict inside me.

Irene's gentle eyes meet mine, and although she doesn't know all the details, I can tell she senses that something isn't right.

"How are you really doing, Asha?" she asks softly, her tone caring yet cautious.

I bite my lip, fidgeting with my sleeve. "I'm . . . okay," I say, though the word feels hollow.

Irene sighs. "Well, your heart is telling me something different. It's okay to not be okay."

Her words send a shiver down my spine, like we are the only two people here. I glance away, unwilling to admit how conflicted I truly am. "I—I just don't know what the future holds," I whisper. "I love him. I always wanted this . . . but sometimes I wonder if I'm just trying to hold on to something that isn't really working." Something breaks inside me as I speak—the weight of every promise, every tender moment, mixed with memories of pain.

Her gaze softens further, and she pulls me into another hug. "Sweetheart, you deserve to be safe and happy. Trust your instincts. Sometimes, if you have even a little bit of uncertainty, it might be a sign to slow down and really think about what you need. It's not about making a rash decision but about making sure you're not ignoring those small warnings."

Her words echo in my mind. *Have I been ignoring the small signs all along? What about the times when he's kind? What do I do with those lingering moments of tenderness, when they seem to make me forget about all the times he's hurt me?* My heart is like a seesaw, tipping back and forth between hope and despair. Every day it's as if I'm leaning more toward despair.

"I told Zara and Malachi, don't ever marry someone unless you feel complete peace about it, unless you've talked to God about it. It's easy to say 'I do,' but so hard to get out of it when things go wrong."

Her words, firm yet gentle, offer me both comfort and a painful reminder of the choices ahead. I know deep down that I must choose what's best for me and for Liv, even if that means facing the truth I've been too afraid to admit.

"Baby, is this what you really want?" She leans in, her eyes glossy.

"I don't know," I finally say.

Chapter 20

CHRISTMAS HAS ALWAYS BEEN my favorite time of year. "Silent Night" and "Let It Snow" by The Temptations have been on repeat for days. Between the twinkling lights, the scent of cinnamon candles, and mugs of hot chocolate warming our hands, everything feels magical.

Outside, soft flurries of snow drift lazily from the sky. After two years of casual Decembers, we're finally getting the wintery Christmas I've been wishing for. I hope the snow sticks. I can already picture Liv bundled in layers, her tiny hat slipping over her eyes as she runs through the snow, squealing with laughter. She'll play until her cheeks are pink and her gloves are damp.

Between the gifts from us and her godparents, Liv is going to have more toys than she knows what to do with. I'll probably need to start boxing up her old ones for donation. It's a good problem to have, I guess.

Still, this Christmas feels . . . different.

I'd planned for us to spend this morning as a family, Russell and me curled up on the couch, Liv crawling between us, Christmas movies playing in the background while she opens one of her gifts.

Instead, it's just Liv and me, on our way to church to meet Akin, Zara, Malachi, and their parents. Phoebe, finally getting a day off, meets us outside with her usual burst of energy.

"Merry Christmas Eve!" she squeals, pulling me into a hug and then leaning in to gently squeeze Liv's cheeks. "Hey there, little Livvy."

Liv giggles, filling the air with her joy.

"Merry Christmas Eve," I reply. Right before getting out of the car, I slipped the engagement ring into my dress pocket. It felt too heavy this morning, a secret I couldn't carry in front of everyone. "Where's Russell?" Phoebe asks, glancing behind me.

Hesitating, I bite the inside of my cheek. "He got called into work."

Russell's been distant again. Working late, barely speaking, and highly tense. He's cold. Detached. Like some version of Scrooge that only I can see. I keep wondering when he'll soften again, when the man who used to bring me flowers and talk about wedding plans will come back. Even though I'm still unsure about our future.

"I love your dress," Phoebe says, snapping me out of my thoughts.

I glance down. It's a simple white sweater dress, loose enough to be comfortable but cinched at the waist with a brown belt. My boots match, and I've added a few gold pieces to pull it together. My curls are soft and defined, falling just to my shoulders.

"You look cute too," I reply, taking in her bright green dress with glitter at the hem and her bold red heels. It's festive, like her, and very Phoebe—impossible to ignore.

I shake off the thoughts tugging at me. Today is about more than what's missing. It's about being surrounded by people who love me, who love Liv. My second family. And being in the place where I feel most comfortable.

"Let's get inside. It's chilly," Irene says, reaching for Liv and cradling her close.

Inside, the church offers a warm and inviting space. The Christmas Eve sermon is centered on the birth of Jesus. Pastor

Quinton speaks of the prophecies that led up to that holy night, how God orchestrated every moment with purpose—even the painful ones. Despite Herod's attempt to kill Him, despite the whispers about Mary and Joseph, despite the uncertainty surrounding His arrival . . . everything unfolded just as it was meant to.

His message is simple, but it settles deep in my soul: God has a plan—even in the chaos.

And I wonder, sitting in that pew with Liv curled beside me, what that plan is for me. For Russell. For our daughter. *How do all the broken pieces—my doubts, my fears, the heaviness I carry—fit into something greater?*

I don't have the answers. Maybe I won't for a long time. But Pastor Quinton's words stay with me. A quiet reminder that even in this challenging time, this aching season . . . there is still hope.

After the service, people trickle out toward their cars, chatting and laughing as they go. Pastor Quinton and his wife, Mrs. Charlene, stand by the double doors, offering warm hugs and holiday blessings to each member of the congregation.

"Asha!" Mrs. Charlene's warm smile greets me. "Sweetheart, how are you?"

Manuel has Liv in his arms. "I'll catch up with you all," I say as they give me a brief moment alone with her. "I'm doing well. How about you?"

"Oh, never better. It's such a beautiful time of year," she replies. "I pray all is well with you."

I hesitate for a second, then decide to be honest. "I'm still trying to figure things out . . . from our last conversation."

She squeezes my hand. "Remember what Pastor preached this morning—God has a plan. Even when we can't see it, He's always working. I'm praying for you, sweetheart. Stop by anytime."

Her kindness soothes something in me. "Thank you, Mrs. Charlene. Merry Christmas Eve."

"Merry Christmas Eve."

When we get to Zara and Akin's apartment, the smell of roasted turkey, savory spices, and something sweet fills the air. Everything is either in the oven or simmering in slow cookers, and the house already feels full of life and laughter.

After a long church service and a few snacks from Irene's purse, Liv finally crashes for a nap.

Phoebe and I settle at the kitchen table while Irene and Zara move seamlessly around the kitchen in sync. The guys are tucked away in Akin's man cave, no doubt watching football or talking smack over a pool game.

"So, how's work at the hospital?" I ask Phoebe just to make small talk.

Her nails—painted in alternating red and green—tap against her glass as she beams. "It's hectic but amazing! I mean, it's exhausting most days, but I feel like I'm actually doing something that matters, ya know?" She takes a sip of her drink. "How are things—" She hesitates as if she was going to ask me a similar question but realized I don't work. "How are you doing?"

"I'm good," I say.

"So, Malachi tells me that you used to want to be a teacher after college?"

"Yeah . . . I did."

"What changed? Or do you just prefer being home with Liv?"

My eyes drop to my hands in my lap. "It's complicated. I got pregnant, and everything sort of shifted. At first, I wanted to stay home for her first year, then get back into work. But Russell pushed for me to stay home longer." I pause. "He was pretty adamant about it."

She studies me for a second. "Malachi said you were always one of the smartest in class. That you helped him study sometimes."

I smile faintly. "That was a long time ago."

"He talks about you a lot," she adds casually, but her eyes search mine.

"Oh?" I keep my voice light.

She nods, but her lips twitch slightly. "He's so sweet. I really hope things work out with us. My last relationship . . . wasn't easy."

My curiosity perks up. I don't know much about her past. "What happened?"

She sighs, her finger tracing the rim of her glass. "I was engaged once. We were together for two years, then—just two months before the wedding—he ended it. No warning. No explanation. Just . . . gone."

My heart aches for her. "Phoebe . . . I'm so sorry."

She shakes her head with a strained smile. "It was the worst heartbreak I've ever felt. I didn't leave my bed for days. I kept wondering what I did wrong, replaying everything." She looks up, her eyes softer now. "And then I met Malachi. He's been so kind."

"Malachi's not that kind of guy," I tell her without hesitation. Because I know him. Deep down, I always have. "He wouldn't do that to you."

She tries to smile again, but her eyes flicker. "I want to believe that. But . . . sometimes it feels like he's not all the way in."

My chest tightens. "What do you mean?"

She hesitates, blinking fast like she's holding back tears. "It's just . . . the way he is around you and the others—it's different. When we're alone, I don't know. Sometimes I feel like he's keeping part of himself hidden."

A strange heaviness settles in the room.

I place a gentle hand on her shoulder. "I'm sure he's just trying to figure things out too. He's been through a lot."

She nods, brushing under her eyes with a napkin. "Yeah. You're probably right. I just . . . I really don't want to lose him."

Before I can say anything else, the guys walk into the kitchen—Malachi among them. Zara and Irene follow behind, balancing trays and dishes.

The moment Phoebe sees Malachi, she straightens, pasting a bright, effortless smile across her face. It's almost convincing—*almost*.

But I recognize that kind of mask. The one that says *I'm fine*, when inside you're anything but. It's the same mask I've worn too many times before. And she's good at it. Better than me actually.

Malachi leans in and plants a kiss on her cheek, and for a brief second, I want to believe that it's enough to reassure her. That she's worrying for nothing.

But then his eyes flicker to mine. And my stomach stutters—but I don't know why. I quickly drop my gaze, focusing on the porcelain plate in front of me.

The conversation shifts, the warmth of food and laughter filling the room. After Zara says a quick prayer, Malachi takes a bite, then glances at me. *You okay?* he mouths.

I force a smile, nodding as if to say *I'm good*.

But from the corner of my eye, I notice Phoebe watching. Her bright eyes dart between us, and I turn away before Malachi can mouth anything else, shifting my attention to Zara and Akin.

"So," I say, lightness to my voice, "are you two ready for your trip tomorrow?"

Zara perks up instantly, her eyes shining with excitement. "Girl, I'm so excited! Ever since Mal told me he bought us tickets, I've been counting down the days. I can't wait!"

"It'll be nice to get away for a few days," Akin adds.

"Well, my gift better be just as good," Malachi jokes. Zara rolls her eyes at him before taking a bite of her turkey. "It better be just as expensive too."

"I got your gift from the dollar store," she fires back, and the room bursts into laughter.

After dinner, I slip onto the balcony, taking a deep breath of the crisp night air. The city lights twinkle in the distance. I close my eyes, letting the cold air clear my thoughts.

From my pocket, I pull out the ring and stare at it. By now, I thought I'd feel more at ease—hopeful, maybe. But I'm still just . . . confused. I slide the ring onto my finger, holding my hand out. This is what I've always wanted. Russell is the man I imagined building a life with. But now?

Now, I'm not sure. I don't think I can live like this forever—always fearful, always anxious, always tired.

Before I can slip the ring back off, the door creaks open behind me and Malachi steps out. I cover the ring with my right hand.

Malachi doesn't say anything, just leans against the railing beside me. Filling the silence I say, "Zara mentioned you and Phoebe might be getting pretty serious."

Malachi sucks in a breath, folding his fingers together. "I'm not sure yet."

"Well, you two make a beautiful couple," I say, even though something tugs at my chest. I don't think it's jealousy—but it stings in a way I can't explain.

Malachi glances at me. "Thanks."

I shift, wrapping my arms around myself. "Phoebe told me about her ex-fiancé." I hesitate before continuing. "She was devastated."

"Yeah," Malachi says, exhaling. "She doesn't talk about it much, but I know it really messed her up."

I turn to him, searching his face. "She loves you, Mal."

His eyes flick to mine and linger for a second too long. He doesn't answer.

"Don't break her heart," I say softly. I don't know why I say it. Maybe because I'm thinking of my own heart. Or maybe I just want another woman to get the fairy tale she deserves.

Something shifts in his gaze. My stomach flips.

"I won't," he says finally, but his voice is quieter, like the words aren't his own. His shoulder brushes mine. "So . . . are you good?"

"Yeah," I answer quickly. "Why?"

"You've been . . ." He tilts his head from side to side. "Different lately."

I blow out a breath through my nose. "I'm fine."

He smacks his lips as if to say *yeah, right.* "And I actually passed algebra senior year."

I snort, then cover my mouth. "You barely passed algebra."

"Exactly." He grins, nudging me. "What's got your mind?"

I shake my head, smiling despite the truth behind his words. "You always think you know me so well."

He shrugs. "That's because I do." His expression softens. "I can read you like a book." A moment passes. "Is it Russell?"

I swallow. *How do I answer that question without unraveling everything?* I can't, so I go with the easiest response. "Russell and I are fine."

His jaw ticks. "Since when did lying come so easy for you?" He looks away. "I talked to Mom the other day. She didn't say much, but . . . she's worried. About you. Should I be?"

Should he? I run a hand through my curls, tucking my bottom lip between my teeth.

"No," I say. "I'm fine."

His gaze drops—down to my left hand.

Oh no.

I shove my hand into my dress pocket, heart hammering, but it's too late.

His voice hardens. "Is that what I think it is?"

I freeze. My mouth goes dry, my throat tightening.

"You're engaged?"

I open my mouth, then close it. "I—"

"Russell proposed, and you said yes?" He steps back, eyes stormy with disappointment and something else I can't name.

"I was going to tell you."

He scoffs, shaking his head like I said something ridiculous. "But you didn't."

"I told Zara and Irene. I just . . . didn't know how you'd react."

He laughs, bitter. "My sister and my mom knew. But me? Why would *I* need to know something like that?"

I expected disappointment. Maybe even frustration. But not this. Malachi looks . . . hurt. "Why are you acting like this?"

"Like what?"

"Like it bothers you so much."

He flicks his thumb over his nose and sniffs. From the cold or something else.

"Because it does," he snaps. "I've known you forever, Ash. I care about you. And I know men like Russell." His voice rises slightly. "I just—"

I blink, caught off guard. I want to explain why I said yes, to explain how my life has been behind closed doors these past few months. But if he's reacting this way *now*—I can't imagine how he'd react if he knew the truth.

"Malachi—"

He looks like he might cry. His eyes search mine, desperate. But then he shakes his head, mutters something I don't catch, and storms inside.

He's never been mad at me before. And I hate how it feels.

I rush in after him, heart pounding.

Zara and Akin are curled up on the couch. Phoebe is organizing gifts. All eyes turn when we burst in. I silently beg Zara not to say anything. But Malachi turns to her, eyes blazing.

"What's wrong?" Zara asks.

"How could you not tell me Asha's getting married?"

Phoebe gasps, clapping her hands. "Oh my gosh! We have a wedding to plan! Congratulations!"

I bite my lip, looking at Akin.

"What?" he asks, sitting up.

Malachi shakes his head. "Yeah. She's going to marry *him*."

"You don't understand," I cry out.

"No, you don't, Asha. You don't see it, but everyone else does." He walks out, and before I can follow him this time, Phoebe grabs her coat and rushes after him.

"Babe, wait up!" she calls out.

The door slams behind them, and I feel it slam into my chest.

"What's his problem?" I ask Zara.

She stands beside me, wrapping an arm around my waist. "He's just worried, that's all."

Akin's voice cuts through the room, firm and serious. "Zara, you knew and didn't say anything?"

"I wanted to, but that's not my place to tell," she explains.

"Asha, are you sure this is something you want to do?" His words make my stomach churn. Akin is the *only* one who knows about the hole in the wall. The only one who knows *how* it got there. He knows something the others don't. I know why he doesn't understand my yes to Russell's proposal.

"Don't worry about Malachi," Zara says. "He'll calm down."

I shake my head, trying to make sense of it all. "He's acting like I did something wrong."

Zara gives me a knowing look. "Ash, you *know* how Mal is. Overprotective, stubborn. Akin, can you check on them?"

Akin stands, but before he leaves, he looks at me.

It's not just concern in his expression—it's disappointment.

My cheeks burn. I feel *exposed*, like everyone can see something I don't want them to.

After a long silence, I swallow hard and whisper, "Should I have just told him no?"

Zara doesn't answer right away.

"If you want to marry him, you should," she finally says. "No one can tell you what to do. You're the one who has to become one with him. But like I told you before, I want you to be happy. We all do."

I nod slowly, but her words don't settle the unease in my chest.

"Even Irene thinks it's a bad idea." I exhale. Russell has his anger problems, and his drinking habits . . . but he's working on those things. He's *trying* to get better. For me and for Liv.

He hasn't hit me since the last time. That's progress, right?

Chapter 21

THIS MORNING, I WOKE up feeling light. Hopeful, even. Despite how last night went. Malachi eventually came back inside with Phoebe and Akin, but when he did, the tension between us was undeniable. He wouldn't even look at me.

I pushed those confusing feelings aside because, after all, last night was about Liv. She opened so many gifts, they barely fit in the trunk. Zara and Akin got me a nice sweater and a pair of boots. Malachi handed me a gift, but before I could even react, he walked away—back to the tree to hand out the rest of his presents.

I still haven't opened it.

It's sitting in my car, on the front seat, untouched.

Opening it doesn't feel right. Not when he's upset with me.

I barely slept, tossing and turning, wondering how to make things right between us. But I know Malachi—he needs space. Time to process. His reaction still felt a little strange, but I know he only wants what's best for me. He always has.

Although, I never imagined him being this angry at me. When we were younger, we played harmless pranks on each other—like the time I sprayed a can of men's shaving cream in his locker to get back at him for stuffing my car with so many balloons it took forever to clear them out. He'd been annoyed, sure, but he never treated me any differently. We'd even had disagreements over the years, but he was always himself. But now . . . I don't know.

He seemed so hurt.

But no one knows how I truly feel.

It's hard being in this position—trying to do the right thing. I want Olivia to have a two-parent household, something I never had. And I want to marry the only man I've ever loved. *That's ever loved me.*

I'm giving Russell grace. A second chance. He deserves that, doesn't he?

But it's hard to feel confident in my choices when everyone disapproves. They don't have to say it. I see it in their eyes.

Still, it's Christmas Day, and I bury the weight pressing on my chest under hope and joy. Today is going to be a good day.

As I stretch and get out of bed, my phone dings.

Trina: *Merry Christmas! Welcome to the world, Demetria Collins!*

Attached is a picture of a tiny, wrinkled newborn, swaddled and peaceful, her eyes closed. She's beautiful.

A smile tugs at my lips as I respond.

Me: *I'm so happy you had a safe delivery! Congrats to you and your family! She's so precious! Merry Christmas!*

For a moment, I just sit there, staring at the screen. A new life. A fresh start. And on Christmas Day.

It makes me think of Liv, how small she once was. It feels like just yesterday she was placed on my chest for the first time, warm and crying, our first skin-to-skin moment. A moment I wouldn't mind reliving.

I glance at Russell. He's still asleep, his chest rising and falling steadily. Even from here, I can smell the liquor on him.

My stomach tightens.

I push the feeling away. *Not today.*

I head to the kitchen and start breakfast, letting the warm scents of maple syrup, butter, and crispy bacon fill the house.

While cooking, I glance at the refrigerator. Russell's new counselor's card is pinned neatly with a magnet—*Tony Brooks.* Russell's initiative to follow through with his promise tugs at the strings of my heart. Though I can't quite put my finger on it, the tension has lightened a little. Things are starting to get better, at least on the surface.

He had his first session a few days ago, and I can't wait to hear all about it, whenever he's ready to open up. If things are going great, this could be the fresh start we need.

He's been kinder overall and taking actual steps toward change. But I want to ensure he's going to keep trying. Russell's still adamant about having a Valentine's wedding and isn't budging on the idea. At this point, the day will be here before I know it, and I'm still as unsure as I was the day he asked me. But nonetheless, even if I didn't want this—I don't see a way out of it now. I said yes, and he's trying, so . . . there's that.

When I open Liv's door, she's already rubbing her sleepy eyes. Her little face lights up when she sees me. "Good morning, sweet girl," I murmur, pressing a kiss to her wild curls. "Merry Christmas." When we get downstairs, her gaze immediately shifts to the glowing Christmas tree, her excitement bubbling over.

She wiggles in her highchair, happily munching on eggs, strawberries, and pieces of pancake.

Then, footsteps come up behind me. Heavy. Slow.

"Dada!" Liv cheers, her tiny legs kicking.

I don't turn around, but his presence is strong—the weight of his hand on my shoulder, the rough press of his lips against my neck.

"Good morning," he mumbles, voice hoarse with sleep. He smells like spice and soap. I glance at him. He's showered and wearing a fresh pair of blue jeans and a plain brown sweater.

I force a smile. "Morning."

Russell plops down beside Olivia's highchair, making silly faces at her. She giggles, trying to feed him strawberries. He pretends to eat them, chewing dramatically, and she bursts into uncontrollable laughter.

My lips curve into a smile. *See? Today is going to be a good day.*

After breakfast, we sit on the floor together, Boyz II Men's Christmas album playing softly from the speaker. Liv rips through her presents, her squeals filling the room. Russell and I both got her new outfits, bows, and shoes, but he focused mostly on toys—some of which she already has. I'll just donate the extras.

As Olivia examines a learning tablet that plays music when you press the buttons, I hand Russell his gift.

"Let's see . . . what'd you get me?" he teases, shaking the box slightly.

He opens it, and his expression shifts. His brows knit together as he lifts a gold Rolex from the box.

I sit cross-legged, my fingers fumbling in my lap. "Do you like it?"

His jaw tenses. "I do . . . but how'd you pay for this?"

I swallow. "I've been saving."

He flips the box over as if looking for a price tag. "With what money?"

"The money you give me for gas or groceries. Anything left over, I put aside." I force a chuckle, trying to ease the tension. "When we went to the mall a few weeks ago, I saw you looking at this exact one."

His lips press into a thin line.

Something about the way he's staring at the watch causes a knot to form in my stomach. I thought he'd be happy. Thought he'd appreciate the effort.

Instead, he lets out a low laugh, shaking his head. "So instead of using the money for what you're supposed to, you're blowing it on expensive gifts?"

I blink. "I mean . . . it was for you."

Russell exhales sharply, shaking his head. "That's not how this works, Asha."

I gulp. "I just wanted to do something nice for you."

He scoffs, tossing the watch onto the couch like it's nothing. Then, without a word, he reaches under the tree and grabs a wrapped box, shoving it into my hands.

"I'll take it back and get the money refunded."

Russell doesn't respond, but his irritation fades, replaced by something else. Possessiveness? Satisfaction? I can't quite tell. Instead of answering, he drags a warm hand down my face, his fingers brushing my neck.

"Open it," he says, voice softer now.

I nod and carefully peel back the wrapping paper, revealing a sleek black box. I lift the lid, and my breath catches in my throat.

Lingerie.

Delicate lace, deep red, barely there. It's sexy and it's too small. It's definitely not what I was expecting. I shove it back in the box, for some reason fearful of Olivia seeing it, as if she'd know what it is.

"Oh," I murmur, forcing a smile. "Thank you."

Russell leans in, pressing a deep kiss on my lips, his hand resting heavy against my thigh. "Since we haven't been intimate in a while, I was thinking you can save it for our honeymoon," he whispers against my skin. "Just two more months."

February. Valentine's Day. Our wedding. He has everything all figured out. Getting married at the courthouse, with an invitation extended to Darnell only as a witness. He wants all three of us to wear white. I haven't given him an answer, but he is adamant on doing it soon.

I swallow hard, my heart pounding. I should be excited, but instead, I feel trapped. The reality of it all sinks in. I still don't know if this wedding is what I truly want. But Russell does. And that's all that seems to matter.

Guilt pierces my heart like a knife. This is the life I've always wanted, but now that it's here, I can't shake the uncertainty gnawing at me.

After a long day of playing in the fresh snow with Liv and watching her play with her toys, eating meals together, and lounging in front of Christmas movies, exhaustion weighs on all of us. Liv is freshly bathed and in her pajamas, curled up against Russell's chest. I sit beside them, my head resting on his shoulder, soaking in this rare moment of peace.

I hesitate before speaking, not wanting to ruin the moment. But this is important.

"How's therapy going?" I ask casually, keeping my tone light. I really do want to know. With everything that's happened, I haven't had the chance to check in. And with the wedding coming up soon, I need to know if we're headed in the right direction.

Russell stretches his arms across the back of the couch, exhaling slowly. "It's fine."

I wait for him to say more, but he doesn't.

"Just . . . fine?"

He shifts, pulling at his beard. "I mean, yeah. It's whatever."

"Are you still going every week?"

His jaw twitches. "Asha."

I sit up a little. "I'm just asking."

He rolls his eyes. "I go when I can."

I press my lips together, debating how to approach this. "Russell . . . what does that mean?"

He exhales sharply, clearly irritated now. "It means I go when I feel like I need to."

"So, you're not planning on going anymore."

"I didn't say that."

I swallow the frustration bubbling up. "You kind of did."

Russell leans forward slightly. "Look, I don't know if I need all that, okay? I'm good."

I blink. "You're good?"

"Yeah." His tone is defensive now. "I don't see why you keep pushing this."

I stare at him, my heart sinking. "Because you said you wanted help, Russell. You said you were committed to this, and if you want to get married in less than two months, I need to make sure you're keeping your promise."

He scoffs, shaking his head. "If I don't, what are you going to do? Call off the wedding?"

"That's not what I'm saying."

"That's exactly what you're saying." His voice hardens. "What, you think I need therapy to be the kind of man you'd actually want to marry? I'm the one who wants to marry *you*, and what do I get in return? Nothing." He scowls. "I work my behind off to take care of you and Liv. *I* make all the money. *I* provide for this family. And I've been patient with you, especially with all the weight you've put on since having Liv."

I flinch. "That's not fair—"

"Oh, isn't it?" He lets out a cold laugh. "You question every move I make, waiting for me to mess up. You act like I'm not trying. But what are you doing?"

I open my mouth, but he cuts me off.

"No, you know what? It doesn't even matter. Nothing I do is ever enough for you."

His voice is rising now, and my heart pounds. I glance down at Liv, who is in his arms. Regret sinks in. I should've kept my mouth shut.

It's like I can't talk to him about anything without it turning into a fight. *Aren't couples supposed to work through things together? To talk, to disagree, but still love each other through it. Isn't love about sacrifice and compromise?* But it's like I'm the only one sacrificing. The only one compromising. My peace of mind. My heart. My friends. My worth . . .

"Russell, keep your voice down."

He throws his hands up. "Of course. Always gotta be quiet. Always gotta tiptoe around your feelings."

I wipe my cheeks, surprised that they're damp. His words cut deep, harsh and belittling. I've done everything I can. He's trying, and I've acknowledged that. The wedding plans are in motion, despite the fact that he slapped me . . . because I love him. Or maybe because I'm afraid he's the only man who ever will love me. I don't know anymore.

"I'm going to put Liv to bed."

"No, you're going to sit down and let me talk." Russell puts Liv down at his feet.

I ignore him, holding out my hand for Liv, who's obviously tired. "Come on, let's get you into bed."

But before I can scoop her up, she takes a step forward just as Russell stands up too fast.

His knee knocks into her tiny frame, sending her stumbling backward. She lets out a startled yelp before landing on the floor with a soft thump.

My breath catches.

Liv's face crumples, her eyes filling with tears. "Mama—"

I'm already gathering her in my arms, my heart pounding. "Shh, baby, I got you." I run my hands over her arms, her back, checking for any signs of injury.

She buries her face in my shoulder, whimpering. I whip my head toward Russell, fury burning in my chest. "Russell—"

He scowls, but he doesn't reach for her. He just stands there. "It was an accident," he grunts. "Dang, Asha, don't start." I stare at him in disbelief. He rubs his hand over his face. "She wasn't watching where she was going."

Heat courses through my entire body. "Are you serious?"

His eyes flick to me, frustration simmering beneath the surface. "Yes, I'm serious. You act like I threw her across the room."

I clutch Liv tighter, her sniffles still warm against my neck. "You should at least apologize."

Russell exhales sharply, shaking his head. "For what? Asha, let it go."

"No," I snap, standing up with Liv still in my arms. "I can't do this."

His eyes darken. "What does that mean?"

I don't answer. I turn toward the hallway, ready to take Liv to her room.

But before I can take a step, Russell grips Liv's arm, tugging her toward him. She cries out, sending a sharp pain up my chest.

"Russell, stop!" I yank back, but his hold is firm.

Liv starts sobbing, thrashing between us.

"Give her to me!" I plead, my voice breaking.

Russell's grip tightens. "No. You don't get to act like I'm some monster, Asha."

"She's scared!" Panic rises in my throat. "Russell, let go!"

He yanks her one last time before I relinquish her. She flops to the couch, curling into herself, hiccupping between sobs. I rush toward her, but before I can reach her, Russell grabs me.

He wraps his hand around my throat, slamming me against the wall. Air catches in my lungs.

His face hovers inches from mine, his grip tightening just enough to make my pulse hammer against my skin.

"What did you mean?" he demands, his voice eerily low. "You can't do this? Huh?"

Tears prick my eyes as I try to push against his hold, my chest heaving. "Russell—" His grip tightens, and I can't get the words out.

"You think you can just leave me?" His fingers press harder. "You think I'll let you?"

I try to speak, to explain that I didn't mean I was leaving for good, I just can't do this tonight. I don't want to argue. I don't want to yell. It's Christmas. Today was supposed to be a good day.

I wasn't planning on leaving him. Even though I'm starting to think I should.

But I am angry, furious that he yanked Liv's arm like that, that he tossed her onto the couch like she was nothing. And beneath all that anger, I'm terrified.

Liv's wails fill the room, piercing through the haze of panic in my mind. *I have to get to her.* I continue clawing at his wrist, my vision blurring at the edges.

"Let me go," I choke out, my voice barely above a whisper.

Russell doesn't move at first. His eyes bore into mine, searching, challenging, daring me to fight back. I don't recognize him.

Then, suddenly, he releases me.

I stumble forward, gasping for air, but I don't waste a second. I scramble toward the couch, scooping Liv into my arms.

She clings to me, her little body shaking. "Mama," she whimpers.

I hold her tighter, my own body trembling.

Russell steps back, his breathing heavy, his expression unreadable.

For the first time, I see it clearly—this will never get better.

Not with him.

Not like this.

And I know, without a doubt, I have to get us out.

Chapter 22

MY VOICE SOUNDS LIKE sandpaper scraping against a chalkboard. It's raw, sore, and every swallow is a painful reminder of last night. The bruises on my neck, dark red and purple, throb with each movement, a cruel reminder of Russell's hands around my throat.

This morning, I woke up to the sound of Russell moving around the bedroom. I hadn't been able to sleep much, but I was too afraid to move. So I lay there in the dark, pretending to be asleep, my eyes squeezed shut as he showered and then left the room. I didn't dare move, but the only reason I forced myself out of bed was because I couldn't leave him alone with Liv.

I took a quick shower, my fingers trembling as they grazed the bruised skin on my neck, tears filling my eyes. It hurt to cry, so I pushed down the sobs threatening to break through. I need to keep it together—for Liv, for the day ahead.

I wrap a teal scarf around my neck, doing my best to hide the marks from the world. In the mirror, I see myself for a moment—flushed cheeks, a raw throat, a face trying to pretend everything is fine. I slip on a white cardigan, flared blue jeans, and boots, hoping the outfit hides the emotional mess beneath.

Liv's soft cries echo from downstairs. She's awake, and Russell is with her. I hurry downstairs, praying—no, *desperately hoping*—she's okay. After everything last night, I can't help but wonder how much he would hurt her in my absence. And I hate to think that way, but I can't control the thoughts that enter my mind anymore. He's proven time and time again why I can't trust him.

When I reach the kitchen, I find Russell sitting at the table, feeding Liv oatmeal and berries. She lights up when she sees me, and the urge to hold her tight nearly overwhelms me. To put distance between her and him. That thought alone convicts me.

"Good morning," he says, setting the bowl down like nothing happened. He stands, moving to the stove as if it's a regular morning, cooking breakfast as if everything is perfectly fine.

I instinctively touch the scarf around my neck, my throat throbbing. "Thanks," I manage to whisper, though it's an effort to speak at all.

I sit at the table as he brings over my plate of French toast and scrambled eggs. He pours syrup over the toast, and I focus on the dark liquid moving in slow, deliberate circles. For a moment, I feel paralyzed, unsure if I should eat.

"How'd you sleep?" he asks casually, as if he didn't just inflict violence, fear, and pain on me.

"Fine," I lie. My stomach knots as I push a forkful of food into my mouth. The taste is drowned by the bitterness, the dread that's settled deep in my bones.

"I got you some new flowers this morning," he says, nodding toward the windowsill. A fresh bouquet of red roses sits in the vase, vibrant and full of life.

The sight of them brings a lump the size of a tennis ball to my throat. I've come to notice the pattern. He hurts me. He buys me flowers. Or does something nice like make breakfast. It's a cycle, and cycles like this aren't meant to be broken.

"They're lovely," I whisper, but the crack in my voice betrays me. The facade is cracking too.

I manage only a few bites before he finishes feeding Liv and starts to get ready to leave. He sounds normal, unaffected, but I know better. I push the plate away, too tired to pretend to eat anymore.

"I've got to get to work, but I'll be home soon," he says, patting Liv on the head in a way that makes me sick. Then, without warning, he leans in for a kiss. I flinch, my body going stiff as his large hand slides up my neck, pulling me closer, deepening the kiss.

Don't cry. Don't cry, I tell myself.

"I'll call and check on you later," he adds, his eyes scanning me. I used to find warmth in those eyes, a kindness that made me feel safe. Now, all I see is darkness and coldness.

I nod as he grabs his coat and keys. When the door shuts behind him, I let out a shaky breath I hadn't even realized I was holding. I release my grip on the table, the tension in my body slowly uncoiling, but my heart is still racing.

Pushing the plate back, I scoop Liv into my arms. She's not crying, but I am. I rock her gently, the tears flowing freely now as I break down in the quiet of our kitchen. *How did I get here? How did I let this happen?*

Never in a million years did I think I'd find myself in a relationship like this, justifying my reasons for staying in it. But here I am. I was blind—blinded by love, blinded by the hope that things would get better. It wasn't until he hurt Liv, until he hurt me in front of her, that the truth finally hit me.

I knew something was wrong from the very first moment he punched the wall in a fit of anger, but I didn't want to see it. The arguments. The fear. Mrs. Charlene and Irene warning me. The way none of my friends liked him. It all makes sense now. My mom probably would've seen it too, and that thought stabs at my heart.

What would she tell me? What would she say?

A thought comes to me like a whisper in the dark.

Later that day, after lunch, I grab Liv and leave the house. It's been nearly a year since I've been here, since I've visited her grave. The air is cold, the sky heavy with dark clouds threatening rain. A thin layer of snow crunches beneath my boots as I walk, Liv wrapped tightly in my arms.

When I reach my mother's headstone, a wave of grief crashes over me. I want to collapse right there on the ground. Coming here is both a comfort and a torment, reminding me that she's gone and I'll never see her again.

Tears start to fall uncontrollably as I stand there, my voice a hoarse whisper. I don't know if she can hear me, but I speak anyway. "When you left, Mom, my whole world changed." I wipe my cheek, sniffing back more tears. "It was the worst day of my life. There were so many things I wanted to do with you. You never got to meet Liv." I shudder, the weight of losing her crashing over me again. "You would've loved her. I know you would've. You two would've been best friends."

I gulp, searching for the truth I'd buried.

"I was so lost," I continue, my voice shaky. "Zara and Irene tried to be there for me, but I pushed them away. Even Malachi tried. They were so kind, so patient with me, but I didn't want to let anyone else in. I just wanted you back. I'm sorry. For not coming sooner. I couldn't." Because I was too scared to heal, thinking it meant I'd have to let her go. But maybe I should've come sooner. That's when things started changing between Russell and me, yet I ignored them like I did everything else. I visited a few months after having Liv, introducing them to one another, but that had crushed me.

The words stick in my throat, but I finally let them out. "Mom, he hits me. Russell hit me in front of Liv." I can barely say his name without disgust piercing my heart.

I sob, my body wracked with the pain of the confession. Liv looks up at me with wide, concerned eyes, and I know right then that I can never let her see me this way again. I can't let her grow up in a world where she thinks this is normal. That this is love.

At some point, my cries turn into a prayer. I beg God for help, for guidance, for strength. I ask for a way out. I can't keep living like this. "I don't want to hurt anymore."

And then I hear it. Her voice is a soft memory, smooth like honey, comforting me even though she's not here. *"Baby, God is near to the brokenhearted. He bears our burdens with us. Give it to Him, and everything will be okay."*

I close my eyes, letting her words baptize me, and I know what I have to do. She would want me to leave. To get out. To find safety, to find love that doesn't hurt. Because, despite everything, I deserve better. I'd been lying not only to my friends but to myself.

I deserve a love that lifts me up, not tears me down. I deserve someone who sees me, who knows me. Someone who loves me, not just because I'm there, but because they truly care. I deserve someone who knows what kind of chocolate I like and who pours into me, not drains me. I deserve someone who makes my heart warm with joy and not cold with fear.

I place my hand on her headstone, whispering goodbye. I let Liv touch it, too, before we make our way back to the car.

As I buckle Liv in, the gift from Malachi catches my eye. I open the bag, pulling out a pink sweater, size XL, not the medium I used to wear before Liv. It's a small thing, but it matters.

I pull out a tiny box and open it, gasping when I see what's inside. It's a gold bracelet with a cross and crown, with a simplicity that screams *put me on*. My hands tremble as I slide it onto my wrist. Inside the box is a note: *May this be a reminder that Jesus is always there.*

Tears fill my eyes as I pull out the rest of the gifts—a women's study Bible and a box of chocolates filled with strawberry fudge. One of my favorites. I laugh softly when I find a pack of tissues tucked inside, a note scribbled on the back: *Figured you're probably crying while opening these gifts. P.S. Why are women so sensitive?*

And in that moment, I realize something important: I'm not alone. Malachi's care for me, even as a friend, has shown me something I've been missing—the kind of love that's gentle, thoughtful, and real. If he can care for me like this, imagine what someone who truly loves me will do.

Chapter 23

REGRET SEEPS DEEP INTO my bones as soon as we get home. I should have left this morning when I knew Russell would be gone all day, but it wasn't until after visiting Mom's grave that I realized this was the right—the *only*—answer. I expect Russell to get home a little after five o'clock, so when I pull into the driveway, I immediately hurry inside. I leave the car unlocked, the window slightly cracked, and the engine running as Liv sleeps soundly in the backseat.

My plan is to only grab the necessities: a few clothes, our toothbrushes, some personal items . . . and my mom's wooden bamboo box where I keep our pictures and her necklace. I can't live without it. I haven't called Zara yet, but I know she won't mind me showing up. I'm ready to talk to her, to tell her everything that's been going on. Though she may be upset with me, I know she'll be proud that I'm finally getting out. Her, Akin . . . even Malachi, though he might still be angry with me . . . *they* will be there for us. I won't have to face this alone.

Ten minutes. That's all the time I need to gather our things. Adrenaline floods through me like a cold drink. My hands are shaking, my mind foggy as I throw clothes into a duffel bag—Liv's, mixed with mine. *What will Russell do when he comes home and finds us gone?* The thought still lingers: he has friends in high places, knows the laws, has everything in his favor. *Will he try to take Liv from me? Come after us?* So many questions plague my mind, but all I can focus on is leaving. I'll have to deal with everything else later.

I take a photo of my neck. Never really knew why I took a picture of the hole in the wall and the bruise he left on my arm, since I never planned on showing anyone. But now . . . if he wants to come after me, if he tries to hurt me again, I'll tell anyone who'll listen. I *have* to, if it means keeping Liv safe, keeping me safe, so I can remain in her life.

When he pinned me to the wall, squeezing me so tight I thought my eyeballs would pop out, the sand settled. Russell could end me if he wanted to. *And then who would take care of Liv? Who would make sure she's safe?*

When I finally finish in Liv's room, I rush back into my room, almost forgetting Mom's box hidden in my closet. That's when the sound of a car door slamming causes me to freeze. My breath stops. My ears become hyper-aware. At first, I think it might be the neighbors, but then I hear the sound of the door unlocking downstairs, heavy footsteps, keys sliding across the counter.

Those footsteps are coming up the stairs.

There's no time to think. The duffel bag, with our things scattered, still lies open on the bed. Drawers are half pulled. I clutch the box under my arm as Russell's shadow appears in the doorway. His face is unreadable, eyes scanning the chaos around him.

"Wow. Asha." He snickers, shaking his head in disbelief. Then he yells, "You were going to leave while I was at work? Take my daughter away from me? Got her in the car, what, so you could just grab your things and leave me?" Veins bulge in his neck.

I stand frozen, my chest rising and falling heavily. I'm so scared, it feels like everything I've eaten today is about to come up, but I force it down.

"Russell," I start slowly. "I can't do this." This time I'm not talking about this conversation but about our relationship.

I pull away the teal scarf, letting it fall to the floor, exposing the bruises. I want him to see what he's done to me, the woman he claims to love.

"You've hurt me too many times. And you hurt me in front of Liv. It's not safe," I cry out, but no tears come. Not right now, at least. I need him to *hear* me, to know that I'm not just some weak woman. So, I stand a little taller, pushing my shoulders back, keeping my head up, even though I've never been this scared.

"We can work this out," Russell says in a calm voice, stepping closer, trying to soften his tone. "Let's talk this through."

But I know what that means. I know what he's capable of. He'll be nice for a few days, maybe even a week or two, and then he'll hit me again.

"No, Russell. I want you to get the help you need, but you'll have to do it without me."

I start moving slowly, my eyes flicking between the duffel bag and the door. Russell is blocking it. *How am I going to get out of here?* I'm angry at myself for not leaving earlier.

Russell's voice raises, yelling again, telling me I'm not going anywhere, that I need to get our daughter and get back in the house. My body shakes, but I tell him no.

"We're leaving, Russell. You can't stop us," I say, my voice trembling but firm.

Then all of a sudden, he starts to cry. "I can't live without you. I need you, Asha." He sobs, tears streaming down his face, and if I weren't so desperate to escape, I'd want to give him a trophy for his performance. "I'm so sorry. I never meant to hurt you."

He steps closer and lays his head against my chest, but as he mutters, "I won't do it again. I'm so sorry. I love you," I tell myself—no, *love doesn't hurt.*

I think of the Bible: *love is patient, love is kind.* This isn't love.

With all the strength I can muster, I shove him off. Grabbing the duffel bag, I race down the stairs, heading for the front door.

But just as I reach it, Russell slams it shut, dragging me back. I drop the box and the bag. He begins hitting me, punching, kicking me so hard it radiates through my bones. "Stop!" I scream as loud as I can. "Let go of me!" Russell's fists are strong, the heels of his shoes solid as they kick my ribs. I taste blood in my mouth as his fist comes in contact with my lip.

He climbs on top of me, straddling me, his grip tightening around my face as he squeezes my cheeks together. His breath is hot and heavy against my neck. "You're not leaving me," he whispers, his damp cheek pressing against mine, sending a shiver down my spine.

I scream, trying to get away from him—until something inside me snaps.

This time, I fight back. I punch, I kick, I do whatever it takes to break free, knowing I have to get to Liv. The rage that he'd been building up is finally escaping. I knew he was capable of so much more, and tonight he's showing me I was right. It'll never stop. *Ever.*

I finally kick him in the nose, and with a sharp cry, I break free. I grab the box and bag and sprint for the car.

Russell follows me outside, his nose bloody. He bangs on the car, shouting for me to get out, telling me I can go, but I need to leave Liv behind.

"No!" I scream.

He curses, hitting the car again. "Don't you take her from me!"

I ignore him, just as I ignore the pain radiating through my body.

"Don't take her from me! Don't you leave!" He points an accusatory finger at the car, veins bulging from his neck and forehead.

"Move!" I yell. Russell's in the way, and he's standing his ground. My fingers tighten around the steering wheel, and the last thing I want to do is hurt Russell, but I'm determined to get us out of here. I warn him again, tears pouring from my eyes.

"Do it!" he yells. His eyes bulge from their sockets. Anger boils over, and I press on the gas. Russell jumps out of the way, shock on his face as I speed off. In the rearview mirror, I see him chasing after me, his voice carrying into the night. Liv's cries echo from the backseat, but I can't stop. I won't stop.

I take back roads, weaving through the city, making sure he's not following me. What should have been a ten-minute drive to Zara's house turns into an hour of driving in circles, my paranoia eating away at me.

Finally, I park down the block, out of sight. He'll look here first, trying to spot my car. But when he doesn't see it, hopefully he'll assume I took Liv to a shelter or that I got a hotel with some of the cash he gave me for those last-minute gifts. Because he can't find us.

Clutching Liv to my chest, I stumble to the door and knock.

It swings open, and Malachi stands there, shirtless in sweatpants. His eyes widen in horror as he takes in my appearance. Without a word, he pulls us inside, locking the door behind him.

He speaks through gritted teeth. "Did he do this?"

I look away, letting the silence speak for me. His gaze travels over my bruised skin, my trembling hands. He clenches his fists, his entire body tense with fury. "I swear to God, Asha, I'm gonna—"

He stops, his rage faltering as he really looks at me. Anger drains from his face as his eyes take in the bruises. "Are you okay?"

I swallow hard. I don't know how bad I look, but now that I've stopped running, the pain ignites like a flame. My head drops, my voice barely above a whisper. "I had to go."

Malachi exhales, his own eyes glossy with unshed tears. We sit on the couch, Liv playing on the floor, recovered from tonight's turn of events.

Malachi listens as I finally tell him everything, how Russell punched a wall that Akin had to fix, how he was right to worry when he saw Russell grab me in the hallway, how Russell shoved me so hard I hit the ground. I tell him about last night. About the bruises. About the yelling. I show him the red marks still lingering on my neck.

Before I can continue, Malachi's strong arms pull me into a hug, careful of my injuries. His bare chest is warm against me, and for the first time all night, I feel safe. *Secure.*

"You're okay now," he murmurs. "He won't hurt you again. I won't let him."

He lifts Liv into his arms, holding her close. He presses a gentle kiss to her forehead, his jaw still tight with anger.

With everything going on, it isn't until now that I remember Zara and Akin are out of town at the art event. Malachi offers to call them, but I shake my head. "No . . . this trip is important to her. I don't want to ruin it. I'll tell her when she's back."

Malachi doesn't argue. "Then you're staying here. You and Liv. You can take my room. I'll sleep on the couch."

My body sags with exhaustion. "I'm so tired, Mal." My voice cracks. "And I'm scared."

His expression dims. "I'll help you get cleaned up. I'll grab your stuff from the car later." He pauses before asking, "Are you hurt anywhere bad? Do you need a doctor?"

I shake my head. "I don't think so." Then, after a moment, "Can you . . . help me take pictures?"

His brows furrow.

"For proof," I explain with a trembling voice. "I think he's going to come after Liv now. Try to take her from me. I have to go to the police." The thought terrifies me. I don't know who to trust. "Maybe I can talk to Trina and Darnell . . . but I don't know if Darnell will try to cover for him."

Malachi's throat bobs, then he gives a small nod. "I'll help you."

He settles Liv in front of the TV with cartoons before leading me to his room. It smells like him—clean, warm, familiar. I sit on the edge of his bed, and he kneels in front of me, his eyes dark and stormy as he scans the bruises on my legs and my arms. I lift my shirt just a few inches so he can take photos of my stomach and back.

His hands shake as he lifts his phone. The camera clicks. Each flash feels like another wound reopening, but I let him do it.

Malachi exhales sharply, his voice thick. "I'm so sorry, Asha." He looks away for a moment, as if staring at me any longer will break him. "I wish I'd been there. I wish I could've stopped him."

I force a small, broken smile. "It's okay. I fought back." My hand comes to his face, and I guide his gaze back to mine. "I fought back," I repeat.

He gives me a smile that doesn't quite reach his eyes. "I know you did."

And this time, he doesn't try to hide the tear that slips down his face.

Malachi takes care of Liv the rest of the night while I shower, washing away the dried sweat, blood, and fear clinging to my skin. I change into a nightgown, the only sleepwear I managed to grab before leaving. I don't look in the mirror, not once. I'm not ready to see what he did to me.

When I return, I tuck my legs under me on the couch, staring at nothing in particular. My body aches, exhaustion pressing down on me like a weight.

Malachi walks down the hallway, stepping back into the living room. "She's finally asleep."

"Thank you," I whisper.

He nods, rubbing the back of his neck. "Maybe we should put ice on the bruises—to help with the swelling."

I don't argue as he disappears into the kitchen.

Then, suddenly, a knock at the door.

I jump, my pulse skyrocketing. My breath catches in my throat. It has to be him. *He's here. He's come to take us back.*

Malachi's eyes flick toward me, immediately catching my panic. "It's okay," he says gently. "I called Phoebe."

I blink, confused. "Phoebe?"

"I want her to check you over, make sure you're okay. I know you don't want to go to the hospital, but I need to know that you don't have any serious injuries."

I'm not ready to explain what happened to anyone else. Before I can protest, Malachi unlocks the door, and Phoebe steps inside. She starts talking before she even fully enters, her voice a flurry of concern.

"Oh, Asha, sweetheart. I came as fast as I could." She kneels beside me, scanning me with wide, worried eyes. "Oh, honey, I'm so sorry. I can't believe—" She stops herself, inhaling sharply. "Let me check you over, okay?"

I appreciate her kindness, but her voice is too loud, her energy too much. My head is pounding, and all I want to do is sleep, but I'm thankful that she came all the way here to check on me.

Malachi clears his throat. "I'll, uh . . . give you some privacy." With one last glance at me, he steps out of the room.

Phoebe carefully examines me, checking for anything serious. "How are you holding up?"

"As good as I can right now."

She sighs, shaking her head. "I'm so sorry, Asha. No one should have to go through this." A bitter laugh escapes her. "This is worse than when my ex left me before our wedding, and I thought that was the worst thing that could happen."

I don't have the energy to respond, so I just nod.

She hesitates before asking, "Are you staying here?"

"Yes," I say, but I notice something in her eyes. A flicker of something I can't quite place.

Suddenly I feel uneasy. I don't want to cause problems between her and Malachi.

When Zara gets back and we go to the police, I'll talk to Irene or Mrs. Charlene at the church. Maybe they'll know somewhere I can stay. Somewhere safer.

Phoebe presses a bag of ice into my hands. "Keep this on the bruises. It'll help with the swelling."

"Thank you," I murmur.

She stands, heading toward the door. Malachi comes back into the room, and Phoebe takes his hand in hers. "I really think she should go to the hospital," she whispers loudly enough for me to hear her.

"No. I can't go," I explain. "If I go, Russell will find out and come there. They'll call the police, and I just—no. You don't know Russell. He's going to try and cover this up, make it seem like my fault somehow and take Liv from me. I can't let him do that."

"You might feel okay now, but what if there's internal damage? What if something gets worse overnight? Plus, the hospital will document your injuries. Without it, it's your word against his."

I can tell Malachi is considering her words, but my eyes plead with his. I can't go.

"We've already taken pictures. Besides, I'll keep an eye on her. If anything changes, I'll bring her in," Malachi says.

She presses her lips together, eyes narrowing. Phoebe clears her throat. "Well, if you feel lightheaded or weak, call an ambulance immediately. And if you need anything at all, call me."

She pauses just before stepping out, leaning to whisper something to Malachi. I can't hear what she says, but when she pulls away, she gives me a look that makes me shift my focus elsewhere.

Then she's gone, the door clicking shut behind her, leaving me and Malachi alone in the quiet living room.

He stands there, leaning against the door, now wearing a black hoodie. His arms are crossed over his chest, muscles tense. Fury burns in his eyes. A storm brewing, ready to unleash it on Russell immediately.

Without a word, he walks me to his bedroom. With each step I take, it hurts. The sheets have been changed. At some point, he moved Liv's crib from Zara's room into his, making space for her beside the bed. She's lying on her belly, bottom in the air, drool trickling from her mouth.

I climb under the covers, my body aching with every small movement. Malachi helps me into the bed, then moves to the door. He leans against the frame, watching me with pain in his expression. Having him here with me, I feel better somehow.

He reaches for the light, switching it off. Moonlight spills in through the window, silver and soft. He turns to leave, and as he does, a quiet groan escapes me before I can stop it.

Malachi freezes. "Asha, you okay?"

I gulp, my face hot with embarrassment. I feel like a child, but I ask anyway. "Can you stay for a bit?"

"Of course," he says with no hesitation in his voice.

He crosses the room and sinks onto the small loveseat beneath the window, pulling his hood over his head. He leans back, eyes on the ceiling, silent.

I lie there, staring at the shadows stretching across the room, absentmindedly fumbling with the bracelet on my wrist Malachi gifted me. Despite the agony burning through my body, relief washes over me.

I'm not alone.

Malachi is here.

Chapter 24

I DON'T KNOW HOW long I've been asleep, but when I wake, the golden glow of morning is long gone. My entire body feels as if it's been hit by a train. The vision in my right eye is blurry, and my head pounds like someone is knocking against my skull.

Pain radiates through me. It takes a moment to remember where I am, and then panic grips my chest.

Liv!

My breath catches as I turn my head, heart hammering, only to find the crib empty.

I try to sit up, but the moment I do, a sharp pain shoots through my arm.

"Agh!" I cry out.

Heavy footsteps pound down the hall, and within seconds, Malachi is there, standing in the doorway with Liv in his arms. She's clutching her cup in her tiny hands, resting her head against his shoulder.

"You okay?" Malachi asks, his brows furrowed.

Tears blur my already fuzzy vision, and the tension in my shoulders melts away seeing Liv safe in his arms. I press a trembling hand to my chest, nodding shakily. "Yeah . . . I'm fine," I whisper.

Malachi steps forward, lowering himself onto the edge of the bed. I reach out, my fingers brushing Liv's soft cheek. She blinks at me, her round eyes filled with quiet curiosity. Malachi's gaze moves over my face, and I know I must look as bad as I feel.

"She woke up a few hours ago," he says gently. "I thought I'd let you rest."

"Thanks." I exhale, sinking back into the pillows.

"How are you feeling?"

I stare at the ceiling. "Like crap. What time is it?"

"A little after one."

I can't believe I slept that late, but even now, my body begs for more rest. My eyes feel swollen, my limbs sluggish.

Malachi adjusts Liv in his arms. "Just rest, Asha. That's all I want you to do today."

He stands, placing Liv back in the crib before walking over to me. His movements are careful as he helps me sit up, his strong arms steadying me. Even though I grit my teeth against the pain, I don't protest when he guides me out of the room and down the hall.

By the time we reach the living room, my body feels like it's on fire. Malachi eases me down onto the couch, wrapping a soft blanket around my shoulders.

"Here." He hands me an ice pack, placing another gently against my ribs.

I wince but nod. "Thank you."

He disappears into the kitchen and returns minutes later with a small tray. A bowl of yogurt topped with granola and fresh fruit, a bottle of water, and some pain medication.

I shake my head. "You didn't have to do all this."

"I did." His voice is firm. "And I'm not going to work today. I'm staying here with you."

I look up at him, startled. "Malachi, you don't have to do that. I'm fine."

He scoffs. "You could barely make it to the living room on your own. You think I'm just gonna leave you here by yourself?"

My body is in too much pain to argue. He kneels in front of me, holding out the medicine. "Take this, Asha. Please."

Reluctantly, I swallow the pills and take a sip of water. As I settle against the cushions, I eat my breakfast. The smooth yogurt soothes my throat.

After I'm done, Malachi takes the dirty dishes from me, and moments later he returns with Liv.

"Can I hold her?" I ask softly.

Malachi hesitates but nods, carefully placing her into my lap. I suck in a breath as her tiny foot grazes my bruised hip. The pain is sharp, but it's nothing compared to the ache in my heart when she looks up at me with those wide, innocent eyes.

I blink back tears, pressing a shaky kiss to the top of her curls.

Malachi watches quietly, then pulls out his phone when it buzzes. He glances at the screen, then at me. "It's Zara."

Panic rushes through me. "Don't say anything."

Malachi debates for a second, then nods. Malachi and Zara tell each other everything, and I've been creating a chasm of secrets between them.

He steps into the hallway to take the call, leaving me with Liv. I stroke her back gently, breathing in her warmth.

A few minutes later, Malachi returns, slipping his phone into his pocket.

"She said they're having fun, and she told me to check on you because you didn't answer your phone last night."

My stomach twists. I turned it off so I wouldn't have to see if Russell was texting or calling. But knowing him, he probably is, and he might even be looking for me . . . the thought terrifies me.

I swallow the lump in my throat and say nothing.

***

THE NEXT DAY, I'M still glued to the couch, and Liv is playing on the floor beside me. Malachi paces near the door, slipping on his watch. "I won't be gone long," he says. "Just a few hours."

I nod, but an uneasy feeling rests in my chest. Just yesterday, I longed for him to go to work, but now I wish he could stay.

Malachi steps closer, his gaze searching mine. "You sure you'll be okay?"

I nod, forcing a small smile. "I'll be fine."

He doesn't look convinced. "Mom and Dad should be here any minute. If you need anything, call me." His voice is firm, but there's an unmistakable edge of worry. "Are you sure you're going to be fine?" he asks again, his eyes dark with concern.

Before I can answer, someone knocks on the door.

Malachi opens it, and Irene and Manuel step inside. The moment Irene's eyes land on me, they well with tears. "Oh, sweetheart . . ."

I don't even realize I'm crying until she rushes forward, wrapping me in a careful hug. Manuel follows, his face tight with emotion. They don't ask questions. They don't demand answers.

Instead, Irene cradles my face in her hands, her eyes searching mine. "My poor baby." She presses her forehead against mine, her voice thick with sorrow. "I'm so sorry."

I sniffle. "I'm fine."

Manuel gently rubs my back. "We need to call the police."

230

"No!" I say quickly, my voice rising in panic. "Not yet. Not right now." The thought of it leaves a sour taste in my mouth. I'm not ready. It's too much. I need to talk to Zara before I do anything else.

Manuel grinds his teeth, but his voice is steady. "Whenever you're ready, we'll be there every step of the way."

Irene brushes a strand of hair from my face. "Let me make you some tea." She grabs her bag, and I know without a doubt she's brought her own ingredients, determined to nurse me back to health.

Malachi turns to me, his expression unreadable. "I have to get going, but I'll be back in a few hours. Don't open this door for anyone else."

His tone is sharp, protective, his dark eyes piercing into mine. I lick my chapped lips. "You're going to work and coming right back home?" I ask, needing reassurance. Because the look in his eyes tells me he wants to do more than just go to work. He wants to confront Russell. To show up at our house or his job and unleash wrath on him. I can see it. I can feel it.

"Yeah," he says, but I'm not sure I quite believe him.

"Promise me you're not going anywhere else."

He looks down at his feet for a second, then back up at me. He nods.

But that isn't enough to ease the tension in my chest. Manuel whispers something in Spanish to Malachi.

Malachi squeezes the bridge of his nose. "I promise," he groans. "I'm not going anywhere else." Manuel places a strong hand on his shoulder, giving him an understanding nod.

Malachi lingers a moment, clearly torn, wanting to stay. But eventually, he sighs and forces himself to leave, hesitating at the door before finally stepping out.

Manuel sinks onto the couch beside me, his expression heavy with worry. "How are you doing?"

I exhale shakily, staring at my hands. "I'm hurting," I admit. "I don't know how he could do something like this to me."

Manuel's jaw clenches. "Men aren't supposed to put their hands on women. Ever. They're supposed to protect them, love them." His voice is edged with anger. "I want to talk to the police."

"I'm scared," I confess. "Because of Russell's job. He's a cop, Manuel. What if nothing happens? What if they cover for him?"

Manuel's eyes darken. "That doesn't matter. This is going to be handled." His tone is firm, leaving no room for argument. "Look at what he did to you, m'ija." His voice cracks, thick with emotion. "You're too precious for something like this . . . no man should ever lay a hand on you."

Before I can respond, Irene walks in carrying a steaming cup of tea. "Here, sweetheart." She eases down beside me, wrapping an arm around my shoulders as she helps me take a careful sip. The warmth spreads through me, soothing in a way I didn't know I needed.

Manuel gets down on the floor with Liv, making her giggle as he plays with her, giving her the attention she deserves. Irene presses a kiss to my temple, and something inside me cracks.

"Malachi tells me you don't want to go to the hospital, but I think it'd do you some good." She traces my jaw with her thumb tenderly.

I shake my head. "No, I'm fine. I'm feeling better already. Thank you for taking care of me," I whisper, my voice carrying weighted emotion. "You remind me of Mom so much."

Irene's lips tremble into a soft smile. "Before she passed, we made a promise to each other. I'd take care of you like you were my own, and she'd do the same for my two. You were always family, Asha. That hasn't changed."

My throat tightens. "Did you . . . did you suspect something?"

Irene sighs, her hand tightening around mine. "I thought something was going on, but I wasn't sure what. The way Russell behaved, I couldn't put something like this past him. I tried to give him the benefit of the doubt for the sake of you and Liv. When Malachi called and told me what happened, my entire heart dropped." Her voice wavers slightly, her eyes shining with empathy. "He sounded so heartbroken on the phone. He worries about you so much."

Tears sting my eyes, and I look away. I can't bear the weight of their concern, of their love. I don't deserve it.

Irene squeezes my hand. "Everything is going to be okay now, sweetheart. You won't have to go back to that. Not ever again."

Time ticks by quickly, partially because I sleep most of the day away, and when I wake up, Irene and Manuel are gone and Malachi is sitting on the couch. He's watching me, and when I grunt, his stare intensifies as if he's trying to solve a puzzle.

"Where's Liv?"

"I hope you don't mind, but Mom and Dad took Liv with them to give you a break tonight."

"Oh," I whisper. I don't mind at all because she's been there plenty of times, but a pang of unease settles in my chest. The thought of her not being here makes me nervous. A small part of me wonders if Russell will try to find her. But the odds of that are slim. He probably doesn't even remember where they live. And even if he did, I know they'd do everything to keep her safe.

Silence lingers between us, thick with something unspoken. Malachi watches me, his expression unreadable. But there is something in his eyes, something deep and piercing.

He rubs his palms together before resting them on his knees. "You know . . . even when we were younger, I always wanted to keep you safe." His voice is low, almost cautious, as if he's scared to say what's really on his mind.

He shakes his head slightly, a rueful smile tugging at his lips. "It's just . . . I hated seeing you hurt. Even when it was just stupid stuff—like you falling off your bike or getting into it with Zara over something small. I wanted to step in, to make things easier for you."

His words cause my breath to hitch in my throat. I'm not sure how to respond. Something deeper than concern laces his tone, and it makes me nervous. I don't know what it is, or maybe I do, but it's all too much right now.

Instead, I smile. "Well, you were always bossy," I tease in an attempt to break the tension.

Malachi huffs out a small chuckle, but his eyes never leave mine. "Maybe," he admits. "But I meant it. I still do."

Something inside me stirs, a nervous flutter that I can't make sense of. I swallow hard and look away, focusing on the pattern of the blanket draped over me. Because if I look at him any longer, I might start to wonder what he really means.

"Are you really okay?" Malachi asks after a while.

I don't lie. Instead, I shake my head.

He rubs the back of his neck. The warmth of his presence is steady, grounding. "I wish I could take the pain away," he whispers, his voice rough with emotion.

I know if he could, he would. Because that's the type of person he is.

For a moment, he just watches me. Then, he inches closer, and his voice drops even lower. "I swear to you, Asha, I won't ever let anything like this happen again."

Something about the way he says it, the certainty in his voice, causes my throat to tighten. I rest my head on his shoulder, letting his close proximity bring me comfort.

We sit there for a long moment, something unspoken lingering between us, until I drift off to sleep.

Chapter 25

ZARA AND AKIN ARRIVE a little after lunch, and the moment my best friend walks through the door, the weight of the world lifts from my shoulders. I've been counting down the hours until she gets back, because she's the one person I need right now.

She's laughing and chatting with Akin as he carries their bags inside. Akin sees me first. He stops in his tracks, his mouth falling open, eyes widening with shock. Zara follows his gaze, and before I have a chance to say anything, she rushes toward me with open arms.

Malachi leans against the wall as Zara embraces me. I break down, sobbing into her shoulder. We stay like that for several minutes, clinging to each other, both of us crying.

When we finally pull apart, Malachi hands us tissues. Akin sits on the couch, his leg bouncing, hands clasped together. I can see the questions in his eyes, but he stays quiet, giving us our moment.

Once I finally regain my composure, Zara and I settle opposite Akin while Malachi perches on the armrest beside me. He taps his foot against the hardwood floor as I begin to speak, my voice shaking as I unveil the hidden truths I've kept from them all—especially from her. It's as if Malachi is angry all over again because his jaw clenches so tight I can hear his teeth grind together.

Akin mutters something under his breath, his hands balling into fists. Anger blazes in his eyes—not just at Russell, but at himself. He always suspected Russell was capable of something awful, but he trusted me to walk away before things got this bad. And I didn't. I let him down.

"Asha, I—" Zara's voice falters. She shakes her head as if trying to process everything I just told her. "I'm so sorry you had to go through this alone. That I wasn't there for you and Liv. I can't believe he did this."

"I can," Malachi mutters darkly. "Russell's a coward. I guarantee you he wouldn't put his hands on a man like that." The heat in his words displays his anger. I can't help but sense a deeper meaning behind them.

"Has he contacted you?" Akin asks.

I shrug, glancing toward my bag where my phone still sits powered off. I don't have to turn it on to know it's flooded with missed calls and unread messages. And I can't handle that right now.

"We need to go to the police," Zara says firmly.

I hesitate. "I wanted to talk to you first. I needed time to process everything." My throat tightens. "I'm scared. Do you know how many cops' wives can't report their abuse because their husbands are the law?"

"Who cares about that!? Look at your face!" Akin yells.

My head falls. I can't even look at myself in the mirror. Maybe I'm a coward too.

"Not all of them are like that. Darnell's a good guy. We should call him, talk this through," Zara mentions.

"That was my first thought, but . . ." I exhale slowly. "I don't know how he'd react since Russell is his partner. What if he tries to protect him?"

Zara shakes her head. "I don't think he's that type of guy. But then again, look what else I was wrong about." She buries her face in her hands, her neon-blue nails trembling against her forehead. "How did I not see what Russell was capable of?"

I place a hand on her shoulder. "None of us really knew. It still doesn't feel real."

I lean back against the couch, pulling my legs up to my chest. A dull ache blooms in my lower stomach, and I'm suddenly grateful that Malachi made me take another pain pill earlier.

"I have an idea," Malachi says.

I lift my head. "What?"

"You and Trina are close, right?"

I hesitate. "I wouldn't say that exactly. We talk sometimes. She texted me when she had the baby."

"What if you call her? Tell her what's going on and let her see what Russell did to you. She'll push Darnell to do something. And he'll have to listen to her."

I shake my head. "She just had a baby. This isn't her problem."

"But this could work," Akin chimes in. "A good husband who loves his wife. He'll do whatever she asks. Trust me on that one." He shoots Zara a knowing glance.

I think about it. They have a point. But I've already pulled so many people into this mess, it doesn't feel fair.

"I can try," I murmur, "but not tonight. I'm not ready yet."

Malachi's arm slips around my shoulders, his thumb grazing my skin in a slow, comforting motion. A cold shiver runs up my neck, but I don't pull away.

"All right," he says softly. "No rush."

For the remainder of the evening, Zara stays at my side like we're glued together. I don't think I could do this without her.

Irene and Manuel still have Liv, keeping her overnight, and I finally allow myself to rest. With Zara and Akin here and Malachi's plan in place, things are headed in the right direction. I'm still slightly uneasy and scared, but now I can face this.

As we sit around the dining table, the warm aroma of vegetable soup and grilled cheese fills the air. Zara suddenly looks at me with that teasing expression. "You still look sexy, you know."

I scoff, waving a dismissive hand. "You don't have to lie to me, Z. I know I look like I got into a fight with a bear and lost."

Zara frowns. "You look like a baddie."

"I hope so," I say, brushing a curl behind my ear.

Akin speaks up, his voice heavy with guilt. "I should have done more," he mutters, looking down at his bowl. "I should've done something the day you called me . . . before it got this bad."

Zara clears her throat. "I'm a little upset that you kept that from me. We're supposed to tell each other everything."

Akin reaches for her hand. "I know, babe, and I'm sorry. I didn't have all the facts, but I wanted to let Asha handle it."

I shake my head firmly. "This isn't your fault, Akin. Russell did this. Not you." I force my busted lip into a smile, hoping to ease the weight in his eyes. "Besides, I made you promise not to say anything. I was being stubborn."

"Still are," Malachi says because of my refusal to go to the hospital.

"Liv definitely gets that from you," Zara adds, and we all find ourselves laughing. I'm grateful that the night is ending on something lighter, something that isn't just my pain. Zara and Akin talk about their amazing trip, and it's enough to get my mind off things.

After dinner, as we start winding down for the night, I feel . . . better. Not healed, not whole, but hopeful. Like I can finally breathe, because I'm not alone.

I stand in the living room, rubbing my arms as exhaustion settles in. "You can have your bed back, Mal. I'm feeling a little stronger, so I'll take the couch tonight."

He stands in front of me, a blanket in hand as he prepares to lie down. "Nah, don't worry about it. I sleep on the couch sometimes anyway."

I narrow my eyes. "You sure?"

He shrugs. "Yeah. I'm not going to let you sleep on the couch. And honestly . . ." He hesitates for a moment before continuing, his voice softer now. "I'm kind of grateful my apartment flooded. If it hadn't, I wouldn't have been here when you came looking for help."

"You've done a lot for me," I say, my voice quiet. "So . . . thank you."

"Of course," he murmurs back. Then, with a teasing smirk, he adds, "That's what your best friend's brother is for."

I roll my eyes. "Well . . . I guess you're kind of like my best friend too. But don't let Zara hear me say that. She'll kill us both."

He chuckles. "It's our little secret." He presses a finger to his lips in mock secrecy.

Zara is my bestie. Malachi is just . . . Malachi. I'd never thought to put a label on it. He has always been like family, I guess. But in this moment, I realize just how much he has always been looking out for me, supporting me in ways I never really acknowledged before. And now, with everything I have going on, he is prioritizing my safety in a way that is hard to explain.

Tap. Tap.

We freeze. A sudden, sharp knock echoes through the apartment. My stomach flips.

Zara and Akin rush into the living room, Zara clutching the sleeves of her pajama top. Their eyes meet, the same question hanging between them.

"Who could that be?" Zara whispers.

Malachi shakes his head. "Phoebe's at work."

Zara frowns. "It's not Mom and Dad. They would've called first."

Akin is already moving toward the door. "I'll check." He peeks through the peephole, his entire posture stiffening. "Asha," he says, voice urgent but low, "go to the balcony. Now."

I don't ask why. I don't need to.

Malachi is already guiding me toward the sliding glass door, his hand firm against my back. As I step outside, the night air wraps around me, but the shiver running down my spine isn't from the cold.

From inside, I hear the door open, followed by Akin's calm voice. "Good evening, officer. What can I do for you?"

A beat of silence. Then the officer responds. "We received a call about a welfare concern regarding a woman and her daughter. We just need to confirm that everyone here is safe."

Akin doesn't stall. "Everyone here is fine." His voice is edged with irritation. "It's late, officer. We were just about to turn in for the night."

The officer doesn't back down. "Who all is in the home?"

"Just me and my wife."

Right on cue, the sound of Zara's feet shuffle across the floor. "Hey, officer."

Malachi is in front of me, inches from my face as he peeks through the glass door. My body is pressed against the brick, and I'm gazing up at him. The way we're positioned, I can't peek inside; I don't want to. I'm too scared to move.

The officer pauses, then asks, "Have either of you seen an African American woman and a little girl?"

Akin's jaw flexes. "Why? And who called you?"

"It was an anonymous tip."

A heavy silence fills the room. I can imagine the look Zara's giving him—one that says she knows exactly who sent this officer. *Russell.*

Akin huffs. "Let me get this straight. You show up at our door, this late at night, over an *anonymous tip*? Are you knocking on everyone's door or just ours?"

"We just need to verify—"

"Yeah, well, we're good here." Akin's tone turns to steel. "It's late. My wife and I need to get to bed."

The officer clears his throat. "You two wouldn't keep information from a police officer, now, would you?" His question sounds threatening. It sends a shudder down my neck.

"Of course not," Akin responds casually. "Now, you have a good night, sir."

"If you hear anything, feel free to contact the department."

It takes another second before the door closes. I exhale a breath I hadn't realized I was holding. My heart is hammering so hard it's all I can hear.

Malachi steps back inside first, helping me in. Zara looks like she's just seen a ghost, her lips pressed into a thin line.

"Russell's not stupid. He's just trying to scare you," Akin says.

"Well, it worked. You still think contacting Darnell is the best option?" I ask.

Chapter 26

IT TAKES ME SEVERAL days to finally work up the nerve to look at myself in the mirror.

I don't want to.

I know what I'll see—the pain, the damage, the undeniable proof of what he's done to me. I've felt it in every aching step, in every wince when I move too fast. *But seeing it? Admitting it?* That's something else entirely.

My hands tremble as I grip the bathroom counter, forcing myself to look.

My bottom lip has a small cut running across it, the wound dark and scabbed. A black ring circles my right eye, the swelling finally going down, but the deep purple still lingers beneath my skin. The discomfort hasn't left me, pulsing dully under my cheekbone. My lower stomach and legs are speckled with bruises—some dark green and yellow, fading with time, while others seem to bloom deeper, darker, refusing to disappear.

I barely recognize myself.

The life and light that used to be in my face is completely drained. My eyes, glassy and hollow, stare back at me.

This is what he did to me.

A sharp breath leaves me, and before I can stop them, tears spill over. They roll down my cheeks, hot and relentless, my shoulders shaking under the heaviness of it all.

I press my palm against my quivering stomach. If only I could erase what's already been done, go back in time and leave sooner . . . but I can't. The pain isn't just skin deep. It's *everywhere*.

Closing my eyes, I let myself remember.

The good memories come first, like always. The ones I used to cling to. The ones that gave me hope that things would get better.

I think about the nights we sat outside on the porch, watching the rain. The way he wrapped his arms around me, his warmth seeping into my skin, his breath steady against my neck. I used to think of those moments as perfect, as proof of how much he loved me.

But now, I remember what I chose to forget.

I remember how, after a few minutes, he'd sigh, shifting behind me. *I'm ready to go inside*, he'd say, pulling away, breaking the moment before I was ready. But I'd let it go. I always let it go.

I think about the times he rubbed my feet when I was pregnant, how I convinced myself it was sweet, how I let it be a sign of his care. But now, I recall the pressure of his hands, rough and rushed, like he was aggravated. *Like he couldn't be bothered.*

And suddenly, I see the pattern. How many of our *good* moments had tiny cracks in them, cracks I ignored.

I thought love was supposed to be patient. Kind.

But Russell had never been patient with me.

Even in his kindness, there had always been something else lurking beneath it.

And now, standing here, staring at the proof of what he's done, I finally stop making excuses.

The sob that tears out of me is raw, ugly, and uncontrollable. My knees buckle, and I grip the counter to hold myself up, my body wracked with grief, with regret, with anger so strong I can taste it.

I should have seen it.

I *did* see it.

And I stayed.

It isn't until my grip tightens around the counter that I feel the silver ring pressing deep into my finger. I rub it, twisting it absentmindedly, hating that I'm still wearing it. I want to take it off. I *should* take it off. My fingers tug it past my knuckle, but I stop. As much as I want to be free of it, something in me won't let go.

God, why did this have to happen? Why can't I let him go?

A soft knock on the door pulls me from my prayers. I quickly wipe my cheeks with the back of my hand before opening the door slightly.

"You okay?" Zara stands there, purse slung over her shoulder, her voice gentle but worried.

"Yeah . . ." I sniffle.

"Malachi's in the car. We're ready when you are," she says.

"Give me five minutes. I'll be down."

She nods, pulling the door shut with a quiet click.

I finish getting dressed, choosing loose-fitting clothes that won't irritate my skin further.

I consider putting on makeup but decide against it. *Let them see what he did to me.*

The car ride takes about thirty minutes, but when we arrive, I can't make myself get out. My hands are clenched in my lap, my heart hammering.

"I'm not trying to rush you or anything, but we've been sitting out here for at least fifteen minutes," Akin says, tapping his thumb against the center console. "I don't want anyone getting suspicious and calling the cops."

"He's right," Malachi agrees, though his hands are still gripping the steering wheel.

Beside me, Zara hasn't moved either, but her hand rests on mine, warm and soothing. "Are you sure you want to do this?" Her voice is soft, filled with concern. Akin's eyes ask the same question, but he stays silent.

I swallow hard. "Yes."

I reach for the door handle, but before Malachi can step out too, I shake my head. "No."

Everyone looks at me.

"I'm going in alone."

"But you don't have to," Zara presses.

"I know. But I *need* to." Besides, it would probably feel weird for all of us to show up unannounced.

"I'll be fine," I reassure them. "I'll call when I'm done."

They hesitate, but eventually, they drive off, leaving me standing there, feet heavy as I approach the white steps. Her car is parked outside, so I know she's home. My knuckles tap against the door, and I wait.

"Sit down somewhere!" Trina yells from inside.

The door swings open, and Trina stands there with a newborn baby in her arms. The second she sees me, her face falls.

"Oh my goodness . . . Asha."

She pushes the screen door open, stepping aside without indecision. I walk in, the warmth of her home contrasting sharply with the cold weight in my chest.

"What happened?"

I don't answer. I just *look* at her, my eyes glossy. The moment realization hits, her features soften, her lips part slightly. She knows.

"DJ," she calls out, her voice steady but firm. "Take your brothers in the backyard to play. Give Mommy a few minutes."

Her oldest son, who looks just like his father, grabs the hands of his younger brothers. But before he leaves, his eyes meet mine. He stares at me like I'm unrecognizable.

"Hey, Miss Asha," he says quietly.

"Hi, DJ." I force a small smile.

He doesn't question it, just leads his brothers outside, and Trina ushers me into the living room. She gently places the baby, Demetria, into the bassinet beside the couch. The tiny girl scrunches her knees to her belly, cooing softly before closing her eyes again.

Trina turns back to me, her eyes scanning my bruises, her jaw tightening. "Please, sit. Can I get you anything? Water? Something to eat?"

I shake my head. "No, I'm fine."

My hands clasp together, my fingers nervously twisting that stupid ring again. "I'm sorry for showing up unannounced. Under normal circumstances, I wouldn't do this, but I—" My voice breaks.

Trina doesn't wait for me to finish. She sits beside me, her hands covering mine. "Hey . . . don't you dare apologize."

I let out a shaky breath, glancing at the bassinet. "I should've brought something. A gift for the baby . . . or something to help you." My voice is weak.

Trina shakes her head, her expression tight with disbelief. "Asha, don't do that. Don't sit here worried about a gift when you look like this." Her eyes sweep over me again, and I see it. The disgust, the anger settling into the lines of her face. She presses her lips together, shaking her head again, this time slower. "I can't believe Russell would do something like this." A humorless laugh slips from her lips. "I've always told Darnell something was off about him, but not like this. No offense," she quickly adds.

I look down, my fingers twisting together. *No offense.* But it still stings.

Trina exhales sharply, standing up. "You should leave him."

"I did. I'm staying with Zara," I blurt out.

"Good. How's Liv?"

"She's fine," I say, scratching my neck. My fingers knot in my lap. "He hit me in front of her. I can't go back. And I don't know what to do."

Trina watches me, her face unreadable at first. But I don't need to say anything else—she already knows.

She knows why I came.

She knows what I'm asking.

"You want me to talk to Darnell," Trina says, more of a statement than a question.

I nod. "I don't know what else to do." My voice wavers, and I take a deep breath. "The police came looking for me last night. I know it was Russell. What would you do if it were you in this situation?" I ask because I need to know. Because I feel lost.

She sighs, running a tired hand over her face. Despite just having a baby, she still looks put together. She has dark circles under her eyes, likely from sleepless nights. Her hair is pulled into a short ponytail, and she's wearing what I wore every day the first two months after giving birth: sweatpants and a large shirt.

"I don't know," she admits. "I'd be scared. I wouldn't trust some of the cops . . ." She shakes her head. "But Darnell's a good guy. My husband *hates* men who put their hands on women. I can't believe this." Her voice tightens with frustration.

She paces for a moment before stopping abruptly. "When he finds out his partner is a woman-beating scumbag . . . he's going to *flip*." For some reason, her calling him a scumbag pricks at me.

I lean forward, my hands clasped together. "But when we tell him . . . what happens next?"

Trina exhales, rubbing her temples. "I don't know."

And that's what scares me the most.

"Darnell should be home any minute. We can talk to him together."

"I'd rather not."

The thought of facing Darnell right now makes my stomach turn. He's Russell's partner, his friend. *What if he doesn't believe me, even with the bruises? What if loyalty clouds his judgment? What if he refuses to help?* The questions swirl in my head, each one heftier than the last.

Trina watches me, understanding in her eyes. "I'll talk to him," she says firmly. "Let me tell him what's going on, and then we'll go from there." Her voice tightens. "He needs to be locked up for what he did to you."

Tears well in her eyes as she takes a seat beside me. She hesitates for a second, then reaches for my hand, squeezing it gently. "You're so brave, Asha." Her voice drops to a whisper. "A lot of women don't get out . . . they don't leave."

Her words settle over me, true and painful. She's right. So many women stay. Because their love for him drowns out the fear. Because leaving feels harder than surviving. Because the hope outweighs the pain. Because they don't have the support like I do. It's not fair. No one deserves this.

***

AS I LIE IN bed, Liv curled beside me sound asleep, my mind refuses to settle. I can't help but wonder where Russell is. What he's doing right now. How he's handling all of this.

Has he been drinking? Or is he going to work, pretending nothing happened? Or worse—what if he's outside right now, waiting for an opportunity to drag me and Liv back home?

And then, a quieter thought creeps in.

What if he really is sorry? What if he didn't mean to hurt me?

The endless "what ifs" swirl in my head until my skull aches. I roll out of bed carefully, making sure not to wake Liv, and tiptoe out of the room, avoiding the spots in the floor I know will creak.

I expect to find Malachi asleep on the couch. Instead, he's sitting up, hands clasped together in front of his face. He's praying.

I pause, stepping back toward the bedroom, but the floor betrays me with a creak. His eyes fly open.

"I'm sorry," I whisper. "I thought you were asleep. I didn't mean to interrupt you."

"It's okay. Everything all right?"

I nod. "Just a headache. I was going to get some water and ibuprofen."

"I'll get it for you."

Before I can object, he's already on his feet, moving toward the kitchen. I sigh and follow.

One thing about being a victim, if that's what I am, is that suddenly everyone wants to do everything for me. As if being beaten means I can't function anymore. Or maybe they're just trying to help. But it makes me wonder if I'm a burden.

He takes a glass from the cabinet, fills it with water, then digs through the medicine drawer. He hands me two pills. I take them, swallowing until the glass is empty.

And then, just as I lower the cup, he asks, "Do you miss him?"

I freeze, my head snapping up. "What?"

Malachi holds my gaze, unflinching. "Do you miss him?"

Shock ripples through me, quickly replaced by offense. "That's not really any of your business," I say sharply.

He points to the ring I'm still wearing. "I didn't mean to offend you." He leans against the counter, arms crossed. "But if you do, it's okay. Most women in your situation do."

I narrow my eyes. "What's that supposed to mean?"

"I was looking some stuff up," he says simply. "Trying to figure out how to be there for you. I read up on something called trauma bonding."

I let out a dry, sarcastic chuckle. "Oh, so you're a counselor now?"

"No," he says evenly. "I'm just trying to understand. To be here for you."

I scoff. "It's too late for that." I don't know why I say that, but I do. *Do I miss Russell? Is that why I'm responding this way?*

Malachi's shoulders drop. "I tried," he says, voice quieter now. "I tried in other ways. Like when you were sick, who showed up? Who took care of you?" He stares at me expectantly. "Or did you forget that?"

I look away. Because I know Malachi is the one person who's been there in ways I'd never imagined.

"I've kept Liv for you. I've always been there. Even when your mom passed away. But you—you pushed me away."

I swallow hard. "You don't understand."

"You're right. I don't understand." His expression darkens. "Because every time I tried to be there, you wouldn't let me. You shut me out."

I twist the ring on my finger, heart pounding. "Nothing about my life is simple," I murmur. "No one can truly understand unless they've been in this situation."

Malachi studies me for a long moment. Then, his voice drops to something almost vulnerable. "Maybe if you let me in, I could." He turns from me, and before walking out, he says, "I care about you, Asha. More than you'll ever know."

I gulp, hands sweating as I meditate on his words.

I can't sleep now.

I think about everything, how Malachi has always been there, how he bought me Christmas gifts that actually meant something to me.

And then I think about Russell. How every gift he ever gave me was never really for me but for his own pleasure.

The contrast stings. I should apologize to Malachi, tell him I didn't mean to snap, but I need to understand why I'm upset in the first place. He's done nothing wrong. If anything, his kindness is what's unraveling me.

Being around him, I feel safe, seen and cared for, but it stirred something in me I wasn't ready to face. A guilt I can't explain. Like I'm betraying Russell, even though we aren't together anymore. Even though there is nothing romantic happening between Malachi and me. And that's what makes it worse.

I don't even understand what I'm feeling. Just that it's tangled and messy and heavier than I anticipated.

Without thinking, I grab my phone and turn it back on.

The screen floods with notifications.

Hundreds of messages. Dozens of missed calls. All from Russell, which I expected. I'm not going to open any of them or respond. Not yet.

But then I see two missed calls from Trina. And one text.

Trina: *We need to talk.*

Chapter 27

ZARA FILLS THE TABLE with platters of pancakes, fruit, bacon, cheesy eggs, and biscuits. Containers of orange juice and water sit nearby, and just as I finish helping her set the plates, the doorbell rings. I take a deep breath, bracing myself for what's to come.

"Darnell. Trina. Thanks for coming," Akin says, giving Darnell a firm handshake. I expect their kids to be tagging along, but it's just the two of them and the baby.

"No, thanks for letting us come," Darnell replies.

"Where are the kids?" Zara asks.

"My mom is watching the older ones," Trina explains, Demetria enveloped in a baby wrap carrier snug to her chest. "I figured it'd be best if we didn't bring the boys. They'd tear your place apart." She provides a warm smile.

Phoebe and Malachi are the first to take their seats. I sit across from them, keeping my head down, scared of Darnell's reaction—still unsure of how this will go. Irene and Manuel come in, holding Liv, and everyone else quietly takes their place. This feels like an intervention . . . my stomach is queasy. But I'm grateful that they are all here.

Then, a firm hand lands on my shoulder.

"Asha."

Darnell's voice cuts through the silence. I slowly lift my head.

"I swear . . . I never knew he could do something like this," he says, his voice heavy with guilt. "I'm so sorry."

Relief floods over me, hearing those words from him.

"I'm not going to let this slide."

I nod, managing a small smile. The room falls into a deafening silence, everyone avoiding the giant elephant in the room—*me*. Plates are passed around, but no one really eats. Zara's nerves led her into cooking way too much food. She had to keep herself busy. Even Phoebe, who is usually chatty, is quiet.

I clear my throat, finally breaking the tension.

"We all know why we're here," I say. "So, there's no need to stall things."

Trina puts her fork down and pats the baby's back gently. "I wanted to make sure you were ready. To do things on your terms." She nudges Darnell.

Darnell wipes his mouth with a napkin—though it's already clean. He exhales, finally meeting my gaze. His eyes scan over me, like I'm fragile.

"I want to start by saying I'm sorry," he repeats. "I've known Russell since the academy, and I never thought he was capable of this. When Trina told me what happened, I couldn't believe it . . . or maybe I didn't want to." He pauses. "You have options, Asha. I know you're scared, but you should file a report."

I hesitate, my stomach twisting.

"But what happens when Russell lies?" Irene asks, her elbow propped on the table as she bounces Liv on her knee. "What if he says Asha attacked him first? What if he claims self-defense?" She's asking all the right questions, the same ones I've been asking myself.

Darnell shakes his head. "He can say whatever he wants, but she's the one with the bruises. You should get a lawyer."

He carefully explains the legal process, but my biggest fear tightens around my throat.

"What if nothing happens to him?" My voice cracks. "What if he takes Liv from me? I don't trust him."

"We have to try. I can't stop him from retaliating, and I'd talk to him if I could . . . except he hasn't been at work."

I frown. "What do you mean?"

Darnell sighs. "Russell's missed work all week. He took personal time. I went to check on him, but he wouldn't open the door. He's been ignoring all of my calls."

He glances at Trina, as if asking for permission to continue. She gives him a small nod. Darnell coughs, then takes a sip of water before speaking again.

"I'm not saying this is what you should do, but . . ." He pauses. "If you could convince Russell to turn himself in, it may be easier. If he finds out there's a warrant for his arrest, he could run."

"Absolutely not," Malachi snaps. "Asha's not talking to him. He had the chance to take accountability and get help, but he didn't."

Darnell licks his lips, leaning back in his chair. "Men like Russell . . . they run. If we can convince him to turn himself in—"

"Then *you* go talk to him—" Malachi cuts in.

"Honey, calm down," Phoebe says, putting her hand on his shoulder.

"I am calm," he spits, but the tension in his shoulder says otherwise.

Akin sits up straighter. "I think this should be Asha's choice."

"Akin, don't," Zara warns. "That didn't work the last few times."

A stunned silence falls over the room.

"I don't know what I want to do," I admit. "I need time to think."

"Well, don't take too long," Darnell says with a sigh. "We need to figure something out soon. I'll try to talk to him again. But the last time I saw him . . . he was drunk and upset. Barely coherent."

I swallow hard, the weight of it all pressing down on me.

"Tomorrow, we put an end to this," Malachi says.

"Asha hasn't said if that's what she wants to do yet," Zara interjects.

"He's right," I whisper, head down. "Darnell will try to talk to him again, and if he won't turn himself in, I'll file a report."

Later that night, I sit on the edge of the bed, staring at my phone. The conversation at breakfast still plays in my mind, looping over and over. As I piece the details together, worry washes over me.

I should go to the cops. I know that, but even as Darnell laid out my options, explaining the process, warning me about the risks, something inside me locked up. Filing a report means making it real. It means war. And I'm not sure I'm ready for that yet. But Darnell stated he'd be there with me the entire time. All of them will be.

My fingers hover over my phone screen. My heart is heavy, my mind racing, so sleep is far from me. I try to push the thought of him away, but the memories of his hands on me—both gentle and violent—occupy my every thought. It makes no sense why I have this urge to check on him . . . to make sure he's okay. The revelation that he isn't handling this well and has no one makes me worry.

I press my palms into my temples.

Maybe I should talk to him. Maybe . . . just maybe, if I reach out, I can stop things from spiraling even further. *What if I can convince him to turn himself in? To cooperate and get real help?*

Taking a shaky breath, I open my messages. The unread messages stack into an overwhelming barrier I'm not ready to climb over. Hundreds of them. Missed calls. Voicemails I can't bring myself to listen to.

My hand trembles as I start typing.

Me: *Are you okay?*

I stare at the words, like I betrayed myself, Liv, and my friends just by writing them. But before I can overthink it, before I can talk myself out of it, I press send.

The moment the message goes through, my heart pounds in my chest. If anyone found out I'd reached out to him, they'd be furious. They would tell me I'm being reckless, that I'm undoing everything. Maybe they'd be right.

I need to hear from him. Need to know if he is okay, if there was a reason he'd changed. To know if I'd truly lost him. The man I fell in love with.

Tucking my phone under my pillow, I lie back down, staring at the ceiling. The response could come at any moment. Or maybe it wouldn't come at all.

Either way, there is no going back now.

The phone dings, and my heart stops.

Russell: *I need you. Can we talk?*

I know I should tell them—should have someone go with me. *I shouldn't even be doing this.* But I am. *What am I doing?*

I move quickly, slipping on my jacket while everyone is hopefully asleep. My body is betraying me, moving against the tug in my mind telling me not to go. *He hurt you, and he can do it again. Don't believe his lies.* Yet, I put on my shoes.

By the time the sky is swallowed by darkness, Malachi is in the shower, and Zara and Akin have retreated to their room. Irene and Manuel took Liv to their house again so we could meet Darnell early in the morning. I take a deep breath and step into the hallway, my heart pounding in my ears.

Just as I reach for the door, Malachi comes down the hallway, shirtless, water glistening over his skin, a towel slung over his shoulders. His sweatpants hang low on his waist, but it's his eyes that stop me—the way they narrow slightly, scanning me.

"I thought everyone was in bed," he says, his voice thick from the heat of the shower. Then his gaze drops to my jacket. "Where are you going?"

My pulse skyrockets. I *hate* lying to him. "Just stepping outside for a bit. Getting some fresh air."

He tilts his head, suspicion creeping into his expression. "Why not just go on the balcony?" he asks, voice even but probing. He rubs the towel over his damp curls.

Now's my chance to tell him the truth. Maybe even have him go with me or talk some sense into this delusional heart of mine. Deep down I know this is a mistake, but on the surface, I have to do this. Russell needs me, and I need to know that he's okay. Even after everything, I still care. It makes me sick.

"I just need a short walk," I say quickly. "Not going far. Just outside for a minute."

Malachi's jaw tightens. His arms cross over his chest, the battle happening in his mind evident on his face. Finally, he exhales sharply, shaking his head.

"I don't think that's a good idea."

I want to tell him that he's right. I know I shouldn't be doing this, but I am. In fifteen minutes, I'm meeting him at the house . . . *our house*. The place where he hurt me.

I need to go. Need to see him. Need to make sure he's going to get help and get himself out of this mess he's in. I hate myself for it, but I have to do this.

"I'll be fine. Don't worry about me."

Malachi bites his bottom lip, breaking our gaze. He sighs. "I'll go with you then."

"No," I say a little too quickly. "I would rather be alone. I don't need you following me around like some bodyguard." I regret them the moment the words escape my lips. I don't mean them. I just needed to say something to have him stay.

My words hurt him; he studies me with soft eyes. "You're right. You don't need me," he says, brushing past me.

I'm sorry, I think to myself. *I didn't mean it.* I'd try to explain myself, but I don't have time.

The drive there is long and nerve-wracking. I can't believe I'm doing this. After everything he's put me through, I'm going to check on him. *What's wrong with me?*

I sit in my car outside the house, my fingers gripping the steering wheel so tight my knuckles ache. My heartbeat pounds in my ears as I stare at the dimly lit windows. *I shouldn't be here.* Every fiber of my being tells me to turn back, to leave, but something—some twisted part of me—still wants to save him.

I take a shaky breath and step out into the cool night air. My hands tremble as I knock on the door. At first, there's no answer. Then, just as I'm about to turn away, the door swings open.

Russell stands there, shirt wrinkled, eyes bloodshot. The stench of alcohol rolls off him in waves. His hands shake, and a wild look is in his eyes.

"Asha."

His voice cracks like he can't believe I'm really here.

I swallow hard. "Russell . . . I—"

Before I can finish, he pulls me inside, crushing me against his chest. "I've missed you so much, baby," he sobs into my messy curls. His arms tighten around me, trembling with emotion.

Against my better judgment, I return his hug. My hands rest on his back, soothing him, if only for a moment. The place reeks of alcohol, and my eyes dart around the room. Empty bottles clutter the table, papers crumpled and strewn across the floor. It looks like chaos. I've never seen the house like this before.

Russell finally pulls away and stumbles to the couch, running a shaky hand over his face. "I knew you'd come back." He gives me a weak smile. "We just needed a little space."

I don't respond. I can't. My body stays tense, feet planted near the door in case I need to *run*.

He looks up at me, his eyes glossy. "I wanted to give you a good life, Asha. I wanted to be the man that made you feel safe. But I ain't that man. I never was." He exhales shakily. "My mom . . . she was killed by her boyfriend when I was a kid. I never knew my father. I swore I wouldn't be like them, so I became a cop. Thought that would make me different. But deep down . . ." He swallows hard. "I think I'm just like the men my mother dated."

His words slam into me like a punch. After all this time, I never knew the truth about what happened to his mother. I never knew what kind of childhood he lived. I never knew him at all.

"You're not them, Russell," I say gently. "You can get help."

He shakes his head violently, gripping his hair. "It's too late for that. I hurt you, and I hurt Liv. I kept calling you, texting you. I needed you."

"Look at what you did to me," I whisper, taking a small step closer so he can see the damage his hands caused.

His face twists into something dark, something unhinged. A chill slithers down my spine. Russell grabs the beer off the table and takes a long swig before sighing heavily. "I never meant to hurt you. I want us to work things out."

He stands suddenly, making his way toward me. "Baby, we can start over. Me, you, and Liv. I promise I'll be a better man. I just need you."

His trembling fingers cup my face, and he presses his lips against mine, kissing me desperately. "We can start over."

I grab his wrists, pushing him away. "Russell—" I gasp. "No!"

His entire body stiffens. He steps back, his expression darkening. "What?"

"You need help," I say firmly. "Darnell can help you."

"No one can help me."

I take a step back. "Russell—"

"We need to leave. We can start over. These people are brainwashing you. Turning you against me. Against us. We need to get away from them. Everything will be better when it's just the three of us." He grips my arm. "We're getting Liv, and we are leaving right now."

"No," I say firmly. "I didn't come here to run away with you. I came to make sure you were okay."

Russell's grip tightens. "You *are* coming with me," he growls. "I love you, Asha. I'm not losing you two again."

His shadow looms over me, the moonlight casting eerie shapes across the room. My pulse hammers as his fingers dig into my arm.

"Russell, let me go!" I struggle against his grip, but he yanks me toward the door.

A truck screeching to a stop outside grabs my focus. Headlights blaze through the windows, flooding the room with white light.

Russell turns around just as the front door slams open. Malachi.

Before I can process what's happening, Malachi storms in, ripping me from Russell's grasp. He shoves him back, his fist colliding with Russell's face with a sickening crack. They crash into each other, a tangle of fists and anger. Malachi is driven by rage, Russell by desperation and alcohol.

Malachi lifts Russell off the ground and slams him onto the coffee table. Glass explodes in every direction, shards raining to the floor. But neither of them stop. Russell swings wildly, his punches sloppy yet landing, one striking Malachi's stomach. Malachi barely reacts. He rears back and delivers another hard blow to Russell's face.

I scream. "Stop! Stop it!" My voice is drowned beneath the sounds of their fists hitting one another.

Malachi pins Russell down, hammering into him. Blood streaks Russell's mouth, his nose. This isn't a fight anymore, it's a beating. I grab Malachi's arm, yanking with all my strength. "Malachi, please!"

Finally, he jerks back, breathing hard, his knuckles slick with blood. He steps away, his chest heaving.

Then—

Russell spits blood onto the floor. His hand moves.

Reaches.

I see it too late.

The gun fires.

Malachi staggers, his body jolting. A rasping sound escapes him as he crumples to the floor.

A scream rips from my throat. "No! No, no, no!"

I rush toward him, but Russell's gun swings to me. I freeze, my breath ragged. In an instant, he grabs me again, dragging me toward the door.

My fear turns to fire. I claw at him, kick, thrash, doing anything to break free. Malachi lies motionless on the ground, his blood darkening the floor. No matter how hard I try, I can't get to him.

I have to survive. I have to live. I have to see Olivia again.

Russell manages to open the door, tightening his grip, but I twist loose. My heart slams against my ribs as I throw a wild punch. I grab a vase, the only thing within reach, and I swing it at him. Hard. It hits the top of his head.

The gun flies from his hand, landing on the front porch. I lunge for it, snatching it up before he can.

Russell straightens, his face smeared with blood. He grins. "Don't do anything stupid."

"Don't move." My hands shake as I raise the gun. Tears blur my vision. "I don't want to hurt you, Russell. I just—I just want this to stop."

He steps forward. And I take a step back, down the stairs.

"Don't make me do this!" I sob, my grip unsteady. Despite everything—the pain, the fear, the bruises—I don't want him dead. But I don't want Malachi to die either. I have to get to him.

Russell takes another step. Before I can pull the trigger, sirens wail in the distance. Flashing red and blue lights slash through the darkness like a scalpel.

A car screeches to a stop.

The driver's door flies open.

Darnell steps out, gun drawn. "It's over, Asha. Drop the gun."

Russell staggers, swaying on his feet, his body wrecked from the fight. Blood drips from his mouth. His eyes are hazy.

My knees buckle.

"Malachi's been shot," I choke out. "Help him!"

More cars flood the driveway. Officers swarm the house.

The last car pulls up. *Zara and Akin.*

Darnell moves swiftly, cuffing Russell and handing him off to another officer. But my focus is on the house. I can still see the blood on the floor, on Malachi's motionless body.

I run inside, Zara and Akin close behind me.

Zara notices Malachi and screams. Akin grabs her, holding her back as she fights to reach him. "Noooo! No, no!" Her cries cut through me like a knife.

"Malachi!" My voice is raw, breaking. I drop to my knees beside him, my hands pressing against his face, his blood warm against my skin.

Darnell kneels next to me, urgency in his voice. But the words don't register.

Malachi isn't moving.

Paramedics burst into the house. Hands pull me away, but I cling to Malachi's hand until the very last second, until his fingers slip from mine.

Chapter 28

FIVE MONTHS LATER

"Happy birthday to you! Happy birthday to you! Happy birthday to Olivia Willow Steffens! Happy birthday to you!"

We all harmonize in an imperfect tune, some of us loud and off-key, while Irene and Trina hum with a sweet, perfect tune. Either way, we all sing with love in our hearts for my baby girl. Liv sits in her highchair at the center of attention. Her eyes are round, shining with joy. Her curls bounce as she claps her hands. The flicker of the two pink candles atop a buttercream-covered cupcake dances in her brown eyes.

She reaches for the flame without hesitation.

"No, baby—careful." I gently pull the cupcake back before she can burn herself. "Make a wish," I say, even though she doesn't understand. But I wonder if she did . . . what would she wish for?

For a puppy? For a new doll or those fruit gummies she likes? Or maybe for her dad to be here?

The thought slams into me like a brick wall. My throat quivers as I struggle to swallow what feels like glass. I blink quickly, forcing the tears back. I can't cry today—not today. Not on Liv's birthday.

"Cake," Liv demands, sticking out her bottom lip in a dramatic pout.

My little drama queen.

A hand touches my shoulder, and I jump at the touch. I know it's not Russell, but for some reason it still scares me. I turn, and Akin stands behind me. He offers a reassuring, apologetic smile.

"We'll all blow it out together," he says.

Zara leans in on the other side of Liv, and the three of us bend down, holding the cupcake carefully between us.

"One . . . two . . . three!"

We blow. The candles flutter, then die. Laughter and applause fill the room.

"Yay!" Zara chimes, swiping a bit of the icing and dotting it on Liv's tiny nose. She squeals. I place the cupcake in her hands, and she giggles.

Liv dives in immediately, smearing icing across her cheeks. It covers her fingers and lips. Her joy is contagious, like it always has been. I let myself smile because I'd do anything to make her happy.

The room is full, yet a strange vacancy travels through me. Trina is chatting with Darnell by the table. He's holding their only girl, Demetria, in his arms, and she's sucking on her pacifier. Their boys are nearby, tearing through goodie bags and swapping their least favorites for their favorite pieces of candy.

Ms. Mildred is organizing gifts behind me, her usual sweet soulful hum filling the room. Phoebe stands quietly in a corner, sipping juice and smiling. Akin busies himself making balloon animals for the other kids.

Irene and Manuel are sitting at the table, eating and watching Liv make a mess with her cupcake.

Everything looks perfect. Everything should feel perfect.

But it doesn't.

Because Russell isn't here . . . and neither is Malachi.

The ache gnaws at me, and no matter how hard I try to suppress it, it bubbles in my chest.

"Girl, where are the napkins?" Zara's voice slices through my thoughts. "Liv is getting frosting all over my favorite jeans." A streak of white frosting covers Zara's right pants leg. She's wearing a pink ruffled off-the-shoulder top, skinny jeans, and matching pink heels. Of course she looks as beautiful as ever.

I blink, snapping back into the moment. "Uh—on the counter," I say, turning around to grab the pink polka-dotted ones hiding behind a tray of fruit. I hand one to her and start helping Liv wipe her sticky little fingers.

The sunlight streams through the window and casts a warm glow against Liv's brown skin. "Mama," she coos, her voice soft and sweet like the frosting on her cheeks. Her big brown eyes lock with mine. Her innocence squeezes something tender in my chest. For a split second, I let myself feel grateful. She wants me. Needs me.

Then she points to the floor. "Down."

Of course. I chuckle, then finish wiping her sticky fingers and chubby cheeks. I unbuckle her from the highchair and place her gently on the ground. Before I can adjust the tiny white tutu around her waist, she takes off, bare feet pattering across the hardwood floors. Her curls bounce, arms outstretched toward Irene.

"Gotcha!" Irene laughs, sweeping her up with ease. Liv plants a kiss on Irene's cheek with a dramatic "Mwah!" before snuggling into her embrace.

"Nana." She giggles.

That word—*Nana*—lands right in my heart. Not because it hurts, but because it heals something in me. My mom isn't here, but Irene is. Zara is. This family that chose me, that chose Liv. I press my palm to the counter to compose myself in that gratitude before the next wave of emotions hits me like a ton of bricks.

Manuel says something in Spanish that floats through the air. I don't understand the words, but Liv nods along like she does. "Papa!" she squeals.

The house is a mess, so before it gets too late, I start cleaning up the trash around the house. "Need any help?" Phoebe's voice breaks through the noise. She's standing near the table and places her half-finished juice down.

"Sure," I say. We begin picking up the clutter: half-empty plates, crumpled napkins, and plastic cups that the kids left behind.

The silence between us is thick. Ever since the incident, something's changed. Things have felt off. I don't think she's angry or upset at me, but there's this awkward tension between us. She's still her same chatty and energetic self, but it's not the same.

"So . . . how have you been?" she asks finally, her voice light but her eyes probing for answers.

I hesitate, licking my lips. Everyone keeps asking that. And I never know how to answer.

"I'm . . . as good as I can be," I answer. It's the truth. Some days, I feel like I'm drowning. Other days, Liv's laughter pulls me to the surface long enough to breathe again.

Phoebe nods slowly. "I can't imagine how hard this must be—" she whispers. Her eyes dart around like she's afraid someone might overhear her. "You know . . . with Russell not being here. Since he's in jail."

A sharp breath escapes me. I didn't mean to let it out, but it came anyway.

Leave it to Phoebe to throw salt on the wounds still burning in my chest.

"It's hard," I say, placing another plate in the trash, "but we're managing just fine." I hand her a stack of paper plates. "Give me a sec—I'll be right back."

Before she can respond, I slip outside onto the front porch.

The breeze caresses me like a blanket.

May is warm, but not heavy. Summer in its gentler form. The scent of freshly cut grass mingles with barbecue smoke and wildflowers, thick with nostalgia. I grip the wooden railing and let the stillness overtake me.

I close my eyes.

I don't want to think about Russell. I don't want to remember the way Liv cried for him every night for the first few weeks after he was arrested. The way she clung to his shirt that still carried his favorite cologne on it. I don't want to remember how many nights I stayed up convincing myself it wasn't my fault.

You didn't put him in jail. You didn't make him lie. You didn't make him hurt you.

I echo my therapist's voice inside my head, over and over.

Asha, it's not your fault.

But the guilt is eating at my heart.

My sundress flutters around my knees, the yellow fabric catching the light like a sunflower. My curls, half shoved into a bun, tickle my cheeks, but I don't brush them away. I let them twirl with each breeze.

I remind myself: this day won't come again. Liv will only have one second birthday. I can't waste it buried in the thoughts of these past few months.

Still, I wonder if she remembers him. It's been five months. No visits. No calls.

And slowly, heartbreakingly, she's stopped asking for him.

The front door creaks open, and the soft scent of Zara's perfume announces her before her arms do. She slides one around my waist and leans into me.

"You okay?" she asks quietly.

I shake my head, biting the inside of my cheek. If I speak, I'm pretty sure my voice will crack.

"It's okay," she murmurs, giving me a firm squeeze. "I know there's a lot going on in that head of yours. But don't let it pull you under."

Taking a shaky breath, I respond, "I took her father away from her. He should be here." My words wage war against my thoughts. I know I did nothing wrong, but I can't help but carry some of the guilt.

Zara pulls back just enough to look at me, her eyes sharp with sentiment. "Asha . . . there is no way you really believe that."

I open my mouth, but nothing comes.

"Russell was a narcissist. Manipulative. Controlling. He hurt you. He hurt Malachi. He made this mess. You didn't. He deserves everything he got."

There's anger behind her words. I know what image she's holding in her mind—Akin restraining her as she screamed at the paramedics, tears streaking down her face as Malachi lay bleeding in my living room.

"I just—" I pause, swallowing. "Maybe."

Before she can argue, Akin opens the door. His voice is low. "Babe, Trina needs you."

Zara gives me one last squeeze, then disappears inside with him.

I stare up at the baby-blue sky and the white fluffy clouds.

This can't be what I prayed for. I asked God to help Russell. I asked Him to give me strength, and yet . . . I feel weaker than ever. More alone than ever.

Despite everything, some part of me still misses the way things used to be. Not Russell, not who he is now, but who I thought he was. The man I fell in love with. The man I wanted to build a future with.

I wipe under my eyes carefully, not wanting to smudge the makeup Zara helped me put on.

Then a familiar deep voice says, "Hi." Heavy steps crunch against the gravel. His voice sends tiny chills up my arms.

"Hi," I say, almost breathless as if I've been jogging.

"Hope I'm not too late."

Time stands still. I turn slowly, and there he is. *Malachi.*

A neatly wrapped gift is tucked under his arm. He wears a crisp white T-shirt, dark jeans, and a fresh pair of Jordans. His black curls are edged up with a sharp temp fade, and a neatly trimmed beard frames his face. A gold chain shimmers at his collarbone.

My breath catches the moment I see him. Even though he's an hour late, all I can say is, "No. You're not."

He gives a single nod. "Good."

Silence settles around us, holding space just for the two of us. It's the kind of silence that pulls you in and doesn't leave room for anything else. His gaze drifts over me, from the worn sandals on my feet to the messy bun on the top of my head. My knees threaten to buckle, and I lean on the railing for balance.

My eyes dart away from his captivating gaze.

Because seeing him here again . . . it burns. All I can see is the blood soaking through his shirt, his eyes wide with panic the moment he realized he'd been shot. That memory is carved into my brain. *Forever.*

Since that night, everything between us has been altered.

"I didn't think you were coming," I manage to say. When I sent the invitation to his apartment, he didn't RSVP. Then he was an hour late. But I'm glad he's here.

"I wouldn't miss it for the world."

The first few weeks after being discharged from the hospital, he drifted away like a ghost. Locked himself in Zara's guest room. I'd show up, bring soup and comfort items, but he wouldn't answer.

It took another month before he started gradually coming around again. Even when he was physically present—mentally he was elsewhere. *Here but not really here.* That was my fault.

When he found another apartment, because his was nowhere near finished being renovated, he moved out. Zara begged him to stay with her longer because she was worried about him. We all were. *Are.* After going through what he did . . . he needed us.

But he assured us he could manage on his own. Now, I realize how he must've felt when I pushed him away, when all he wanted to do was help. My heart ached.

Zara says even Phoebe doesn't know where they stand anymore. She still comes around, but the chasm between the two is as obvious as night and day, I think because of the undeniable friction between her and Malachi.

Most days, he's holed up in his office at the Good Brew, staying hours after closing. I only see him at church . . . on the rare Sundays I can get there now with my busy schedule. He comes to Zara's house like usual, but he leaves early.

All of it is my fault. I should've never gone back home. If I hadn't gone back home, Malachi would've never been hurt.

"Thanks for coming," I whisper.

Another long pause.

He steps closer, his tall frame casting a shadow across me. "So . . . how've you been?"

I haven't seen him in two weeks because of my new job. Zara makes sure to take Liv to church with them every Sunday, so at least he still gets to see her often.

I meet his gaze, his deep brown eyes soft at the edges.

I clear my throat. "Shouldn't I be asking you that?" But what I want to say is, *Are you angry at me? Do you blame me for what happened?* And I want to tell him that I'm so sorry. That I bear that burden daily. Because even when he's around me, he doesn't stay in the room long. "How are you, Mal?"

His expression shifts. "I'm fine."

I glance at his shoulder. "How's it healing?"

His eyes follow mine to his shoulder where the bullet tore through him. He grimaces, his fingers instinctively reaching up to rub it.

"Better."

That's it? Better.

I nod, but it isn't enough. I want to reach in and pull more from him, make him talk to me, but that's not fair to him. I want to fix this, fix him, but maybe I don't have that right anymore. We haven't talked about what happened at all, dancing around the subject like it'll just go away if we ignore it.

"How are you doing, Asha?" he asks again.

The question feels too big coming from him. *How do I tell him that I hate myself? That I relive that night over and over again, and every time, it ends with him bleeding on the floor, his hand slipping from mine?*

"I'm good."

He hesitates at the door. His eyes widen slightly. I follow his line of sight and realize—this is his first time back here. The place where it all happened. I should've thought of that, should've opted to do it elsewhere.

"I can take it inside for you if you'd like," I say, nodding toward the gift.

He shakes his head. "No. It's fine. I can't leave without seeing Liv. She'll be mad at me." His lip twitches into a grin.

He creeps inside like the floor might crack beneath him.

Then suddenly—

"Mal!" Liv squeals, launching herself from Irene's lap.

She barrels toward him, arms wide. Malachi sets the gift down, scoops her up, and spins her around. He gives her a bright smile, one that I don't see often.

"I didn't think he was gonna come," Darnell says, stepping beside me.

"Me neither."

"The trial took a toll on him, plus the surgery and physical therapy . . ." Darnell sighs.

I nod, eyes fixed on Malachi as he tickles Liv. Then flashbacks of us being in the courtroom—hearing the words *attempted murder*—hits me like a freight train. Russell's face as the verdict was read. It haunts me. Makes my blood run cold.

"I did this to him," I whisper. My voice cracks like glass.

Darnell gently places a hand on my shoulder. "No. Russell did this."

He and Trina have become close friends of mine, helping out more than I ever expected. In this strange new life as a single mom, I've learned that I need all the help I can get.

The rest of the evening is beautiful. We unwrap Liv's presents. We dance. We laugh and eat some more. Liv falls asleep in Manuel's arms midway through a game of musical chairs, and he's out cold with her, their soft snores filling the room.

Ms. Mildred leaves early, mumbling about her blood pressure meds and needing her mid-afternoon nap. She kisses Liv goodbye before heading out the door. Zara and Irene take over the kitchen like they always do, cleaning, laughing, and helping me in ways that make my heart swell.

As I walk Trina, Darnell, and the kids out, I catch a glimpse of Malachi and Phoebe standing near the side of the house. The moment between them is heavy and unsure.

Phoebe's face is downcast, her arms crossed tightly, her lip trembling like she's fighting back tears. Malachi stands still, head bowed like he's saying a prayer, hands stuffed in his pockets as he kicks at the grass mindlessly. Whatever's happening between them, I hope they find a way through it. Malachi's been through so much, and if he won't let us in, maybe he'll let her.

"Thanks for coming," I say as Darnell finishes buckling Demetria into her car seat.

"Of course," he says with a deep chuckle. "The kids had a blast. They'll be out cold by the time we get home."

"Oh, they'll sleep in the car, but when we get home, they'll be wide awake. I'm pretty sure DJ and Drew will be doing backflips on the couch immediately."

"Luckily, we're already home so Liv will probably nap for at least two hours. I think she's still in the phase where she enjoys her naps."

"Demetria's over it. The only time she naps now is when her daddy walks through the door. They curl up on the couch together, but during the day it's like dealing with baby Jack-Jack from *The Incredibles*."

I burst into laughter.

I've babysat Demetria a few times, and she is very hyper, especially after breakfast.

"But hey, it is what it is. I'll see you later, girl." She gives me a quick hug before climbing into the car.

I wave as they pull off, then just . . . stand there.

The wind brushes against my skin like a whisper.

I close my eyes, and then everything around me begins to spin.

Red and blue lights flash behind my eyelids. Sirens scream from nowhere. My chest constricts, and when I look down, I see blood on my hands. It's bright red, sticking to the insides of my fingers.

A hand touches my arm and I jerk back, stumbling a little.

"Asha, you okay?" Malachi asks, Phoebe standing beside him with a worried expression.

I blink. The lights are gone. My hands are clean.

"Yeah," I whisper. "I'm fine."

These episodes come and go. I could be washing dishes, and all of a sudden, the water turns red. I could be driving by the precinct, and I'll swear I saw Russell heading inside. That's why I started therapy two months ago. My therapist is great . . . but I'm still waiting for the healing to stick.

"Thanks for inviting me," Phoebe says, giving me a quick hug. Her voice is soft, sad almost. "I'll talk to you later."

She walks to her car without looking back. Malachi watches her go, then turns his attention to the yard, which is overgrown and slightly wild.

"I can take care of this for you, if you'd like," he offers gently.

"No, no. It's okay. I've been meaning to ask Manuel or Akin, but I kept forgetting. Honestly, I'm embarrassed to admit I don't know how to work a lawnmower. Russell used to—" The name slips out quickly before I can stop myself. I brush a curl behind my ear, heat traveling to my cheeks.

I can't tell if hearing Russell's name affects him.

"It's okay. I don't mind. Just let me know when."

"Are you sure? You don't have to."

"I'm sure."

"Thanks," I say.

"You'll let me know when?" he asks.

"Yeah."

"Cool." As he turns and walks away, he pauses and looks back at me. "It was good seeing you."

"You too, Mal," I whisper so low I'm not even sure he heard me.

Chapter 29

"PANCAKES WITH SCRAMBLED EGGS and grits with cheese? The usual, right?" I ask, scribbling the order down for Mr. Bennett, one of our elderly regulars who's here every Sunday morning.

"That's right, sweetheart. And I'll take a black coffee, no sugar." he says with a chuckle, patting his round belly. "Trying to watch my figure."

I smile politely, then make my way behind the counter to hand the order to the cook. I've been working at Earl's Diner for three months now, and the only things I halfway like are the regulars who make me laugh and Brittney, one of the waitresses on shift. Although we don't talk outside of work, she makes this job bearable.

Grabbing the empty bucket and washcloth, I begin making my rounds through the diner, clearing dishes and wiping down tables. The breakfast crowd is just thinning out when I hear my name being yelled from the back.

"Asha! My office, please!" Mr. Wilbert, the manager, calls out from his office near the kitchen.

I roll my eyes.

Brittney walks past and grabs the bucket from my hands. "What now?" she mutters, already annoyed on my behalf.

I shrug and head toward the office.

Mr. Wilbert is short and in his mid-forties, with wide hips and a shiny bald head. His glasses sit low on his large nose, and he's always chewing grape-flavored gum. He's perched on the edge of his desk, arms folded.

"You wanted to see me?" I ask, closing the door. I don't bother sitting. The chairs have holes and smell like old mop water.

"You were late again this morning," he says, smacking his gum.

I press my lips together, already tired of this conversation. "I've communicated my availability multiple times. I've asked not to work Sundays because I want to attend church, and I have to wait until my friend can pick up my daughter."

"Well, everyone has to work when I schedule them. You were also late Friday night."

"Because my sitter isn't available until six on Fridays. I've already explained this." Between Zara and Irene, I try not to ask too much of them, and with Ms. Mildred getting older and having more doctors' appointments than she can keep track of, I try not to put too much on her. I know they'd be willing to help out more, but they're doing more than they should already.

"Sounds like you need to find a new sitter or put your daughter in daycare."

It takes everything in me not to roll my eyes again. I pinch the bridge of my nose, recalling how I didn't even want this job in the first place. But after sending out applications everywhere, Earl's was the only one that responded. Even though I have a college degree in education, I have no work experience . . . *thanks to Russell.*

I don't have access to any of his accounts, so all I've got is what was left in the safe at home, and that won't last much longer.

"I'll just figure something out," I say with a scowl. I hate that I let Russell convince me not to work. That I let him cut me off from being able to support myself and Liv. I should've used my degree and gotten a job at the elementary school like I had planned. Now here I am, grateful just to be able to afford diapers.

"Well, if you don't, this won't work out," Mr. Wilbert says, peering at me over the rim of his glasses. I force a nod and leave before I say something I'll regret.

If he gave me the schedule I asked for, we wouldn't even be having this conversation.

***

LATER THAT EVENING, AFTER being on my feet all day, I head to Zara's to pick up Liv and enjoy a home-cooked meal, something I haven't had the energy to make much lately.

"Sunday is for going to church and worshiping," I grumble as I step into her house. "I want to be there with you guys, but instead I'm getting coffee spilled on me and dealing with a manager who doesn't even know how to build a decent schedule."

Zara finishes changing Liv's diaper on the couch and places her gently on the floor. My daughter immediately toddles over to a fuzzy ball on the rug. "Mama—ball!" she shouts, picking it up and throwing it into the wall.

I giggle softly, resisting the urge to scoop her up in my coffee-stained uniform.

"You want to change?" Zara asks.

I nod. She disappears and returns with a soft oversized T-shirt and some joggers. I kiss Liv's cheek before heading to the bathroom to clean up.

By the time I come out, Akin's finishing the last touches on dinner. We gather around the table—me, Liv in her highchair, Zara and Akin across from me. Malachi would still be here, but he left early. I can't help but wonder if he doesn't want to be around me. Because he blames me for what happened.

We say grace before digging into a hot meal of baked chicken, cabbage, cornbread, and pinto beans.

"You should tell Mr. Wilbert he needs to respect the availability he promised when you were hired," Akin says, breaking his cornbread. "He can't just do what he wants."

"I've already told him. He doesn't care," I reply, stabbing at my cabbage like it offended me.

Zara sets her fork down. "You know, you could just work with Malachi. The cafe's closed on Sundays, and it's down the street from the gallery. Liv could even come during your shifts. Mom and Dad could help watch her there too. Malachi would definitely work with your availability."

I shift uncomfortably. "I'm not sure that's a good idea."

"Asha," she says gently. "He doesn't blame you. He's just . . . going through it. I looked it up. I think he has PTSD or something."

"I've been trying to talk him into therapy," Akin adds. "He says he has someone he's talking to, but I don't know who it is. He says he's fine, but I don't believe him."

I go quiet, guilt welling up in my throat.

"It's my fault. If I hadn't pulled you guys into my mess—"

"Don't do that," Zara interrupts. "You didn't ask for any of what happened. That's on Russell, not you. We just wish you'd told us sooner. That's something no one should have to go through alone." She reaches across the table, placing her hand on mine.

I nod, but the weight lingers in my chest.

"Don't worry about Malachi," she adds. "We'll take care of him. You need to focus on you and baby girl."

Working with Malachi would give me Sundays off. I could go to church again. Attend my counseling sessions without rearranging everything. Liv could be close. I may actually make more working there than I do at the diner. It might actually be . . . the better option.

"I'll think about it,"

Zara smiles.

"While you're thinking about it," Akin says, "how are you holding up with everything else? You heard anything else about Russell?"

My stomach knots.

I shake my head slowly. "No. Not since court. In all this time he hasn't reached out . . . and honestly, I don't even know what I'd say to him if he did."

They exchange a glance but say nothing.

I look over at Liv, who's babbling to herself with a mouthful of mashed beans. I lean over, wiping her cheeks with a napkin. I want better for her, to give her the childhood I never had. I'd do anything for her.

After dinner, I help wash the dishes. My back is aching, but I try my best to ignore it. It's the least I can do after everything they do for Liv and me.

By the time we pull into the driveway, Liv is babbling about a ball and a car. The porch light flickers slightly as we walk up to the door, and a strange wave of loneliness washes over me.

Walking into the house, I pause at the door. The silence is thick. Even though I know Russell's not here, some part of me still braces to hear his voice or feel his presence. It's unsettling how a place that once felt full now echoes with silence. If things had never happened the way they did, Russell would be watching the football game on the couch or roaming around the house, but now there's just stillness.

I move through the house carefully, locking every window and double-checking each door. I peek through the blinds twice, scanning the street for any parked cars or unfamiliar shadows hiding in the dark. It feels weird not having a man in the house.

With Liv tucked against my hip, I head upstairs.

I run her bath, adding lavender-scented bubbles and a few of her favorite rubber ducks and toys. As the tub fills, I sit on the edge and watch her play. Her chubby fingers wrap around a plastic cup as she scoops water and pours it out with a dramatic splash. A loud, innocent giggle bursts from her lips, and I can't help but laugh with her.

She's perfect.

Wild curls, tiny toes, soft cheeks that brighten when she's excited. I stare at her, wondering what her future holds. I think about how the choices I've made—who I loved, who I trusted—have already shaped the world she's growing up in. My chest aches with a combination of guilt and unwavering love. Liv can't grow up thinking chaos and pain is normal. I don't want that for her. She should only know peace, stability, joy, and love.

After drying her off and dressing her in a mint-green onesie, I lay her in the crib. She hugs her little plush bunny and blinks up at me as lullabies float from the baby monitor. I smooth her hair, give her a soft kiss on the forehead, and dim the lights. Slowly, I back out of the room, leaving the door cracked open.

My own shower feels like a release. I stand under the hot stream, letting the steam rise around me like a comforting blanket. I wash the diner's grease from my skin, scrub away the stickiness of exhaustion, and let my thoughts spill down the drain.

By the time I step out, my fingers are wrinkled. I wrap myself in a towel and sit on the edge of the bed, rubbing shea butter onto my arms and legs in slow circles.

The room is quiet. Empty.

I glance up at the wall across from me—the one that used to have a hole in it. Months ago, I had Akin patch it up as if I could erase the truth behind it. The truth I chose to ignore.

I wanted to make things work because I loved him.

Maybe I still do in some broken way.

But I never loved myself enough to walk away until it was too late.

I pull the towel tighter around me, swallowing the lump rising in my throat.

My phone lights up on the nightstand. I wonder if Zara is calling to check in.

An unfamiliar number flashes across the screen.

I freeze.

It's late.

My first instinct is to let it go to voicemail, but something in me whispers for me to answer it. My thumb hovers over the green button for a beat, and then I press it.

A robotic voice fills my ear:

"You are receiving a collect call from an inmate at River Falls Detention Center. This call is from—Russell Steffens. This call will be recorded and monitored. To accept this call, press—"

I don't press anything.

The phone slips from my hand and lands on the bed with a soft thud.

The sound of his voice when he stated his name sends a chill over my entire body.

He hasn't called once. Not when he was arrested. Not when his face was plastered across the news. Not after the trial. Months of silence, and now he calls.

My chest rises and falls too fast. My hand finds its way to my stomach, anchoring me, even as everything inside feels like it's spinning.

He doesn't get to do this to me.

But still . . . a small part of me aches to hear what he had to say.

Chapter 30

I'M SITTING DOWN ON the couch, my body half sunk into the cushions. One arm is draped over my stomach, the other resting limply by my side. My eyes are fixed on the yellow-and-white floral painting hanging on the back wall of the office.

The room smells faintly of old books and honey, with soft jazz playing low in the background. It's meant to be calming, I think, but it only intensifies the thoughts in my head.

Rachel sits across from me, her physique calm and assuring. A beautiful Black woman in her late fifties, with light brown skin that gleams softly in the warm light. Her hair is pulled into a sleek bun, a few silver strands catching the light. Her blouse is emerald-green today, a modest complement to the dark slacks that hug her long legs. One leg is crossed over the other, and her black heel points in my direction. She holds her notepad close, the pen in her hand moving in slow, deliberate strokes.

The sound of her pen scratching the notepad fills me with anxiety.

Sometimes I wonder what she's writing about. I imagine pages filled with harsh truths, summaries of all the things I've been suppressing. I wonder if she sees me as fragile. Or foolish. If she thinks I'm "emotionally unstable" or "insecure."

"So . . . how did that make you feel? Getting a call from Russell," she asks gently, her voice velvet-soft but firm.

Her eyes are on me, steady and patient. Not judging. Just waiting.

I trace my bottom lip with the tip of my tongue, trying to summon the right words.

"I felt . . ." I pause, deciding how much of the truth I'm willing to share today. "Sad. Angry. Scared." Then the one emotion that was more subtle. "And . . . hopeful."

I don't look at her. I can't. I keep my eyes locked on the painting, afraid of what expression will be plastered on her face. *Disappointment? Surprise?*

But Rachel hums low, and then the pen moves again. She doesn't speak right away. I've learned by now that silence is a part of her tactic. She leaves space, not to push me, but to let the rest rise to the surface.

I breathe in deep. "I regret not answering the phone," I admit. "It's been eating at me. I keep wondering why he called . . . wondering if he's okay. If he's scared. If he misses Liv."

A wedge grows in my throat now, making it hard to swallow. I gulp, but it doesn't budge.

"Even after everything . . . a part of me still cares. And I hate that. I hate that I still care."

Rachel just nods slowly.

"I shouldn't care, right?" I ask her.

She sighs, leaning back in her brown leather chair. "You know, Asha . . . people think that love disappears the moment someone hurts them. But that's not true. What you and Russell had, although messy, was real. You had a daughter together, a home and a routine. Even when the relationship became violent and unhealthy, the love you two shared doesn't just disappear. That's why so many survivors find themselves emotionally tethered to the very people who hurt them."

Her words land like bricks. But everything she said is true.

I press my fingers to the corners of my eyes, trying to catch the tears before they fall. "But I don't want to care."

"You can care about someone while still being angry with them. While grieving the loss of what you thought you had. These emotions don't cancel each other out—they coexist. The sooner you allow them to do that, the more you'll learn to manage them."

"But I don't know why I still care, when I shouldn't. He—" The words get stuck in my throat like jagged glass. I have to clear it before I continue. "He choked me. He beat me. He shot Malachi." My voice drops to a whisper. "He deceived me."

Rachel's eyes soften, and she leans forward a little. "We believe what we are shown. He showed you the version of himself that he needed you to fall in love with. That's not your fault, Asha. A part of you still cares because you believed in that version of him. You wanted that version to be real. Letting go means admitting it might never have been."

The ache in my chest swells until I can barely breathe.

Rachel flips back a few pages in her notebook, her pen resting on the arm of her chair. "You said something a few sessions ago." She flips through the pages, then reads aloud. "'If I would have been more supportive, asked fewer questions, been less stupid . . . maybe Russell would've never started drinking. Maybe he wouldn't have hit me in the first place.'" She looks up. "Do you still believe that?"

My lip trembles, and I shrug.

Rachel's voice softens even more. "This is not your fault. None of it."

And just like that . . . I start to cry. Not a silent, pretty cry, but a full-on ugly cry. My face scrunches, chest shaking, nose running. The kind of cry that comes from deep in the soul, which I tend to do every single session.

She pushes the tissue box closer, and I reach for it with quivering hands. She doesn't speak. She just waits, like she always does.

"It's hard to believe that," I whisper, voice cracking.

"Why?"

I don't answer. Because I don't know why. Because maybe I do still blame myself.

"Russell made his own choices, Asha. He chose to drink. He chose to lie. He chose to abuse his authority and hurt you. Just like Malachi made his own choice to come after you that night. You didn't make them do anything. Their actions are on them."

Her words hit hard. Like waves dragging remnants of guilt I've carried for too long back into the ocean.

"Grieve him," she says. "Grieve what you thought he was. But don't let that grief turn into shame. God can't heal what you won't let go of." She touches the cross pendant around her neck for a moment.

I sit up straighter, wiping my eyes and nose, tossing the used tissue into the trash can beside the couch. My elbows rest on my knees, fingers laced. I glance down at my worn black Converse rubbing against the carpet. My black tank top clings to my skin, and my jeans are ripped at the thigh and calf. My golden-brown skin used to glow—now it looks dull from stress. I barely recognize myself anymore.

Rachel sets the notebook down and leans in. "So, what's new?" she asks.

I let out a weak laugh, wiping the corner of my eye. "I quit my job."

She raises her brows. "What happened?"

"He scheduled me again for this Sunday. And then he denied my time-off request. I'm tired of not being respected. He accommodates everyone but me."

"Look at you." She smiles. "Setting boundaries."

I nod, then sigh. "Now I'm jobless. Zara thinks I should work at Malachi's coffee shop."

Rachel's eyes narrow thoughtfully. "And what do you think?"

I run a hand over my wild curls, catching my reflection in the mirror behind her. My daughter has the same hair. Darker. Thicker. But still wild like mine when I don't brush it.

"I told her I'd think about it. But honestly, I don't know if it's a good idea."

"Why not?"

I chew the inside of my cheek. "He's been so distant with me. After the shooting . . . everything changed between us. He talks to me when I'm around, but I don't know how to be around him anymore."

Rachel flips through her notebook again. "Tell me about the night you visited him. After his surgery."

I close my eyes. The memory stabs at me.

"It was late. When the paramedics left with Malachi, I jumped in the car with Akin and Zara."

My voice grows quiet, like I'm talking from somewhere far away. "Akin didn't say a word, but I saw the tears in his eyes through the rearview mirror." I press my palm against my thigh. "Zara cried the entire ride, and that broke me."

Rachel watches me closely, but she doesn't interrupt.

"When we got to the hospital, I was still covered in his blood." My fingers shake, just remembering. "My shirt . . . my hands . . . it was everywhere. I couldn't breathe. The walls were caving in on me."

I blink hard, trying not to cry. The image is still burned into my mind: Irene holding Liv tightly, rocking her back and forth in the waiting room. Her eyes red and swollen, like she hadn't stopped crying since the call. She whispered prayers to God. Manuel was on his knees, praying out loud, hands raised in surrender, repeating, "Dios salve a m'ijo!" God save my son! His voice cracked with each word.

I swallow the lump rising in my throat.

"Everyone else went in before me. I waited . . ." My lips press together. "And when I finally walked into the room . . ."

I stop. My mouth opens, but no sound comes out. I stare at the floor, seeing it all play out again like a video.

"He was shirtless," I whisper. "His shoulder was wrapped up and he looked so lifeless. His skin was dull, lips dry, and his eyes . . . red and glassy."

I blink again, and this time, the tears come. "He saw me and—he tried to sit up." My hands mimic the motion unintentionally. "I ran to him, begging him to stay still, to rest."

My voice cracks. I wrap my arms around myself, rocking slightly in the chair.

"I sat beside him, my hands at his side, crying so hard I couldn't speak. There were a million things I wanted to say, but the words got stuck. He looked at me, and he asked me if I was okay."

I can see it in my mind—his good arm lifted, fingers brushing my bruised cheek. "My face was still swollen from where Russell hit me. I'd forgotten all about my own pain. I was so focused on Malachi . . . but can you believe that? He'd just been shot but was worried about me." I cry some more. Silence sits heavy in the room.

"Before I could even answer him, Phoebe walked in." I exhale shakily. "And the way she looked at me . . . like this was all my fault. Everyone looked at me that way, or at least that's how it felt at the time. I couldn't take it. So I cleaned up in the bathroom, got Liv, and left."

My hands clench in my lap, knuckles white. "Phoebe had been working when they brought him in. She ran into the waiting room asking questions, crying, begging for answers none of us could give."

My voice lowers. "It took two weeks for all the bruises and swelling to fade from my neck. From my arms and ribs. But Malachi took months to recover—even now I think he's still in physical therapy." My shoulders sink. "If it weren't for me . . . maybe he wouldn't have almost died."

Rachel's voice cuts through the haze.

"This is weighing on you, Asha. Deeply. I think that's why you keep seeing him in your dreams. You're carrying guilt that isn't yours to carry."

She picks up her pen and scribbles something down. "So here's your homework."

I blink.

"Talk to him."

My heartbeat quickens. "What?"

"Not for him. For you. For closure, for peace and healing." Her tone is firm. "Don't bring up that night unless he does. Just talk. Like you used to. When the time is right, I believe the moment will present itself."

I nod slowly. My hands tremble in my lap. I rub them together. My voice is thin. "We do talk . . . but it's not the same." I look at her, eyes burning. "I'd go back and change everything about that night if it meant things could go back to the way they were."

Rachel smiles gently, then rises to her feet, brushing off her slacks. "That's the good thing about healing. They can. It just takes time."

"I see why Mrs. Charlene recommended you," I say, smiling. Somehow, I'm lighter than when I first came in.

"I'm glad you came. I think we're moving in the right direction."

"Two weeks?" I ask, standing slowly.

"Two weeks," she confirms.

Chapter 31

I'M SITTING OUTSIDE THE Good Brew, stomach tight, feeling like I'm going to vomit. My hands grip the steering wheel as I take slow, deep breaths, willing myself to get out of the car. I've known Malachi my entire life, and I've been here hundreds of times, yet a flutter dances in my chest.

He used to pull my pigtails in preschool. I called him "brace face" in sixth grade when he got braces. We went through college together and awkward phases. This is just a conversation. We don't have to talk about that night. *Not now. Not here*, I remind myself.

My phone buzzes. A message from Zara, with a photo of her and Liv at the park, pops up on my phone. Liv is mid-laugh, eyes squinting against the sun.

Zara: *You've got this! Good luck!*

I smile and take a final deep breath before stepping out.

Inside, the Good Brew is warm and welcoming. It smells like espresso, vanilla, and something rich and chocolatey. People are scattered throughout the shop typing on laptops, chatting over coffee, and reading books in corner booths.

I make my way to the counter, adjusting my purse strap on my shoulder. "Hi. Is Malachi here?"

The barista wiping down a cup looks up. "Yeah, he's in his office. Are you here for an interview?"

"Um, something like that. Can you let him know Asha's here?"

She gives me a quick once-over, then nods and disappears through the swinging door behind the counter.

Another employee offers me a polite smile. "Can I get you anything, ma'am?"

I shake my head. "No, thank you."

"All right. Just let me know if you change your mind." He waves the next person forward in line as I step aside.

A minute later, the barista returns and gestures for me to follow her. "He said to bring you back."

I follow her through the bustling space behind the counter, careful not to bump into anyone. Staff move like busy ants while working and laughing.

Malachi's office door is slightly ajar. When I step in, he straightens from his slouched position in a black swivel chair, surrounded by scattered papers and open books. His eyes land on me, softening instantly.

"Hey," I say cautiously. "Should I close the door?"

"Yeah. Sure."

I shut it gently and sit across from him. My palms are sweaty, so I rub them against my pants. I'm dressed casually—jeans, a loose T-shirt, sandals, gold hoops, and a couple of studs lining my ear. Nothing fancy, but just right for a warm day.

"You okay?" he asks immediately.

"Yeah. Yeah. I'm good." *Why is this so hard?*

A moment of silence passes, then I blurt it out. "I was wondering if I could work here. With you. I mean—just a regular job. I can make coffee, clean, bake cookies, whatever you need. I just . . . really need something stable right now. As you know, my last manager didn't respect my schedule. So, I quit. Zara thought maybe I should come here, and I know you're probably fully staffed, so if you're not hiring, I totally understand—"

"Asha," Malachi says, lips twitching into a half smile. "Slow down."

I suck in a breath and nod. "Sorry."

He leans back in his chair, watching me quietly. "Okay."

I blink. "Okay?"

"When can you start?" he asks.

I sit up straighter. "Wait, what? I didn't even apply. You don't have to hire me just because of my situation or the fact that we grew up together or because of Zara—" *And if you're still angry at me, I'd understand*, I want to add.

"I'm not hiring you out of sympathy or because Zara asked me to. I'm hiring you because I know who you are. I trust you," he says calmly. "You've got a degree, you're smart. You care about people. You're overqualified, honestly."

My shoulders relax, tension easing as warmth spreads through my chest. "Thank you," I whisper. "So . . . what do you want me to do? I can take orders, wipe tables, or whatever you need me to."

He clicks his tongue thoughtfully. "Actually, I had something else in mind."

"Oh?"

He leans forward, resting his elbows on the desk. "I've been meaning to hire someone for a Community Events Coordinator role," he says. "Someone to plan and organize outreach—open mic nights, book clubs, community brunches and donation drives. I want the Good Brew to be more than a coffee shop. I want it to be a place where people connect. But I haven't had the time or energy to make it happen."

He pauses, eyes flicking briefly to his shoulder. His voice drops slightly. "With everything going on . . . I think it's time."

"That sounds amazing," I say, heart racing. "You sure you want me for that?"

"You're thoughtful, organized, and you're likeable. It's a good fit. If you want it, it's yours. And if it doesn't work out, we can try something else."

I press a hand to my chest, overwhelmed. "Thank you, Mal. Really. I was scared to come talk to you," I admit.

"Why?" His eyes narrow.

"I . . . um . . . I just wasn't sure if you'd want me working here."

"Why wouldn't I?" His eyebrows furrow, head tilting to the side. I'm not even sure why I said anything. This conversation doesn't have to happen right now.

"Never mind. I don't know why I said that."

Thankfully, he drops it, but the curiosity in his expression lingers. "We'll figure out the pay and details later."

He rises, walking to the office door. I follow, hovering a moment.

"So . . . when do I start?"

He leans against the door frame, arms crossed. "I'll let you know."

And just like that, the air shifts. That space between us returns. He looks away, staring at something in the distance.

"Sounds good" is all I manage to say. "Did you still want to come by and cut the grass?"

"Oh, yeah. I've been waiting for you to let me know when a good time would be," he says.

"Does Friday work?"

He nods. "See you Friday."

As I step outside and get into my car, I do a little victory dance. I can't believe he gave me the job, one I didn't expect to get. But even in the celebration, guilt picks at my heart.

Because it's not lost on me that this is the same man who nearly died because of me. And still, he's been nothing but kind. Even when I lied to his face and said things I didn't mean. The guilt tries to linger, but I tuck it away and drive to the store.

I grab Liv's favorite juice, snacks, and a frozen cheesy pizza topped with pepperoni and beef. Tonight, we celebrate, and maybe tomorrow I'll figure out how to accept Malachi's unconditional kindness that makes me feel both seen and unworthy all at once.

After picking her up, we head home. I toss the pizza in the oven; we clean up and change into our pajamas. By the time the pizza is finished, we curl up on the couch in the living room. The day's stress melts away as I cuddle Liv in my lap, pressing tiny kisses to her cheeks.

"Mama got a new job today!" I squeal, hugging her tighter.

Tears brim in my eyes as I say it again. *I have a job.* One where I can give back and make a difference.

"We're going to be okay," I whisper.

"Mama," Liv coos, pointing at the warm pizza. "Eat—eat."

I laugh. "You read my mind."

We settle in, watching a cartoon filled with tiaras and sparkly dresses. At some point, we both doze off, Liv drooling on my shirt, her little body sprawled across my chest. One of my legs is lifted on the couch, the other dangling off. My hand cradles the back of my head as I drift into sleep.

But this time, the nightmares don't come. No visions of Malachi lying bloody and near death. No shadows lurking in the dark. Just peace.

I wake the next morning to the stiffness in my back and neck. The blinds let in a dim morning glow, and Liv is still asleep beside me, lips pouty and arms spread wide.

I slip away gently, careful not to wake her. I clean up the pizza box, juice cups, and snacks. Liv sleeps longer than usual, and I take full advantage. I fold laundry and clean the bathrooms before she wakes up.

When Liv finally wakes, she's all smiles and energy. I whip up French toast and eggs, and she devours it all.

After washing up, I dress her in blue overalls and a white T-shirt. As I close her dresser, my eyes freeze on a pink shirt shoved in the back. *Daddy's Girl* is written on the front of it. I trace the letters, my stomach twisting. Then I slam the drawer shut.

"Mama—park!" Liv beams, pointing at the door. "Go!"

I swallow the knot in my throat. "Yeah, baby. Let's go."

***

BY THE TIME WE arrive, the sun is bright, and the park is bustling with activity. A breeze keeps the May heat from being too much. Liv squeals as I push her on the swing, clutching the sides like we're on a rollercoaster.

"Up!" she demands each time the swing dips low, and I gently push again.

It doesn't take long before Liv is asking to get off and racing to the slide. She slides down by herself several times, her laughter echoing through the park. Once she grows bored of that, she notices a group of toddlers gathered at the sandbox. They're digging with colorful buckets and plastic shovels, their faces lit with joy.

A boy with chestnut curls scoots over to make room. Liv plops down beside him and grabs a shovel, immediately joining in. My heart swells. I love seeing her interact with kids her age—carefree, playful, innocent.

I take a seat on a nearby bench, keeping my eyes locked on her while a soft smile settles across my face. Reaching into my handbag, I pull out my Bible and begin reading from Psalms. The verses wash over me like a gentle wave.

While I'm reading, I notice a woman sitting on the bench across from me, eyes straining as she stares. She looks slightly familiar, but I can't place her. I offer a small, polite smile, but she doesn't return it.

Instead, she scowls, shoving her items into her purse. I remain seated as the woman storms over to me.

"You ought to be ashamed of yourself," she says, jabbing a finger in my direction.

I close the Bible and sit up straighter. "Excuse me?"

"My husband worked with Russell for years. There is no way those allegations are true. You don't know what you've done—you've ruined a good man's reputation. Women like you give the rest of us a bad name."

She can't seriously be defending him.

I recognize her now. I'd seen her at the precinct a few times, at department events like the badge-pinning ceremonies. We never spoke, though. Russell made sure of that. He always kept me close to his side, brushing off conversations he didn't personally initiate with anyone.

The only reason I ever got to know Darnell was because he was Russell's partner, and even that came with side-eyes and subtle warnings when we got home.

"I'm sorry," I say, calm yet dense. "But I'd appreciate it if you didn't speak to me that way. Especially not in front of my daughter."

She huffs. "You could've just kept your mouth shut. Now your daughter has to grow up without her father."

"You have no idea what you're talking about." I shake my head, my blood boiling.

"Russell was one of the best detectives in this county. And because of you, the whole community—and even the state office—are questioning the integrity of every officer he worked with, including my husband."

Her words cut like glass, and she says them loud enough that nearby parents start glancing over. Their stares send a cold shiver crawling up my spine.

"Maybe they should be questioned." I lean forward, my voice dropping so Liv can't hear. "Because if Russell could break the law and hurt me behind closed doors . . . there's no telling what he did on the job—with men like your husband watching his back."

Her mouth falls open.

I stand up, grabbing my things. The woman takes a quick step back, clutching her purse like she expects me to swing. But I don't. *I won't give her that.*

I bite my bottom lip so hard it stings—anything to keep from crying or shouting. I scoop Liv into my arms, her small body folding into mine like second nature. She clutches my shirt, sensing something's off.

We begin to walk away, and I pray that this is the end of it.

But it's not.

The woman yanks her son from the sandbox and follows behind me. "I hope you realize what you've done!" she calls after me.

I freeze mid-step. Liv buries her face in my neck. The last thing I want to do is end up in jail for assaulting this lady.

I turn just enough to meet her eyes. Her mouth twists like she wants to say more, but she doesn't. Instead, she spins on her heel, muttering under her breath as she drags her son away.

I sit back down on a different bench, heart pounding. The playground noise returns, but it's faint, like I'm underwater.

I cradle Liv closer, kissing the top of her curls.

That lady's words rub salt into my wounds, even though I wish they didn't. Anger spreads through me like wildfire, and it takes the rest of the day to calm down.

Chapter 32

"I CAN'T BELIEVE SHE had the audacity to approach you like that," Trina says, "Katherine has always been a pain in the butt. Darnell's told me so many stories about that woman it's not even funny. It's actually just sad."

"You're better than me," Irene adds, dragging both hands across the table in a dramatic motion. "I would've pulled her all across that playground."

"Mama," Zara scolds, sipping from her water bottle, "you know the Lord doesn't like ugly. Asha did the right thing."

I sigh, one foot tapping against the floor, the other propped up on the kitchen chair. "I'm just so tired of paying for Russell's mistakes. And then for her to verbally attack me and to accuse me of lying . . ."

Trina sits across from me, discreetly breastfeeding Demetria under a light blanket while nibbling on a few grapes.

"And in public too," she mutters. "I'm definitely going to have a word with Darnell. He can let Officer Whitley know to check his wife before I do."

I glance around the room at these women. *My circle. My support.* Zara and Irene have always been there, and now Trina's part of this sisterhood too. When Russell was around, I could never be this vulnerable.

Now, once a month, we all gather at someone's house or meet up for lunch. We vent, we pray, we dive into mini Bible studies. Sometimes we just cry. It's been healing. Refreshing. Everything I needed.

Liv plays in the living room, tossing her toys into a basket, only to dump them out and start over again. The sound of her giggles fills my heart with gratitude.

The window is cracked open. Birds chirp in the distance, but the low rumble of thunder warns of an approaching storm. Still, my mind is louder.

"Don't let her words get you down," Irene says gently. "Russell made his own decisions. Liv isn't going to follow that path because she has *you*. You're a great mother who's raising her right."

She reaches across the table and squeezes my hand. Her touch calms me.

"I hope so," I whisper, blinking back tears. "Until recently it feels like I've been failing her. I just want what's best for her. I want her to see my strength and to never settle."

"All of us good mothers want the same thing," Irene replies with conviction. "You do your best and let God handle the rest."

"So, Zara, how have you been?" Trina asks, shifting the conversation.

Zara smiles, setting her water bottle down. "Things are going great. The gallery's doing really well, and we are looking at partnering with a few art institutions in a few years. Akin's marketing firm is landing big clients." She clasps her hands together. "With how things are going, I think we'll be ready to start trying for our own little family."

Irene nearly bolts out of her seat. "Girl, don't play with me!" she shouts. We all laugh because Irene's been counting down the days for Zara to have a baby.

"I'm serious," Zara says, grinning. "Give us another year or two, and we'll be giving Liv a godsibling."

"I can't wait!" I say. "The way you and Akin treat Liv like your own, I already know your child will be so blessed."

By the time everyone leaves, the thunder outside has grown louder. Katherine's words keep replaying in my mind, but it's not what she said that bothers me. It's the uncertainty of Liv's future. The worry that somehow I might fail her. That she may follow in Russell's footsteps. Irene's words brought some comfort, but doubt still finds a way to creep in, like it always does.

Later when Liv is upstairs playing, a knock at the door causes my heart to jump. My friends are gone, and no one ever shows up unannounced.

Relief floods me when I notice Malachi standing on the porch.

I swing the door open, one hand on my rapid heart. "You scared me," I say with a nervous chuckle.

"Sorry," he replies. "I thought we agreed on Friday. The grass?"

"Oh, yeah. We did. I just forgot." I offer a shy grin. "I'm sorry."

"It's cool."

I shift from one foot to the other, licking my lips. "You wanna come in for a bit?"

He glances at the darkening sky. "I think I should get to the grass before it starts pouring."

"Yeah, of course."

He spins on his heel, heading toward his truck.

I close the door and walk to the kitchen. I try not to stare out the window, but it's impossible not to notice how his muscles flex as he pulls the lawnmower from the back of his truck. He's wearing joggers and a black T-shirt that hugs his shoulders and arms.

Heat rises up my neck. It takes everything in me to pull my attention away. I focus on prepping a quick dinner, which includes pasta with a side salad. I feed Liv in the living room while the steady buzz of the lawnmower hums in the background.

By the time I get Liv upstairs and give her a quick bath, Malachi's already finished the front yard. I didn't expect him to do the backyard, but there he is pushing the lawnmower through the overgrown grass.

I pause at Liv's window, which overlooks the backyard, and watch him for a moment. Liv's already in her crib, holding one of her stuffed animals. Malachi must sense me watching him, because he looks up, eyes meeting mine through the window. I pull back quickly, closing the curtain against the soft glow of the setting sun.

Thunder rolls across the sky as I tuck Liv in. I kiss her forehead, then slip into my room. Stripping down, I place my jewelry on the nightstand. My fingers hover over the engagement ring—Russell's ring. The one he gave me not long after he hit me.

It's still here. Still mocking me. I took it off that night I got home from the hospital, after I'd washed Malachi's blood from my hands. And yet, I haven't gotten rid of it.

I don't know why. I just haven't.

The hot water stings as it rushes over my skin, but I welcome the pain. I let it wash the weight of today down the drain.

Afterward, I slip into a sports bra, oversized shirt, and a pair of soft sweatpants. Downstairs, I pour a glass of water and grab some grapes. I'm just about to sit when the soft patter of rain starts up, echoing through the house like a hushed symphony.

The door jiggling makes my heart skip, but it's just Malachi, having finished the backyard as the rain started to pour.

"Sorry," I say as lightning flashes, briefly illuminating his drenched body. "I must've locked it out of habit."

He's soaked, water dripping from his curls, his shirt clinging to every line of his frame. His shoulders are tense, one hand gripping the door. He carries a black bag in the other.

I tell myself not to stare. But my breath still catches.

"It's all good," he says, brushing it off.

"Let me get you a towel." I rush to the downstairs bathroom, returning seconds later. I consider offering him clothes, but all of Russell's things have been donated. I wouldn't want Malachi wearing anything of his anyway.

He takes the towel, rubbing it over his hair, face, and neck. Then he walks into the house, wiping his feet on the welcome mat. He lifts the black bag. "I've actually got a change of clothes in here. Do you mind?"

I shake my head, watching as he goes to the bathroom.

I dart to a nearby mirror, suddenly checking my hair, wiping under my eyes, rubbing my lips together. *What am I doing?*

Malachi returns just as I stop.

"You can stay a while, until the storm calms down," I say.

"You sure?" he asks, setting the bag down beside the couch, his Adam's apple bobbing as he swallows.

"Yeah. Can I get you something to eat or drink?"

"Nah, I'm good."

His eyes flick to the living room, then back to me.

"We can sit in here for a bit," I offer, heading toward the kitchen.

We sit at the kitchen table. Again, his eyes drift to the living room before landing on me. "Did you have a busy day today?" I ask, trying to draw him back.

"Um . . . kind of. Ran some errands this morning, worked for a few hours. Then I had a meeting with Pastor Quinton before I came here." He clears his throat, like he wasn't sure he wanted to share that with *me.*

"Oh?" This must be who he mentioned to Akin.

"Yeah. He's been helping me work through some things."

It's the most he's shared in months. I smile a little. It's a start. I wonder if he's told Phoebe about this, or just me.

"That's good," I say softly. "His wife helped me a lot when things started getting worse. But I'm seeing a therapist now. She's great."

"Zara mentioned that. That's good."

I think about the therapist's advice: *talk to him.*

That was my assignment.

"Do you want to talk about the position? Monday is my first official day as Community Events Coordinator. I've been researching and preparing, but maybe you can give me more insight into your expectations."

"Sure. The job's full-time," he says. "But you can telecommute. I'd like you in the shop once or twice a week, just to stay connected to the team."

That flexibility means everything. I can stay home with Liv while working.

"Malachi, this is . . . amazing."

He leans in, arms resting on the table, the scent of rain still clinging to him—warm and earthy. "I don't micromanage. After your training, it's yours. Whatever you need, I've got your back."

I study his face. His eyes don't waver, but that ripple of doubt stirs inside me. "Are you sure you want me in this role?" I ask. "I mean . . . I know what it entails, mostly. But there's a lot of room for me to mess this up."

His brows draw together, not in frustration, but in confusion. "Yes. I'm sure. I wouldn't have offered it if I wasn't."

He shifts slightly in his seat, water droplets still clinging to the curve of his jaw. "Monday we'll do a full tour, introduce you to the team, and get you set up." His voice softens. "Any idea what you want your first project to be?"

I tap my nails lightly against the wooden table. I've brainstormed plenty of ideas—community dinners, art showcases, book clubs—but none of them feel like the one. Not yet.

"I'm still thinking about it," I admit, glancing down. "I want the first event to really count. It needs to make an impression. So . . . I just need a little more time."

"No rush," he says with a faint smile. He pulls out his phone, opens a document, and hands it to me. "Here's your contract. Look it over if you want."

I skim through it, and that's when I see it. My name, printed clearly, followed by a salary figure that makes my breath hitch.

My brows lift. "Mal . . . I think you made a mistake."

He leans in, close enough that his breath warms my cheek. I point to the number, waiting for him to realize the error.

Instead, he just nods. "That's right. That's your salary."

I blink in disbelief. "You can't seriously think I'm worth that much."

"You're right," he murmurs.

My heart sinks—until he lifts his smoldering gaze to mine.

"You're worth much more."

I forget how to breathe. Heat blooms in my cheeks. I glance away, reaching for my water. My fingers tremble.

With this salary, I can pay the bills. I can take care of Liv. This is surreal. *Thank you, God.*

"If I could pay you more, I would. But I've set aside a budget just for events this year. I want you to have the space to create something meaningful without worrying about funding. I want to support you, however I can."

I fan my shirt at the collar. "Is it . . . warm in here?" I ask, already checking the thermostat. It reads 71. Definitely not the house—*it's me.*

Back at the table, I try to calm my racing pulse.

"Any more questions about the job?" he asks, scooting closer.

I shake my head. "Nope. I think that's everything for now."

"Good. We'll go over more Monday."

But then I notice it, that subtle wince as he rubs his shoulder. He always does that when he thinks no one's looking.

My throat tightens.

I want to reach out. To help. To touch him. But I don't. Not here. Not in the house where he was hurt. And he's not mine to touch.

So instead, I whisper, "Does it hurt every day?"

His hand falls. He looks at me, startled. "No," he says quietly. "Not really. Just aches when it rains . . . like tonight. Some days it gets sore. That's all."

I nod even as emotion rises in my throat, impossible to swallow. So much I want to say, so much I've buried since the hospital.

And when the silence stretches too long, I panic. "How are things between you and Phoebe?"

The moment the question leaves my lips, I regret it.

Malachi freezes. Then slowly, he leans back and folds his arms. "We haven't been talking much. I mean . . . we're still friends. But I—" He stops, blinking hard.

"I'm sorry," I blurt. "I wasn't trying to pry. I just . . ."

"It's okay to ask." He meets my gaze. "Zara and my parents have been on me about it too. Said I've been shutting people out."

I say nothing. Because I've noticed that too.

He's been quieter. Distant, sometimes. A little slower to smile. *But who wouldn't be, after experiencing what he had?*

That bullet could've ended everything.

Could've gone through his heart.

Could've taken him away.

The silence stretches between us again, but it doesn't feel empty this time. It feels full. Heavy with everything we're not saying.

His eyes drift and his brows tug together slightly.

"That shirt," he says suddenly, voice lower than before.

"What?"

He nods toward me. "That's mine . . . isn't it?"

I follow his line of sight and blink, realizing what I'm wearing. A soft gray T-shirt, worn and slightly oversized. A faded coffee mug is printed across the chest with the word *Blessed* underneath it.

My mouth opens slightly. "Oh . . ."

The memory hits me all at once.

The date Russell canceled. My bruised hip. Crying at Zara's house and her offer of Malachi's clothes.

His slippers are still upstairs in the closet.

I glance up at Malachi again. "I forgot," I murmur, tugging at the hem. "You told me I could keep them."

His expression softens, lips curving just slightly. "Yeah. I remember."

I brush my fingers over the fabric, suddenly self-conscious. "It's comfy. I guess it just got folded into my laundry and stayed there."

A corner of his mouth lifts. "Looks better on you anyway."

The air shifts again, thicker and warmer. My pulse thuds in my throat. I don't check the thermostat. I don't need to. My heart's doing enough to make me sweat.

"You really forgot?" he asks.

I nod, a little breathless. "I forgot a lot about that night. Or maybe I just wanted to."

His smile fades, like clouds creeping across the sun. His voice cracks. "That night . . . I was worried about you."

"I know."

He hesitates. "That night you said you two just argued. But . . . was it more than that?"

My shoulders stiffen. I stare into the cup of water on the table, a light ripple spreading across its surface. My voice doesn't come, but I nod once.

Malachi lets out a slow breath and leans forward again. His jaw clenches, and his eyes close. "I wish I could've done more."

I reach across the space between us, my hand brushing his shoulder before I can talk myself out of it. His eyes open slowly.

"You saved my life," I whisper. "You've done more than enough."

Chapter 33

AFTER CHANGING MY CLOTHES a hundred times, I finally settle on a white button-up with the sleeves casually rolled up to my elbows, wide-leg khakis that fall just below my ankles, and clean white Nikes. I considered heels but didn't know what the rest of the day would look like. Comfort easily won.

I slide on my usual jewelry, small gold hoops and diamond studs climbing my ear and my mother's necklace from her box. I grab the gold bracelet Malachi gifted me last Christmas and put it on. I pause for a moment, brushing my fingers over the delicate charms. Even though it was a simple gift, it made me feel . . . special.

I finish getting ready with a few stacked rings and a final glance in the mirror. My curls are freshly defined, parted slightly to the side, falling past my shoulder in soft coils. My makeup is light and natural looking.

Trina's watching Liv today. She wanted to have a playdate with her daughter and picked her up an hour ago so I could have time to get ready. I didn't realize how nervous I'd felt until now.

It's just Malachi, I remind myself. I've known him my entire life. There's no reason for me to be nervous, right?

By the time I arrive at the Good Brew, the place is packed. The morning rush is in full swing. A line stretches nearly to the door, every seat is full, and the staff are a blur of motion from taking orders, steaming milk, and wiping down counters. The air is warm and fragrant with the smell of espresso, vanilla, and donuts.

And there he is.

Malachi's standing behind the front counter, sleeves pushed up, black apron slung around his waist. His light brown skin glistens slightly from the heat and movement, and his focus is intense as he scribbles names on cups and prepares orders.

The owner, right there in the mix with his team. It stirs something in my chest.

He spots me from across the room, and a soft smile spreads on his face. He waves me toward the back. I make my way to the counter, hesitating.

"I can wait," I say as I approach. "You all seem really busy."

"You don't have to wait. Go ahead and sit in the office. You're a part of the team now," he says. "I'll be back once we get through this rush."

I nod, strangely reassured by his tone. As I walk toward the back, several team members greet me. A few smiles, a wave or two. I feel . . . welcomed. Like I belong.

I wait in the office for about fifteen minutes before the door creaks open. Malachi steps in, his shoulders slightly slouched from the weight of the morning chaos. He lets out a tired breath and flashes a quick grin.

"Is it like this all the time?" I ask.

"Mostly in the mornings between seven and eight, then again around lunch, and right after five. But we manage. I figure I'd train you in everything just in case you ever want to help out on the floor."

I smile, nerves prickling at my skin. "Perfect."

He sinks into the leather chair behind the desk, the sound of keys clicking quickly filling the space as he logs into the system. He grabs a folder from the corner of the desk, my name printed neatly on the tab.

"All right. Let's get down to business."

The next half hour is a whirlwind. Malachi gives me a tour of the shop, and it turns out to be much bigger than it looks from the front. The break area is cozy with two tables in the middle, chairs pushed in neatly, a long couch pressed against the far wall. A refrigerator and microwave sit beneath a shelf of mugs, and a bookshelf is tucked in the corner with a soft rug beneath it.

He walks me through the small conference room, the employee restrooms, and the back exit that leads to the alley behind the shop.

Then we circle back, and he introduces me to the seven employees working the morning shift. Everyone's kind, smiling, cracking light jokes, and offering hugs.

"Glad to have you be a part of the team!" says Wynter, a petite girl with bright hazel eyes and box braids twisted into a high bun.

"Malachi's told me so much about you," Greg adds, bumping Malachi with his elbow and giving me a playful wink. "Didn't tell me how beautiful you were though."

"She's too old for you," Wynter says. "No offense!" She gives me an apologetic grin. "You are gorgeous!"

"Thank you," I respond. Malachi glances at me with a sheepish look, rubbing the back of his neck. The gesture makes my stomach flip just a little.

After the intros, we return to the office and go over the menu, the ordering system, and the basic responsibilities of each role. He explains opening and closing procedures, then hands me a few printouts. One for upcoming events, another for budgeting guidelines.

"So," he says, "whenever you're ready, we can start planning your first event. You'll fill out one of these for every event. List the details, theme, projected costs, and put it on my desk for review. The only thing I'll be checking is the budget request. Once your probationary period is over, you'll have access to the funding accounts directly."

I nod, absorbing every word. It still feels surreal. Just a few months ago, I was a stay-at-home mom, and recently I was clocking long hours at a diner with stained toilets and microwave meals. Now, I'm sitting across from my friend, someone I've known since forever, being trusted to coordinate events for his successful coffee shop.

"Thanks again. I'm so excited," I say, smiling. Then I pause, fingers twisting slightly as I lean forward. "I actually had an idea for our first event."

He perks up. "I'm listening."

"Okay, so . . . I have a few, but these two stood out." I take a breath, tucking a curl behind my ear. "The first is an open mic night. Something warm and creative. We could dim the lights, create a cozy stage vibe, invite people from the community to share poetry, spoken word, acoustic sets or whatever moves them. I was thinking we could call it 'Voices at the Brew' or something like that."

Malachi's brows lift, intrigued.

"And the second idea is more service-focused," I continue. "We could do a canned food drive with the church. Maybe set up a donation station here in the shop and collect food for the homeless or low-income families. I want us to give back to the community. Plus . . . it lines up with the heart behind what you built here."

He leans back slightly in his chair, nodding slowly, weighing both options.

"I like them both," he says. "One builds community. The other serves it."

"Exactly." I smile. "And maybe we can do both. Start with the open mic to build momentum and follow it up with the food drive. We can announce it after and start taking donations."

A slow smile spreads across his lips. "This is why I hired you." The way he looks at me sends an unfamiliar warmth through me that I can't explain.

After sitting in the back of the booth sipping on a latte and eating a muffin, I finish a rough draft for the first open mic. Excitement courses through me as I think about how fun it's going to be.

I go ahead and make a note to talk to Mrs. Charlene and Pastor Quinton Sunday after church about the donations.

"Need anything?" Malachi's voice cuts through the quiet.

I tap my pen on the edge of the table and glance up. "No, I think I'm good."

"All right," he says, sliding into the seat across from me.

He's sat this close plenty of times. But today, it feels . . . closer somehow. I shift in my seat, brushing it off.

"I was thinking, you could use the office while you're here," he says, nodding toward the back.

"I don't want to be in your way."

"I don't mind. But if you need a quiet place, you can use it. Or if you'd feel more comfortable, you can use the conference room when it's free."

I nod. "Thanks." I'm not sure where I'll spend my days working, but I am considering the options.

My fingers fidget with the bracelet he gave me, and he looks down at it—his eyes lighten and he smiles . . . maybe because I'm wearing it.

Malachi looks up, eyes widening slightly as he looks at something or someone behind me. I glance over my shoulder, surprised to see Darnell walking inside.

"Hey, man," Malachi says, standing up to bump his fist with Darnell's.

"Hey," he says. "Trina told me I could find you here."

"Everything okay?" I ask.

Darnell's eyes dart between me and Malachi, and I know what this is about. Who this is about.

"Can we talk for a minute? Somewhere private," he asks.

I get up, grabbing my things.

"We can use my office," Malachi offers. Darnell follows us behind the counter, and when we get to the office, Malachi stands at the door. "Do you want me to stay?" he asks.

Darnell shrugs his shoulders. "Yeah, sure."

My heart flutters when Malachi steps inside and closes the door.

"I went to the jail to see Russell," Darnell says, his voice low. "He's been calling nonstop." He shifts his weight, eyes dropping for a second before continuing. "Russell got beat up pretty bad. I mean, being locked up with people you used to put away . . . it was bound to happen."

The question rises in my throat before I can stop it—*is he okay?* But I swallow it down. That part of me doesn't exist anymore. He doesn't hold that place in my heart. "What does this have to do with me?"

"He wants to see you," Darnell says. "He wants to talk."

The room goes still. The air thickens, pressing into my chest like something too heavy to hold.

I blink, heart pounding in my ears. "He wants me to come?" *So that's why he called me.*

Darnell nods. "Yeah."

I press my back against the wall. My head swims with memories I've tried to bury of Russell's violent hands. His fists, his voice rising above mine, his eyes cutting through me like I was nothing. I've spent months trying to forget that version of myself. The one who tiptoed around him. The one who flinched at slammed doors.

"No way," Malachi says, stepping between us like a shield. "She's not going."

Darnell throws up his hands. "I don't like it either. I'm not saying she *should*. I'm just saying . . . he asked. Maybe it could give her closure."

I stare at the floor, trying to ground myself. But my body's already betraying me. I'm covered with chills, my hand instinctively rubbing my neck, remembering how it felt when he wrapped his hands around it.

Tears sting the corners of my eyes. The room sways.

I *don't* want to see him. Not after everything he did.

I *hate* how even now, he makes me feel small . . . afraid . . . but maybe if I face him, I can finally leave it all behind.

A firm hand settles on my shoulder. "Asha, you okay?" Malachi asks gently, his eyes searching mine.

He's worried. Protective.

"You don't have to do this," he says.

But I do.

"I'll do it," I whisper.

Chapter 34

NOW THAT I'M OLDER, I understand why my mother kept me rooted in church. She knew there'd come a day when she wouldn't be here, but He still would. She knew I'd need Him. And she was right.

Now, it's my turn to pass that on. No matter where life takes Liv, I pray she'll always find her way back to Jesus. Just like I did.

Working with Malachi has been one of God's greatest blessings. Having Sundays off means no more missing church. Not just for the music or the familiar faces, but because here, in God's house, I feel closer to Him.

I know He's with me everywhere, but there's something about walking through these doors . . . a peace settles over me. One I thought I'd never feel again.

And the Word—oh, how I crave it now. Even one day without prayer, without scripture, feels off. Like I'm not fully myself.

As Pastor Quinton closes the service with an altar call, people shuffle toward the front, carrying their Bibles and notepads.

I lift my hands, tears sliding down my cheeks. Not because of the job. Not even because of this peace. But because God is so good.

There was a time I couldn't see that. When it felt like my storm would never pass. But now, on the other side, I see what I couldn't before. He never left me. Not once.

The pew shifts beside me as Malachi rises slowly, his eyes glistening with tears of his own. He steps past me, careful and quiet, and makes his way to the altar. When he kneels, hands lifted, head bowed, my breath catches.

He's surrendering. Finally.

And something in me breaks open. I want that too. I want to forgive Russell. To let go. To forgive myself. To live free.

I stand and follow. Not even thinking, I stop near Malachi, not on purpose, but maybe not on accident either. I close my eyes—a single tear escapes.

"God, I give it all to You," I whisper.

After the service, while Zara and the rest of the crew take Liv home to start dinner, Malachi and I hang back.

Pastor Quinton and Mrs. Charlene finish greeting the last of the congregation and wave us into their office. The room smells faintly of clean linen and coffee. We sink into the comfortable chairs across from them.

"Asha, you look so . . . different. Full of joy," Mrs. Charlene says, reaching for my hand. Her palm is warm, her voice even warmer. "How have you been, baby?"

"Thank you. I've been doing better."

"I knew you could do it," she says with a knowing smile, squeezing my hand gently.

Pastor Quinton lets out a chuckle as he shifts in his chair. "So, Malachi, you here to tell me you two are getting hitched?"

"What?!" I laugh, caught completely off guard. "Oh my goodness!"

I glance at Malachi, who's already trying and failing to hide his grin. He clears his throat, adjusting his tie. He glances at me and shakes his head. "Actually, we're here to talk about a community project," Malachi says, turning the conversation over to me.

After regaining my composure, I open the folder on my lap, smoothing the flyers inside. My heart races, but I clear my throat and dive in.

"We want to start a neighborhood canned food drive," I explain. "We'll have donation bins set up at the Good Brew and here at Truth Center Ministries. All the donations will go to local families in need, the homeless, low-income families . . . anyone who needs help."

I describe how we also plan to partner with a soup kitchen, hosting a dinner event to distribute extra goods.

The more I talk, the more excitement builds in my chest. It spills over in my words, my hands moving as I paint the vision.

I want more than a one-time project. I want a partnership with ongoing support. A real community.

When I finally stop talking, my face is heated with embarrassment.

But Pastor Quinton's eyes gleam with pride. "Now that's how you pitch an idea," he says.

Mrs. Charlene smiles so bright it reminds me of sunlight. "It's an incredible idea. The church would be honored to partner with you."

"We've needed more hands, more hearts willing to do the work," Pastor Quinton adds. "You two might just be the answer to some prayers."

My heart swells. Maybe this is what God's been preparing me for all along. And this is just the beginning.

As we wrap up the details, Pastor Quinton glances at me thoughtfully. "You know, Asha, we've got an outreach team that could really use someone like you. If you ever want to get involved, say the word."

I nod, smiling.

When we finally head outside, Malachi walks ahead with Pastor Quinton, deep in quiet conversation.

I linger by the doors with Mrs. Charlene. "I wanted to thank you," I say. "That day I showed up here months ago . . . the way you spoke life into me, I've never forgotten it."

"That wasn't me," she says softly, touching her heart. "That was the Holy Spirit." She squeezes my hand again. "I'm so glad you're still here. That you made the right decision, even though I know it cost you."

After a moment, she adds, "After we heard the news, we prayed for you. Every day. You and Malachi both."

Tears sting the backs of my eyes. I blink them away.

"I know I wasn't coming to church for a while. It wasn't because of what happened. Things were intense, then I started working at the diner near the shopping center," I explain. "But now, with Malachi at the Good Brew . . . God's leading me somewhere I never even thought to go."

"God is good," she murmurs.

Her words are laced with a soft fierceness. "When all hell breaks loose around you, baby, that's usually when God's up to something big."

We glance over at Malachi and Pastor Quinton, still in quiet conversation by the car.

"He seems like a good man," Mrs. Charlene says, watching Malachi. "My husband speaks very highly of him."

"He is," I say without hesitation. "A wonderful boss. And a great friend."

Mrs. Charlene gives me a knowing look, one eyebrow arching high. Heat creeps up my cheeks.

Malachi pulls the car around and hops out to open the door for me. His hand brushes mine briefly, but it's enough to send my heart skittering.

"Have a good evening, Pastor and First Lady!" he calls out, waving before closing the door carefully.

I sit there, stunned for a moment as he jogs back around to the driver's side.

What . . . just happened? Did he just open my car door? It's just Malachi. He's always kind. *Don't overthink it, Asha,* I tell myself.

We drive in comfortable silence for a while until Malachi glances over at me.

"You're the right person for the job," he says simply. "You did an amazing job in there."

"You think so?" I ask, a ridiculous surge of giddiness spreading through me.

"I know so. Pastor's already brainstorming new ideas to run by you next meeting."

I let out an excited squeal, and Malachi laughs. A real laugh, one I haven't heard in a long time.

"It's good seeing you smile," he says softly, eyes flickering to me before focusing back on the road.

"You too," I murmur.

***

DINNER WAS GOOD AS usual. I'm stuffed and satisfied. We're all relaxing in the living room now, Liv asleep in Zara's room. The laughter has died down, and we're just sitting there in comfortable conversation.

I glance around the room, staring at their faces. I know I can't keep it to myself any longer. After surrendering to God this morning at church, I made up my mind.

I sit up, licking my lips. "I'm going to see Russell tomorrow," I blurt out, ripping it off like a bandage.

Zara stiffens beside me—Akin frowns and leans forward in his seat. Malachi doesn't move, but his gaze darkens slightly.

"I know I shouldn't ever speak to him again . . . but I need to. I have to hear him out. I have to see what he wants. And I need to do this for myself."

"Asha . . ." Zara starts, her voice heavy with worry.

"I'm scared," I admit, the words falling from my lips like weights. "I don't want to see him. I never thought I'd have to again. I never imagined raising Liv without him . . . but here we are. And I can't let him have this power over me. Not anymore."

Malachi moves to sit on the opposite side of me, putting me between him and Zara. He places a hand on top of my knee, reassuring and comforting. "I'm going with you," he says.

And for some selfish reason, I want him to.

Chapter 35

"THANKS FOR SEEING ME on such short notice," I say, stepping into Rachel's cozy office.

She waves me in, smiling warmly as she gestures toward the couch, the one spot that somehow feels safe even on the worst days.

"I always try to be available for my clients," she says, crossing one leg over the other, her green-framed glasses sliding a little down her nose. "Luckily, my morning appointment was rescheduled, so we've got time. What's going on?"

I sit down, stiff-backed, trying to ignore the way my heart is about to punch a hole through my chest.

I lick my dry lips, my voice coming out too fast. "I'm going to see Russell," I say. "Today."

Rachel freezes for a second. Her eyes go wide, lips parting like she's not sure if I'm serious. "That's . . . interesting."

I lean back, picking at a loose thread on my jeans, and start filling her in on Darnell's visit.

She listens without interrupting, her face unreadable. When I finish, she taps the arm of her chair lightly. "I see," she says quietly. "Do you really think he'll talk?"

I shrug. "I think he just wants to see me."

Rachel's gaze sharpens. "Do you want to see him?"

I press my lips, caught off guard.

"Do you want to see him so you can finally move on with your life?"

"I mean . . . I *have* moved on. It's just—" I pause, staring down at my hands. "It feels like he still has this hold on me."

Rachel watches me carefully. "How do you feel about seeing him?"

I open my mouth, then close it. She reaches for her notebook on the table beside her, then picks up her red pen. She scribbles something down.

I'm about to walk into a burning building with no way out.

"Do you want the truth," I ask, forcing a shaky laugh, "or some half-truth to make it sound better?"

Rachel chuckles. "Let's keep it real, Asha."

I pick at my nails for a second before I answer. "I'm scared," I admit. "I'm nervous. I don't know what to expect when I see him."

Rachel nods. "It's completely normal to feel that way. You're walking into a situation that once caused you a lot of pain and fear. It's okay to be scared."

I swallow the lump in my throat. "I just . . ." I hesitate, searching for the words. "I'm hoping after today I can put this behind me. I don't want to be scared of him anymore."

She tilts her head slightly. "Is that the only reason you're going?"

I look down at my hands, at the raw bitten skin around my thumb. The real answer hides deep beneath the surface of my heart, but it's too heavy to ignore.

"No," I whisper.

"And . . ."

I draw a suffocating breath. "I need to do this. I need to show him that he didn't win. That he doesn't control me anymore. Even if I'm still scared . . . even if seeing him brings all of it back . . . I need him to see that I'm not broken. I need him to know that I've forgiven him."

Rachel leans forward a little. She speaks with a firm voice. "You don't have anything to prove to him, Asha."

The words should feel empowering, and maybe someday they will, but right now, I still feel like some small child. "I know," I whisper. "But I need to face him. So I can move on with my life."

Rachel nods, seeming to understand more than I can explain. "Malachi's going with me," I say after a moment.

Rachel raises an eyebrow. "Malachi? Given . . . everything, are you sure that's a good idea?"

"He insisted. He's not coming inside the room. He's waiting in the lobby. Darnell will be there too."

Rachel hums thoughtfully. "It's good Malachi's being supportive. You shouldn't have to do this alone." She scribbles something on her notepad again, then looks back up at me. "And how have you been since things between you two started to feel normal again? Plus, you're also working with him now."

Warmth creeps into my chest, up to my neck to my cheeks. I duck my head, trying to hide the tiny smile I can't hold back. "It's been . . ." I search for the right word. "Good. Better than good, honestly. He's always been kind, but working with him, we've been spending more time together."

Rachel smiles knowingly. "Oh, really?"

I nod "Yeah, almost every day."

Rachel sets her notebook and pen aside, her fingers interlocking as she leans back slightly. "Just an observation I've had over our last few sessions, since things with you and Malachi have gotten better." She adjusts her glasses, smiling thoughtfully. "You seem, I don't know, happier?"

"Yeah, I guess I am."

Rachel's smile grows. "You deserve that, you know."

My eyes burn, and I have no idea why I'm on the verge of tears. "It's just different," I say after a moment. "With Russell, it was like walking on eggshells every day. I was constantly trying not to upset him. Trying to keep everything perfect."

"And with Malachi?" she prompts gently.

I breathe out slowly. "I don't have to try so hard. I don't have to be perfect. He's always been a part of my life, and then this situation happened. But now . . . things are different. Better. He makes me laugh, trusts me, and confides in me. It's so natural."

Rachel nods, studying me carefully. "That's what safety feels like Asha. That's what I call love."

Chapter 36

"I DON'T KNOW IF I can do this anymore," I say, heading for the exit. Darnell stands up abruptly, moving to block my way, his hands lifted in a calming gesture.

"Asha," he says carefully. "I know this is hard. But you're already here."

Behind me, Malachi's presence is a towering anchor. "She doesn't have to do it if she doesn't want to," Malachi states.

I glance over my shoulder at him. His hands are shoved into the pockets of his dark jeans, the fabric of his neatly ironed polo stretched across his chest.

I notice the faint dark circles under his eyes, and a sharp pang of guilt twists in my stomach. Maybe it was selfish of me to allow him to come. To ask him to be in the same building with the man who almost took his life.

"I'm sorry," Darnell says, sincerity written all over his face. "I know this isn't easy for either of you. If you don't want to do it, we understand. All he's asking for is five minutes. You don't even have to speak; just hear him out."

I chew on my bottom lip, searching Malachi's face for an answer I know he can't give.

Rachel's words float through my mind from our session just hours ago. *You don't have anything to prove to him, Asha.*

And she's right. I don't have to do this, but I'm going to. I don't have to prove anything to him anymore, but I need to look him in the eye. To prove to myself that he doesn't control me anymore. *You can do this.*

Even though I repeat the words to myself like a prayer, they don't ease the churning sickness in my stomach or the heaviness pressing down on my chest.

"Okay," I whisper. "Let's just get this over with."

I turn toward the door, but my feet hesitate, almost as if the air around me has thickened into concrete.

Darnell scans his badge. The heavy door buzzes and swings open, revealing a narrow hallway with cold gray cement walls that seem to shrink the farther we walk.

"I can come in there with you," Malachi says behind me.

I swallow hard, forcing back the tears burning at the corners of my eyes.

I can't cry. Not here. Not now.

I shake my head. "I can't let you do that, Mal."

His hand gently grazes my arm. "Asha—"

"No, Malachi," I cut him off, my voice cracking. "That wouldn't be fair to you. You shouldn't even be here right now." I take a shaky breath, blinking up at him. "You can't keep saving me."

"I'm just trying to be supportive," he whispers, sadness bleeding into every word.

"I know." My chest contracts with guilt. He's been nothing but good to me, and here I am pushing him away, *again.* I squeeze his hand gently. "Thank you, Mal. But I need to do this alone."

"I'll be right here."

The hallway stretches endlessly before me. Every step feels like dragging my body through quicksand. When we finally reach a door on the left, Darnell scans his badge again.

Inside, it's even darker. The small room is warmer than the hallway, almost suffocating. A thick glass window cuts across the far wall, and on the other side, chained to a bolted-down metal table, slumped in a chair too small for his frame, is Russell.

The sight punches the air from my lungs. Breathing suddenly feels impossible.

"He can't see you from here," Darnell explains. "When you're ready, go through that door. I'll be right here. He's chained. He can't get to you."

It's meant to reassure me, but it doesn't. My skin crawls. I move closer to the glass, heart pounding painfully in my chest. Russell's hands, those same hands that once held Liv so gently, that once held me with love, now rest, shackled, on the table. But those were also the hands that bruised me, choked me, and broke me.

Russell's hair is wild, tucked into uneven cornrows. His beard is longer now. His eyes are closed, head tipped back like he's sleeping, but the tension in his body tells me otherwise.

I rest my hand lightly against the wall beneath the glass and inhale deeply. *God, please help me. I know You're with me. Please help me not to be afraid anymore.*

A special verse, 2 Timothy 1:7, comes to mind—*God has not given me a spirit of fear.* And for the first time in a long time, I believe it.

I exhale slowly, steel my nerves, and step toward the door.

As soon as the door clicks open, Russell's eyes snap wide. For a second, it looks like he's about to stand, but he doesn't.

"Asha," he breathes, genuine surprise flashing across his face.

I fidget with my fingers, forcing myself forward until I sit across from him. Up close, he looks different. Thicker around the middle. A fading bruise under one eye and a cut on his lip.

He scratches under his bruised eye, then lets out a dry, humorless laugh that makes my skin crawl. "Perks of being locked up with guys you put here yourself," he says. "But don't worry about me. I can handle myself just fine."

I'm not worried. Looking at him now, shackled and worn down, I just feel . . . sorry. Now he knows how he made me feel. What it's like to be beaten and bruised.

"How've you been?" he asks.

I don't answer. My mouth is so dry, I'm afraid the words will crack.

"It's like that, huh?" He nods, almost like he expected it. "How's Liv? How was her birthday? I imagine she misses me."

"She's fine," I say sharply.

He leans back in his chair, sighing. "I miss her like crazy. I think about you two every single day."

My heart twists painfully. I know he misses her. There were times, early on, when I missed him too, before I remembered the bruises, the fear, the nights spent crying on the floor.

"We're both fine," I say firmly.

Russell studies me. His eyes linger on my blue floral dress, my pearl earrings, the delicate bracelet on my wrist. Malachi's bracelet.

"You look good," he says, that familiar sly smile tugging at his lips. "Lost some weight?"

I stiffen. Fury bubbles up inside me. His words threaten to open old wounds, but I don't let it. It's evident he's trying to get under my skin.

"I'm not here for compliments," I say flatly. "I'm here because you said you needed to talk. You wanted me here, so here I am."

His tone sharpens, controlling again, just like before. "How's everybody else? Zara? Akin? Malachi?" The way he spits Malachi's name makes my stomach drop.

"They're fine," I say, then add, maybe a little cruelly, "Malachi's here with me."

Russell's nostrils flare. His whole body tenses. "Of course he is," he mutters. He looks up at the ceiling, searching for words. "He's always been . . . fond of you." His eyes darken. "You know . . ." His voice drops. "I never meant to hurt him. Or you. I was drunk. Angry. Outta my mind. If I'd wanted him dead . . ." He looks up, eyes cold. "He would be. I don't miss."

The chill that runs down my spine reminds me exactly who I'm dealing with. "You almost killed both of us, Russell."

He slams his chained hands against the table. I don't flinch. Not this time. Tears well up in his eyes. "You don't think I know that?" Russell snaps, veins bulging from his neck. "I know what I did! I think about it every day!"

"Things could've been so different," I whisper. "I tried so hard to be the woman you wanted me to be. I followed your rules. I stayed when I should've left. But it was never enough. None of this is my fault. It's yours."

Saying it aloud lifts a weight from my soul I didn't know I was still carrying.

"I tried to get help. I really did. When my mom's boyfriend killed her, it broke me," he rasps. "You know that. I never wanted to be like him. I swear to God, Asha—I never wanted to be that man."

He presses the heels of his hands to his eyes, wiping the tears away like they shame him. He runs a hand over his hair. His voice breaks. "I wanted to be better for you. For Liv. I tried. I wanted to give us a better life. I'm sorry. I'm so sorry. But I'm glad I'm locked up, because if Malachi hadn't shown up that night . . ." He hesitates. "I probably would've killed you too."

The words slice deep, but I force myself to stay strong. I swallow hard, blinking back tears.

"Russell," I whisper. "I was so angry at you. I hated you after everything you did. But I want you to know . . . I forgive you. For the drinking. The hitting. The lies. I forgive you for it all."

I pause, taking in a deep breath. "That night, before Darnell and the cops showed up . . . I had the gun. I could've pulled the trigger, Russell." I meet his eyes. "But I didn't."

A glimmer of hope lights his eyes until I keep going.

"I prayed for you. Every day. That God would help you and heal you. That He would save you. But there's no place for you in our lives anymore. Liv has a family who loves her. Forgiving you doesn't mean forgetting. It doesn't mean trusting you again."

His mouth twists into a sneer, but it quickly crumbles into grief. "You can't keep my daughter from me."

"I'm keeping her safe," I correct. "And when I leave this room, you won't see us again. Goodbye, Russell," I say, standing.

"Asha, please—" he croaks. "Don't do this! You can't keep her from me!"

But I'm already walking out.

An officer badges me out—Darnell stays behind.

I don't feel heavy anymore. I don't feel stuck. I feel free, lighter than I've felt in months. My heart pounds, but it's steady.

When I step into the waiting area, Malachi shoots to his feet and rushes forward, eyes wide with worry. Without hesitation, he pulls me into his arms, wrapping me up tight.

I bury my face in his neck, his heartbeat drumming against my own.

"I'm proud of you," he whispers into my ear.

Chapter 37

I'M HEALING. AND FOR the first time in what feels like forever . . . life is good.

Bills are no longer a crushing weight, thanks to my new salary. Liv has everything she needs and more. Things at the Good Brew are blossoming, and in just a few days, we'll be hosting our first open mic night. I've even got a surprise planned for the end of the night, something none of my friends will see coming.

After so many months in the dark, I'm finally stepping into the light. And it's beautiful.

I get Liv from the babysitter and head home.

When we arrive at home, I fix Liv a simple lunch and put her down for a nap. Her soft snores are the sweetest sounds in the world. I head for the shower, scrubbing away sweat and tension under a stream of hot water that fogs up the mirror. Then I slip into leggings and an oversized tank top, ready for a nap of my own, but there is work to be done. The open mic night is just a few days away, and I have to make sure everything is perfect.

Knock. Knock. Knock.

I rush to the door, surprised at the visitor waiting on the other side. *Phoebe?*

Her blonde hair is pulled into a ponytail, and she's still wearing scrubs. No makeup except a bit of mascara and lipstick. She looks tired.

My eyebrows furrow.

"Hey, Asha," she says.

"Hey." I glance behind her almost instinctively, half expecting to see Malachi or Zara. But she's alone.

"Sorry to pop in unannounced. I hope I'm not interrupting anything."

"Not at all," I say, stepping aside. "Come in. Can I get you something to drink?"

She shakes her head, arms crossed over her chest as she walks in. Her eyes are glassy. Her lips tremble as she takes a seat on the couch.

Something is off. My chest tightens with unease.

I sit beside her, careful to leave space.

"Is everything okay? Is Malachi okay?" I ask carefully.

Her head snaps toward me, eyes sharp. "He's fine. That's actually . . . why I'm here. I need to talk to you. About him."

My heart stutters. "Phoebe, if you're worried I know something about your relationship, I don't. Malachi doesn't really talk to me about you two." I say it gently, trying not to assume too much. I know things have been strained between them since the incident. The first time I saw them together again was at Liv's party . . . and even then, it didn't look like things were going well.

"I know," she whispers, swallowing hard. "You probably noticed we're . . . not really a thing anymore." She wipes her nose with the back of her hand. "I thought this time would be different," she says. "I thought this relationship would be the one. But the truth is . . . it was never going to work out."

"I'm so sorry, Phoebe."

She gives a weak smile. "I'm not. We both deserve to be loved wholeheartedly. And I'm glad he told me the truth instead of letting me keep hoping for something that was never going to happen. The night he got hurt . . . it just confirmed everything I'd already suspected."

"Suspected?"

She nods slowly, tears beginning to slip down her cheeks.

"This might sound crazy or jealous, but I'm not trying to be. The way he looks at you, Asha. The way he always talked about you . . . it made me feel invisible."

My breath catches. "I never knew you felt that way, Phoebe. I mean, Malachi and I have known each other since we were kids."

"I know," she says with a shaky voice. "But it felt like I was always competing for his attention when you were around. Then, when you weren't around, it was as if something was on his mind, like he was thinking about you."

"I don't know what to say."

She laughs, bitter and soft. "That night you showed up at Zara's. After you left, he couldn't even finish the movie. He went straight to his room. He seemed so worried. He cares for you more than I think he knows how to say."

I stare at her, stunned into silence. Words refuse to form in my mouth.

"Even before I met you, he talked about you. I saw the way he looked at you at Zara's grand opening. You left before he could introduce us, but I noticed."

I shake my head slowly, disoriented. "We are just friends. He's never said anything to me."

"No. Because he respects you. And maybe because you were with Russell at the time. But Asha, come on, have you ever asked yourself *why* Malachi didn't like him? Even before he knew what Russell had done to you?"

I pause. I never really had.

"From what I heard he didn't like any of your boyfriends. You think that's just a coincidence?" She tilts her head gently. "He was jealous."

I lean back, folding my arms tightly across my chest. My heart is racing.

"I'm not trying to make this awkward," she says softly. "I just think you deserve to know."

"Know what exactly?"

Phoebe hesitates. Then her voice breaks. "The night he got shot—the first person he asked for when he woke up was you. Every single night in that hospital, he had nightmares. And every time, he cried out *your* name."

My breath hitches like I've been punched in the chest. This is my first time hearing this, and I'm not sure how to feel about it.

"That's not even the hardest part," she whispers. "He took a bullet for you, Asha."

The world tilts. I grip the cushion to steady myself, tears suddenly stinging my eyes.

"I don't think he ever expected anything in return," she continues. "But someone who takes a bullet for you . . . someone who carries your pain like it's his own? He loves you."

He loves me?

I don't know how to process that. Everything in me is unraveling.

She stands and smooths her scrubs. "I already talked to him. He didn't know I planned to come to you. But I had to say this for my own peace. You must think I'm crazy, right?" She chuckles sadly.

"No," I whisper. "Of course not."

I stand up, chewing on my bottom lip.

She walks over and takes my hand. "Don't let Russell's mistakes keep you from being loved right. If a man took a bullet for me, I'd be all over that in a heartbeat." I know she's trying to make light of the bombshell she just dropped, but I have to force a smile.

Guilt eats away at me. I can't believe she's felt this way all along. *What kind of friend was I to not see it?*

She pulls me into a hug. "Take care of that sweet girl of yours."

Then she's gone.

The front door shuts behind her with a quiet click, and I just stand there, dazed. My mind is spinning. *None of this feels real.*

Why couldn't I just say it? No, I don't have feelings for Malachi . . . right?

But a quiet voice whispers back, *Are you sure?*

My thoughts spiral as I think of all the times Malachi was there for every heartbreak, through my mother's death, and for Liv's birth. He'd been the first to see the bruises Russell left behind. He's always seen me. Protected me.

Even now, he's here. He gave me a job with an amazing salary. He came to my house after he'd experienced something so traumatic here. He showed up even when he didn't have to. Malachi came with me to see Russell just to make sure I wasn't alone.

The memories press down on me.

I stumble outside, gasping for air. The sunlight feels too bright. I lean against the porch railing, pressing a hand to my chest, staring down at my bracelet as it glints in the light.

Chapter 38

I'M SITTING ON THE back porch, legs pulled up to my chest, wrapped in a sweater. The night breeze carries a chill, and I pull the sleeves over my hands, tucking my fingers in.

The screen door creaks open behind me. Zara steps out, balancing two mugs. "Malachi made this calming tea. It's so good, I already had two cups."

She gives me one, and I curl my hands around it, letting the warmth seep into my skin. I stare at the steam rising in swirls before vanishing into the air. "Thanks."

"This is why I miss having Malachi live with us. He was always in the kitchen." She laughs softly, settling into the chair beside me. "Right now, he's inside making an apple pie."

I manage a small smile. "He makes the best pies."

I take a sip, and she's right, it's good. The tea has an earthy and sweet taste with a warm cinnamon finish that lingers on my tongue.

"I haven't seen him this way in a long time. He seems happier lately." She slides closer to me and nudges my knee with hers. "How are *you* holding up? You look . . . surprisingly calm. It must have been hard seeing Russell."

The Asha from earlier this year would be having a complete meltdown all while isolating herself away from those who matter most. I'd be depressed and terrified.

I inhale slowly. "I'm just tired, Zara. Of being scared. Of waiting for something bad to happen. My life, it's changed so much. Some of it was awful, yeah, but some of it has been beautiful too. Seeing Russell again made me realize he only had power over me because I gave it to him. And I can't keep living in fear. God is doing something new in me, I can feel it. And I don't want to waste it."

Zara smiles, her eyes warm. "Look at you. All grown up and getting in the Word of God. You started working for my brother and now you're living like a Proverbs 31 woman." An expression crosses her face that is far too smug to be innocent.

I burst into laughter. "What was that?"

"Nothing," she says, taking another sip. "I'm just saying . . . I'm glad Malachi's coming around more."

"I beat myself up for a long time because of what happened to him. I still can't believe he did that for me."

Zara sucks her teeth. "Shoot, nobody told him to follow you back home that night. But girl, I hate to say it. That man would walk into a burning building for you."

"No, he wouldn't." I say it too quickly, like I'm trying to convince myself more than her. "He's just—he's always been kind. Protective. That's who he is."

Zara gives me a pointed look and rolls her eyes. "Sure. He's that way for *everyone*, right?" She raises an eyebrow.

I avoid her gaze and focus on my tea, which suddenly feels too warm in my hands.

"I forgot to tell you, Phoebe came by earlier," I say, steering the conversation elsewhere.

Zara's head snaps toward me. "That's not weird at all." Her voice drips with sarcasm. "What'd she want?"

I hesitate, scratching the back of my neck. *How do I explain that Phoebe, of all people, came here to drop a truth bomb I wasn't ready for?* So instead of filtering or sugarcoating, I just tell her everything, word for word.

By the time I'm done, Zara's eyes are huge, and her jaw is practically unhinged. "*Shut up*," she squeals. "No way that actually happened."

I nod slowly, some of the burden lifting now that someone else knows. If anyone can help me untangle this, it's her.

"I hate that it came from Phoebe," she says, "but seriously, *about time* someone told you."

I choke on a sip of tea. "I'm sorry—*what?*"

Zara grins. "Malachi has been in love with you since he was pulling your pigtails in kindergarten. This is not news."

I blink at her. "Okay, I think I'd remember that."

"You don't remember how your mom used to tease you? Say you two would get married someday?"

I shake my head, smiling faintly. "I vaguely remember her joking about that. We were like eight."

Zara shrugs. "Doesn't matter. Everyone knew. Even when I started dating Akin, he thought you two were already a thing. Malachi has always looked at you differently. Even Mom would say how she wished you'd just leave that no-good man alone and date someone like Malachi."

I laugh despite myself because I can definitely hear Irene saying something like that.

I go quiet, staring through the back window. Inside, Malachi is at the counter, sleeves rolled, focused as he moves around the kitchen. Akin says something, and they both laugh. And suddenly I feel like I'm standing outside of a story I was part of all along but never realized.

"How did I not see this?" I whisper.

Zara doesn't answer right away. Then, gently, "The real question is, do you have feelings for him too? But you're my best friend so I already know the answer."

The words land in my chest like a stone. I don't answer. Not because I don't know, but because I realize I've been trying to ignore them. It's all somehow terrifying.

Because if I'm honest with myself, it's not just that he took a bullet for me. It's not just the way he shows up or the way he makes Liv laugh. It's not the job or the quiet safety I feel when he's nearby. It's deeper than that.

It's the way he's always seen me. Even when I didn't know how to see myself.

I think back to my sessions with Rachel, the way she'd sometimes smile when I talked about him, like she already knew something I hadn't put together yet.

And now that I let the possibility of it settle in my heart, I can't unsee the signs.

Like the little tugs in my chest when he dated someone new. The subtle ache I'd bury so deep I convinced myself it wasn't real. I remember the night at the gallery, Phoebe beside him. I'd told myself that I was just curious, but I wasn't. I was longing. I felt it again the night they came to my house and Zara introduced them as a couple. That sting wasn't just surprise. It was betrayal. Not because Malachi owed me anything, but because something in me, hidden and quiet, had desired him long ago.

And it all makes sense now.

He even remembered my favorite chocolates—the strawberry fudge-filled ones he'd bought me for Christmas. I never told him they were my favorite; he just knew.

A realization blooms inside me. This thing between us has always been there. Waiting for the right moment to take root. And it took everything with Russell, the abuse, the pain, the silence between us, for me to finally see it.

Our lives had taken different turns—I met Russell, had Liv, and got swept into something I thought was love. Malachi was focused on opening his coffee shop. We were on our own paths.

But now we're here. Both of us are single, carrying scars from our past. And I know how he feels. The amazing part about it is that I feel the same way too, and I don't think I can keep pretending I don't.

Zara jumps to her feet, her face lighting up like a Christmas tree. "Oh my gosh! We're going to be sisters!"

"Z!" I grab her wrist, dragging her down beside me, my finger pressed to my lips. "Stop before they hear you!"

"Sorry, sorry," she whispers, though the grin on her face says otherwise. I can practically see her mentally planning our wedding and Liv's flower girl dress.

The back door creaks open, snapping us out of our laughter. The guys step onto the porch.

"Hey," Akin asks, eyeing us, "you two all right?"

Zara clears her throat, trying to suppress her excitement. "Yeah. We're all good."

"You ready to go, babe?"

Zara looks at me, squeezing my hand as she stands. "I'll see you both at open mic night this weekend!" She plants a playful kiss on Malachi's forehead before disappearing into the house with Akin.

"Good night," I call out. "Drive safe, lovebirds!"

"Night!" they both call, and the door shuts behind them. I just know Zara is telling Akin everything in the car.

Malachi still stands in front of me, thumbs hooked in the front pockets of his jeans. The porch light catches in his eyes, and for a second, he doesn't speak. He just looks at me like he's trying to memorize this moment.

I tuck my legs beneath me, suddenly feeling like a schoolgirl with a crush far too big to hide. His gaze lingers a moment longer, then he sits down beside me. His knee brushes mine.

A spark jolts up my leg. I freeze, breath caught, and dare a glance at him to see if he felt it too. But he's already glancing out into the quiet of the night.

"It's a little chilly out here," he says.

Without waiting for a reply, he slides off his jacket and gently drapes it over my shoulders. His fingertips graze the back of my neck, light and warm, and my body betrays me with a shiver.

I inhale sharply, barely masking the sound. "Thanks," I whisper, fingers clinging to the soft sleeves. "For everything."

"No problem," he says with a deep voice. His words wrap around me like the warmth of his jacket.

When I glance up at him, his eyes are already on me. His gaze is intense and aching. It's so familiar my heart throbs. I've seen it a hundred times before but never had the courage to believe it was real.

Now I know. I feel it. *Oh my . . . I do have feelings for Malachi. How did I not see it?*

I break our gaze before the emotions swallow me whole. My fingers twist into the fabric of his jacket to anchor me.

"Can I talk to you about something?" His voice is rough, and the nerves are obvious.

"Of course," I manage, heart thudding wildly.

He leans forward, elbows on his knees, head bowed. His foot taps a restless rhythm on the ground. I don't rush him. I just wait.

"Life's short, Asha." His voice cracks on my name. "It's hard for me to talk about what happened. That day . . . when I followed you back here, I was terrified. I thought he was going to hurt you again, and I couldn't let that happen."

I gulp.

"Seeing him grab you like that . . ." Malachi shakes his head, hands clenched together. "I hated him. I hated him in a way I didn't know I could. I wanted him to suffer for what he did to you."

I don't even think before my hand reaches for him, resting gently on his back. His shoulders are tense under my touch, but he doesn't pull away.

"When he shot me," he continues, voice quieter now, "I could hear you crying. I could hear him hurting you. And I couldn't move. I was bleeding out, and all I could do was pray. I begged God, begged Him to save you, because I couldn't."

Tears slip down his cheek, and he wipes them away with the back of his hand. In all our years, I've never seen him like this before. So vulnerable and exposed.

"And God did. He saved you," he breathes, almost to himself. "But after that . . . I pulled away. I had to distance myself."

"Malachi," I whisper, my hand still on his back. "I understand. I'm not mad."

He lifts his head, eyes rimmed red. "But I was. I was mad at myself for feeling so much. For caring so deeply. It scared me." He swallows hard. "Because even after all that, I didn't regret taking that bullet. Not for a second."

I press a hand against my chest, trying to calm the wild flutter of my heart.

"I would do it again, Asha. A thousand times. Because keeping you safe, being there for you, that matters more to me than anything else. And that scared me too. That loving you . . . could cost me everything, and I'd still do it without hesitation."

Wow. Phoebe was right.

I stare at him, the air thick with emotion. My pulse pounds in my ears.

"I didn't want to tell you how I felt," he admits. "Things were still complicated with Phoebe. And there was a lot going on. I didn't want you to feel obligated. I wanted you to choose on your own. To heal. To breathe. To come back to yourself. But the truth is . . . I never stopped wanting to be the man you felt safe with."

Something inside me cracks open. The dam I'd been building to protect myself from Russell, every layer of numbness, every wall, they crumble under the weight of Malachi's words. I feel seen. *Wanted.*

My lip's part to speak, but nothing comes out at first. I clutch the edge of his jacket tighter.

"Mal—" I start, but the rest gets caught in my throat.

Then, it happens.

An invisible thread pulls us together like gravity. The space between us shrinks without warning, and his eyes flick down to my mouth. There's a pause, just long enough for doubt to flicker in, just long enough to feel the air thicken around us.

"I don't know if you feel—"

Before he can finish, I close the space and kiss him.

It's not rushed, not desperate. It's soft, slow, and tender. But underneath it, a yearning storm breaks inside me. My hand lifts to his chest instinctively, fingers curling into the fabric of his shirt like I need something to hold on to.

Malachi's hand finds my face, cradling it gently, his thumb brushing just beneath my eye as the kiss deepens.

I sigh against his mouth because this feels like nothing I've ever felt before. Even though I can't explain it, this feels right.

Chapter 39

I'M SITTING AT THE kitchen counter sipping on my tea as the morning light spills softly through the curtains, casting a golden glow across the room.

I haven't felt this way in a long time.

My fingers drift absentmindedly to my lips, and I catch myself smiling. It's been a few days since the first kiss—the one that made me whole again. And every kiss since has felt like the very first one.

I keep replaying it in my head: the way his hand caressed my face, the way he kissed me like I was fragile and sacred all at once. Hands that were tender and safe. Hands that would never hurt me.

Even when we are working together or around others, our eyes speak in a quiet language only our hearts understand. Any moment we can steal alone, we do, sneaking quick kisses that melt my insides. I catch myself wondering how I ever went so long without feeling something this soft . . . this safe. I never knew I could feel this whole.

For the past few days, he's been coming over. And at night, when it's just the two of us, Liv upstairs asleep, we do our best to set boundaries. Boundaries that are hard to keep but so important to our faith.

We haven't really talked about what this is or what we're becoming. We're still cautious, unsure how or when to include Liv in all of this.

I can't wait for the day we can share this openly. To show our friends, his family, the truth: something's brewing between us. Something we may not know how to name just yet, but it's real. And it's growing.

Every morning, Malachi comes over to make breakfast. He leads us in prayer, and afterward, we lounge on the couch or take walks at the park with Liv. It's become a routine, one that feels effortlessly familiar, as if things have finally fallen into place. It's strange, but it feels like we've been living this way all along.

Liv's still curled up in her crib beneath the thin blanket, one arm wrapped tightly around her stuffed bunny, the one her father gave her. The sight of it stirs something bittersweet in my chest.

She'll grow up not knowing him, even though he's alive. That reality still stings. But I know it's for the best.

"Good morning, beautiful," Malachi says as he walks into the house, wearing a slightly wrinkled beige button-up, blue jeans, and a fresh pair of white shoes.

"I love it when you call me that," I say, blushing. "Good morning."

He rounds the counter where I'm sitting, and my eyes lift to meet his just as my stomach does a backflip. His hand slides gently to the back of my neck, and his lips find mine.

The cup nearly slips from my hand. Just as quickly as the kiss begins, he pulls away. "Any plans for this morning?" he asks casually.

I place a hand on his chest, still a little flustered. "Nope. Just preparing for open mic night. You?"

"I've got a meeting with an investor at nine." He opens the fridge and grabs a carton of eggs. Breakfast is usually his thing, while preparing dinner is mine.

"You're going like that?" I nod toward his wrinkled shirt.

"Oh, yeah. I didn't have time to iron it."

"That's okay. I can do it for you."

"Are you sure?" he asks, pausing.

I extend my hand, waiting. I'm not sure if he's going to give me the shirt now, letting me see him shirtless, or grab a different one out of the room. I've seen him shirtless before, but not since we've started . . . whatever this is.

Slowly, he begins to unbutton the shirt, starting from the top, revealing his toned chest. He slides it off his shoulders and hands it to me. I keep my eyes down.

I take the shirt to the laundry room where the iron and board are already set up. I run the iron over the fabric quickly, trying to compose myself before going back to face a shirtless Malachi. I've always admitted he's handsome, but now that truth is taking on a whole new meaning.

When I return to the kitchen, his back is to me—broad and strong. The morning sun casts a golden sheen across his skin. My gaze drops to his shoulder.

And I see it. The scar.

It's round and slightly indented. It's a shade lighter than the rest of his skin. My breath catches. It's a reminder of everything he risked for me.

He turns slightly, and our eyes meet. I shift, instinctively taking a step back. "I'm sorry," I say quickly. "I didn't mean to stare. I just . . . I hadn't seen it before. Not until now."

Tears sting the corners of my eyes.

His expression softens, and he turns to face me slowly. He sets a whisk and bowl on the counter. "It's okay," he says gently. "You can look."

I lower my gaze, unsure if I'm crossing a line. Then his footsteps approach. When I look up, he's standing in front of me. So close my heart flutters.

Malachi takes my hand and carefully places it against the scar on his shoulder. His skin is warm. The texture beneath my fingers is slightly uneven but still smooth.

I swallow. "I hate that he did this to you."

His breath grazes the top of my ear as he leans in. "I already told you, Asha. I'd do it again. As many times as I need to."

My hand lingers on his shoulder as I close my eyes, centering myself in the weight of this moment.

His fingers glide along my neck, tilting my chin gently. Before my gaze meets his, I see his toned abs and hard chest. "I've been looking at this scar every single day since it happened, and every time I do all, I think about is you."

And when he kisses me again, it's everything.

He kisses me with hunger and desperation. Like he knows exactly what this means.

When we finally part, I can barely catch my breath. I bite my lip, surprised by how this kiss is just as electric as the first.

Malachi steps back and puts the shirt on like he didn't just completely undo me. "After tonight, maybe we should talk about what this is. If that's okay with you."

I smile, my chest rising with quiet hope. "I'd like that."

***

THE GOOD BREW IS full of energy and anticipation.

I'm moving nonstop, checking on every detail. The tables have been rearranged to make room for a small stage in the front, with a soft rug, a tall stool, and a simple mic stand. Twinkling lights hang across the ceiling, giving the space a cozy glow. The scent of cinnamon and fresh espresso lingers in the air.

"Mic check, one, two," the sound man says as I lean in beside him, adjusting the levels. "I think we're good to go."

"Perfect, thank you!" I tap my phone and check the schedule.

"Jazz playlist ready?" I ask Wynter. She gives me a thumbs-up. I nod, satisfied, and turn, only to catch Malachi leaning against the counter, arms folded, watching me.

There's that smile again.

"What?" I ask, arching an eyebrow as I walk over to him.

"Nothing." He shrugs. "I just wish I could kiss you right now," he whispers, low enough that no one else hears.

"Maybe later," I say.

"I just love seeing that beautiful smile on your face. You've been glowing all day."

I try to hide the grin, but it's hopeless. My cheeks warm as I glance down. "Maybe our kiss this morning has something to do with that," I say.

"That's definitely a good reason to be happy."

"Shouldn't you be working on something? This starts in fifteen minutes, you know."

"Don't worry," he says, lifting both hands in surrender. "Everything's handled. You did that."

I shake my head, a smile tugging at the corners of my mouth as I walk away, heart skipping.

One by one, familiar faces begin to walk through the door.

Zara and Akin come first, both dressed in warm earth tones and looking stunning together. Trina and Darnell follow, Trina already snapping photos of the space while Darnell heads to the coffee bar. Irene and Manuel walk in just after, holding hands. Mrs. Charlene and Pastor Quinton arrive minutes before the show begins; they'll announce the upcoming canned food drive when the night wraps.

Through the window, I spot Ms. Mildred holding Olivia's hand. I blow her a grateful kiss before returning to my post near the stage.

By the time the lights dim and the music fades into silence, the place is packed. More guests than I expected fill the chairs, with others standing against the walls sipping warm drinks and nibbling on cookies.

I take a deep breath and step up to the mic, my nerves dancing in my chest.

"Good evening, everyone," I begin, my voice a little shaky. I hadn't realized how nervous I'd be, standing in front of all these people. "Thank you so much for coming out to our very first Open Mic Night here at the Good Brew, which we will call Voices at the Brew. Our goal tonight is to create space—for honesty, expression, healing, and most of all . . . love."

A ripple of applause. Then we begin.

First up is a young woman named Kiera, who shares a powerful piece on acceptance and God's love. Her words send a chill up my spine as she talks about loving yourself and seeing yourself the way God does.

Next is Julia, delivering a heartfelt poem about overcoming obstacles. Her voice trembles as she speaks, but by the time she finishes, goosebumps trail my arm.

After one more performance, I step back to the center of the stage.

"We've already heard some amazing voices tonight," I say, heart pounding. "You all have been incredible, and tonight feels like a dream."

Snaps echo softly around the room, making me smile.

"We've got one more piece before we wrap things up," I continue. "And . . . this one's mine."

Gasps echo through the crowd. I catch Zara's wide-eyed surprise, Trina already holding up her phone to record. Malachi leans forward, his smile shifting into something softer, more curious.

I take a breath and begin.

"I call this poem 'Escaping the Shadows':

Shadows can only exist in the presence of light.
They are dark and scary,
Inflicting pain and heartache that linger in your soul.
While you hide in a corner,
It's a loud song that you sing every single night,
Hoping that one day the flicker of light
Becomes so bright
It erases the presence of darkness.
It held me in captivity, wrists bound in a dark room—
A constant reminder of the four-letter word called pain.
And where that pain lay,
A suffocating shadow followed,
Blinding me, holding me underwater
Making it impossible to escape.
It wasn't the darkness that scared me most,
But the monster that lived there . . .
The one that tried to dim my light,
And the only way to become free
Was realizing the monster didn't have control over me."

I glance at Malachi as I read with raw emotion.

"But as long as I stayed in the shadow—
in the pain, the misery—
healing and hope
couldn't deliver me.
I found the light.
In the midst of the storm,
in the middle of pain and scars . . .
It's finally time for me to . . . embrace the light."

The room is silent when I finish. For a brief second, it's just Malachi and me. His eyes lock on mine, and even the way he looks at me reminds me that I'm safe.

Then the applause hits, loud and echoing, full of love, but I barely register it.

I step off the stage and head straight to Liv. She's clapping, too, with her tiny hands—I kiss the top of her curls. "Did Mama do a good job?" I whisper, laughing quietly.

Malachi appears then, arms open. I walk straight into him, and he wraps us both in his arms. I melt there, not caring who sees us.

This is home.

As the night winds down, laughter echoes through the café while everyone helps tidy up. Boxes of donated canned goods are stacked near the door, and the last of the flyers are tucked into bags and purses for later distribution.

"You did amazing," Malachi says, slipping his keys into his pocket. He leans in close, gently brushing a loose strand of hair behind my ear. His fingers linger for a second longer than they need to.

"I need to drop one of the teens off. I'll see you at the restaurant?"

I nod, still smiling. "Yeah. I just need to grab something from the office. Z's going to let Liv ride with her."

He gives a soft smile and presses a light kiss to my temple before heading out. I watch him for a moment, heart fluttering, then turn toward the office, still warm from his touch.

Inside, I flick on the small lamp near the desk. The soft light casts shadows across the papers scattered around. My planner should be right here, and my purse too. I sift through the desk, moving stacks of books and flyers aside. No sign of either. Maybe Malachi moved things earlier in the rush.

I open the drawer. Inside are stacks of papers, a folder, some office supplies.

Tucked in the back, nearly hidden beneath some papers, is a small velvet box.

My heart stops.

I stare at it, frozen, unsure whether I should even be looking, but something inside me already knows. My hand trembles as I reach for it. The moment the box opens, I stop breathing.

A ring. Gold. Oval diamond. It's simple yet elegant and breathtaking.

My knees go soft.

Was this . . . for Phoebe?

Did he buy this before we ever admitted anything to each other? Before the kiss? Before everything happened?

I close the box gently, my fingers cold and trembling. I find my planner under a pile of books and my purse on the chair behind me, but I feel like I'm moving underwater.

The drive to the restaurant stretches forever. My thoughts won't stop spiraling. *Was I just a byproduct of trauma? Did Malachi only step in because he felt responsible for me? For Liv? Was Phoebe the person he truly saw a future with, and I just . . . got in the way?*

When I walk inside, the restaurant is already erupting with life. Liv is giggling with Zara, trying to dip her whole hand into a water glass. Akin laughs beside them, sipping lemonade. Darnell is talking to Akin, one hand working through a basket of bread and butter. Trina is deep in conversation with Ms. Mildred, while Irene and Manuel sit at the far end of the table. Manuel speaks quickly in Spanish, making both Irene and Malachi burst into laughter.

For a moment, I forgot that Malachi is fluent in Spanish too.

There's only one empty chair, right beside him. He must've saved it for me.

He gives me a soft, knowing smile as I slide into it, his hand finding my knee under the table. The waitress arrives to take my drink order, and I try to focus, to be present. This moment is supposed to be full of joy. But all I can think about is that ring.

Trina and Zara rave about my poem, eyes wide with surprise, and I smile, but it doesn't quite reach my eyes.

Malachi leans in. "You okay?"

I hesitate, then nod toward the door. "Can we step outside for a minute?"

He's already standing before I can finish the sentence.

The air outside is humid with a soft breeze. I wrap my arms around myself and turn to him.

"Tonight was wonderful," I say softly. "Everything felt . . . right."

He smiles, slipping his hands into his jacket pockets. "Yeah. It really did."

I pause, then take a shaky breath. "I was looking for my planner and . . . I couldn't find it. I didn't mean to snoop, I promise, but I found something. The ring."

His expression shifts to something neutral and unreadable. His eyes are slightly narrowed.

"I wasn't trying to invade your space," I continue, heart pounding. "I just saw it. And I thought . . . maybe it was for Phoebe. And I know we said we'd talk about what this means. But she talked to me recently. She told me about the conversation she had with you. She was devastated, Malachi."

"She talked to you?" His brows lift slightly.

I nod. "She told me you had feelings for me. And I didn't know. I probably wouldn't have even let myself consider it if she hadn't said something. But if that ring was meant for her . . . I won't get in the way of that. I won't let what happened between us, what I feel, be the reason she is heartbroken. I don't want you to be with me out of guilt. Or obligation. Or because I'm a single mom and you feel like you need to protect me."

I pause, voice shaking. "I just want you to want me for real."

He lets out a soft laugh, then takes both of my hands in his. The warmth of his touch calms me instantly.

"Asha," he says gently. "Are you finished?"

I press my lips together. "Yeah."

He exhales slowly, like he's been waiting for this moment. "That ring's not for Phoebe. It never was."

My knees nearly give out.

"I bought it a few weeks ago. That night when I got shot, everything changed. It was terrifying, yeah, but it clarified something for me. I couldn't imagine a life without you in it. That's what I told Phoebe after the incident. That's why I ended things."

I stare at him, speechless.

"That's also why I seemed so distant . . . right after it happened." He pauses, the words pulling me in.

"I knew I wasn't imagining things," I say, my eyes meeting his.

"It was already hard being around you when Russell was there. But when you became available . . . being near you was intoxicating. I wanted you. I've always wanted you. I just didn't know if you felt the same way. I wasn't going to give it to you now," he adds quickly, rubbing the back of his neck. "I wanted to take you out properly. To take our time. But the truth is . . . I already know you. I've known you my whole life. I've loved you longer than I ever admitted to myself."

Tears sting my eyes as everything inside me softens. It's not just me. He feels it too.

I reach up, cupping his face. "I don't need the ring. Not now. I just want this. You."

His arms wrap around me, pulling me in, and I melt against his chest. The world fades for a breathless, sacred moment, until shouting and laughter burst through the restaurant windows.

I didn't realize they could see us from this angle. So much for trying to keep things private. Everyone inside is clapping, cheering, faces pressed to the glass. Irene is the loudest.

"About time!" she shouts, grinning from ear to ear.

Malachi tilts my chin, pulling my attention back to him. He presses his lips to mine, despite the audience. When he breaks away, he whispers, "Asha, I want you. I want to marry you."

Our foreheads touch, our breath mingling as we soak in the moment.

"I love you," he says.

"I love you," I respond, and I truly mean it. Because Malachi is everything I prayed for.

I escaped the darkness that held me captive.

And now, I will embrace the light.

The End

Acknowledgments

I want to thank God for trusting me with this story. Without Him, this book wouldn't exist. I pray He finds me a faithful steward of every story He gives me to write and that they always point back to Him.

To every beta reader, ARC reader, and friend or family member who contributed your time, prayers, and encouragement—thank you. Your feedback gave this story depth, and your support gave me the courage to keep going. To my amazing editor, thank you for helping me believe this story matters.

To those who see themselves in Asha—you are not alone. You deserve more than what the Russells of this world have to offer. You deserve a Malachi. God sees you, and it is my prayer that you find your way out of the shadows.

And to my amazing husband—thank you for standing beside me through every late night, every moment of frustration, every rewrite and doubt. Your love is steady and true, like Malachi's. You are my light on the dark days. I'm so grateful to walk this journey with you.

About the Author

Aleah is an indie author with a heart for storytelling that reflects faith, healing, and real-life struggles. She writes fiction that places Christ at the center while capturing the complexities of human emotion through authentic, relatable characters.

For every novel she writes, she works to uplift and encourage readers through honest and grace-filled stories.

She is a Christian wife, writer, and foster mom. She loves her godchildren and her large family.

Aleah resides in South Carolina with her husband and their beloved dog.

Let's Connect!

Sign up for my newsletter here: aleahwrites.com.
Follow me on tiktok @ aleahdonaldauthor.

***

Loved Asha's journey? Share your thoughts! Your review helps other readers find the story.

www.ingramcontent.com/pod-product-compliance
Lightning Source LLC
Chambersburg PA
CBHW050615110726
47899CB00001B/116